A Conspiracy of Silence

A Conspiracy of Silence

DONALD F. MEGNIN

Contents

Foreword

The saga of the Malin family continues with their arrival in America. Friederich and Emilie continue their bifurcated life: Friederich searches out new ways to make a living, especially eager to buy a farm; Emilie, the consummate homemaker, wonders how they'll ever survive in these increasingly difficult circumstances in which they find themselves repeatedly as a consequence of Friederich's search for economic success. Emilie finds out about Friederich's early sexual escapades which shock her but she's at a loss to know what she should do. In Germany her defense mechanism was to remain silent; in America it would be appropriate to label it a conspiracy of silence. Other family members knew what Friederich had done but none of them is willing to make an open charge or break with him over this silent issue. The family "knows" what he's like, but no one is willing to hold him responsible for what he has done. Were his behavior only related to the distant past, it might be more forgivable. But it continues, probably unbeknownst to Emilie and the other members of his family, with his daughter.

For a man and woman who have to learn how to survive not only in farming, which they had never learned or experienced before, Friederich and Emilie must learn by hard experience how to maintain and care for cows and horses. They must milk by hand themselves when the rest of the family returns to the city. A devastating fire consumes their barns, hay and ensilage which puts the family to a test of sheer endurance. Emilie would have retreated and followed Friederich's siblings to the city; but Friederich would have none of it. He was determined to stick it out and succeed on the farm in spite of the ruinous losses and additional hard work he has to undertake.

Emilie continues to defer to Friederich's judgment in everything. She continues to speak of "Papa" as if her husband were her father. She makes suggestions which occasionally are accepted by Friederich, but mostly he choses and directs what she and the rest of the family are to do. He will not tolerate anyone countering what he prefers. If anyone disagrees with him, it's just too bad. He does what he wants. Even such a little thing as taking off his boots before coming into the house after being in the barn, is not something he's likely to do. He seems oblivious to Emilie's feelings and desires. Life, for him, is to be enjoyed solely on his terms and conditions. He doesn't seem to understand nor care that other persons can have feelings and concerns also. His life's objective is to make money and he doesn't care how many lives he steps on on his way to the top. For a person who survived an abusive childhood Friederich has long felt he was exploited and used by other people for their own benefit. He becomes the very kind of man whom he had deplored as a boy.

Emilie remains the quiet, passive, loving and relentless hard worker who learns to put up with everything she never expected to encounter in her life growing up as the eldest daughter of an important family in a small German village. She was groomed to become "a lady". How ironic. No one has ever had to work as hard as she doing a man's work day after day in addition to caring for her family, household, and garden. If anyone can ever be forgiven for becoming an unwitting accomplice to a Conspiracy of Silence, it is Emilie Malin. She really did not know what she could do to stem the appetite of her husband for young girls. Indeed, it seems inconceivable that she didn't know what he was doing under the very same roof she was living. But was it fear that prevented her from confronting her husband? Or was it truly exhaustion and ignorance of what was transpiring in her daughter's bedroom?

The Malin children were a curious threesome. The oldest was by far the most intelligent of the whole family (including his parents) and also was, physically, the biggest of the cousins. The second child was not only a very good student, but an attractive one. Unfortunately for her, she was also a girl. Her father's appetite for her knew no bounds. She had to put up with his predilections whenever he felt in the mood. She did not believe she could say anything to anyone. It would "break up" the family. Both of the older children were given corporal punishment as youngsters, although the daughter was slapped much less than her older brother by their father. The youngest son was the favorite of his father. He took him along whenever he could to the woods or fields. He let him sleep with him in the winter to make sure he was warm enough. He inadvertently encouraged his young son to become attracted to his mother's thighs by stroking them during meal times while he was present as a little boy. The experience has had an impact throughout his lifetime. His eyes have been directed towards the legs of pretty women ever since.

Preface

In many ways this novel may be termed by some of the readers as "nasty, brutish and short". It reflects the types of experiences which, unfortunately, are all too often kept hidden and silent for fear of losing the respect and continued relationship with those persons with whom we wish to remain good neighbors and friends. It should be noted, however, in every novel there are resemblances drawn to persons living or dead. The reader should keep in mind the names, places, and events are the product of the author's imagination. Therefore, any relationship to persons living or deceased is to be viewed as accidental. The types of human situations and experiences are universal and, therefore, used extensively throughout this novel. As in all fiction, the characters, the plots, and the activities which consume the lives of the characters are bound to reflect what happens to persons in every day life. Therefore, the names, places, events, and characters may be found anywhere at any time. It is hoped the reader will be understanding and considerate in her/his appraisal of what has consumed the lives of these characters. The author hopes the reader will find the novel edifying and helpful in understanding the multitudinous ways in which human beings have attempted to cope with their natural and human environments throughout the centuries. We need to understand the standards and mores of earlier times were much different from those of today. What has transpired in the past would no longer be tolerated today.

For any family that moves to another country, the environment becomes a paramount obstacle to overcome. Not only are the mores different, but the language, the culture, and the day to day interactions between "old timers and newcomers" influences perceptions for the next generation. Until a person has lived, gone to school, and worked in a foreign country for an extended period of time, he/she will always be on the outside of the community into which they have moved. It is even more difficult for immigrants to make this adjustment. When a person has a physical disability (such as the loss of voice) in addition to the baggage of a foreign language, the result can be difficult at best and overwhelming at worst. The novel attempts to portray what happens as cultures and peoples collide when they interact (which they must) with each other. The frustration of these circumstances, unfortunately, can have a devastating effect upon the persons involved.

The Author
Donald F. Megnin

iii

Dedication

This novel is written for the express purpose of honoring my mother, sister, aunts, and the thousands of other girls and women who have had the tragic experience of being abused and/or exploited, verbally and physically, by their fathers, uncles, brothers, cousins or any man who has used his physical strength to overpower them. The history of female exploitation has been, and still is, very much an unfortunate part of a woman's experience. Her freedom has been curtailed, manipulated and twisted, not only physically, but also mentally either by limiting her opportunities to develop into the potential person she could have become, or by denigrating her status as a person by denying her the opportunity to find her fulfillment in pursuing a satisfying career which she has personally chosen. While women have gained status, recognition, and value for being themselves in most western societies so that they are achieving comparable goals to that of men, the condition of women worldwide, unfortunately, is still one of subjugation and humiliation at the hands of men. They have too long been oppressed by men in every aspect of life. While men believe themselves entitled to the freedom to become whatever they choose and are able to achieve, women still do not have the same privileges and opportunities that men take for granted due to the machinations of men who seem to believe that women were "placed on this earth to be their handmaidens".

Chapter I

Preparing for Departure

Unfortunately, Frau Bartholomae didn't know her son-in-law. Once Friederich made the decision to emigrate to America, there was no way it would ever be altered. He made boat reservations through an agent in Stuttgart. He arranged for a shipping firm to pick up their things in Vaihingen after he had packed them in boxes for shipment to the pier in Bremerhaven. The shipping agent asked,

"Do you want us to do the packing?"

"No, that won't be necessary. Just send me the boxes. I'll do my own packing."

Friederich began packing very systematically. There were certain items he wished to take to America about which he didn't want anyone to know. He literally rebuilt some of the wooden boxes provided by the shipping firm. He created secret compartments in which he placed his guns, gems, and money without being discovered. The guns were partially his, and partly his brother's. He had been issued a Luger pistol together with a rifle during the war. Because of his medical discharge, he had had to give these back to the government. When Karl was drafted, he was also issued a pistol and rifle along with a knife, bayonet, uniform, overcoat and mess kit for use in the field. All of these items, together with shoes and boots, were simply taken home after the Armistice was declared in 1918. Since there was no real discharge for the veterans who returned home in November and December 1918 (the war was not officially declared at an end until after the Versailles Treaty's acceptance by Germany in April, 1919), millions of German soldiers simply kept their weapons (including hand grenades). There had been the possibility of renewed conflict should the Armistice agreement be broken off by either side. The German government did not call for the return of these weapons until after the Versailles Treaty had been ratified. Karl had been wounded, but had recovered in time to be reassigned to the Western front. He was one of those millions of soldiers who returned home fully armed. He had decided not to try to take these arms to the United States when he emigrated. Instead, he sold them to Friederich for twenty Reichsmarks. Friederich had also inherited his father's rifle which he had had as a young man and wanted to use for hunting. His brother and brother-in-law had written game was plentiful in America and anyone who wanted, could go

1

hunting. Friederich thought he would like to do so especially if he should buy a farm. He was unsure whether or not an import license might be required to import firearms. He didn't bother making enquiry. He simply built a false bottom on a couple of their bedding boxes and nailed the guns securely to the bottoms. He also did the same with his collections of gems and money. He took a quantity of cartridges along so he would not run short too soon in case he couldn't buy any in the United States. These he also nailed down with strips of metal to keep them from rattling around.

All Malin household goods and supplies were taken along; bedding, kitchen utensils, pots and pans, towels, washcloths, whatever could be put into four by four wooden boxes. Friederich also packed all of their books, photo albums, dishes, glasses, and tools. Whatever he had accumulated and felt were necessary to have should he ever have to go to work as a tool-maker again in America were crated. Emilie asked "Can we take the piano and beds along?"

"Nothing doing! We can buy those things in America. It would cost far more than they're worth to ship them. We can sell the piano to a neighbor."

"What?" she asked indignantly. "You want to sell Mama's piano? I think we should at least give her the option of buying it back if she wants it, Papa. After all, she didn't really want to sell it in the first place."

"That's stupid sentimentality. But if that's what you want, we'll give her first crack at it."

Friederich almost had an argument with his mother-in-law over it.

"Frau Bartholomae, would like to buy your piano back? We can't take it along. It's too big."

"Yes, I'll take it. I'll give you the same price you gave me."

"I want one hundred forty Reichsmarks for it."

"What? That's twenty Reichsmarks more than you paid me! That's not fair, Friederich!"

"If you keep arguing with me over the price, Frau Bartholomae, I'm going to sell it to a neighbor."

"Papa, please!" Emilie said pleadingly. "We can't sell it to anyone else. It was Mama's piano to begin with. We can't expect her to pay anymore for it than we paid!"

It was the first time Emilie had ever crossed him. He just looked at her dumb founded.

"Don't forget if we should ever need her help, she'll remember this episode over the piano longer than anything else!"

Emilie was amazed at her own audacity. Friederich conceded.

"All right, Frau Bartholomae, if you give us what we paid for it, you can have it. You're getting a real bargain. It's worth far more than you're paying for it!"

"That's exactly what I tried to tell you a few years ago!" she retorted.

It was a hot July day when the packing was completed. The shipping firm took the last of their boxes on a truck to the railway station. The shipping manager told Friederich "Herr Malin, your boxes should leave at least two weeks before your departure so when you arrive in Bremerhaven you and your boxes will all be together on board the ship. You wouldn't want to have things arrive after you've landed in New York. It would only cost you storage until you could pick them up."

"That's a good idea. We'll leave at the same time."

This meant that for the last two weeks of their stay in Germany, Emilie and the children lived with her mother. Friederich stayed with his aunt Katharine Vischer. He used the occasion to try to persuade her and his sister to come to the United States. They had halfway made up their minds to do so. It was just a question of when. Because of Friederich's rather quick sale and departure date, they did not have an opportunity to arrange their affairs quickly enough, especially the sale of Aunt Katharine's house. Much as they would have liked to join them, they couldn't.

"If I can sell the house in the next two years, Friederich, I may join you," Aunt Katharine said.

She was older than her sister (Friederich's mother). She had helped her sister raise her children. Shortly after Emilie and Friederich were married, he told her his aunt had long ago decided not to marry. She had seen what a hardship it was for her younger sister being married to such a man as Gottlieb Malin. Friederich related a story to Emilie which had her upset for some time. It was such a shock to her. It took her some time before she could face aunt Katharine, she felt so embarrassed for her.

"She always made sure someone else was around when she visited mother's house whenever my father was at home," Friederich related. "She remembered what had happened to her when she was alone with him once. She was an attractive woman in her younger days. While she was taking care of me and my younger sisters, my father raped her in full view of us children. My father had been drinking and when mother went shopping, Aunt Katharine was left in charge of us. I was eight years old at the time and all of us were in the kitchen with Aunt Katharine when my father came in.

"'Father asked, 'Is Maria here?'

Aunt Katharine said no. My father's words were somewhat slurred. Aunt Katharine asked, 'Gottlieb, have you been drinking again? You know your wife doesn't like that! What'll she say when she comes home and finds you drunk?'

'I don't give a shit what she says,' he told her. 'She isn't here anyway . . . '

He then went over to Aunt Katharine and grabbed her around the neck and kissed her.

'Now stop it, Gottlieb!' she said and pushed him off. 'The children are watching!'

He ignored her words and pulled her towards him again . . . This time,'" Friederich continued, '"he reached inside her blouse and stroked her breasts. She tore away from him and pushed him so hard he fell backwards. He caught his balance on a chair. He grabbed her arm and twisted it behind her back. He dragged her into the bedroom off the kitchen. I tried to help her, but he kicked me in the stomach so hard I doubled up from the pain. Father closed the door behind him and told us, 'Stay out, or you'll get what Fritzle got!'"

He proceeded to tear off her clothes. He laid her down on the bed and forced his way into her. I went to the door and looked through the keyhole. I watched as he kept struggling with her on the bed. His penis was very hard and forced his way in. He had taken off his pants. I was amazed what a large penis he had. The more my aunt struggled, the more he forced her down and kept his body going up and down on top of her. My aunt was crying, but she couldn't speak above a whisper. We couldn't hear what she was saying. I only saw my father gradually stopped and fell asleep on the bed. Aunt Katharine got up and dressed again. She cursed him a few times, but he only grunted as he continued to fall asleep. I got away from the door just before my aunt came out. When she saw us sitting there and looking as though we were afraid to move, she said, 'Don't tell anyone what you saw! Your father's drunk and doesn't know what he did. Don't even tell your mother. It'll only upset her!'

I was bothered by this admonition at the time. All of us children agreed we wouldn't say anything to anyone. We liked our aunt. If she really didn't want us to say anything, then we wouldn't. Even though I told my sisters later, to forget what we had heard and seen, I've never forgotten this episode. In spite of what my father did, I used to dream about my aunt and what he did to her. I wanted to do the same thing, even if it was violent. She appeared not to like it. She was a beautiful woman. I'd often dream that someday, I'd like to do the same thing."

Emilie didn't know what to say, she was so shocked. Friederich looked at her as if to gauge what kind of a reaction it had produced in her. She realized she had to say something.

"That must have been terrible for you and your sisters to watch. Your father must have been a really wicked man to do something like that!"

"Actually," Friederich went on, "I did something very similar to her when I was eighteen. My father had been dead for a little over a year. I wanted to visit my Grandfather and Grandmother Vischer shortly after I returned from Switzerland. I had hiked through the countryside from Basel to Schaffhausen and then to Winterthur where I spent nine months studying at the Institute. I had walked the entire time I was in Switzerland. Upon my return, I took the train back to Vaihingen. I had been gone until my money ran out. As an apprentice at Robert Bosch, I had been well paid. Not only had these funds financed my trip, but I was able to give my mother some Reichsmarks each week to help support my sisters and brother. I always enjoyed visiting my grandparents. I lived with them because my father and I couldn't get along. My mother had asked them if they would take me. They agreed and I started living with them when I was eleven. It wasn't much fun at home when my father was there. We always got into an argument. I couldn't stand him and my mother couldn't understand why we couldn't get along. My grandparents treated me more like a son than a grandson. I was much younger than their own son had been when he left Germany. I seemed to fill the void left by his death."

Emilie had never heard Friederich talk so much about his family before. Even though she was shocked by what he related, she felt he needed to tell her about them. What does he mean he did something similar to her, she thought to herself?

"When I returned from my trip, I found my grandparents had gone to Stuttgart for the day and wouldn't be returning until evening. My Aunt Katharine was the only one home. She was glad to see me again and asked me all kinds of questions about my trip. I was pleased she was so interested. While she made dinner, I helped myself to Grandfather's wine. We had an enjoyable time together. As we ate, drank, and talked, the image kept coming back to me of the scene ten years earlier. I had never forgotten what I had seen through the key-hole. Whenever I saw my aunt after that, I felt a twinge of excitement. I had long harbored the same desire to do to her what my father had done. She was in her forties at the time. She was well built with a very full bosom. Her hair was jet black and made up in very long and attractive braids. Her skin was a very smooth and silky white. Her lips, while somewhat narrow, were plump and rosy. I felt attracted to her as we sat together at dinner. She had never married and I always thought it was too bad. She was really a much more attractive woman than my mother. I felt sorry for her. She should have experienced some of the joys and pleasures of sex as I had, I thought to myself. I had helped myself to my fourth glass of wine and filled hers as well. The more I thought about her and looked at her, the more the scene of ten years earlier came back to me. I reached over and put my hand on her knee. She didn't remove it. She seemed to like it. I had spent a lot of time in their home and, of course, she lived there, too. I was more like a younger brother than a nephew. She used to let me snuggle in bed with her on cold winter nights even after I was a teenager. I enjoyed these warming sessions. As I lay next to her I noticed my penis would get hard. She didn't seem to mind. She would simply hold it until it got soft again. I thought this was just about the most enjoyable experience I had ever had. I looked forward to getting in bed with her so we could do this over and over again. There were certain times when she didn't let me climb in bed with her. It must have been during her periods.

"You must have really enjoyed that." Emilie couldn't help but think of their own intimate times in bed together.

"I was great. I really looked forward to doing it with her as often as possible. When I started to move my hand up her thigh, she didn't do anything about it. I had gotten pretty far up when she took my hand and put it back on my own lap. But this time, instead of leaving it there, I put it back on her thigh again. I kept moving my hand up her thigh. She told me to stop, but I couldn't. I had gone too far. I continued to rub my hand over her thighs and reached with my other hand under her dress. Her thighs excited me, just like yours do, especially when they're so white! My excitement increased and so did her's. She said, 'Stop this Friederich! I'm your Aunt, don't forget!'

She started to get up, and I pulled her down again. I put my other hand under her dress again and lifted it so I could see her thighs. I stroked them repeatedly with my left hand while holding her down with the other. She tried to push me away.

'So, you want to do to me what your father did? she said. 'Well, I'm not going to allow it! Get out!'"

Emilie was dumbfounded. She blanched noticeably. Oh my God, she said to herself as she put her hand over her mouth. Friederich continued.

"I put my hand inside her pants as she pulled it away. I was surprised she was so strong. I grabbed her arm and twisted it behind her back. She couldn't move. She tried to get away from me but each time I twisted her arm.

Emilie thought she was going to faint. How could you do something like that to your own aunt, she thought over and over again? What kind of a man have I married?

Friederich continued his story.

'Friederich!' she shouted. 'You're breaking my arm!'

'Then don't resist,' I told her.

I continued the stroking and this got her very excited. She tried to yell, but it didn't do any good. Her voice is like mine; it couldn't be heard outside of the house. I gradually turned her around and forced her to the floor. Her dress was already open at the top because I had reached in to play with her breasts. She didn't struggle anymore. I pulled her pants down and got on top of her. I didn't bother taking off my trousers. I just forced my way in. She tried to move away, but I was too strong for her. I told her how much I had wanted to do this ever since I was a little boy. She just looked at me and said nothing. After a few more thrusts, she stopped trying to move me off. I continued and it seemed she actually was moving with me. You know, Emilie, it almost felt as good as it does with you. I thanked her for letting me have it."

Emilie couldn't believe what she had heard. How could my husband have done something like that? She felt sick. She wanted to leave, but Friederich wasn't through.

"What I couldn't understand was how she could compare me with my father. I can still remember how she accused me. 'Don't ever forget, you had to take it, just like your father! I wouldn't have let you, if you hadn't forced me!'

She was very angry with me. I couldn't understand why she had forgotten all of those pleasant times we had in bed together when I was growing up. She told me,

'Go to your mother's house! I don't want you to stay here anymore!'"

Emilie didn't say anything for a long time. She really didn't know what to say. She felt sick from what he had told her. It was a strange mixture of shock, disbelief, fear, sadness, and repugnance all mixed together. She wished he hadn't told her. It made her feel very uncomfortable, and uncertain what she should say or do. She did notice it seemed to take a load off his conscience. Still, she didn't want to believe it. Did this mean I've married a rapist, she thought to herself? Surely not! He had drunk too much! Yes, that was it. Aunt Katharine had also drunk wine. She finally said,

"Papa, you both must have been drunk to have done something like that! Surely you didn't' rape her?"

"No I didn't! She liked it just as much as I did!" he responded vehemently. "She's always had a soft spot in her heart for me!"

It was probably true, Emilie told herself. Only then did she recall the brief conversation she had had with Aunt Katharine shortly after she and Friederich were married. She had wondered why Aunt Katharine said what she did to her.

'I like Friederich a lot. He's done a lot for his mother and his family. But you've got to watch him like a hawk. He'll never admit it, but he's his father's son. He's bull headed and determined to do whatever he thinks he wants to do, just like Gottlieb. The only difference between the two of them was a matter of age. Once Friederich gets upset about something, there's no stopping him, Emilie. He has a mad streak in him. I know I've never wanted to be alone with him ever since he was a boy. He did something to me I don't want to talk about. Just be careful. Don't get him so upset that he gets wild."

"Oh? What did he do, Aunt Katharine? I'd like to know."

"I can't tell you. But it was something he did to me just like his father did, years ago. As far as I know, he's never done anything like that since, but I still feel ambivalent towards him. He's a very good provider. He'll help someone who's down and out, but just be careful. He's not himself when it comes to sex," she said firmly.

Ask as she might, Aunt Katharine told her nothing further. Emilie wondered what had happened between the two of them. It was only after Friederich related the story to her that she finally understood what his aunt had meant. When Emilie talked with her about what had happened between the two of them again some years later in America, Aunt Katharine told her

"I never even told my sister anything about it. I was so embarrassed. Yet, in spite of what he did, I still like Friederich. I was deathly afraid of becoming pregnant. It was remote, because of my age, but I didn't want anyone to know I had ever done anything like that. Even though it wasn't my fault, I still felt guilty about it. He said he loved me. No one else had ever said that to me. I guess I've forgiven him. I felt badly for years that he raped me, but I feel much better about it now that I've told you. Let's just keep this a secret between us, Emilie. I've never told anyone else about it."

Now, more than twenty years later, Friederich was trying to encourage his aunt and sister to join them in America. Aunt Katharine was much older now. She still had a soft spot for Friederich. When he suggested they should go to America with them, she listened.

"If I could sell my house, I'd go. Elise would almost certainly go with me since she has no where else to go. She'll never go back to Kassel. As soon as she has enough money saved, I'm sure she and Waltraude will be going to America, too."

The Malin family left for America on July 18, 1927. It was one of those rare, hot summer days in southern Germany in which a person actually feels too hot for his clothes. The men have to take off their jackets. The women wish they didn't have to wear hose. Because Friederich had booked passage for the 19th, they had to leave Vaihingen on that date in order to catch the boat on time.

The train trip was uneventful. It was the first long train ride for Volkmar and Inge. They looked out the train windows for several hours until they fell asleep. When they awoke, it was time to eat. Emilie unpacked the sandwiches she had made before leaving Vaihingen. They were baloney on butter smeared, black bread. She had also made jelly sandwiches which meant butter spread on white bread with a thick layer of jelly on top. The children ate their sandwiches gladly. It had been a long time since breakfast in the early morning. Whenever the train stopped, Friederich got off and bought coffee for Emilie and himself, and apple juice for the children. Friederich always needed some liquid when eating anything ever since his operation. If he didn't have any, he couldn't swallow. The food was likely to lodge in his throat.

They arrived in Bremerhaven and went directly to the pier. The ship was already taking on passengers. Friederich and Emilie found most of the lower compartments had already been taken. They did find a couple of berths near each other, but there were no longer any four berth compartments left. Friederich and Volkmar found two berths with a family of six in one compartment. Emilie found two berths for Inge and herself in an adjoining compartment of eight. While the family was next door, they were, nevertheless, separated. Emilie and Inge occupied an upper and a lower berth in their compartment while Friederich and Volkmar occupied two upper berths next to each other. Volkmar thought this was great fun especially since there were two other boys his age in the family sharing the compartment. The boys immediately set off to explore the ship. They found several other boys their age in the other third class compartments. Volkmar discovered his family was actually one of the smallest in this part of the ship.

After Emilie and Inge moved into their compartment, Emilie decided Inge had best sleep in the lower bunk in case she had to get up during the night to go to the toilet. Inge slept in the berth directly below her mother for the first night. Before the second night she asked,

"Mama, can I sleep on the top bunk? I can see much better from up there."

Emilie changed bunks with her. Inge enjoyed looking all around the compartment. She could see virtually everyone from her bunk. There were mostly older girls and women in their compartment. Inge was the youngest. The others took an immediate interest and liking to this little four and one-half year old. Emilie didn't have to worry about her since the others took turns taking her to the toilet, or helping her wash herself in the wash-basins. This interest on the part of the other compartment mates turned out to be very fortunate for Emilie. She spent practically the entire trip in her bunk due to seasickness. The other women took Inge to the dining room for each of the meals, particularly after the ship entered the North Sea. The motion of the ship was simply more than Emilie could take. She began to vomit after the fourth hour underway and didn't stop until the ship docked in New York! The other women brought her water to drink or juice, with a little bread to eat occasionally. Each time she tried to stand, she felt dizzy and would begin to vomit. She had to lie down again. The other women and girls saw to it that Inge was washed and put to bed each evening during the trip. Emilie simply wasn't up to it. Friederich was concerned about her. She lay in her bunk day after day. Even when he came to visit her, she couldn't get up. The women assured him they would look after her and Inge. Friederich only saw Inge when the women brought her to each of the meal times, or on their long evening walks around the ship before going to bed. Ingele seemed to be getting along all right, he thought. I don't have to worry about her.

Volkmar and the other boys in his compartment also had a good time together. They took long walks along the passages deep inside the ship. It was a real adventure for them. Friederich noticed Volkmar was getting along with very little help from him. Occasionally, when the weather permitted, Friederich took him to the upper deck so they could watch the ocean waves and the wake left by the ship coursing its way across the Atlantic. Volkmar enjoyed these topside excursions with his father and was glad he didn't get seasick.

"If I got as sick as you are, Mama, I wouldn't be able to go anywhere!"

He actually had a very good point. Only children sixteen and older were allowed on the deck unless accompanied by an adult. On sunny days, when they went topside, Volkmar marveled at the sunlight reflecting off the water. It was so bright he had to close his eyes or turn in the opposite direction. During these topside visits, Friederich did his calisthenics of push-ups and sit-ups. He liked the briskness of the sea air and breathed it in deeply for several minutes each day. He wanted to expel the bad air, as he called it, from the ship below. He hated the close quarters of the compartment and came up as often as possible to clean out his lungs. He and Volkmar ate each meal regularly. Friederich saw to it that Volkmar ate something at each of the meal times. He had learned this from his previous passage to Brazil.

"You need to eat something at each meal time, otherwise your empty stomach is going to get the best of you," he told his son.

On those rare occasions when the storms at sea made the ship roll, as well as everything in it, they slept for a few hours until the motion sickness passed. For Emilie, however, the two weeks on board seemed like an eternity. She lost fifteen pounds and was only a shadow of herself. She became extremely pale as well as weak by the time they reached New York. It was only with the greatest of care and urging that Friederich got her to get up from her bunk. She couldn't believe the ship had actually berthed at the pier. She kept feeling the motion of the ship even after Friederich got her down the gangplank and seated on their baggage. She could hardly stand. He told her,

"You stay with the boxes, while I get the rest of our things from the ship."

Volkmar had the job of looking after his little sister while also watching the bags Friederich was unloading on the pier.

Chapter II

Arrival in America

"Can I go into the dock area and help my brother and his family go through customs?" Karl asked the customs official.

"Sure. Go ahead. He probably doesn't speak any English?"

"No, he doesn't."

As Karl walked up along the pier, the first person he saw was Emilie. She was very glad to see him.

"Emilie, what happened to you? You look so pale!"

"Oh Karl! How good to see you again!"

They hugged and kissed each other.

"It was about the worst trip I've ever taken! I haven't eaten anything for two weeks!"

"Is this Volkmar and Ingele?"

Both children ran to their uncle and gave him a big hug.

"My, you've both gotten so big. The last time I saw you Inge, you were just a little baby! Volkmar, you stay here with the baggage. I'm going to take your mother to the waiting room."

"I feel so weak, Karl. Is it very far?"

"No. It's just down the pier a little ways. We've got to get you something to eat, Emilie. As soon as get you settled in the waiting room, I'll go back later and get the children. The bags should be okay with Volkmar until I get back."

Karl took Emilie to the waiting room and found her a comfortable seat.

"I'll go get the children, Emilie, you wait here."

Karl went to get the children.

"So, Volkmar and Inge, come along with me. I'll take you to your mother. I think we can leave your things here. Your father should be coming back soon with more of the baggage."

He took them to Emilie. "Now that you're all together, I'm going to get all of you something to eat."

"I don't feel like eating anything, Karl. I just want to sit here and get used to the boat not rocking any more."

Karl laughed. "You're not on the boat anymore, Emilie! I'll be back pretty soon."

Karl found a fruit vendor and bought some oranges. He brought them back to Emilie and the children.

"I've found the best fruit after a long trip like you've had, Emilie, is an orange. You really ought to eat one. You must be starved!"

Emilie peeled an orange and slowly began to eat it. It was the first food she had had which stayed down since Bremerhaven! The children ate their oranges with gusto.

"Well, I better get back to the baggage. Friederich will be wondering what happened to all of you," Karl laughed as he went back to the pier.

Friederich came down the gangplank with another of their boxes when he saw Karl standing where Volkmar had stood.

"Hello, Karl. I was wondering if you were going to come in here to give me a hand."

"Hello, Friederich. It's great to see you again! I've got a truck just outside the gate. As soon as we've gone through customs, we'll take the baggage to the train station for the trip to Syracuse."

"Where are Emilie and the children?"

"I took them to the waiting room. It was a much better place for them to wait than here. Have you got more stuff on the boat?"

"No. This was the last box."

"Then I'll find a customs inspector so we can take your things to the truck."

It took another two hours until Friederich had opened all of the boxes and bags. The inspector checked them over and approved all of them for release.

"I'm surprised, Karl. Your English is very good. Aren't there any customs officials who speak German?"

Karl laughed. "Occasionally, you'll find one. I was lucky enough to have one at the pier when I came over in twenty-three. The man had served in France and had learned some German from the German prisoners of war."

Friederich didn't answer. He just shook his head. After the formalities at customs and after all the declarations as to contents were completed, Karl got the truck he had rented.

"It's a good thing I didn't try to drive my car down here. Syracuse is a long ways away and I didn't think my car could have made it. The roads are poor and it would have taken more than two days. Besides, with all of the stuff you've brought, I couldn't have put all of the boxes in the car anyway. We can take a load over to the train station and then come back for the rest of your things. I'll drive you, Emilie and Ingele over first with this load and then come back for the next. Volkmar can stay here, Friederich, with your baggage and boxes. After we've unloaded the truck, we can come back for the next load."

It took three trips from the pier to the train station before Karl had transported all of the Malins' belongings. Emilie stayed with Inge and the boxes at the train station; Volkmar waited at the pier until they had taken all of their things. After the last trip, Karl said "Why don't you get yourselves something to eat in the railway dining room while I return the truck to the rental agency. I'll be back by the time you've finished."

They waited until Karl returned. Friederich was leery about exchanging any Reichsmarks. He wasn't sure what the exchange rate was, nor could he speak English.

They ate the fruit Karl had bought and waited. As they sat in the waiting room, Emilie had to go to the toilet. She didn't know what to to do, nor where to go. She noticed several women and girls going in one direction down a long hallway and then came back. She didn't know how to ask for a toilet, but she and Inge followed the other women with their young daughters. They went through a door and found exactly what she were looking for. Inge and Emilie went to the toilet as did the other women. Emilie was much relieved. She was glad she had followed the women and made the discovery she expected. After washing and drying their hands, they went back to the waiting room. As she went out of the door, she noticed there was a little metal sign with the letters L-A-D-I-E-S on it. She made a mental note of it. The next time we have to go to the toilet, I'll know which room to enter. When they returned, she told Friederich,

"I've learned my first English word, Papa. It means toilet for women."

She proceeded to spell L-A-D-I-E-S for him.

"I don't think it's for men. There were only women and girls in it." When Friederich and Volkmar had to go to the toilet, they did exactly what Emilie and Inge had done; they followed the crowd of men and boys this time. As they went through a door, Friederich noticed there was a long English word also on a metal plate which spelled G-E-N-T-L-E-M-E-N. When they returned, Friederich was pleased to tell Emilie, "I've learned my first English word, too. G-E-N-T-L-E-M-E-N means toilet for men."

They both laughed.

"At least we won't have any problem finding a toilet in the future," Emilie told him.

Friederich was becoming concerned by Karl's long absence.

"He'll come when he's finished," Emilie suggested. "Maybe he's had a problem with the truck."

It was more than two hours before Karl reappeared. Since Friederich was never one to have to wait for anything, he took Karl to task for coming back so late.

"Where were you so long?"

"I had a flat tire on the truck. I had to buy a new tire before I could return it. Otherwise, I would have been right back."

Friederich was somewhat mollified by Karl's problem.

"I'll pay you for the new tire," Friederich offered.

"Forget it. I've already taken care of it."

"I'd like to change some money so I can pay for the train trip to Syracuse."

Karl went with him to the exchange window in the station. Friederich carried most of his money in a leather attache case and never let it out of his sight. Since he had locked it, he couldn't get it open. Emilie reminded him. "Papa, you carry your key in the inner pocket of your vest."

He took it out and opened his case. Karl was surprised

"You carry that much money with you?"

"I've sold everything in Germany, Karl. There's no sense in leaving it there. I'm not going back again and I'll need a lot of money over here."

Karl helped him get the exchange rate of four Reichsmarks to the Dollar. Friederich cashed five thousand Reichsmarks to buy not only the train tickets to Syracuse, but also to have plenty left over for the meals and the initial weeks in Syracuse.

They all boarded the train at 4 p. m. and settled down for another long train ride.

"It will take about ten hours to get there since the train stops at every station," Karl said.

"That's about the same time it took to go from Vaihingen to Bremerhaven," Friederich replied. "That means we won't get to Syracuse until tonight."

"That's right," Karl said. "It's a big country."

The children were glad to get on the train. They could look out the windows and go for walks in the different railway cars. Since they hadn't eaten anything other than the fruit from Uncle Karl, they were very hungry and wanted something to eat.

"When can we eat?" Volkmar asked. "I'm hungry."

"There's a dining car on the train. I'll be glad to take the children to get something to eat," Karl offered.

"Why don't we all go?" Emilie suggested. "Maybe you could ask the people here in the car with us to look after our things while we get something to eat?"

Karl's English was quite good and although he spoke with a heavy accent, he could get around very well. He talked with a fellow passenger who had been on the same ship with the Malins.

"Could you look after our things while we go to the dining car?"

"You can talk to me in German. I haven't learned any English yet!"

Karl laughed. "Where are you going?"

"I'm going to a place called Buffalo. I have relatives there. Go ahead, I'll look after your things. Could you bring me back something to eat? I don't care what it is, just so long as it's edible!"

The Malins made their way to the dining car. They had to walk through several coaches to get there. The swaying almost caused Emilie to lose her balance a few times. Karl and Friederich caught her before she fell.

"Friederich, why don't you take Emilie by the arm and I'll hold Ingele's hand so she doesn't fall," Karl said.

Volkmar walked by himself, reaching out both arms to steady himself on the seats as the swaying continued. When they got to the dining car, they had to wait a few minutes until a table was available. Friederich didn't care for the wait, but Karl said,

"There's nothing else we can do, if we want something to eat."

Friederich was all for turning around and going back to his seat.

"The children are hungry, Papa. We'll wait until a place is available."

Friederich was furious with Emilie. He walked back and forth several times to the adjoining car until a place at a table was cleared.

"I see Friederich's still as impatient as ever, isn't he?" Karl said to Emilie.

"Yes. But he's got to think of us, too. We haven't had anything to eat all day other than the fruit you bought us."

Friederich would have gone back to his seat, except for the fact they had promised their fellow passenger in the coach they would bring something back for him to eat. Friederich noticed it was impossible to talk on the train. No one could hear him and even Karl had difficulty understanding him. Karl and Emilie carried on a conversation while Friederich walked back and forth. Volkmar and Inge stood by the door of the dining car and looked out the window.

"Anne and I are building a house on the outskirts of Syracuse. It's in a place called, Lyncourt. You'll like Syracuse, Emilie. There are so many Germans living in our neighborhood. The Haussmanns are expecting you and so are the Kesselrings. For the first few days, we'll all be living together, until you can find something for yourselves."

Karl was enthused about Syracuse, Emilie thought. She enjoyed hearing about how much money they were earning at the Easy Washer.

"There are several hundred employees who work in the factory. I'm not the only relative working there. Richard and Gustav work there too, and we make twenty dollars a week! This is more than enough to live on because food and housing are so cheap. There's plenty of housing available, Emilie. You shouldn't have any trouble finding a place of your own. You probably don't know this, but originally, Gretel and I thought you would stay with the Kesselrings. They've been here the longest and are the most fluent in English. They would be in the best position to help you get located in the city. But the more Bertha, Gretel and I talked about it, though, the more we realized Friederich and Gustav would never get along together. Gustav likes to drink. He gets abusive sometimes. Friederich wouldn't stand for that even if he is a guest in our house Bertha told us."

"Where will we be staying, Karl?"

"Gretel has offered her place, Emilie. She's not too keen on having Friederich there. Her house is very small. She doesn't think Richard and Friederich will get along together that well either. The more she thought about it, though, the more convinced she became. She thinks she can put up with him for a few days, so long as Richard is around."

Emilie didn't say anything for a long time. She was deep in her own thoughts. She remembered what Margaret (or Gretel as most of the family called her) had told her once, on one of her visits to her in Stuttgart. Friederich had often mistreated his younger siblings.

'When he was a teenager, he beat us if we didn't do what he wanted. He even forced Elise and me to have sex with him! Your husband can be a real tyrant,' Emilie, she recalled Gretel telling her. Oh my God, Emilie thought to herself. First I heard him tell me about his Aunt and now his sister tells me what he did to them as little girls! She was shocked by this revelation at the time, but didn't know what she could do about it. She had even confronted Friederich with this information and he had gotten so angry with her she thought he was going to hit her.

'They only got what they deserved. If they hadn't been so fresh and hard to live with, I might have treated them differently. When she asked him, 'Did you have sex with your sisters?' he got enraged. 'What kind of lies is she spreading about me now? I don't ever want to hear about this again, do you understand?' He was literally yelling at her at the time. Now with this conversation with Karl, Emilie again had this frightening recall. That was a long time ago, she told herself. She gradually discounted Gretel's story. They were just young girls. Surely the stories were much more vivid and graphic than what really happened, she assured herself. Yet, in spite of these alleged episodes, Emilie felt very uncomfortable. The more she found out about Friederich, the more fearful of him she became. She didn't know what she could do. She was totally dependent upon him. She only hoped he would get along with his siblings. She didn't want to be all alone in this new country where the only people she knew were her husband's relatives! She hoped they wouldn't be living with the Haussmanns for long.

"So, for the time being, Karl, we'll be Gretel's house guests? I hope it won't be for too long."

"Yes, that's the way it looks. Anne and I wouldn't mind having you live with us, Emilie, but we're just in process of building our house. It won't be finished until next spring. We're also living at the Haussmanns. The house is small, but it's a congenial place to live. Grandmother looks after the children. We're all getting along very well. Wilhelmle, Riche and Grete have someone to look after them while the rest of us all go to work. Gretel works for a family doing general housework. Anne works as a cook in a nearby restaurant. Actually, Riche and Grete are in school all day. Grandmother really only has little Wilhelmle to look after. Oh incidentally, we call him Billy now. Wilhelmle is too hard for Americans to say. School is out at present and doesn't start up again until September. The children are under my mother's care during the day. I'm sure you'll enjoy the company of the ladies during the evening, Emilie. Grandmother won't mind having your two children during the day, either."

Emilie really had her doubts about this arrangement, although she said nothing to Karl. Friederich likes his peace and quiet, she reminded herself. It's good Karl has evidently forgotten Friederich's attitude towards his wife, she thought to herself. If we're all together each evening, will Friederich's attitude towards Anne change? she asked herself. The more she thought about it, the more uneasy she became. Friederich couldn't stand her! If we're all living together so closely, Emilie thought, won't his anger at her come out? Well, for now, we'll have to make the best of it. But I think we'll have to move as soon as we can. She continued to listen to Karl and, fortunately, he never guessed what she was thinking.

They finally got a seat in the dining car. Friederich had only caught some of what Karl and Emilie were talking about, for which she was thankful. We'll cross that bridge when we come to it, she told herself.

"What's on the menu, Karl?" Emilie asked.

"It looks like a good menu. There are fish and chips; roast beef with noodles; hamburgers with French fries; and New York strip steak dinners. There's also milk and a variety of soft drinks. Maybe the children might like to try a hamburger and French fries with an orange drink. That's what Billy likes the most."

"Who's Billy?" Friederich asked.

"That's Wilhelmle, Friederich. I told Emilie about it, but I hadn't told you. In America Wilhelmle means Billy. They used to call our old Kaiser Wilhelm, Bill. We thought we'd better shorten his name to one that Americans can easily use."

"So Wilhelm mean Bill in English?" Friederich asked.

"Yes. Well, what will you and the children have, Emilie? Do you want the hamburger, French fries, and orange soda?"

"That sounds like a good idea, Karl, for the children. What will you have, Papa?" Emilie asked.

"I'll take the roast beef and noodles."

"I'll take the same," Emilie said.

"I'll take a hamburger, French fries, and a orange soda pop, just like the kids," Karl told the waiter.

"What do you want to drink?" Karl asked Emilie and Friederich.

"I'll take some hot tea," Emilie answered.

"I'll take glass of red wine with my meal," Friederich said.

"Well, it's good that you asked, Friederich," Karl responded. "Unfortunately, neither beer, nor wine, nor any liquor is allowed in America. None of these drinks can be legally sold here. There's a prohibition against them. Maybe you can do what Richard does once you have your own place. He raises his own grapes in his back yard and presses them for wine. He has his own little barrel in his cellar. The law can't stop you from making your own. You just can't sell it," he laughed.

Friederich was amazed at this news. "What kind of a place is this where you can't even buy a glass of beer or wine?" he asked incredulously. It wasn't that he drank too much. He was just used to having an occasional glass of beer or a glass of wine practically every day in Germany.

Emilie was surprised Volkmar and Inge ate so well. They had never had this type of food before.They did leave most of their French fries. Emilie helped to eat them.

"It would be shame to leave them on the plate," she said out loud.

Friederich ate the roast beef with the gravy. The noodles were quite hard and he had difficulty swallowing them. He left most of them on his plate. Karl ate everything he had ordered and helped Emilie finish the children's French fries. They also had salads with their meals so that there was plenty to eat for all of them. Emilie didn't appreciate Friederich's comment to Karl.

"It looks like Emilie's going to make up for her lack of eating these past two weeks."

"I'm just very hungry, Papa. You don't know what seasickness is!"

She was still so ravenously hungry, she helped herself to Friederich's noodles. Before they were through eating, there was nothing left on any of their plates.

Karl ordered a roast beef sandwich and coffee to take back to the man who was guarding their belongings in the coach. He had also not had much to eat that day. After eating his sandwich in four bites, he asked Karl "Where's the dining car? I've got to get another sandwich."

"I'll go with you so you get what you want. You don't speak any English, do you?"

"Thank you very much. No, I don't know any English. It would be a help if you could come along to translate."

While Karl and the other passenger went to the dining car, Friederich and Emilie were left watching the baggage. Volke and Inge soon fell asleep. Emilie also fell asleep and even Friederich took catnaps for the rest of the ride to Syracuse. Karl came back with their seat-mate and when he saw the Malins were all asleep, he sat and looked out the window. He, too, couldn't help but wonder how the next few weeks were going to work out with so many people under the same roof. They are all so different, he thought to himself. He still remembered what Friederich had thought of Anne and how upset he was that he had married her. Oh well, he thought, Friederich's in a new country now. Maybe he's changed . . .

When the train arrived in Syracuse, it was twelve o'clock midnight. There were many people stirring about the railway station. Those who were getting off, had family and friends meeting them. The Malins didn't have anyone, other than Karl, who drove a car. Karl said to his brother, "Friederich I'm going to walk to Haussmanns' and get my car. I didn't want to leave it here at the station until I came back. I took the streetcar from the Haussmanns down here when I went to New York to get you. But at this time of the night there's no streetcar. I'll come back and pick up Emilie and the children first and then your baggage."

"I'll go with you, Karl," Friederich suggested.

"No, Fritz. I'll make better time by myself. I'm familiar with the streets. You better stay here with Emilie and the children. What if she and the children fall asleep? What would happen to your baggage? Someone could easily steal it!"

The argument worked. Friederich stayed with the family to guard their things. Karl went home alone to get his car. It took him almost three hours from the time he left until he returned with his Model T Ford. He had had trouble getting it started. It was only after Richard came out to crank it, while Karl worked the choke, that it finally started. The streets were lighted but his headlights were so dim, he couldn't see very far ahead. He had to drive very slowly.

When he reached the Malins, he took the children and Emilie first with as many bags as they could squeeze in the trunk. He made eight trips before he brought all their belongings to Haussmanns. He then went back and got Friederich. Fortunately, his car ran well that morning and by the time he had brought everything to Knaul street, all of their things were stacked in the cellar, the garage, and front room of the house. Grandmother Malin was already up and had prepared breakfast by the time Karl came back with Friederich. Emilie and the children were still sleeping, as were the Haussmanns, and Karl's wife and son. Grandmother Malin was very glad to see Friederich again. After all, he was her eldest son. She gave him a hug and kiss. He was also genuinely glad to see her. They sat in the kitchen and drank coffee, ate eggs, bacon, toast and sweet rolls while she asked him all sorts of questions about Germany. She had not heard from her sister for several weeks and wondered how they were.

"Are they coming, too?" she asked. "Is Elise going to come with her daughter? Did you sell the garden? Did you get what you wanted for your business?"

"Now wait, Mother. We'll still be here tomorrow. Why don't you let me get some sleep first?" Friederich asked.

His mother didn't want to quit, but noticed he was almost asleep even as they were talking. Karl, too, was beginning to feel the effects of the trip to New York and back and was nodding at the table. When the Haussmanns came down for breakfast, they said hello to their most recent relative from Germany. At that point, both men went off to sleep for several hours.

Friederich awoke at two in the afternoon. Emilie was still asleep. Volkmar and Inge were playing with their young cousin, Billy. Grandmother Malin worked in the kitchen preparing the evening meal. Riche and Grete had also been there for a while, but left to play with their friends. Their newest cousins were so much younger than they. Gretel, Richard and Anne had already gone to work. Karl slept until ten a.m. and then went to work late. Friederich woke Emilie and they looked around for the first time. The house was, indeed, small. Much smaller than Emilie imagined. There were two bedrooms downstairs, one of which was occupied by Karl, Anne and Billy. The other, by Gretel and her daughter. The large front room was actually a living room, but had been set aside for Friederich and his family. It was the largest room in the house and was used as their bedroom. The room, immediately adjacent, was the dining room. It was also larger than the bedrooms and almost as large as the room in which Friederich and Emilie were located. They soon discovered there were two more bedrooms upstairs just under the eaves. One was shared by Richard and his son, Riche; the other was used by Grandmother Malin. The kitchen was to the rear of the house as was the bathroom. For the first time ever, the Malins saw that the toilet and the bath were in the same room. In Germany these two functions were always separated.There was also a staircase leading from the kitchen into the cellar with a small hallway covering the staircase. A person could either go outside through a back door, or down stairs into the cellar. It was a small, but cozy house, they thought. They weren't sure there was really enough room for all of them there, too. Friederich and Emilie decided they had best start looking for their own place as soon as possible.

"If we're ever to have sex, Emilie, it'll have to be at night when everyone else is asleep! We can't do anything in this crowded situation . . ." Friederich whispered.

They got up and went into the kitchen where Grandmother Malin was already cooking the evening meal. It was her job to have supper ready when the menfolk came home at five-thirty. She packed a lunch for each of them each morning. When they came home in the evening they could count on a good hot meal.

"Good morning, Grandmother," Emilie said

"So, you've finally slept out, have you?" She gave Emilie a hug and kiss. Emilie actually felt her mother-in-law was glad to see her, too! Grandmother asked her all sorts of questions about Vaihingen and what her mother and sisters were doing.

"What do you think, Emilie? Will my sister come to America, too? And what about Elise and her daughter? She said she wanted to come when she had enough money."

"She told me that, too, Grandmother, just before we left. I can't imagine they'll stay in Vaihingen by themselves very long."

"I'm going to go for a walk around the neighborhood," Friederich said. Emilie knew what was bothering him. He wondered how he was going to react when he saw Anne later this evening. He told Emilie before they came out to the kitchen "I don't think I can stay very long under the same roof with her. It's just too crowded! I'm going to look for another place as soon as possible. Maybe Gretel and Richard don't mind, but I certainly do. I'm not going to stay cooped up in such a little place!"

He walked around the block, or what he thought was a block, only to find it ended at the foot of a very large hill. He went down it again until he came within sight of the house. He then turned left and this time walked until he came to the entrance of a park or a playground. He wasn't sure what this was but did see there were boys playing on the dirty end of the field, where no grass was growing.

"I thought it was odd the boys preferred to play on the dirt instead of the grass," he told Emilie later. "But then, they were doing the playing, not I!"

He continued to walk in the park and discovered the swimming pool of which the Haussmanns had written while they were still in Germany. This must be the swimming area, he told himself. He watched for some time and noticed the girls had somewhat shorter bathing suits than in Germany. A group of boys came over toward him and he wondered what they wanted. He didn't have long to wait. One of the boys addressed him,

"Uncle Friederich, what are you doing here?" the boy asked him in German.

It was only then he realized it was his nephew, Riche, whom he had not seen since two years previously. He had grown tall and was now seventeen years old. He had become a man and was taller than Friederich.

"We shook hands. And then Riche introduced me to his friends. You wouldn't believe it, Emilie," Friederich told her later in astonishment. "They all spoke German!"

"What are you doing, Uncle Friederich?" Riche asked.

"I'm just looking over the neighborhood. I want to get better acquainted with it."

Riche, then, excused himself from his friends and took his uncle all around the north side of Syracuse.

They walked through the rest of the park; the shopping area; the meat market; the bakery; the barber shop; the trolley stop; the furniture and hardware stores; the school nearby where Volkmar would go in the fall; the market where fresh vegetables can be bought each week; and other items from the local farmers who came into town twice a week. Before the tour was over, Riche had shown him every block around his house within a two kilometer radius in each direction.

"Syracuse is big city compared to Vaihingen," Friederich later told Emilie. "I've already located a few houses which were either for rent or for sale. I asked Riche what the signs said and he told me which was which. If anything should prompt an early moving out from here, I now know where other places are available nearby.

Riche liked his Uncle Friederich. He had some difficulty understanding him because of how quietly he spoke, "But if I listen very closely and watch his lips, I can understand almost everything he says," he later told his aunt.

Emilie was glad they got along so well together. Each afternoon, Riche took it upon himself to show Friederich another part of the city. By the end of the summer, they had seen the whole city. Friederich knew where different areas were and what was to be had where.

"Uncle Friederich made notes to himself and when I asked him what he was doing, he replied, 'I just want to know where I might be able to buy some property at some time in the future,'" Riche related to Aunt Emilie.

By the time the summer was almost over (the children went to school in early September), relationships at the Haussmanns had become difficult at best, and filled with constant stress at worst. Friederich had another argument with his sister about how much he should pay each week towards the groceries. He also could hardly contain himself with his sister-in-law, Anne. Emilie thought it was most unusual that Friederich tried his best not to talk to her, otherwise he only became angry with her. He couldn't stand her voice. "Listen to her Emilie," he confided.

"Her words are inane! She supports the position of whomever is talking, even when she hasn't the foggiest idea what's being discussed. She always fits her comments into the subject being talked about!"

"But Papa," Emilie said. "She does try to be as accommodating to others as possible."

"I can't stand people like that! It's the height of insincerity. You can't trust people like that. They'll stab you in the back every time!"

Both Karl and Richard suggested to Friederich he should go with them to the Easy Washer plant.

"You'll get a job without any problem," Karl assured him.

"You mean when people can't even understand me in German, you think they will in English?" Friederich replied caustically.

"I'm not one to work for someone else after having had my own business for so long!"

"There's still time for that, Karl," Emilie volunteered.

"After we learn how to speak English, Papa can think about doing some work. Our English teacher at the Americanization League said just the other night, we were making more progress with English than most of the other immigrants in her class!"

"There's no comparison, Fritz, between working in an American factory and a German factory. You have a great deal more freedom here than you do over there," Karl told him. "The boss gives you your work for the day and you go about doing it however you want. He's only interested in having it done right by the end of the day."

"The wages are good, too," Richard contended.

"We make more than enough to pay all of our bills and still save some on top of that."

Each time the argument came up about Friederich getting a job, Emilie became more and more uneasy. She thought Friederich's relatives were jealous of him. She knew he would not want to work for someone else. Besides, he still had thousands of Reichsmarks left from the sale of his business and Grandmother Malin's garden. It must have angered them, she thought, because they had to work to live in America almost since they arrived, and we do not. Gretel's comment to Friederich one day revealed far more than she thought about how she felt.

"You wander around all over Syracuse every day and we have to go to work! Why don't you do something worthwhile?" she shouted at him.

"Oh, Gretel," Emilie said. "Try to be a bit more understanding. It takes time to learn a new language and to get used to living in a new environment. You, of all people, should know that!"

"That's easy for you to say, Emilie," she shot back.

"You're still living like you did in Germany! Live as comfortably as possible, with as little work as possible!"

Her comment hurt. Emilie knew Friederich had other ideas in mind.

"What do you want?" Friederich shouted back at her as best he could. "Isn't fifty Reichsmarks a week enough?"

"All you do is walk around the whole north side of the city! Why don't you do some work?"

"What I do is my own business!" Friederich told her. "If you don't like it, that's just too bad!"

Emilie knew why Friederich was spending so much time walking all over the north side. He was looking for a good location where he might set up a business of some kind. He asked Emilie not to say anything to anyone until he had found a good location. He stormed out of the house and continued his search for just the right place. When he came back, he and Emilie discussed what Gretel had said.

"Papa, maybe you ought to put those Reichsmarks in a bank. I'm sure it bothers your relatives no end that you have them here in the house."

"No, I'm not going to put them in a bank! I'm not going to run the risk of a bank going bankrupt. None of the banks around here look like anything more than holes in the wall! I wouldn't trust my money to be safe in one of those, if they were the last banks in the world!"

Emilie didn't say anything right away. She had learned some years earlier to be quiet when he became so enraged. After several minutes, she said

"I certainly hope you find something pretty soon, Papa. I don't think we should stay here much longer. We're all getting on each others' nerves! It's just too crowded having all of us living here."

"Yes. I know it!" He answered crossly.

"We may have to move into an apartment first before I find some place to set up a business. The property around here is more expensive than I thought."

Towards the end of September, Friederich came back from one of his tours around the neighborhood.

"I've found a place for us to move into just five blocks from here. I didn't want to buy it. It's just a temporary place for us to move into."

"That's a good idea, Papa," Emilie said. "It's just too crowded for all of us here."

He had found a place on Butternut street which was not at all far from the Haussmanns. It was an upstairs, three bedroom apartment, with a living room, dining room and bathroom plus a kitchen. Emilie thought it was a very nice apartment and about the size of Haussmanns' house. It's just right for us, she thought. It was also furnished which meant they didn't have to buy any furniture. Friederich saw this as an additional plus because he wouldn't have to part with any more Reichsmarks than necessary for the rent.

After they moved from Knaul street, Friederich let himself be talked into going down to the Easy Washer Company to apply for a job. Since Karl, Richard and Gustav were already working there, he had no trouble getting a job.

"What can you do?" the foreman asked.

Karl went with him to translate.

"He's a master tool-maker."

"The machine's over there. Go to work. We need two thousand of these screws by Saturday."

Without further ado, Friederich went to work. He not only completed this first assignment by Saturday, but two other assignments as well. The other workers looked at his speed and workmanship with amazement.

"Why is he working so fast?" they asked Karl. "Why doesn't he slow down? He has a job now . . . There's no need to hurry things! There's plenty of work. Tell your brother to slow down!"

"Friederich," Karl said. "The other workers think you're working too fast."

"Karl, I have other plans than working here very long. As soon as my English improves, I'll do something else. I don't want to say what it is just yet, but I'm not going to loaf on the job! I've never done that and I wouldn't want any of my own workers doing that! That's not my way of doing things."

The other workers thought Friederich was a bit odd, Karl told Emilie later.

"But since I get along so well with them, they said they'd leave him alone. They don't like it at all that he does his work so fast," Karl chuckled. "They also can't understand him when he speaks, so they pretty much ignore him."

When Emilie told Friederich what Karl had told her he said,

"Those guys are lazy! If I were the boss, I'd have them work a lot harder. They stand around their machines and spend more time talking to each other, than they work. They seem to think they should prolong their assignments as long as possible. That's no way to run a business!"

Karl also confided in Emilie "The foreman likes his work. Whenever we have a rush job to do, he has Friederich do it. I really can't figure out why he's in such a hurry all of the time. He never talks with anyone else in the shop, besides the three of us. It's probably because they couldn't understand him anyway. The noise level is fierce. I can hardly understand him, either."

For Friederich, the work became increasingly routine, tedious and repetitious.

"I'm only going to continue to work there until I have enough money saved, together with my Reichsmarks, to buy a house," he told Emilie after a particularly noisy day at work.

"I have my eye on one on North Geddes Street. I first saw it on one of my tours around the north side with Riche. It's an older house, built around the turn of the century, near the Barge Canal and the oil refineries. This would be a good place to set up a business. It's in an expanding industrial region and it's not far from several factories. There will always be workers around. Business should be good in this place. The city is expanding into this region with several new housing developments nearby."

"What kind of a business do you have in mind, Papa?"

"Do you think you could cook, if we opened a restaurant here?"

Emilie almost fell over, when he asked her. She sat down with an astonished look on her face.

"You mean we would open a restaurant and I would be the cook?"

"That's exactly what I mean. You've really improved your culinary skills to such a point you'd have no trouble building up a clientele in a short period of time."

She was very pleased to have him say this to her. She had improved greatly over the past seven years, she thought to herself. I've learned how to make spaetzle, roast beef, potato salad and lettuce salad so well that even Papa's sisters are envious.

"I think I might be able to do it, Papa. Even your sisters never thought I would ever learn how to cook as well as I have! If you think we can do it, I'd be willing to try."

"It's something to keep at the back of our minds for the future. We don't have to tell anyone about our plans just yet."

"I won't tell anyone."

The apartment was a big one in comparison with what they had experienced at Haussmanns. It was close enough for Emilie to visit Grandmother Malin. It was also close to several shopping areas and Schiller park. It was less than one block to the elementary school where she enrolled Volkmar in first grade. She had barely learned enough English by then to read the directions to fill out the enrollment form. Volkmar almost understood more than she so when the teacher asked her "Where do you live?" he answered, "Nearby."

She wrote out the street and house number for the teacher. When the teacher heard them talking German to each other, she said in German,

"I came from Germany just twenty years ago. It took me a little while to learn English but, as you can hear, I almost don't have an accent any more. Volkmar shouldn't have any trouble learning English."

Emilie was very pleased when she spoke to her in German.

"Where did you come from?" she asked.

"I also came from Wuerttemberg. I was born in Ludswigburg. I came over with my parents as a young girl in 1907. My father didn't want to have to send my brother to the army. He thought it would be better for all of us if we left Germany."

What a pleasant surprise, Emilie thought. Here I'm speaking in my own dialect. I hope I can learn to speak English as well as she can, she thought to herself.

"Volkmar shouldn't have any problem adjusting to school," Miss Weber continued. "He already knows quite a lot for only having been here less than two months."

Emilie also noticed she spoke to Volkmar in English and to her in German.

"That's the best way to learn English quickly," she said. "When he's in school hearing only English sounds, he won't even notice it's different from what he's learned at home. You may find he'll only be speaking English with you after a few weeks, Frau Malin, when he comes home from school. It happens every time. The majority of my pupils have come from some other country. As soon as the children are in this environment every day, for a few weeks, the parents are learning English from them."

Emilie thanked Miss Weber for the advice. She felt very comfortable having Volkmar in her class even though she felt a certain reluctance to see him go off to school each day. He was already speaking more English than German, just as Miss Weber had predicted. By the end of September, he only spoke German with his parents, when he realized they didn't understand what he had said in English. When they visited Grandmother Malin, he only spoke German to her. She really demanded it.

"A woman my age doesn't have to learn English! If anyone wants to talk to me he should do it in German!"

No matter how often the rest of her children told her to learn English, her response was always the same.

"German is good enough for me!"

The papers that Volkmar brought home from school got better each week. Whenever they visited Grandmother, Emilie took his papers along so she could show her the good work he was doing. After starting off with several mistakes in spelling and forming his letters, he no longer had any red marks on his papers by the end of the first month. They were all pleased with the ease with which he adjusted to school. While Inge still spoke only German with him as well as with her cousins, Volkmar spoke only English with them.

Emilie and Friederich continued to learn English at night school. While they made considerable progress in the language, by far one of the best side benefits of the nightly classes was to become acquainted with Ernst and Anna Bochert. They were also immigrants from Germany; in fact, from a fairly large city in the Black Forest (Pforzheim) and not far from Vaihingen. Ernst worked as a carpenter although he was actually a very skilled cabinet-maker. He and Friederich hit it off right away. They were both about the same age; had both served in their respective State Rifles Divisions (Baden and Wuerttemberg) during the war; and enjoyed recounting their wartime experiences. It became a usual practice for the Malins to visit the Bocherts weekly. Either the Bocherts came to Butternut Street, or the Malins went to Oak street. While they were encouraged to use English on each other in class, they never practiced on each other outside of class. They simply enjoyed each others' company over coffee and kuchen. If the conversations went long enough, the Malins would stay for supper, or the Bocherts would stay and eat with them. One Saturday evening Friederich and Emilie thought it would be nice to take the Bocherts by surprise and pay them a visit. Volkmar and Inge had gone to sleep, as usual, at nine o'clock. Friederich suggested, "Why don't we take a walk over to Bocherts? It's a warm autumn evening. We won't stay long."

"Can we leave the children alone, Papa?"

"Certainly. We won't be gone long."

As they walked along, they both agreed they were glad they had come to America.

"You've made good progress with your English, Emilie."

"You have too, Papa. And the children use nothing but English. I don't think it'll be too much longer before we can speak it well, too."

"I really don't like working in the factory. I'd much prefer to be out of doors on these beautiful fall days. As soon as I've learned enough English to get along on my own, I'm going to buy that place we looked at on Geddes Street and set up our own business. I don't see how Karl, Richard, and Gust can continue to work in the factory. They'll never get anywhere working for someone else!"

"At least they're earning money and have homes of their own. It won't be long before Karl has finished his house. That's something to be proud of, Papa."

"Yes, but Karl is spending all of his spare time working on his house. Richard and Gretel, Gust and Bertha are all working to pay off their mortgages. I don't think they're looking far enough into the future. Where will they be in twenty years? Sure, they'll have their own homes, but not much more!"

Emilie could see Friederich was getting upset. She didn't want to antagonize him but she felt she had to ask.

"What do you think we'll have twenty years from now, Papa?"

"What I want to do is make a lot of money. There's no substitute for it. I want to own land or a farm. There'll always be value in land. The more land you have the richer you'll be."

"That's not a bad idea. My Grandfather Meyer also became a rich man because he had so much land.

"Exactly! I'm going to look around the Syracuse area and see if I can find a farm to buy."

Neither of them said anymore. They were both lost in their own thoughts about someday buying a farm. Neither of them knew anything about farming, but it did seem like a good idea as an investment in the future. The last few blocks were covered in silence. Emilie was holding Friederich's arm as they arrived at the Bocherts.

"Oh, it's dark, Papa. They must have gone to bed. It's already ten o'clock. Maybe we ought to go back home."

"Nonsense!" Friederich said, and rang the doorbell. Ernst opened the upstairs window and called out "Who is it?"

"Tell him who it is, Emilie."

"It's Friederich and Emilie Malin, Herr Bochert."

"I'll be right down, Frau Malin."

They always called each other Herr and Frau. Only Friederich and Ernst allowed themselves the right to call each other by their first names. Friederich also addressed Anna as Frau Bochert.

Herr Bochert came and opened the door in his night shirt.

"Well, what a surprise this is! Anna, get up! Herr and Frau Malin are here!" he called up the stairs to their bedroom. They were really taken by surprise.

"I didn't think you'd mind, Ernst, if we stopped by and paid you a visit this late. Tomorrow's Sunday and we can all sleep in anyway," Friederich said reassuringly.

"No, no. We're glad to see you any time," Ernst replied.

"Oh, hello Herr and Frau Malin. I'll put on the coffee pot and we'll eat some of the kuchen I just baked today. Else, Anna and Gustav are sleeping so there's no reason why we can't enjoy drinking coffee and talking together," Frau Bochert said.

"Who's looking after your children, Frau Malin?"

"They're at home sound asleep. Friederich didn't think we would be gone too long. So long as they're asleep, I guess it's all right to leave them alone."

"Is you mother-in-law there in case they wake up?" she asked.

"No. There's no one there."

"Well, they're probably all right," Frau Bochert said reassuringly.

Over coffee and cake, the Malins and Bocherts rehashed what their children were doing in school. Gustav, their son, was one year older than Volkmar and went to the same school. The Bochert girls were a few years older, more of the age of Riche and Grete Haussmann. They were enrolled in the fifth and sixth grades in the Garfield school some distance further towards the city's center.

"Frau Malin, our girls have to walk such a long way to school. Their English is still rather rudimentary. I wish they were going to the school your children and Gustav are attending," she said with some concern.

"We've told them never to go through the Schiller park on their way to school. There are just too many pathways that are over grown where no one can see who is going through. It's just not safe for little girls to go there alone."

"We're along the route to their school. Why don't you tell them to stop in and see us on their way back and forth?" Emilie offered.

"They could stop in as they take their little brother to school in the morning and then in the afternoons, after they come to pick him up. It would break up their walk very nicely."

"Oh thank you, Frau Malin. As you know, it takes time for them to learn English. It would be good for them to be able to stop in on their way back and forth to school. They're always glad when they come home. Then they can speak German again!" Frau Bochert explained. "We'll tell our girls to stay on the main streets and go by your house on Butternut street on their way to and from school."

Shortly after the Malins arrived at the Bocherts, Volkmar awoke. He looked all over the apartment and the cellar for his parents. Not finding them, he awakened Inge and helped her get dressed.

"Why are we getting up?" she asked.

"We've got to find Mama and Papa. They're not here."

"Where are we going to look?" she continued.

"Let's go to Uncle Richard and Aunt Gretel's place. Maybe they're there," he tried to reassure her.

He had gotten dressed before he awakened Inge. He took her by the hand and together they turned out the lights and shut the door. As they walked along the sidewalk, Volkmar asked a man, "What time is it?"

"It's ten-thirty. What are you two doing out on the street this time of night?"

"We're looking for our Mama and Papa," Volkmar answered.

"Do you know where they are?" he asked.

"I think they're at our aunt and uncle's house on Knaul street."

"Well you shouldn't be out here on the street so late at night," he said and continued on his way.

When they arrived at Haussmanns, they knocked on the door.

Gretel came and asked, "What are you two doing up so late? You shouldn't be out this time of night!" she said in some exasperation.

"Are Mama and Papa here?" Volkmar asked. "They're not at home so I thought they were here."

Gretel couldn't believe her ears.

"What? Your parents are not at home? I don't know either where your mother and father are!" she exclaimed.

Grandmother Malin had come to the door and heard what Volkmar asked. She became very angry and blamed Emilie for neglecting her children.

"See," she said. "That's the way it is with these educated women! They neglect their children for their own enjoyment! Friederich would never do such a thing!"

"We said good night to Mama and Papa before we went to bed," Volkmar told his aunt and grandmother.

"Friederich must have had to go somewhere and Emilie just left them alone," Grandmother said in disgust.

"Well, we don't know why they left the children," Gretel said.

"I'll wake up Richard and after we get dressed, we'll take them back home again. You stay here with our kids."

With Gretel holding Inge's hand and Richard holding Volkmar's, they took them back to their apartment and put them to bed again.

"Are you going home again Uncle Richard?" Volkmar asked

"No," Aunt Gretel said. "We'll wait here until your parents come home. I want to find out where they went and why they left you both all alone!"

The Haussmanns were both angry. Not only because the children had been left alone, but because they had had to get up in the middle of the night! Volkmar and Inge quickly fell asleep. It wasn't until one a.m. that Friederich and Emilie returned. They were shocked to find Gretel and Richard asleep on the living room couch. When Friederich turned on the light, Gretel woke first.

"Well, you're two good ones! Leaving your two little children all alone here in the house and going out! Where in the world did you ever get the idea you can just take off and go wherever you want?" she scolded.

Emilie was upset.

"I really didn't think they'd wake up . . . and we were just over at Bocherts. It really wasn't very far and we were only gone a couple of hours."

"You can't just do that here! Either you have to stay home with your kids, or get someone to stay with them! But you never leave them alone! They're much too young for that!" Gretel said angrily.

Friederich felt put out

"You don't have to yell like that! Volkmar knows where you live and he found your place without any trouble."

"Yes," Gretel shot back. "But you can't just let little kids wander around the city at night! You have to make sure they're all right! Someone could have taken them and then what would you have done? You were just lucky Volkmar knew his way. He even told us he had asked a man what time it was. Suppose that man had taken them with him? Then what?"

Friederich got really upset with his sister.

"You can go home now! We're here and you don't have to worry about them any more!"

"I'm sorry Gretel," Emilie apologized. "If I had known Volkmar would wake up, I would never have left them alone. We didn't mean to cause you to get up and come over here in the middle of the night!"

Gretel and Richard left with Gretel still muttering about how two irresponsible grown-ups could leave their children all alone . . .

Emilie felt very sheepish.

"Papa, I'll just stay home from now on. It could have turned out as badly as Gretel said, but fortunately it didn't."

"Don't be a fool," Friederich responded. "The kids were okay . . . Gretel just thought she could make us feel ashamed, but I don't have to take that from her . . . They go out all of the time! If Grandmother weren't living there, they would still go out and leave Riche and Grete alone! We'll have to tell Volkmar the next time he wakes up, he is to go back to bed and not leave the house! He'll stay here if we tell him."

Emilie didn't say anything. It was several days before she put in an appearance at the Haussmanns. She knew they would just start in all over again about leaving the children all alone at night. Friederich saw Richard everyday but he never said anything about that evening. He knew it would only get Friederich angry. While he shared his wife's concern about not leaving the children alone at night, he also knew they had a built-in baby-sitter with his mother-in-law living with them.

"Gretel, forget about the episode. It only makes matters worse every time you bring it up," he told his wife.

Gretel was not one to forget something like that too quickly. She reminded him and Friederich repeatedly about the event for the next several months. Whenever the arguments became too loud, Richard retreated to the cellar. He found solace in his own home-made wine. While he had a workshop down there as well, he spent most of his time sitting in an old easy chair drinking one glass of wine after another very slowly. He could shut out the noise of the world above him with a couple of good cigars and several glasses of his home made red wine.

After working at Easy Washer for a few months, Friederich decided he had saved enough money. Together with his Reichsmarks, he returned to look at the house he had seen on North Geddes Street. It was still for sale. It was about three miles from where they were living. It was an older house built around the turn of the century, but in good condition. It had had a new roof put on only the previous year. It was in an area Friederich thought was gradually going to expand. There were some new houses being built nearby; the Barge Canal terminal was within one-half mile; and most of the factories of Syracuse were located within a two mile radius. He thought starting a restaurant in such a location would be a very good idea. Mr. Cambridge, the owner of the house, was interested in selling. His wife had died and he didn't have any heirs. He wanted Friederich to buy the furnishings as well. Friederich had been told by some of the workers at the Easy Washer plant that this area was one of the nicest in Syracuse. It was just one and one-half blocks from West Genesee Street with its huge old homes and large American elm trees. Genesee Street, together with James Street, he was told, were the elite sections of the city. Friederich thought if he and Emilie located a restaurant within a short distance of such an area, it would surely draw clientele from among the rich of Syracuse. What they didn't know, however, was that this area of the city was predominantly a Polish ghetto. Some of the older people on West Genesee Street were already selling their large and expensive homes to businesses, particularly automobile dealers. These people intended to move to other sections of the city still inhabited by wealthy people like themselves. The Polish quarter was another workers' quarter like the area around the Haussmanns. The difference between this neighborhood and that around the Haussmanns was the population. It was predominantly German rather than Polish.

Mr. Cambridge was eager to sell. The house was large and he suggested to Friederich "How would it be if I continued to live upstairs and paid you rent? The house is big enough. You wouldn't need the whole house for yourselves. I just need one of the bedrooms and access to the upstairs bathroom. If your wife could prepare three meals a day for me, I'd pay you extra for that, too."

Friederich thought this idea was too good a deal to lose. He told Emilie about it that evening.

"Emilie, you won't believe it, but we can buy the house for half the price Mr. Cambridge had originally asked. All we have to do is let him stay there and you cook three meals a day for him. Since his wife died, he hasn't been eating very well. He really needs someone to cook for him. You know that would fit perfectly with what we talked about earlier. We might just as well open a restaurant. After all, we'll have a built-in customer each day. It won't be much more difficult to cook for a few more people."

Chapter III

Two Brief Business Ventures

It was true. Friederich and Emilie had talked about opening a restaurant earlier, but she had almost forgotten about it. She was floored by Friederich's suggestion. She had really improved her cooking over the seven years of their marriage.

"Your spaetzle and roast beef combination is the best I've ever eaten," Friederich often complemented her. "Even my mother can't cook as well as you can."

"I guess I can try, Papa," Emilie said wistfully. "But I'll need help with the house work. I can't do everything by myself."

"Once we get the business started, I'll find someone to help you clean the house."

As an entrepreneur again, Friederich quit Easy Washer. He set up a little soda shop in front of the house where he planned to sell snacks, soft drinks, and ice cream. Having bought Mr. Cambridge's furniture, they had acquired a huge oak dinner table with four leaves that could seat fourteen people around it in the dining room. They prepared this room as the main one in the restaurant. They set up two little tables in the living room just to the right of the main dining room. The kitchen was to the rear of the house. With Mr. Cambridge living upstairs, they had to use the first floor bath room for their other guests, as well as for themselves. There were two bedrooms on the first floor; one for the children, and one for Friederich and Emilie. When Friederich and Emilie told the Haussmanns and Malins what they had done, they practically laughed them out of the house!

Grandmother Malin raised the question which was on everyone's mind.

"Can you cook for so many people, Emilie? You've never had any experience doing anything like that! How are you going to be able to cook for guests, when you hardly have time to take care of your own family?"

"Who's going to look after the children when you're working in the kitchen all day long, Emilie? You won't have time to do anything else, except cook and wash dishes! Besides, you've only recently learned how to cook!" Gretel said.

She then turned to Friederich.

"What makes you so sure she can cook for so many people? It takes years to acquire the skill to cook for a lot of people."

"There you go again, Gretel. Every time we want to try something new, you're the first one who's against it! You seem to forget I'm going to help her! I'm quitting my job at Easy Washer so I'll have plenty of time to help!"

"If you find yourselves in over your heads, I'll look after the children," Grandmother offered. "But they'll have to stay here because I can't leave the Haussmanns."

"Well, whether you like it or not, that's what we're going to do!" Friederich said self assuredly.

Friederich hired a truck to make the move from Butternut Street to North Geddes Street. They still didn't have much other than personal belongings. Everything fit on one small truck. They moved in over a weekend and were ready for their first customers the following Monday. Friederich painted a sign for the restaurant which he placed over the doorway on the front porch. He opened his soda and snack bar along the curbside for business which might come either on foot or by car. Their first and only customer, for over a week, was Mr. Cambridge. He was very satisfied with Emilie's cooking. He told his friends about the new restaurant on the north side where one could buy a very good dinner for about one dollar. This recommendation helped their business. They soon had regular clients by the end of their second month. Most of the customers were older people who wanted a hot meal each day at noon. Friederich took care of the curbside business, what little there was. He sold an occasional orange soda, or an ice cream cone.

Since Emilie had to cook meals for Mr. Cambridge every day, some of his friends began to make the dinner hour a regular stop, too. She didn't have any help other than what Friederich was able to give in the house and kitchen. She found herself working day and night to keep up with the demands of the restaurant. Not only did she and Friederich have to clean up the kitchen daily, but she also kept track of the daily receipts and expenditures. When she suggested to Friederich they should clean the rest of the house, too, he said "No, no. That won't be necessary. You can do that on weekends."

Fortunately, the meager amount of business, permitted her time to do both the cooking and waitressing. Mr. Cambridge helped her occasionally when she had to prepare sandwiches or some special meal. He liked taking the orders and telling her what the guests wanted. He also helped sweep out the dining room each day and dusted. Other than Friederich and Mr. Cambridge, Volkmar was also called on to help. She often sent him out, at the last minute, to a nearby grocery store to buy those items she needed. Volkmar also spent time in the curbside stand with Friederich. He much preferred to do this than having to stay with his sister at their Grandmother's. There was enough business to make it necessary to have someone else look after Inge. Since Grandmother Malin had volunteered to look after her, Friederich took her there each morning. Another of the acquisitions which Friederich made after buying the house was the purchase of a nineteen twenty-five Willys-Knight four door sedan. It gave him the flexibility to come and goes as he pleased. In taking the driver's test, he paid the official an extra five dollars to make sure he wrote passed on his application. If Friederich needed to take anyone anywhere are get anyone, he had the means to do so. He brought his mother once a month to help clean the house.

Emilie actually enjoyed the restaurant. It gave her a chance to meet other people. Even though the work was hard, and the hours long, she did think she was learning how to become a successful business woman. She had picked up book-keeping from her mother. Friederich even acknowledged she knew more about it than he did. He had already seen this in Germany. She began doing his book-keeping shortly after they got married.

With the restaurant, however, she soon discovered the receipts and expenditures at the end of each month, were out of balance. How can we go on like this, she thought to herself? They were spending more than they were taking in. If it weren't for Mr. Cambridge and his friends, there wouldn't have had any business at all!

After the second month, she said "Papa, unless business picks up, there's really no need to try to continue. We're not making as much as we're spending three weeks out of every four!"

Her dour assessment of the restaurant, started Friederich looking around for some other business opportunities. With his new Willys-Knight, he started driving around the city looking for another business to buy. He found a garage with an apartment overhead. It reminded him of his business/home combination in Vaihingen. It was a battery/automotive shop on South Avenue. The more he looked it over, the more he envisioned it being transformed into a machine shop.

"I think I've found just the right place," he told Emilie. "It's similar to what I had in Germany. The shop and store are downstairs and the living quarters are upstairs."

"It might be possible, Papa. But we've got to sell this business first. How would we pay for it otherwise?"

Friederich didn't want to hear about how they were going to pay for it.

"That's no problem! I still have several thousand Reichsmarks! What's this about how are we going to pay for it? Of course, we'll sell this one and buy the other. We'll have plenty of money with which to negotiate."

Friederich put up a for sale sign on their place at North Geddes Street. Mr. Cambridge was concerned. How am I going to get my meals, if the Malins move? he thought to himself.

"You mean you want to move already, Frederick? You've only been here for a few months and now you want to give it all up? What's the problem? What am I going to do about getting my meals, if your wife doesn't cook for me anymore?"

"I want to try something different. I'd like to set up a machine shop like I had in Germany. That's really what I'd like to do, Mr. Cambridge. We'll see if we can get a buyer who'll continue with the restaurant so you can continue to get your meals here."

After only two weeks, Friederich had a buyer who also had in mind continuing the restaurant. This meant Mr. Cambridge could continue to have his meals at home and allowed the Malins to move on with no hard feelings from Mr. Cambridge. Friederich sold the house for two thousand five hundred dollars more than he had paid for it. He felt overall it was a successful venture. He had also been able to buy the new place on South Avenue for two thousand dollars less than the owner had originally asked. According to Friederich's calculations, he had actually made four thousand five hundred dollars on the two transactions.

Emilie was both surprised and pleased Friederich had done so well and he had done it on his own. She didn't have to help him in the negotiations. She actually felt relieved they were rid of what was becoming an onerous burden for her. She had even talked Friederich into having another baby as a way out of the continued cooking and cleaning she had had to do in the business. When he told her he had sold the house, she was pleased to tell him her secret.

"I have something to tell you, too, Papa. I'm expecting our third child some time in early December!"

Friederich was surprised but pleased. He had often said, "We should have another child."

But whenever he suggested it, she said, "Let's wait until we've settled down somewhere permanently. If we stay somewhere here in the United States in a place that's really going to be a home for us, then I'll be willing to have another child, Papa. But we've already moved twice since we left Germany. I don't want to have to move again with a baby.

On the 29th of May, 1928, they moved for the third time since coming to America. By this time they had accumulated their own furniture (from Mr. Cambridge) as well as the personal things they had brought over from Germany. Emilie liked the new house. It was close to two different parks and an elementary school was only two blocks away.

Elmwood school was where Inge began her first days as a kindergartner. Emilie enrolled both children in the spring for the next fall. All during the summer, she read to the children from the German books they had brought with them and, occasionally, from simple English story books. Emilie felt her English was improving, but she still spoke it with a heavy German accent. She also didn't know the meaning of many of the words she read. Because she could pronounce them adequately, the children understood the meaning of the stories. She also read the daily newspaper, but, again, felt she only understood about forty to fifty percent of what she read. In their new home, she spent most of her time sewing, cleaning, and improving her baking skills. She finally had both the time and interest to content herself with the things which her mother-in-law thought were appropriate for a housewife.

After Friederich opened his car battery shop, by the third day, he felt it was a going success. He had charged several customers' batteries and also sold a few.

He didn't know too much about batteries other than what he had experienced in Vaihingen selling them with his motorcycles.They didn't seem that much different; just the brand names. Occasionally, Friederich whistled upstairs and Emilie knew he wanted her to come down to the shop. Whenever he had difficulty making himself understood, she had to tell the customers what Friederich had said. His English was actually better than hers and his vocabulary was much greater. But, because of the loss of his voice, people had difficulty understanding what he was saying to them.

Several months went by. The business was going very well. Returning customers asked for Emilie when they came into the shop. Friederich was getting increasingly angered with this aspect of the business. It grated on him that people asked for his wife rather than trying to deal with him. He resented and disliked the fact that a woman was asked for in his own business! Emilie tried her best to sooth his feelings.

"I don't mind being your interpreter, Papa. Your business is going well. And so long as I'm able, I can easily come down stairs when you need me."

Try as she might, nothing seemed to help. She was always so enthusiastic and friendly with the customers. What she didn't realize was her response to other people made him very jealous of her.

"You don't have to be so friendly, Emilie! Just tell them how much it costs and and that's all. You don't have to try to interest them is buying something else. All the men want to do is talk with you. We've got more important things to do than talk to them all day!"

"I'm sorry, Papa, that you feel that way. It gives me good practice with my English and I know a lot more about batteries because you've told me so much about them. You know, if I don't help you in the store, I hardly ever get a chance to use my English."

"That's not the point! You ask them all kinds of questions about their families and how long have they've lived here. That's none of your business! I don't want people to know those things about us!" Friederich replied angrily. "I only want you to come down here in the afternoons from now on. I'll take care of the mornings!"

Emilie understood the technical details about batteries very well, she thought. She did like talking with the customers. If Papa's only going to get angry at me being helpful, I'd better let him handle the business by himself. It's just like in Germany all over again, she told herself. The customers can't understand him and yet, he doesn't like it when I do all of the talking!

When people came in the mornings and asked for Emilie, Friederich said,

"My wife isn't here."

"When will she be back?" they asked.

"This afternoon."

"Then I'll stop back this afternoon, Fred," was the usual response.

During weekdays, it was rare anyone stopped in any more in the mornings. Only people who came for the first time appeared in the mornings. Emilie often had to leave her house cleaning and baking to go downstairs to help him. She really didn't like this either because after her housework was finished, she liked to take Volkmar and Inge for a walk in the nearby parks. Since Friederich opened the store at seven a. m. she was often called down before the children had even finished their breakfast. Friederich finally said, "Look, this is crazy. You stay upstairs on Saturdays. That'll be your day off from the store. If people don't want to do business with me, they can go to hell!"

After several weeks of having difficulty making himself understood, Friederich made another decision.

"Emilie, I'm going to look for a farm. I'm sick and tired of having people ask where you are all of the time. When I tell them you're not going to be in the store anymore, they get upset. They say, if your wife's not here how can we understand you? You can't talk loud enough to be understood. I hate it when they say that!"

The event that set off his explosion occurred that morning in the store. A man, who had come to have his battery checked a number of times, came in and immediately asked for Emilie.

"Fred, where's your wife? I need to talk to her."

"What is it you want?"

"Is she upstairs? Can you get her? I've got a battery out in the car that needs to be checked and probably charged. Maybe I need a new one."

"Let's take a look at it," Friederich said as he started towards the door.

"Go get your wife, Fred. I can't understand you. There's no sense talking to you. I can't hear what you're saying anyway!"

Friederich, seething with rage, charged upstairs to get Emilie. It took him several hours to cool off, especially after she greeted the customer with a smile and asked him, "What can we do for you?"

"Good morning, Emilie," the customer said. (It bothered Friederich even more when people called them by their first names. People would never do that in Germany!)

"I think I may need a new battery. Could you have Fred check it to see if the old one still works?"

Friederich went storming out of the shop and checked the battery.

"Tell the bastard he needs a new battery. The old one's dead!"

"My husband says you need a new battery. The old one's dead."

"Well, tell him to put in anew one for me. I'll just wait in here and talk with you while he does the work."

Emilie went out and told Friederich he should put in a new one. He didn't say anything but looked very cross at her.

"What's the matter, Papa? Did I do something wrong?"

He didn't respond with words. He simply waved his hand at her to go away.

"I'll talk to you later!"

After he put in the new battery, the customer paid and left. Friederich came back in the store again and confronted her.

"Why is that you have to be so friendly with every person that comes through the door? That man insulted me and you carried on with him as if nothing had happened!"

"I'm sorry, Papa. I didn't mean anything by being so friendly. I just wanted to be helpful."

Friederich didn't say anything for what seemed an awfully long time.

"I don't want you to spend so much time talking to each and every customer! Couldn't you see? He had deliberately only wanted to talk to you, and not to me? He knew what I said. He just didn't want to talk to me! I'm not going to put up with this nonsense any longer!"

Emilie knew what was coming. It was going to be the "silent treatment" again. She had first experienced this in Germany while she helped him the store. He had gotten so angry because she spent so much time talking with a customer, he didn't talk to her for over a week. She talked to him, but he never responded with more than the shake of his head or a wave of his hand. There was literally nothing she could do that would make him talk to her. The only respite came when one of their relatives came and started talking to him. Then, begrudgingly, he would say, "Make some coffee for our guests."

It was a big relief to her when he started talking with her again. It was a very sad time for her when he was in one of these moods. She really couldn't help herself. She just liked people and enjoyed talking with them. The only times he didn't get upset with her talking with the customers was when a man came in with his wife. Friederich, then, seemed very interested in what they had to say. He paid close attention to what Emilie relayed to him. While she talked with the wife, Friederich went out to check the man's tires, or battery, or whatever else seemed to be giving trouble. The relationship between Emilie and Friederich was much better this way. But it was seldom a man came into the store with his wife. Friederich was so angry with her on one occasion he shouted as best he could "Silence!" and stormed out of their apartment. He slammed the door so hard it almost fell off its hinges! She was so frightened of him even she didn't say another word to him until two weeks had passed. They simply sat and ate their meals in utter silence. She did talk with the children and told them "Your father's not feeling well," when they asked

"What's wrong with Papa? He doesn't say anything."

She also cautioned the children not to say anything to him while he was in one of these moods.

"It'll take some time until Papa's feeling better. Try and be as quiet as you can while he's around.

The children did what she asked. They were even more frightened than she was after he slammed the door shut. It shook the whole apartment! When she was alone in the store during the afternoons, Friederich often went upstairs to rest or get something to drink. One day after he had gone upstairs, she went up to get him.

"Papa, there's someone downstairs who needs you."

This request usually put him into a receptive mood to see what the customer wanted. Before going downstairs, Friederich told her "I'll take care of this myself. You stay here."

After about twenty minutes, Friederich came steaming back upstairs.

"That son-of-a-bitch! He wanted me to check his battery but he insisted I call you to come down. I finally took his battery outside the shop and told him if you can't do business with me, take your battery to someone else!"

Friederich lost several customers that way. He didn't care. He felt he had at least showed them who was in charge of the business! He had already decided he was not going to continue in this business much longer.

"I've had my fill of these idiots who say they can't understand me! I'm going to look for a farm and sell this place!"

Emilie agreed with Friederich.

"I don't like this arguing all of the time over customers any more than you do, Papa. Maybe if we were on a farm, you'd feel better about not having to meet and talk with people. Ever since we've moved here to South Ave., we've had nothing but arguments and problems all of the time. I don't like living this way!"

Sundays became a real treat for the Malins. Friederich drove the family out to the surrounding countryside looking for farms. Volkmar and Inge had a chance to get out of the car and run around the barns and yards of the different farms. It gave all of them an opportunity to see something different than the business and the south side of Syracuse. It also provided Friederich an excellent opportunity to look over what farms might be available for purchase around the greater Syracuse area.

One Sunday morning in late August of 1928, Friederich drove, for the first time, towards the eastern countryside around Syracuse. He had gotten a map of the city and since they had never been on East Genesee Street, he wanted see where it would take him. Emilie noticed this street was still called by the same name even beyond a place called Fayetteville. They had never driven this far from the city. The scenery was beautiful. There were rolling hills, valleys, streams and trees everywhere. There was literally one farm after another between Syracuse and Fayetteville. As they drove around, they decided they would look for farms only on main roads. The reason they decided on main roads only was that's where Friederich could drive directly with his car. They also agreed they would take their time looking at farms in order to see as many different ones as possible.

"You agree, don't you, Papa?" Emilie asked imploringly, "You won't make such a fast decision as you did these last two times? I'm still somewhat in shock with how fast we've moved since we arrived here in America."

"No, it's not going to be as quick as the last two times. A farm costs a lot more than a house and a little business. We'll take our time but I don't want to stay in the battery business too much longer. I don't like it anymore than you do when we argue all of the time."

Emilie was pleased Friederich felt the same way. She had become somewhat unnerved by the rapidity with which he bought the last two places. She wouldn't have known anything about it if the realtor hadn't suggested to him he should put the house and business in her name. Friederich simply informed her he had sold the North Geddes Street house and had bought the South Avenue house. She hadn't even seen the South Ave house before they moved in!

The realtor had told him "If you ever buy a house again, Fred, be sure and put it in your wife's name. If anything should happen so that the mortgage isn't paid, the bankruptcy would be charged to her and not to you. You'll still be able to get credit and buy another place."

Friederich never forgot this advice. Each place he bought, he automatically put in Emilie's name.

Volkmar and Inge enjoyed these outings very much. They got an ice cream cone after each ride into the country. On most occasions, when they stopped to look at a farm, the children usually headed out to the barn. They liked the barns best. Most of the time they found kittens or dogs to play with.

"Kinder, be careful. Be sure the dogs are friendly. Don't get bitten by one of them!" Emilie invariably told them. Fortunately, all of the dogs they encountered were gentle and liked being petted.

Friederich was impressed with how much land came with most of the farms. He didn't know anything about farming, but he did like those farms that had several buildings besides the house.

"The more buildings there are, Emilie, the more room there is for people and animals!"

They looked at one farm in a place called Dewitt. It was just outside the Syracuse city limits. There were over 150 fifty acres for sale with a large cow barn, another separate hay barn, and two silos plus a large, five bedroom, two-story frame house. Friederich liked it very much. There were additional fields nearby which the owner rented so that altogether there were over 250 acres available. Emilie liked the farm, but she didn't think they could afford the price of $25,000! It was just too much money even with Friederich's remaining German Reichsmarks. She didn't see how they would ever be able to raise that much money.

"I'll talk with my relatives," Friederich said. "Maybe they'd be interested in going in with us to buy it. It's got tremendous possibilities and it's so near the city." The children liked the farm, too. There were two dogs there that were about the friendliest they had ever seen. The dogs came up to them with their tails wagging and licked their faces. They followed the children wherever they went. Even the cats were friendly and unafraid of the dogs. There were also lots of cows in the pasture; black and white, and several all red and all white cows. Emilie counted at least fifty all together.

"Now here's a thriving farm," Friederich exclaimed.

The corn stood high in nearby fields. The hay crop was a lush green color with blue tops and had a wonderful fragrance.

"I've never smelled anything quite like it, Papa. Are you sure it's supposed to be hay?" Emilie asked.

"What kind of grass is that green and blue field?" Friederich asked the farmer.

"That's no grass. That's alfalfa. The best kind of hay you can have," the farmer answered. Neither Friederich nor Emilie ever forgot this picture, nor the fresh smell of the fields.

"This is just the kind of place I'd like to own," Friederich told Emilie as they walked towards the car.

"We'll be back," Friederich told the farmer. "We'll have to see if we can raise the money first."

"Don't wait too long," the farmer answered. "I'm going to quit farming before the snow flies. My wife and I are getting too old to do all of the work anymore. You two are young with a growing family. You'd make ideal farmers at your age."

As they drove back to Syracuse, Friederich said, "Let's go talk to the Haussmanns. Maybe if they see it, they'll like it, too!"

He drove directly to Haussmanns and found them at home. Richard was in the basement. Grandmother Malin was somewhat angry because Richard had been down there most of the afternoon.

"He doesn't need to spend all afternoon down there," she told told Friederich and Emilie as they came in the door. "Why doesn't he spend more time with us? All he does is drink down there!"

Gretel was sleeping in her downstairs bedroom. She and Richard had made this arrangement right from the start, she once told Emilie.

"I told him I didn't want anymore children. You sleep upstairs with Riche and I'll sleep downstairs with Grete."

Gretel had a double bed which she shared with her daughter. Richard had a single bed upstairs and Riche also had a single bed right next to his father's. Friederich told Emilie, shortly after they were married, "I don't think they have much sex, if any. She absolutely doesn't want anymore children. She doesn't care whether he wants anymore or not."

After they arrived from Germany and saw the sleeping arrangements at the Haussmanns, Friederich said to Emilie, "Now isn't that convenient for Gretel. They have an upstairs and a downstairs. And guess where Richard has to sleep? That poor guy! And Gretel probably won't even let him use a condom because they're too expensive!"

Friederich shook his head in disgust because of the way his sister treated her husband. "If she were my wife, she wouldn't get away with that!"

Emilie and Friederich both agreed there was little if any sex anymore between the Haussmanns. When Friederich dropped in on them one Saturday afternoon, he knocked on the door. There was no answer.

"I went into the house and found Grandmother asleep and before too long, Gretel came downstairs with Richard. They were both still buttoning themselves up. They must try and do it when there's no one awake. Riche and Grete weren't there, either. You can imagine what kind of sex they must have had," Friederich laughed as he told Emilie the story.

She knew what he meant. They didn't do it any differently than most couples at that time. Foreplay, insertion, and pull out just before ejaculation followed by mutual masturbation. It wasn't much fun that way, but it did prevent couples from having children! One of the stories Richard liked to tell after he had had a few drinks around the dinner table when only adults were around was, "My wife tells me someday we'll be too old to have children. Then we can have all of the sex we want. Until then we'll have to keep working because we can't afford another child. Why do you think I spend so much time down in the cellar?"

Gretel laughed almost as hard as the rest of the adults.

"That's right! We can't take any chances, can we Daddy?" Gretel said.

"All we have to do is go upstairs, Gretel. Whenever I suggest it she says, 'not now'."

"That's where he gets his release," Karl added on one occasion. "No wonder he makes such a good wine!"

"At least he doesn't get violent," Gretel said in self defense. "I like his stories and his laugh is infectious. How could you not love a guy like that? After he drinks a little, I love to watch his antics. He's really not drunk, but acts the part well. I can't criticize him. There's never been a time he hasn't been able to come back upstairs from the cellar by himself."

Gretel woke up first when she heard Emilie's voice and the voices of the children.

"What are you doing here? I thought you always like to take a ride out into the country on Sunday afternoons? We never go anywhere," she said sadly.

Richard didn't drive and really had no interest in learning how. He decided, shortly after they arrived in the country, a car was an unnecessary expense. He wasn't interested in traveling around and if he had to go anywhere, he could always use the trolley, or the train. He also knew his brothers-in-law would take him, if he couldn't get somewhere by means of public transportation.

"It must be nice to be able to drive around wherever you want to go," Gretel said. "My Richard has never been interested in owning an automobile. I've told him any number of times, look at my two brothers? They come and go as they please!"

It wasn't hard to see, Gretel was jealous of Anne and Emilie because each had a husband who owned a car and liked to drive.

"Where's Richard? I want to ask him about something I discovered today," Friederich asked his sister.

"What do you want to talk to him about? It must be pretty important otherwise you wouldn't have come by on a Sunday afternoon."

"Get your husband," Friederich told her.

She went to the door leading to the cellar and called down, "Daddy, can you come up? Friederich and Emilie are here!"

"Yes," she heard, "I'm coming." After a few minutes, Richard came up the steps. Since Friederich wasn't very forth-coming with his sister, she turned to Emilie.

"Where were you today?"

"We've just seen the prettiest farm just outside Syracuse."

"Where?" Gretel asked.

"Near Syracuse, in a place called Dewitt."

"You'd never believe how beautiful it is," Friederich chimed in. "The hay fields smell like a flower garden!"

Richard came into the living room, greeting each one with a hand shake. He sat down in his easy chair near the front door.

"Richard, we saw the most beautiful farm you can imagine," Friederich began. "There are two barns, two silos, and a machine shed in addition to a two story, five-bedroom house. There were at least fifty cows grazing out on the pasture. And it's right next to the city."

The Haussmanns quickly moved their chairs closer.

"There were two very friendly dogs," Volkmar added. "There were two cats, too," Inge chimed in.

"It's obvious your interested in buying this farm," Gretel continued. "But Friederich, you've just bought another place on South Ave! What do you want to do with a farm? You don't know anything about farming! You've never even lived on a farm! How do you think you can work a farm without any training or experience? You can't just buy a farm and work it when you don't even know what has to be done first!"

Richard listened and asked, "Where is it? I've heard of Dewitt, but I've never been there."

"Let me take you over there to see it. You won't believe me unless you see it for yourselves," Friederich volunteered.

"What's the owner asking for the farm?" Gretel asked.

"Twenty-five thousand dollars!" Friederich replied.

Gretel almost fell off her chair.

"What? Twenty-five thousand dollars! And you think you can buy a farm costing that much money? Jesus God! Surely you don't have that much money?"

"That's exactly why we've come to see you," Friederich said matter of fact . . . "We can't swing it alone, but if you go in with us, we might be able to do it and even buy it cheaper!

"From what I've heard at the plant," Richard said, "Dewitt is really going to be the future of Syracuse. I've heard that's one of the newest sections of the region around Syracuse that's going to develop. People are already starting to buy farm lots out there in order to build homes. It's obviously a very expensive area especially from what you've said about the price of the farm."

"Exactly," Friederich responded. "That's why it may not be all that impossible if we all invested in it together and bought it. We could work it for some years and then sell off lots for building if that's what's going to happen to this area in the future."

"But twenty-five thousand dollars is a lot of money!" Emilie said. "Where are we going to come up with this amount? We can't afford it ourselves, Papa. You know that."

"I'll sell my place on South Ave and if you sell your place, we could swing the down payment. The rest we'll borrow from a bank. We could do it if we all work together on it. It takes a lot of manpower from what I've seen and read about farming. The farmer himself said if I had any relatives who would help on the farm, it wouldn't be too much work at all. What do you think, Richard? Would you be interested in buying the farm with me?"

Before Richard had a chance to answer, Gretel had already answered for him.

"We can't afford that much money, Friederich, and neither can you! You need an income to make the monthly mortgage payments and without some knowledge of farming, you'd never make it! You can't just buy a farm! You have to know how to make it work! Besides, you said there was only one house on the property. Who would live in it? You can't have more than one family in a one family house! You saw what it was like here when you lived with us. There just isn't enough room in a one-family house to hold more than the one family at a time. It just doesn't work!"

Grandmother Malin listened intently.

"It would be nice if we could all work together," she said. "Maybe Karl might be interested, too. If he invested in it, there wouldn't be any doubt you could buy it!"

Gretel turned off this idea very quickly.

"What? Have Karl invest in it, too? Friederich can't even stand Anne! Do you think Karl's going to go into an idea like this? Anne can't stand Friederich either, in case you've all forgotten!"

"I'd never ask Karl for anything!" Friederich shouted. "He can't do what he wants anyway. She'd never allow it! That's out of the question."

"That's still too much money for us, Papa. We can never afford that much!" Emilie reminded him.

"What do you mean, we can't afford it? How do you know? We haven't even offered them a price yet! They may sell it for less than twenty-five thousand. You don't have to say we can't afford it when we don't even know what the final figure is going to be!"

DONALD F. MEGNIN

Richard was very quiet. He didn't like these arguments all of the time. "Why is that every time you Malins get together, the first thing you do is argue and yell at each other? Why don't you discuss this like adults? No one has said we have to buy it!" he said slowly. "Then you stop speaking to each other for the next several weeks! Friederich only raised the question about buying it."

He turned to Gretel and reminded her, "We don't have to do anything! He's only asking if we would like to join him in this venture. I think it's not a bad idea. It's in an area which is going to become part of the city's expansion."

Then turning to Friederich, he continued, "I have to say I appreciate your offer to have us go in on this farm with you, Fritz, but I don't think we can afford this one. Even if the owner would sell it for twenty thousand dollars, it's still too much for us. Maybe if you find something cheaper we'll be able to do something like this in the future."

It was the first time Gretel had ever heard Richard say anything about buying a farm. She was amazed he would even consider such an idea.

"What? You'd be interested in buying a farm? Don't you want to keep working at Easy Washer? You've got a good job! You earn a weekly pay check. You'd be willing to throw that overboard and buy a farm? You don't know anything about farming, either! Two stupids don't make one good farmer! You'd better just forget about that idea, Richard. Your place is in the factory, not on a farm!" Gretel concluded.

"You're just too dumb to understand a good investment when you see one! At least Richard understands the potential that's there, even if you don't! Maybe Richard doesn't like working at Easy Washer! Should he stay there if doesn't like it?" Friederich asked Gretel.

"What? Richard, you like working at Easy Washer, don't you? You've never complained to me about working there," she said reproachfully.

Richard was on the spot now and he knew it. He had had just enough to drink to be able to continue this conversation against his wife. He didn't usually do that and she knew it. She said in a very reproachful voice, "Daddy, what do you say? You'd rather work on a farm than in a factory?"

Emilie could see Gretel just couldn't believe what she was hearing from her husband. He rarely, if ever, countered her. She was taken aback by this response and started to cry.

"Now you don't have to cry, Mother," he said as he consoled her. "I didn't mean to disagree with you, Sweetheart. I just think it might be a nice idea to have a place in the country where it's peaceful and quiet and away from the noise and dirt of the factory. The air is clean in the country, even if I wouldn't make a lot of money. I'd really like to be outside again, like I was in Germany before we got married."

Friederich knew that the conversation had come to an end.

"Thanks, Richard, for your support of the idea of buying a farm. I'll keep looking to see if we can find one that's not so expensive. I'll let you know when I do."

Gretel didn't even bother saying good-bye to Friederich. She said good-bye to Emilie.

"Don't take it so seriously, Gretel," Emilie said. "We're just looking at farms. We can't afford this one and Friederich knows it. He just wanted to see what you thought of the idea."

"Thanks for coming, Emmy," Gretel added. "But I could never imagine you working on a farm! You're a lady, Emmy! Don't ever forget that. You haven't any more idea of what to do on a farm than I do! I don't want to leave the city! I like it here! I want to stay here! Talk Friederich out of this crazy idea about buying a farm!"

Grandmother Malin gave Volkmar and Inge each a candy bar before they left. They were always pleased to see their grandmother because each time she gave them something. They liked the chocolate bars especially because the Hershey's were pure chocolate. Emilie let them carry the candy bars out to the car. As soon as they were out of sight, she told them "One candy bar between you is enough. I'll save the other one for another time. Volkmar, give me your candy bar."

She then kept the one and divided the other. She broke off a little piece for Friederich and herself before giving the rest to the children. Volke and Inge ate theirs very quickly. It was rare they ever had chocolate. Emilie knew it wasn't good for children and she certainly didn't want to buy any for just Friederich and herself.

Friederich drove home very quietly that evening. Neither one said anything. They both had their own thoughts about the farm in Dewitt. Friederich still thought it was a tremendous investment for the future, to say nothing of the present. Sure, he thought to himself, I don't know anything about farming, but I think I can learn enough to make a go of it.

Emilie kept thinking about the price. Where in the world would we ever be able to raise that much money she thought? What Gretel had said about our not knowing anything about farming is also true. None of us knows anything about it. Emilie felt a bit uneasy about this last point. She also knew, however, once Friederich had an idea in his mind, it was impossible to turn him from it. If he says he's going to buy a farm, she thought to herself, he's going to buy a farm! She no longer thought it was just another one of his ideas that would not materialize. She had, very early in their marriage learned, once possessed by an idea, he invariably followed through on it. She felt certain he meant it this time just like the previous times. But what will I do on a farm, she asked herself? The more she thought about it, the more unsure she became. Suppose we buy one . . . then what? Can I learn how to take care of animals? Can I learn to work in the fields? I don't even know how to plant a garden! Ah yes, she reminded herself, Papa had always talked about owning a few chickens like his mother and aunt did in Germany. Can I do that too, she asked herself? She really didn't know the answer to these questions. The more she thought about them, the more she wasn't interested in finding out! I've got to think about our third child, she told herself. I still have to sew some more little shirts and jackets for its arrival. I'll be so busy with the baby, she said to herself, I won't be able to help Papa in the business much longer. Maybe the business will improve with time, she mused. If only he could make himself better understood! How easy it would be for him to be a businessman in America! He's willing to take risks; he seems to know when to buy and when to sell; he buys and sells good products; and he's an excellent tool-maker. Even though he didn't know much about cars before we came to America, he seems to have learned quickly enough how they work. Emilie was lost in her own thoughts . . . .

For the next two months, they didn't travel out on East Genesee street on their weekly excursions to the country. Friederich didn't want to go past the farm which he really thought he should buy. He drove in the opposite direction. They looked at farms in the Baldwinsville and Camillus areas. There were a few, but these, too, were over twenty thousand dollars! He had finally agreed with Emilie anything over fifteen thousand dollars was simply too expensive for them. Their price ceiling would have to be $15,000.00.

In late November Friederich and Emilie talked with a realtor in Syracuse about keeping an eye open for farms costing between ten and fifteen thousand dollars. He took them to see a couple of farms in the Pompey area, but these were way up on top of hills. The wind was blowing on one visit which reminded them that in winter it could be bitterly cold at this elevation. The scenery was spectacular. They could see for miles including the distant foothills of the Adirondack Mountains.

"But what about in winter, Papa? It'll be way too cold with a new baby in the house," Emilie reminded him.

"Yes, you're right. We don't want to live on a hill top in the winter. It's cold enough in Syracuse without asking for even worse weather on hill tops."

Chapter IV

Valley Farm

The realtor kept showing the Malins several more farms. There was one, especially, he thought they might like. It was located near Chittenango.

"Is that too far from Syracuse?" the realtor asked.

"Show me where it is on the map," Friederich replied.

As he showed Friederich and Emilie, he emphasized it was on one of the two major state roads, Route Five, to be exact, which crosses New York State from east to west.

"Route Five, together with Route Twenty are the main arteries running through up-state New York. The present owners want to sell the place because they've rented it for years and renters just don't take care of a place the way they should. They're afraid the place will begin to have a "run-down" look." (He had to explain this term to them since they had never heard it before.)

"The owners are willing to extend a mortgage themselves to any buyer who might be interested," the realtor emphasized. "The farm's really worth a lot more than they're asking for it. It's just a long way out of the city and on the very edge of Onondaga County. I think you might be able to get it for fifteen thousand," he continued. "Right after the war, I had seen it advertised for twenty-two thousand dollars. If you're interested in going that far out, I'll be glad to show it to you, but only if you're sure you want to be that far out in the country."

"How many buildings are on it?" Friederich asked.

The realtor responded by saying it had certain unique features.

"There are actually two houses; one is a gigantic mansion built in the late 1700s; the other has been used as the hired man's house in the past. There are two large barns across the road from the big house; one for horses and one for cows. The silo is the biggest one in the entire county! I'm not sure how many stanchions there are in the barn, but I think there are at least thirty, maybe more. I just don't know. The horse barn/garage" he continued, "Is a beauty. There are six stalls with a hay loft overhead and a large garage directly on the road so you can drive from the road into it. Behind the area of the garage, is the horse barn. You can go through from one door directly into the other."

The realtor, Mr. Gorman, saw that both Friederich and Emilie were paying very close attention to his descriptions of the farm.

"As I said before, the silo is the biggest in Onondaga County and it stands just to the east of the cow barn. There's also a small milk house near the road on the same side as the cow barn. Across the road, and just to the southeast of the big house (he used this word instead of mansion because they had asked him twice what a mansion was), there is another combination garage and hay barn."

They were, indeed, very impressed with this graphic picture of a farm which they hadn't even seen. His description of the details intrigued them no end. It sounded far better than anything else they had seen.

Mr. Gorman mentioned, almost in passing, "There are also a few cabins scattered to the east of this combination barn and garage on the same side of the road as the big house. I don't know what they were used for in the past. I'll have to check on that with the owners. But in total, there are at least five buildings in all, including two houses."

After Friederich heard the description, he said, "When can we take a look at it for ourselves?"

Emilie knew exactly what Friederich was thinking without saying anything to the realtor. If this farm has two houses and one of them is large enough, from what the realtor described, then maybe he could get the rest of the family to go into business with them.

Emilie was very large at this point with the baby expected within the next couple of weeks. Should I take this long ride out into the country, she thought to herself, to look over this farm, or not? The more she thought about it, the more opposed she was to taking the trip. After all, she told herself, we've looked at dozens of farms only to find something against buying them, such as the price, or the location. She decided against going this time. Friederich went with the realtor alone. Volkmar wanted to go along, but Mr. Gorman didn't think that was a good idea.

"I don't want the boy to get car sick or something and get my car all dirty. Maybe the next time, when your Dad goes back to look it over again, you can go along," he told Volkmar. "Besides, we might be gone a long time and you'd miss your supper."

The drive out was much longer than Friederich had expected. The entire route from Dewitt, where he looked and looked out the car window at the farm he really wanted to buy, to the farm on the county line, had one active farm after another. Each one was being worked and was just like dozens of others that were supporting families like Friederich hoped he would do at some point. Mr. Gorman couldn't help but notice Friederich looking longingly out the window at the farm in Dewitt as they drove past.

"That's a good farm. It just sold for twenty thousand dollars a couple of weeks ago. I'll bet the owner will get a hell of a lot more for just half of it in a few years. The city's expanding in this direction."

Friederich agreed. "It was a good buy. I just couldn't afford it."

When they arrived at the farm, Friederich was amazed by what he saw. Not only were there all of the buildings the realtor had described, but the main house was even larger than he had imagined. "There are at least twenty rooms in the house!" he exclaimed.

"There's been an active camping program on this farm in recent years. People traveling on Route 5 to New York, often stop here to overnight either at a campsite, or in the house before continuing their journey. So, it's not only a farm, Fred, but a tourist and camping business in the summer as well."

Mr. Gorman showed Friederich the house first, since he noticed he was awe-struck by its size.

"As far as I know, Fred," he continued, "This once was the home of a very rich man who had served as a Colonel in the Revolutionary War with George Washington. For his wartime service, he was given a thousand acre grant on the New York frontier in those days, as payment for his services. Colonel Mabie had this house built around 1796 both as his home, and as a stagecoach stop between Albany and Buffalo. That's why there are these numbers on the doors upstairs."

Friederich had wondered why the rooms were all numbered. Mr. Gorman went on.

"The Colonel sold a part of his huge estate to the Erie Canal Company so the Canal could be constructed through the northern part of his farm."

Friederich noticed the house was solid and well built even if the floor boards were somewhat rough and uneven in various rooms. The basement was earthen although the timbers holding up the main part of the house were simply logs laid across the stone and a concrete like material creating the foundation walls. The bark was still on the logs and were from various kinds of wood which Friederich didn't recognize. He simply noticed they were different from most of the trees he had ever seen. Attached to the main part of the house (the top part of which was in the shape of a T), was a kitchen, a small wash room and pantry, a bathroom with an old copper bathtub built into a wooden frame, a dining room, an adjoining bedroom, and two rather rough but usable bedrooms over head. The kitchen and dining rooms had a common fireplace one side of which (on the dining room side) had been covered up by a wall. To the rear of the structure, and the smallest of the telescopic two units abutting the front T of the house, was a huge garage with the south end open. There may have been a wall or doors at one time, but they had long since disappeared. At the southwest corner of this garage, stood an attached little building which Friederich soon recognized was the toilet. It was the "outhouse", as the realtor called it. The little building was set alongside the garage which was connected by a door that could be closed. Inside, Friederich noticed, were four round holes carved into a very thick plank upon which people sat. There were also four round covers with handles on them for each seat with which to close the toilet when not in use. Returning to the main house, Friederich wanted to go though the rooms again so he could be sure of the number of bedrooms. He wasn't sure if there were ten or eleven.

"Sure, go ahead," Mr. Gorman said. "Look it over all you want."

Friederich went back upstairs and counted them. He, then went downstairs, this time keeping track of how many there were. He counted six bedrooms and a large hallway and staircase upstairs in the main part of the house. There were the two rough rooms over the dining room on the adjacent part of the house reachable from the upstairs hallway; three huge rooms downstairs which could either remain as parlors, dining rooms, or bedrooms, should the need ever arise, he told himself. There was also another little room just off the parlor on the front southeastern corner of the house which served as another lavatory/toilet or privy combination. In total, Friederich counted sixteen rooms, two toilets and one bathroom. But this wasn't the only house. Mr. Gorman took him next through the garden to the "little house", as he called it, where the hired man and his family had always lived. As Friederich walked through the garden, he noticed it was not just large; it was huge and had various bushes bordering it as well as fruit trees. There were huge old apple and pear trees which, Mr. Gorman said, "These must have been planted by the old Colonel himself!"

The "little house" wasn't really so little, Friederich thought upon seeing the inside. It was certainly smaller than the main house, but this house had a detached, free-standing outhouse (for two), another little building which the realtor called a chicken coop which he had to explain to Friederich was a place where chickens are kept away from the house. There was also a small garage separate from the house in which to store either a car or a buggy. As they entered the house from the rear, Friederich later told Emilie, "There was a kitchen, a small room just off the kitchen, which the realtor called a pantry, but I think would be ideal for the baby, a small dining room and living room downstairs, with a staircase leading up from the living room along the west side of the house facing north. The staircase faced south with a landing and a sharp left towards the east leading to three bedrooms and a small lavatory." (This was another new word which Mr. Gorman had to explain meant a wash room with a sink, a stand for a basin, and a jug of water.) "The rooms were much smaller than in the other house but still about the same size as the Haussmanns' house. There was also a cellar which had not been finished with a stairway (more like a ladder Friederich thought) leading down to the earthen floor. The walls seemed solid enough with similar beams to those of the large house, set upon stone, with clay and concrete for the foundation. Actually, Emilie, the more I looked over the small house, the more it reminded me of this place. It may be a bit smaller, but certainly livable."

After Friederich looked over the two houses, Mr. Gorman said, "Now comes the best part of the farm, Fred; the barns. If you thought the houses were something, wait until you see the barns with the biggest silo in Onondaga County right here on this farm and every farmer in the county knows it! If you buy this place, Fred, they'll be green with envy, you know!" (He had to explain what this expression meant.)

"They'll be jealous of you," he continued. "You'll have what they don't have. You'll have one of the oldest and best farms in Onondaga County!"

He saw Friederich's eyes light up. He continued to build up the attributes of what was called "Valley Farm" for Friederich's benefit.

"You're located on one of the most heavily traveled roads in New York State, Fred. Why Route 5 is an old Indian trail which connects you with the State's Capital in Albany and with the second largest city in the State; that's called Buffalo. It's the largest city outside of New York City in the state. When you see the camping area and the little overnight cabins, you'll see right away what I mean about a choice location! People have to overnight somewhere when they're traveling between Syracuse and Albany. They'll want to stop at this place because it's got so much history to it. It's a famous place and around here, only the Gridley farm, on the other side of Mycenae, can compare with it. Do you remember the big place along the side of the road about two miles back towards Fayetteville, Fred?"

"Yes. I noticed the big barn along the side of the road. So this farm is like that?"

"Yes." Mr. Gorman continued as they walked across the road and into the garage and horse-barn. "This place could be equal to that one again. It's been worked by tenant farmers in recent years. The Gridley farm, on the other hand, has been in the family for more than three generations and they've always done their own work. Fred, this farm could be just like that one. All it takes is someone like you to work it and keep the buildings in good shape. Why, in a few years, this place could look even better than the Gridley farm!" he emphasized for Friederich's benefit. He saw Friederich was really paying close attention to what he was saying.

The Gridley farm had been another impressive farm for Friederich. It was similar in so many ways to the one he had looked at in Dewitt. The barns had recently been painted, as had the house. The house, he remembered, was as large as this main house. The only difference was the Gridley house had been built in a huge square whereas this one was in the form of a huge T. The Gridley barns seemed to stretch along the road for several blocks. Friederich was impressed, indeed, with that farm. He thought to himself, if this place could become like that one, what a place this farm could be!

As Mr. Gorman opened the garage door, a huge cat came running out and across the road carrying what looked like an animal almost as big as the cat.

"The old cat's got herself a mouse," Mr. Gorman said.

Friederich thought it was more likely a rat, but didn't feel like contradicting Mr. Gorman. He was showing him a tremendous place even if it did have large rats . . . .

As they walked through the garage, Friederich noticed there was some farm machinery standing around. He didn't ask what types of machines they were, or for what they were used. He didn't want to let on he really didn't know much about farming.

"These mowers are really old and need to be replaced," Mr. Gorman volunteered. "This other one is an old roller."

Friederich described this machine to Emilie as two huge, round rollers that were hooked together on both ends with a seat over the top in the middle and a long pole to which horses are hitched. He was curious what this type of machine could be since he had never seen anything like it. Again, for fear of revealing his ignorance about farming, he remained silent.

Friederich liked the smell of the horse barn. It had the aroma of horse manure mixed with the sweetness of the newly discovered plant that he had found so delightful on the farm in Dewitt; alfalfa. It was slightly different only in that later he recognized it as clover and timothy which also had a pleasant smell. He climbed up one of the ladders built into the framework of the barn and saw the loft was quite full of hay. It reached almost to the roof on one side of the horse barn, and over the top most beam on the other side. He saw another interesting feature about this hay mow. There was a long rope attached to what looked like a large fork which hung from a track running the length of the barn. There was also a smaller rope which hung from this fork-like frame down to the beam near the barn floor. There was another rope, he noticed, which came down the wall and over three different pulleys to the floor of the barn and ended in a big knot just inside the rear door of the barn. He thought, somehow this rope must have something to do with getting the hay up into the mow. But exactly how, he wasn't sure.

The barn door was large enough to bring in a load of hay and then drive right out through the back side again. There were six horse stalls which Friederich remembered Mr. Gorman had mentioned earlier. There was plenty of room for the horses. The stall dividers prevented the horses from reaching each other if they were tied in their own stalls. There was also a grain bin. Mr. Gorman showed Friederich how the horses could be fed their oats every day.

"You don't even have to leave the barn to feed them, Fred."

Mr. Gorman took Friederich next, to the main cow barn. They entered through another large door.

"This can be opened wide enough to let both the horses and wagon pass through."

Friederich saw, on both sides of the center aisle, cows could be kept in stanchions (Mr. Gorman explained meant to hold the cows in the barn). He counted thirty of them and there was room enough for another ten on each side if they were needed, he thought. It was lucky for Friederich he had seen what a cow barn looked like on Grandfather Meyer's farm in Germany. At least he recognized these features of farming and could identify what each item was. He saw the area where more stanchions could be placed, was now taken up by three calf pens and a feed holder filled with grain and corn practically on top of the pens. There were two ladders on each side of the barn to the north and to the south which he proceeded to climb. He quickly saw these must be the openings through which hay could be thrown down to the cows. He also saw the same track with another one of those large forks and ropes similar to what he had seen in the horse barn. There was a slight difference this time in that the track came out of an overhang on the west side of the barn just under the roof. When he climbed down again, Mr. Gorman said, "Fred, now you're going to see the biggest silo in the county! Climb up that ladder and look down inside that monster. It's empty now, but you can imagine how much ensilage you can put in there!"

Friederich climbed up the iron rungs of the ladder which ran inside the barn up to the top of the silo. It was more than fifteen meters high, he thought, and ran right over the barn roof. He had an excellent view of the whole lower farm from the top of the ladder. He looked down inside the silo and was amazed how large it was. It must be about ten meters wide, and it was also hexagonal. It's a very unusual silo, he said to himself. So this is where corn is chopped and stored for cows! He had never seen that done, but thought it was something he was going to look into. It must be quite a machine, if it can throw the ensilage this high, he said to himself.

He climbed down again and Mr. Gorman asked, "Well, what do you think, Fred? Isn't she a beauty? There's not another one like it around here! Let's go back across the road and take a look at the other buildings."

As they walked across the road, Friederich noticed they had to wait for a couple of cars to pass coming from both directions. He had also put it in the back of his mind there were several cars that had driven past slowly, as if they were looking over the barns and silo. Route 5 must be a busy street, he thought to himself. As if to carry on where Friederich himself was thinking, Mr. Gorman said,

"I've heard from the owners that a gas company wants to open a gas station on the farm because of the increasing traffic. They've already agreed to a contract with the Tydol-Veedol Company to have one put in after the first of the year. It probably won't be put in before the middle of March. The ground has to thaw first before they can put the gas tanks underground. But the site has already been picked out. Right over here, just across from the milk house, Fred."

He showed Friederich about where the gas station would be located. There were a couple of huge old maple trees and an elm across from the milk house and well. The owners were already having one of the cabins that was located further up the hill, moved down as the office and little store for the new gas station. Friederich noticed these buildings were rather old, but still usable.

"A group of men from nearby Mycenae are going to move the cabin with four teams of horses and huge wooden rollers. They've already marked off the boundaries where the building will sit. See those stakes over there?"

Friederich followed where he was pointing.

"That's where the gas tanks and pumps will be placed. If you want to take over the gas station, Fred, I think we could arrange that, too. The owners had originally thought they were going to have to hire someone to run it, but if you buy the place, I'm sure they'd be interested in having you run the gas station. Didn't you say you already have a garage now on South Ave? This would be a natural for you, Fred. You could run the farm and the gas station once it's put in this next spring."

Friederich liked the idea . . . This would give us another source of income while we're learning how to farm, he thought. Now if Haussmanns and even Karl would come into the farm with us, we'd really have a family enterprise! The more he thought about it, the better it seemed. Mr. Gorman showed Friederich the large combination garage and hay barn just behind the main house. This garage could be driven into directly from the hill into which it was built. The floor was of a solid construction of planks that were ten millimeters thick. There was still more room underneath this floor if someone would take the time to dig it out, he thought. Near the top of the barn was another floor with planks almost as thick on which some old hay lay. It must have been put there years ago, he thought. It smelled rather musty and old. In the middle of the barn was room for a hay wagon and another one of those odd shaped forks with another long rope leading down to one corner of the building. There was no long track this time, but a pulley attached by a chain to the rafters just under the roof. A large iron fork was again attached to a thick rope similar to what he had seen across the road in the two other barns. This is another good building, Friederich thought. It could be used for any number of things. It might even be rebuilt into a house.

The last of the buildings which Mr. Gorman showed him were the three cabins set under a row of sugar maples lining the edge of a dirt road leading, Mr. Gorman told him, "Up to the top of the hill."

The cabins weren't very large, but at least they had space in them for beds.

"These are rented out to tourists in the summer," Mr. Gorman went on. "They're either for long term, or overnight for those on their way to Albany or New York."

There was another one of those "out-houses" set off by itself which the realtor said was used by the guests sleeping in the cabins.

The last place Mr. Gorman took Friederich was up this same dirt road behind the main house and garage with the nearby cabins. As they walked up the road, Friederich noticed the trees seemed to have scars on them.

"Why do these trees have scars on them?" he asked Mr. Gorman.

"Oh, these trees are sugar maples, Fred. I forgot to tell you. In years past, the owners used to tap sap from these trees in the spring time and made a very sweet maple sugar from them."

"I've never heard of that."

"In the spring of the year when the sap starts running up through the trunks of these trees, you can drill holes through the bark and attach a small wooden tube. You then hook buckets under these tubes and the sap will flow into them. Once the buckets are full, you take them off and heat the sap to a boil until the water is all gone leaving you with a very sweet flavored syrup."

"What's it used for?"

"People like to put it on their waffles or pancakes. It tastes great. You'll have to try it sometime, Fred."

Again, Friederich had no idea what pancakes or waffles were. He had never heard of them. At the time, he didn't know that pancakes were similar to pfannenkuchen which he had long eaten in Germany. Since he was still learning English, he thought this must be another one of those strange things Americans ate!

"Can this be done with all trees, this boring and collecting of sap?"

"No, no!" Mr. Gorman exclaimed. "Don't try to do this on other trees! You'd only poison yourself if you do! Only the sap from sugar maples should ever be used."

As they walked up the road, they talked about a number of things. Mr. Gorman had gotten used to Friederich's heavy accent. If he listened carefully enough, he could make out most of what Friederich asked or said.

"Did you have a farm in Germany, Fred?"

"No, I've never had one."

Mr. Gorman evidently thought he hadn't heard him correctly.

"What did you say, Fred?"

"I've never had a farm."

"What was that?" Mr. Gorman asked again.

"I've never had a farm. I've just always wanted one."

"Say that again? You've never had a farm? Then how are you going to work one if you don't know anything about it?" her asked incredulously.

"I'll learn how to do it when I have one. I can't learn if I don't have one."

Mr. Gorman was quiet for some time. He must have thought to himself, this guy's crazy. He doesn't know anything about farming but wants to buy one in order to learn how to farm? He probably didn't know whether he should warn him about how hard it would be, or let him find out for himself. He must have decided that it would serve Friederich right. He's got to learn what life on a farm is all about. Who am I to try to tell him otherwise? he must have said to himself. I'm just in the business to sell farms. I can't let my feelings get in the way of making a commission. No, if he wants to buy a farm without knowing anything about farming, that's his problem. Mr. Gorman didn't say too much after that to Friederich, except to say

"This farm has a lot more going for it than just farming. There are two big wood lots on the farm at each end; on the north and the south. The trees could be cut for timber."

The road, Friederich noticed, was fairly sound. It could easily be used for horses and wagons. The trees along the side were an excellent buffer for the road and kept it from eroding and washing out in rainy weather. He noticed too, that the trees had had their lower limbs cut off so that large wagons could go under them without hindrance. Friederich thought to himself, even hay wagons could go down this road.

When they got to the top of the hill, Mr. Gorman led him over to the center of the hill, just behind the main house. Friederich could see the cluster of buildings on both sides of the road. It was an impressive sight. But what took his breath away was to look off into the distance.There, before him, was a large lake whose ends he couldn't see. He could catch a glimpse of the distant shore. The lake was reflected beautifully in the sunshine. He could see a whole series of farms and silos spreading out before him in the three directions that he could see without obstruction. Mr. Gorman pointed out the rough outline of the farm which spread before them like a map on a table.

"To the right, along the eastern boundary of the farm, it's almost a mile in length, Fred," as he pointed it out.

"It's also the border of Onondaga county. On the other side is Madison county. To the north is the wood lot I told you about. Along the northern edge of those trees (he pointed to the furthest limits of the woods), is the end of the farm. On the northeastern side you can see where it looks pretty open. That's where a big lumbering operation took place a few years ago. On the west, you can see this rail fence running north to the first cluster of trees. Do you see where I'm pointing?"

"Yes. I see it."

Mr. Gorman continued, "The fence turns left along that line of trees and that old rail fence runs until way off to the corner. "Can you see an old butternut tree with limbs growing in all directions?"

Friederich nodded in agreement.

"Well the border goes right at that point, due north again into those woods. That's the western boundary on the north side of the road. If you turn around, you can see the southern part of the farm. On the left facing south, along that line of trees separating those fields is the eastern boundary of the farm. It runs clear up through those trees to a corner where the woods end and a field begins. Then the fence goes westward across the top of that hill. You really can't see it too well from here, but there's another stake which marks the property off from the John Young place.Then the fence comes north again on your right hand side straight down this line of trees, and that's the western boundary here on the south side of Route 5."

It was a long explanation but Friederich thought he had a pretty good idea where the boundaries of the farm were.

"What do you think, Fred? Do you want to buy it? The owners will take fifteen thousand for it. You can't get it for anything less. They've already come down considerably from what they were once asking. So it's pretty much take it or leave it," Mr. Gorman explained.

"I'll have to think it over, Mr. Gorman. I have to talk it over with my wife. I promised her I would let her see any farm before we buy it. I don't think she can come out to see it until after the baby the arrives. It'll probably be some time in January before she could come, Mr. Gorman. Don't sell it to anyone else and I'll give you an extra hundred dollars," Friederich promised.

"I can't do that, Fred," Mr. Gorman said. "If someone comes along and wants to buy it, I'll have to sell it. I'm under contract with the owners to sell it to whomever comes up with the money. I can't hold it for you."

Friederich reached into his pocket.

"Here's a hundred dollar bill. I expect you to wait to sell it until I see it again in January!"

He gave the bill to Mr. Gorman.

"You're a hard man to deal with, Fred, but I'll see if I can stall the sale along for you. Don't worry. I'll think of this as hand money for three months, until you see the place again," Mr. Gorman promised.

The realtor couldn't help but notice Friederich had several of these hundreds in his wallet. He thought to himself, if he wants to buy the place, he probably will! I wonder where he got all the money? He felt confident he could take this money in good conscience. After all, it was almost winter and it wasn't very likely that anyone would come out looking at the farm this time of year. He'd just hold off showing it to anyone else and tell Pauli and Trant there weren't many people interested this time of the year in buying a farm. Anyway, he told himself, spring is the best time to sell a farm. I shouldn't have any problem selling it then. The more he thought about the one hundred dollar bill, the more convinced he was that Friederich was going to buy "Valley Farm".

On the way back to Syracuse, Mr. Gorman and Friederich didn't say much. Each had his own thoughts about the farm. The realtor felt half-way sorry for Friederich. He still couldn't believe he wanted to buy a farm, especially since he had never worked on one! Mr. Gorman had grown up on a farm himself and had one even now. But he had someone else farming it for him. It was just too much hard work! He wondered how Friederich would ever know what to plant or even when to plow, for that matter! No, the realtor thought to himself, If I were in his shoes, I'd never buy a farm!

Friederich couldn't get the picture of the farm out of his mind. He kept coming back to all of those buildings and two houses! One of them was big enough for two houses by itself, he thought. And then there were the barns and the biggest silo in the county! The more he thought about them, the more he saw himself as the owner who would then be known as having the largest silo in Onondaga County! The gas station with the camping ground, the overnight cabins, and the tourist sign were even more intriguing. He knew it would take time to learn how to farm, but in the meantime, he could make a go of it with the gas station, tourists, and maybe even a garage. There was plenty of work to do. He thought if I can get my relatives involved in the venture, we'd have no trouble making a success of any number of these possibilities.

He was sure he was going to buy it. He just wanted to make sure he could sell his house and business in Syracuse. He could, then, make the down payment, which the owners required, and still have enough left over to buy cows and equipment.

Pauli and Trant wanted two-thousand five hundred dollars down and the rest on a twenty year note. He didn't think that was too much to pay off. If he sold his house for six thousand dollars, he could make the down payment, pay off the balance he still owed on the South Ave house, and still have a couple of thousand dollars with which to start farming. He was glad he told Mr. Gorman that Emilie wanted to see the farm before he bought it. This'll give me time to sell our place, he thought to himself. He felt confident, Mr. Gorman wouldn't sell it to anyone else in the meantime. The one hundred dollar bill would take care of that, he thought.

When Mr. Gorman reached the Malin house he said, "Give me a call, Fred, when you and your wife are ready to take a look at the farm. You said it'll be sometime in January? Is that right?"

"Yes, the baby is expected in early December so it'll be a few weeks after that before she can travel. I'll get in touch with you when we're ready. In the meantime, don't sell the farm to anyone else! Okay?"

"Don't worry, Fred. But if I don't hear from you by the end of January, it'll take another hundred to hold it . . ."

Friederich came in and told Emilie what he had seen on the farm. He was obviously excited, she noticed.

"You can't believe how many buildings there are and the size of the main house! It's even bigger than "Die Rose" where your mother lives."

"What? That big?" She asked incredulously. She almost couldn't believe it. She was sorry now she hadn't gone. I probably could have made it without too much of a problem, she thought to herself. It's just so uncomfortable moving around. My feet hurt and I feel best when I'm simply sitting in the easy chair. She did recall that Friederich was just as enthused the last time when they looked at the farm in Dewitt.

"This farm has many more buildings and more acres than the one in Dewitt."

"But it's such a long way away from the city. If we move out there, Papa, who would come all of that distance to visit us?"

"We're going to take them with us. When they see this place, they'll want to move in with us. It's got everything you could want on a farm. There's also a tourist business and this coming spring, there's going to be a gas station, too. There's plenty of work for all of us. Now all I have to do is convince my sisters and brother this is an enterprise for the whole family. We can all work together and yet, still live separately. It shouldn't be hard to make a living on such a large place with so much to do!"

The next day, Friederich spent the entire day working in the garage. He also sold a few batteries. But his mind was clearly on the farm in Chittenango. He didn't mind at all when people asked for Emilie to explain what they wanted him to do. That was usually another of the annoyances he had had to put up with. Because he spoke so quietly, people also thought he couldn't hear very well. But this time, it was much different. He even joked about it.

"I'll get the boss . . ."

Emilie was amazed with his good mood. It was rare she ever saw him act like that. This must be quite some place to have him in such a positive frame of mind! she thought.

That evening Friederich said, "I'm going over to Haussmanns and see what they would think about the farming enterprise."

"I'll stay home," Emilie said. "I'll do some more reading to improve my English. Besides, Volke and Inge have school tomorrow, Papa. It's better if they go to bed early and get a good night's sleep."

"Yes. You're right. I'll go see the Haussmanns alone."

When he arrived, Karl was also there. That's great, Friederich said to himself. I'll get a chance to hear what he thinks of the proposal.

"You'll never believe what I did yesterday," Friederich explained after greeting all of them.

"I looked over one of the biggest farms I've ever seen! It's a lot bigger than the one we looked at in Dewitt. There are two houses. The larger one has enough room in it for another house! There are five major buildings and five smaller ones and there's going to be a gas station put in next spring. There's also a tourist business on the farm."

"How much does it cost?" Karl asked.

"It's in the range Richard suggested when we looked at the other farm in Dewitt," Friederich replied.

"Fritz, how much do they want for it?" Karl repeated.

"Only fifteen thousand. That's not too much when you think of what's out there."

"It sounds as if it's big enough to have more than one family live on it," Richard said.

"I'd like to see it first," Gretel chimed in. "What's big to you men may not be much for a woman. Don't forget, we're thirteen people all together now and you're soon to have another, Friederich. It takes a lot of money to support that many people!"

"It sounds like quite a farm," Karl said thoughtfully.

"If it's as big as you say it is with all of these additional aspects to it, maybe we could be involved, too. The other farm you talked about in Dewitt didn't have all of these advantages, did it?"

"No. This one is much bigger and cheaper, too."

"It's an excellent idea," Grandmother Malin added. "I'd like to see some enterprise where we could all work together. Aunt Katharine is coming this next spring and so is Elise and Waltraude. They'd be able to live and work there, too. My sister wrote me just last week, she finally has a buyer for the house and they'll come over in March. If they already had a place to live and work, that would be ideal for them, as well as for us. It sounds like just the perfect place."

"Why don't we all go out there in my car this next Saturday," Karl suggested.

"We can't make a decision until we've seen the place. You say it's out near a place called Chittenango?"

"Where's that?" Gretel asked. "I've never heard of it. Can we get there by the main road, or is it out in the country somewhere? It's no use to have a tourist business if you're not on a main road!"

"Why don't we wait and see, Gretel?" Richard suggested. "It may be better than you think. We won't know until we've seen it."

They all agreed the following Saturday they would take a ride out to Chittenango to look over this farm.

"Okay, I'll pick you up at eight a. m." Friederich said.

"Let me drive, Fritz," Karl said. "I've got the newest car and it's in the best condition."

"Okay, I have a hard time getting mine started on these cold winter mornings anyway."

When Saturday arrived, Karl was at Haussmanns promptly at eight. Friederich was also there. It was a cold, wintry day. They bundled themselves very warmly. While there was the threat of snow in the air, there was none on the ground. Still, the wind was blowing and it looked somewhat threatening on this first Saturday in December. Friederich sat with Karl in the front seat. Richard, Gretel and Grandmother Malin sat in the back. They had a blanket on their laps for which they were glad. The wind came through the cracks of the canvass sides of the Maxwell. There was little spoken during the trip. Everyone was doing his best to keep warm, and with the wind blowing, plus the noise of the car, no one could hear Friederich anyway. It was just too noisy to carry on a conversation.

Karl was pleased with the road. It was concrete and generally smooth. There were the section bumps with which to contend. Twelve feet of concrete roadway was completed at a time and left to harden. Then the next twelve foot section until the road was completed. Each of the individual sections seemed to have a character all its own. The joint between the two sections was usually an inch, sometimes two inches apart. With the cold weather of winter, the sections seemed to shrink even more. The spaces were much further apart than in the summertime. The Malins and Haussmanns took these roads pretty much for granted. That's the way all of the roads were built. At least the concrete wasn't broken up and uneven.

"You should have seen the road I was on going out to Baldwinsville last week," Karl shouted over the noise. "It was pitted and broken up. I thought I was going to have a flat tire! This road is in excellent shape compared to that one! This just goes to show you," he shouted to the others, "The more heavily traveled the road, the better condition in which it's kept! This must be a pretty important road if it's in this good condition."

When they got to Mycenae, Karl said, "I've got to stop and tank up again and check the radiator."

He had five gallons of gas put in the tank. Friederich paid the sixty cents. He also made a mental note not to stop here again for gas. He usually only had to spend fifty-five cents for five gallons. Teft's gas was just too expensive. Karl, in the meantime, also put some water in the radiator and checked the oil. The oil level was okay.

"Before we go home, I'll have to put in a quart of oil," Karl said. "It's getting a little low."

They had all gotten out of the car to stretch and move around.

"It's not very far now," Friederich said. "It's just a little further."

He had remembered the Gridley farm and they all marveled at it as they drove by.

"Now that's a farm," Gretel said. "I could live here without any problem. They must be a rich family," she sighed. Richard simply nodded and kept looking out the window. He noticed the stream which flowed through the entire length of the Gridley farm. It had two stone bridges built over it. These could hold even the heaviest wagons or even trucks, he thought

"I wonder if they had these bridges built by masons, or if they built them themselves?" he asked out loud.

As soon as they rounded the curve from Mycenae and were heading past the second farm to the east of the village, Friederich pointed ahead.

"There it is! That's "Valley Farm"! It's the one with all of those buildings that you can see way up ahead."

"Is it the one with the twin silos?" Gretel asked.

"No. It's the one beyond that barn. You can see it on the left hand side; just beyond that smaller barn on the left."

Karl saw the one he meant. The others, in the back of the car, thought Friederich meant the Meagher farm.

"There aren't so many buildings on it!" Gretel said disappointed.

It was only after they had gone past the Meagher barn and silos that they saw the farm Friederich had tried to point out.

"Why it's almost like a little settlement by itself!" Gretel exclaimed when she saw all of the buildings. "What? There are all of these buildings on it?" She marveled at the number of buildings on the farm. "Why the big house is four times the size of our house, Richard!"

She was clearly impressed with how many buildings there were and the size of the big house was more than she could believe.

Unfortunately, since Friederich had not arranged to have the farm officially shown, all of the buildings were locked. They could only look in the windows. Nevertheless, they did just that. Grandmother Malin was pleased with the place.

"You've picked out a beautiful farm, Friederich. If I have anything to say about it, I'd say go ahead and buy it. I'd have no hesitation."

She walked all around the two houses and into the gardens.

"Each of these gardens is almost as big as mine was in Germany! And look at all those fields! There's plenty of room for even larger gardens!"

Looking into the barn windows, each of them saw there was plenty of room for any number of cows and chickens.

"The building up behind the garage would be perfect for chickens and ducks," Richard said.

After going from building to building and looking through what windows they could, Friederich suggested "Let's take a walk up the hill. We can see practically the whole farm from up there."

Friederich led the way up the same dirt road Mr. Gorman had taken him earlier. They walked slowly so Grandmother could come along.

"I want to see the view from the top, too," she said.

After half an hour, they reached the same spot where Friederich had stood with Mr. Gorman. He remembered the layout very well and pointed out the same boundaries which had been pointed out to him.

"You mean all this land is part of the farm, too?' Gretel asked. She couldn't believe there was so much land included on this farm.

"And so many buildings," she said to Richard. "Look how high the silo is! It's the highest one around! The only thing that's higher is this hill!"

Grandmother was the first to speak. "I've never seen anything prettier, nor as large as this farm!"

Gretel even commented, "Friederich, you've really picked out a beautiful farm. Do you think you can afford it?"

Friederich had hoped they would say they would help buy it. But since Gretel put it that way, he said,

"I think I can. I'm going to put my house up for sale this next week and if I can sell it for the price I want, I'll buy the farm. Aren't you interested in investing in it, too?"

"If I hadn't invested so much money in my house, I'd go right in with you," Karl said. "But I don't have any money right now. Maybe later on, when I've saved some, I might be able to help."

"Friederich, we don't have any money. What we had, we invested in our little house on Knaul Street. If we could save for about two more years, we might be in a position to invest then. But if there's this much business with tourists next spring, maybe we can come out and give you a hand. We could try it and see how it works out," Gretel conceded.

Richard was glad his wife had agreed to give this family enterprise consideration. He very much wanted to give farming a try. He liked his house on Knaul Street, but here on this farm there would be plenty of open space and he could raise some ducks and chickens, and have a big garden. He very much wanted to be out in the country and away from the factory.

"In spite of the fact we don't have any money to invest in this farm, we'll be glad to work on it with you for a season and see where we are next winter. If we can make enough from it, Fritz, we'll stay. If not, we can always go back to the city again."

"Friederich," Grandmother said, "I don't have much, but I'll invest five hundred dollars that I still have in your farm if you can use it. It Isn't much, but at least it's a little to help you buy it."

"Thank you very much, Mother. If you're not in any hurry to have it repaid, I'll pay you back sometime in the future."

They walked across the top of the hill and even went as far as the wood lot behind them. Friederich hadn't done that before. He was pleased to see how large the trees were. There hadn't been any cut for many years. The few stumps they did see were very old and badly rotted. They agreed it must have been a long time ago since any trees had been cut out of these woods.

As they walked back down the road to the farm house, they discussed how best to work out some arrangement for doing the work on the farm. They all agreed Richard's idea about all working together for a season was a good one. Especially since there would be three more people arriving in March from Germany.

"You, Gretel, together with your two children, Grandmother, and the three from Germany could live in the big house, Richard," Friederich offered.

"There would even be enough room for you and your family, Karl, if you wanted to come in with us. Emilie and I will live in the small house and, because your English is so much better than ours, Gretel, you could handle the tourist business as well. Emilie's going to be pretty busy with the new baby. You could also take care the gas station that's going to be built this next spring. In fact, Riche and Grete, are old enough to take care of the gas station. You would only have to be on hand, Gretel should there ever be any problem they couldn't take care of themselves,"

"I'm not sure Anne would want to move out here, Fritz. You know she works at the restaurant in the city," Karl said. "Now that my house is almost finished I could, at least, spend my weekends out here and take a long vacation this summer to help with the farm work. If you need help in buying some farm machinery I know something about American engines in case you're going to buy a tractor," he continued.

"I'll help with the farm work and raise some chickens and ducks, Friederich," Richard said. "I'd also like to work in the garden."

They took one more look at the buildings before they left. As they got into Karl's car, they felt very good about the prospects of the farm and about themselves. Each one, in his own way, thought about the farm and his or her future on it.

"You buy the farm, Friederich, and we'll move out on it," they all agreed.

When Friederich returned that evening, Emilie was amazed when he told her the whole family was in agreement about buying the farm in Chittenango. She hadn't even seen it, and yet she felt the momentum of buying it was already underway.

"Couldn't we, at least, wait until I've had a chance to see it?" she asked. "You told Mr. Gorman it wouldn't be before January was over, we'd take another look at it. Now you've already decided to buy it! How are we going to pay for it? We haven't even sold this house yet! In fact, we haven't even tried to sell it! We don't really know even if we can, Papa," she said reproachfully. "Couldn't we wait until I've seen it before going ahead and selling this house? After all, the baby will be coming soon and it shouldn't be too long before I can go with you to see it!"

Friederich got angry from what he called her "pleading".

"Here I've gotten all of my relatives to agree to do something together, and now you're throwing a road block in the way! What difference does it make if you've seen it or not? You'll see it later at any rate!" he fired back. "I'm going to sell this place and the sooner we do, the sooner we can buy the farm! A farm like that won't be available for long! If even Gretel was impressed with it, what do you think other people are going to say about it, when they see it?"

Emilie had to agree. It was most unusual for Gretel to be impressed with something. If she said Friederich should go ahead and buy it, she thought to herself, well, then it must be quite a farm.

"Do you mind if I talk to Gretel about it, Papa?" she asked. "I want to talk with her about where to go to have the baby, anyway."

The next evening, after the shop was closed, Friederich took Emilie and the children to visit the Haussmanns. Since it was only another week or two before the baby was due, Gretel was very surprised to see her get out of the car upon arrival at 207 Knaul Street.

"What are you doing, Emilie, riding around in a car these days? Do you want the baby to come too early? You shouldn't be riding around like this, not this late in your pregnancy!" she scolded.

Emilie apologized. "I just wanted to talk to you, Gretel. Friederich tells me you've advised him to buy that farm by Chittenango. What's it like? Are there really that many buildings and two houses on it? Is there a tourist business with it? Are they really going to build a gas station there, too?"

"Slow down, Emilie," Gretel said. "One question at a time! I can't answer everything at once! Yes, I did tell Friederich he should buy the farm. There are two houses on the property and a lot of other buildings besides. Yes, there must be a tourist business, since there's a sign out in front of the big house saying, 'Tourists Welcome'. In so far as the gas station is concerned, Friederich told us that. It's supposed to be built this March, or as soon as they can dig into the ground to bury the two big gas tanks," she answered each question matter of fact. She continued on in an even more promising note when she said, "It's really a beautiful place, Emilie. You'll like it too, once you've seen it!"

Emilie felt reassured. If anyone would have any doubts about the wisdom of buying the place, Gretel would, she told myself. Since she approves of it, it must be quite a place.

"Gretel, I have another question to ask you. Where would you suggest I go to have my baby? I haven't chosen a hospital yet because I didn't know which one would be best."

"St. Mary's is one of the best hospitals for child care and it's on the north side, too. It's out on Court Street on the way to Karl's house in Lyncourt," Gretel said without hesitation. "Some of my neighbors have gone there and they were very pleased with the care they received. It's run by Catholic sisters so the care is excellent. There's also a hospital on the south side. It's not too far from where you and Friederich live. But I don't know anything about it."

Emilie felt relieved. Not only had Gretel filled her in on some of the details of the prospective farm Friederich wanted to buy, she had also found out about a good hospital near the Haussmanns and Malins. I guess there's no need for me to be upset about not seeing the farm, she told herself. It must be quite a place if Gretel likes it so much. She felt she no longer should object to Friederich's putting up their house for sale. She would have preferred to see the farm herself, but knew she couldn't this far along in her pregnancy. I'll have to wait until after the baby arrives . . . she thought.

Emilie thought about the baby quite often. It was kicking and moving about quite vigorously. It was going to be the first of her children born in America. She and Friederich had already picked out two names: Mary, if it were a girl; and Donald, if it should be a boy. They had asked their night school teacher about truly American names. She gave them a rather long list from which they had picked out these two. She looked forward to these last weeks of pregnancy. It's going to be another new experience for me, she thought to myself. I'll see what it's like to be in a hospital to have my baby. This is only our second winter in America and we've done so much already, she told herself.

On Sunday morning, December 10, around six o'clock in the morning, she awoke.

"Papa, I think you better take me to the hospital. The baby's coming."

The water sac had broken. She knew from the other two children's birth, it could either be very soon, or it could take some hours before the baby came.

Friederich dressed himself hurriedly and woke Volkmar and Inge. He helped them get dressed.

"Volke, you and Inge have to go to Grandmother's now. I've got to take Mama to the hospital because you're going to have a little brother or sister today. I'll take you there, but you'll have to stay until I come back to pick you up, okay? You do what Grandmother tells you."

"Why can't I go along, Papa? I can see why Inge can't go. She's too little! But I can go! I'm big enough to look after myself!" Volkmar pleaded.

Friederich didn't want an argument from him.

"That's out of the question, Volkmar! You'll stay with your Grandmother until I come to get you, do you understand? We don't have any time to argue. We've got to get going before the baby arrives. Get yourself dressed and don't argue!"

Reluctantly, Volkmar got himself dressed and even helped Inge get her coat and hat on. She always had trouble buttoning her coat, which Volkmar couldn't understand. He thought she was just too lazy to do it right! He buttoned her coat right to the very top even when she objected it was too tight. He did it anyway. She tried to unbutton it, but without success. After they were all ready, Friederich took Volkmar and Inge out to the car first. He then came back and got Emilie. She had gotten her things together to take along. Gretel had told her what she should take.

"It might be a couple of weeks before they'll let you come home again, Emilie. It's not like having your baby at home. The doctors want to be sure you and the baby are doing well."

Friederich drove first to the Haussmanns and left Volke and Inge there. Since only Grandmother was up, Friederich told her where he was going.

"So, you're going to become a father again, Friederich? Don't worry about the children. I'll look after them. Be sure to let us know what it is," she called after him.

He promised her he would come back as soon as the baby was born.

When they arrived at the hospital, the nun who admitted Emilie, asked, "Who's your doctor?"

"I don't have a doctor, Sister."

"What? You've been pregnant all this time and you haven't even been to a doctor?" the nun asked in astonishment.

"Why is that necessary?" Friederich asked. "She doesn't need to go to a doctor when she's feeling all right!"

"It's simply better and safer to have a doctor," the nun continued. "If there should be any problems in the birth, it's always better to have a doctor on hand," she said sternly. "That's the way we do things in this country!"

Emilie couldn't help but think to herself, aha, she probably thinks here are a couple more immigrants who only come to us when they need us! She tried to explain.

"In Germany we never had a doctor except when we were sick. I had my other two children at home on our kitchen table."

The nun didn't say anymore. She simply shook her head. Emilie filled out the admission forms, and was taken to a two-bed suite. The other bed was just being changed. The woman, who had been in the room, was discharged.

"You'll be in this room alone for a while. As soon as the contractions increase we'll take you into the delivery room," the nun said. "We only go in there when the contractions have increased into a regular rhythm."

Emilie had no idea what she meant. "Papa, what does she mean the delivery room?"

"She probably means you will be taken into the birthing room when the baby starts coming out."

"Mr. Malin, you can stay with your wife in this room until the contractions are steady. When we take her to the delivery room, you'll have to wait outside in the lounge with all of the the other expectant fathers," the nun concluded.

"I don't understand. Why can't I stay with my wife right through the birth?"

"We don't allow that here," she said sternly. "It's hospital policy! I'll tell you when you have to leave!"

Emilie and Friederich talked about how different it was being in the hospital.

"I don't like hospitals! And the very idea that you should have had a doctor look after you while you're pregnant! That's ridiculous! All the doctor does is charge money. It was some idiot doctor that left me without a voice! No!" he said thoughtfully, "We don't need any doctors!"

"Well, maybe it wouldn't hurt, Papa," Emilie said slowly. "You know there are times when we don't know how to take care of something ourselves and only a doctor might know what to do," she said diplomatically. "You know, if Roswina and Elise hadn't been available as mid-wives during the birth of Volke and Inge, I couldn't have done it all by myself. Here in America, the doctors must be like mid-wives. I'm glad I'm here in the hospital, Papa."

Two hours passed before Emilie told one of the sisters who checked on her periodically, "The contractions are coming regularly, Sister."

The nun took her to the delivery room while another nun took Friederich to the waiting room.

"Now you stay here, Mr. Malin. When the baby has arrived, I'll come and get you. Is that understood?" She said it as if she were talking to a young boy. Friederich didn't say anything. He sat down with two other men in the waiting room.

As Emilie came into the room, she saw there were already two other women about to be delivered.

"Hello," she said to them. They didn't respond. One was an older woman who was having a hard time with the birth. She cried much of the time. The other woman was repeatedly playing with her rosary beads and praying continuously. Since they didn't appear to want to say anything to Emilie, she kept quiet. She couldn't help but wonder, what will this one be? A boy or a girl? It won't be long now, she told herself. Donald or Mary? She kept repeating. She hoped the delivery wouldn't be as hard as the last time. She had really had to push Inge out, she recalled. As she was thinking to herself, she heard the Sister telling her,

"Push Emilie. Push again. It's almost out!"

At ten a. m. in the morning, the little boy arrived.

"Well look at that, Emilie. You've got a little boy!" the Sister said. She washed him off and put him in her arms.

"I'll go out and tell your husband!"

As she entered the waiting room, all three men stood up. Each one was expecting to be the first to hear the news. Even though Emilie had gone into the delivery room last, she was the first to deliver.

"Congratulations, Mr. Malin. You've got a new boy in the family!" the Sister told him.

She told Emilie later, after he had received the news, her husband smiled and said "Thank you very much for all of your help, Sister. We really appreciate it." He then extended his hand to her and they shook hands.

She ushered Friederich into her room. She smiled wanly at him. He had a broad smile on his face.

"You've done a great job, Emilie. We've got another little boy. Just what we need on the farm!" Friederich beamed. "And he weighs so much, too. The Sister told me he weighs eight pounds twelve ounces. I wonder what that is in German pounds and grams? It doesn't matter. I can figure that out when I get home. He's a real bundle, isn't he?"

It was obvious he was very proud of his new son. He repeated what he had said before, "That's just what we can use on our new farm!"

"Yes," Emilie answered weakly. "Now you can go ahead and buy it. Donald will be a big help to us on the farm."

"Donald," Friederich repeated. "That's a good name. And his second name will your father's and mine. Friederich. Donald Friederich Malin."

They were both looking at the baby as he opened his eyes and looked at them. It was almost as if he were asking, are you two my parents?

The Sister took the baby to the baby room and said, "Emilie, you ought to get some sleep now. The baby will want to suckle in a couple of hours. You can come back this afternoon to visit her, Mr. Malin, after she's rested."

"That's a good idea, Papa. I'm very tired and I could really sleep now," Emilie agreed.

He kissed her good bye.

"I'll stop in later today if it's possible. Otherwise, I'll be here tomorrow."

Friederich drove to the Haussmanns to give them the news. When he arrived, they were all awake. Friederich had purchased a box of cigars before he took Emilie to the hospital. He brought these into the house. He announced, "We've got another son!"

Grandmother was the first to hug him.

"Friederich, now you have two strong sons to help you on the farm!"

"That's what a farmer needs, sons!" Gretel congratulated him. Richard also congratulated him and shook his hand. Friederich gave him one of the cigars from the box and they sat together smoking while he told them about how much the baby weighed and at what time he was born. Volkmar and Inge ran to Friederich after they returned from their walk with Grete. Volkmar asked, "What is it, Papa? A boy or a girl?"

"You have a little brother," Friederich said.

"When can I see him, Papa?"

"As soon as your mother is able to come home from the hospital. When I go to pick her up, you can go with me, Volke."

Volkmar and Inge spent the day telling whomever they met they had a little brother. They told Riche and Grete.

"Okay, so you've got a new little brother! How many times are you going to say it? Enough is enough!" they said in exasperation.

"He'll be a lot more fun than a dog or a cat!" Volkmar told his Grandmother.

Each day Volkmar and Inge asked, "Are Mama and the baby coming home today?"

"They almost drove us crazy," Gretel told Emilie. "Everyday they asked, when are Mama and the baby coming home? Or, why is Mama in the hospital?" Grandmother told them just once, "She's in the hospital to have a baby. That's it. You're too young to understand. When you're older, you'll know why she went there." That was all she would say. If the children persisted, she said, "Wait and see." She ignored any further questions on the subject.

Originally, Friederich had worked out a plan for Volkmar and Inge to stay at Haussmanns while Emilie was in the hospital. Friederich drove back and forth between South Avenue and the hospital. After visiting Emilie and the baby, he stopped to see how Volkmar and Inge were getting along. He discovered Inge was sleeping with Grandmother, and Volkmar slept with his cousin, Riche, in the attic.

Emilie missed the children very much.

"How are Volke and Inge getting along, Papa?" she asked each day before any other question.

"They're getting along just fine. The only thing they're missing is school. And that can't be helped," Friederich asserted. "It's much more important they're being well cared for than going to school."

"Maybe Grandmother could stay at our house, Papa. Then the children could go to school."

"She's going to come over tomorrow. Gretel is staying home over the holidays so these last few days before Christmas, Volkmar and Inge will be back in school."

"That's good, Papa. Grandmother can cook good meals for you. "Have you put up a for sale sign?"

"No. I've not had time. I've had too much business to take care of. The cars all seem to need either new batteries or else recharges on these cold winter days. There's always someone wanting me to do one thing or another to their cars. That's why I've not come during the day. I couldn't just close up shop. There are always customers waiting. I haven't missed an evening's visit yet, Emilie. But, I've literally had to turn out the lights in the store after the last customer left and gone upstairs in the dark, otherwise I just wouldn't be able to leave! I'm going to wait until you come home before I put up the sign. I really can't stop to show the house and keep the shop open, too!"

"Are you eating enough, Papa? Is Grandmother cooking good meals for you? It's good that she's staying with you. You'd hardly have time to do any cooking, Papa."

"On the weekends, we all go over to Haussmanns for dinner. I've already decided, Emilie, when you're ready to come home, Grandmother is going to stay on with us for a while until you're back on your feet."

Emilie was pleased Friederich had made these arrangements. Grandmother came to stay at their home to look after the children only three days after Emilie had gone to the hospital. The Haussmanns were concerned Volkmar and Inge were missing too much school. Grandmother was doing not only all of the cooking, but the washing and house cleaning.

"Emilie, you won't have to worry about anything except taking care of little Fritzle."

She felt greatly relieved when Friederich told her. She had been wondering how she would ever be able to manage taking care of the children, cooking, washing, and caring for the baby all at the same time! She wasn't exactly enthused her mother-in-law would be the one to help. But she did recognize this was a better arrangement than no help at all. I'll try to get along with her and listen to all of her advice, she thought to herself. I know she's going to give me plenty of it every day on how I should take care of little Fritzle! Fortunately, when it came to interacting with her mother-in-law, Emilie had already developed a very skillful habit of listening to her very carefully. While Grandmother thought she would do what she suggested, Emilie usually went ahead and did what she wanted to do in her own way. She had learned when she listened attentively to her, Grandmother seemed very pleased. Emilie's appearance of listening well enabled her to do what she exactly wanted to do. When she went ahead and did as she wanted, her mother-in-law didn't seem to get too upset with her.

Emilie returned home on Christmas Eve. Friederich and the children had bought a Christmas tree at a nearby tree nursery and decorated it for her homecoming. Grandmother had baked cookies and even a cake for the occasion. It was a very pleasant Christmas for all of them. Emilie couldn't help but wonder where they would be spending their next Christmas together. It'll very likely be on this new farm that Papa has discovered near someplace called Chittenango, she thought to herself.

The last days of 1928 went by very quickly. Fritzle was a very hearty drinker. Emilie gave him the breast on demand just as she had done with the older children. Volke and Inge enjoyed their winter vacation playing in the exceptionally heavy snow that fell that winter. They usually came into the house soaking wet. Before Grandmother left, she prepared hot cocoa for them, each time when they came in from the cold. Emilie continued to do this. Volkmar followed up his cupful with another cup, or two, of bread broken into cold milk. On top of the submerged bread, he spread a large spoonful of sugar; a trait he carried on into adulthood.

Friederich put the house up for sale. Within one week, two couples looked it over. One man, in particular, wanted to know how business was going and asked all kinds of questions.

"How much do you make each month on battery sales and car repairs? Have you thought of providing a towing service to go along with the battery shop?"

"I've never considered it," Friederich answered.

"It might be a very good idea. You'd have far more business by adding a new dimension to the shop. I'll come back in January and look it over again," he told Friederich. "Your price is reasonable. I just have to see if I can raise the money first before I commit myself."

Towards the end of January, during one of those yearly thaws that often occurs in up-state New York, Emilie suggested, "Papa, maybe this would be a good time to drive out to see the farm in Chittenango."

"That's fine with me, Emilie. Why don't you call Mr. Gorman and ask him if he can drive us out to see the farm?"

Mr. Gorman agreed. "I'll come by the first thing tomorrow morning, Mrs. Malin."

Friederich made arrangements to bring Grandmother over for the day to take care of the baby. While Volkmar and Inge went to school, Friederich and Emilie thought just in case they should return late, Grandmother would be on hand when they came home. The baby took an occasional bottle although Emilie had already decided he would be breast fed as long as possible. Volkmar had been breast fed for almost a year and Inge for eight months. She thought a bottle or two would not interfere with the baby's usual routine.

Mr. Gorman arrived promptly at nine o'clock in the morning. He drove them out to see the farm. Friederich had told her it was called "Valley Farm" and showed her a card with the name printed on it. On the way out, they noticed the snow was slushy underfoot, but the road was dry in the middle where all of the cars had driven. The snow was rapidly melting, even though it was wet and heavy. They wore leather boots which Emilie had greased the night before to make sure they would be water proof. The drive itself was uneventful although at twenty-five miles an hour, she couldn't help but wonder how long it took to arrive. She had thought it was just a little further than Dewitt. She was amazed it took almost forty-five minutes to reach the farm. She, too, was impressed with the quality of the road. There was one farm after another as soon as they left the city limits. These weren't just little farms, but big ones with big barns, lots of open fields and even occasionally some cows standing in the snowy barn yards taking in the sun and fresh air.

"Why are the cows all outside, Mr. Gorman?"

"The farmers think the out of doors is good for them," he answered. "They need fresh air, too, just like we do."

They drove on most of the way in silence although Mr. Gorman wanted to know more about them and why they were so interested in buying a farm. Because of the noise of the car, Emilie did most of the talking.

"My husband wants to live out in the country where he won't have to engage so many people in conversation," she began. "You've probably noticed his voice," she said as gently as she could. She knew Friederich was very sensitive about anyone questioning his voice.

"Has he ever had a farm, or worked on one?" Mr. Gorman asked.

"No. But he's very willing to learn. You know we had our own business in Germany. My husband is a tool and die-maker by trade. He had his own machine shop and sold bicycles and motorcycles as well. He thinks it won't be too hard to learn how to farm," she said confidently.

"That's what your husband told me last month when we first visited the farm. But does he know how hard farming is? Does he know anything about cows or crops?"

"Not that I'm aware of."

Friederich gave her a sharp look.

"But I'm sure, if my husband sets his mind to it, he'll learn how to farm, too."

"I hear you have three children now? Is that right?"

"Yes, we just had another little boy this past month," she said proudly.

"That'll be a big help to you in the future as they grow up. Do you have any other relatives who might help you on the farm right now?"

"My husband does have a brother and two brothers-in-law who might help him on the farm. We're not sure yet, but it looks like at least one of his sisters and her family will join us this spring, if we buy the farm."

"We're here," Friederich interrupted. Mr. Gorman drove into the yard. Emilie couldn't believe her eyes. Here was this huge house with an equally large set of barns across the road.

"Is this the place? Why it's so big and look at the size of that tree!" she exclaimed. "It's even larger than the house!"

"Yes, that's an American elm," Mr. Gorman said. "There are a lot of them around here. You'll find them everywhere. They grow just about anywhere. Look out along the edge of the pasture and those fields over there."

He pointed to the huge trees growing along the fence lines almost in every direction.

"You'll even find them along the edge of your garden, too."

"This is the same kind of tree that stands in front of Haussmanns' house," Emilie said to Friederich.

"Yes. It's the same kind."

"It was an even larger tree at one time," Mr. Gorman said.

He pointed to the east side of the tree.

"It's been repaired with concrete," he continued. "The whole eastern side broke off some ten years ago. But this part will stand for years. It could lose a lot more limbs and you'd still have a wonderful shade tree. Look how its branches reach, almost to the garage!"

"It must be way over four meters around," Friederich estimated.

"It's way over thirty feet around the trunk," Mr. Gorman asserted.

"Just look at that root system. It has to be that big just to hold up the tree!"

The root system was so massive it gave the tree the appearance of having grown on a hill. The roots had raised the ground around it to such a height, where the tree was growing, a little hill had formed slopping down in each direction from the trunk of the tree. There were not only limbs growing out over the roof of the house, but also over the road towards the barn.

"I've never seen a tree this big!" Emilie said in amazement. "Why didn't you mention this before, Papa?"

"There was just so much to see the last time. I wanted to save this surprise for you!"

And surprised she was! The rest of the farm proved to be just like the tree!

"I like the houses, Papa. But we don't need one this big for just the five of us!"

"We don't have to live in this one. Wait until you see the little house. It's just right for us. Let's take a look at that one first."

Mr. Gorman led the way and opened the door for them.

"When you're through, Mrs. Malin, I'll be back at the car. You can look at the rest of the place after you've seen this one."

"I'm just amazed, Papa. There's all this room here in this house!"

"What do you think of this little room, Emilie?"

He led her into a small room just off the kitchen.

"Wouldn't this be just right for the baby during the day? You could be working in the kitchen and if the baby cried, you could come to see what's wrong."

"You're right, Papa. It would be the perfect place for him during the day."

"Let's take a look upstairs. There are more rooms up there."

Friederich led the way. "Take a look at this room. Wouldn't this be just right for the baby at night? It's right next to our bedroom."

Sure enough there were three bedrooms upstairs with a small closet like room next to the room Friederich said should be their bedroom.

"This is perfect, Papa! I could put him here in the evenings and downstairs during the day. And there are two more bedrooms so Volke and Inge could have their own bedrooms, too."

She couldn't believe how lucky they were to have such a convenient house in which to live!

They returned to Mr. Gorman's car. He drove them over to the big house. It seemed even larger than Friederich had described.

"Is this where the Haussmanns would stay?" she asked. Friederich nodded.

Mr. Gorman opened the front door and they walked into the house.

"Oh, such big rooms! The big house is even larger than you told me, Papa! If the Haussmanns want to live here, that's fine with me. With your aunt, sister, and niece coming from Germany this spring, they could move right in here, too. There'll be plenty of room and then some, even for tourists."

She had been a little apprehensive about living so far out in the country. The distance from Syracuse seemed a long way. She had real doubts about moving this far out as Mr. Gorman drove them out to see the farm. But after she saw it, she could visualize the Haussmanns living right next door. She felt she wouldn't feel so isolated, or alone anymore. She had voiced these fears to Friederich on the way.

"Wait until you see the place before you start worrying about the distance!" was all he would say. For him the distance from Syracuse didn't make any difference at all.

"I can't imagine how anyone would ever be lonely on a farm," he said somewhat angrily.

After they arrived and Emilie saw all of the buildings and the two houses, she felt very reassured. While there wasn't much traffic going by as they walked around the barns, a few cars did drive past, every now and then.

"Are there tourists, Mr. Gorman?" she asked. "I see the sign down by the road."

"Oh sure. You'll be surprised how many cars there are on the road in the summer. There's not too much traffic now, in the winter, but when spring comes, you'll definitely see a big change," he assured her.

Mr. Gorman kept talking almost non-stop about the farm.

"There's a new gas station going in and I just talked with Mr. Pauli and Mr. Trant yesterday. They said as soon as the ground gets soft enough, the gas company is going to dig the hole to put in the tanks for the gas station. They thought it might even be finished before spring. It all depends on the weather," he continued.

"If this thaw continues, why they'll have them in pretty soon, maybe even this month."

He pointed toward the little house that stood next to the road just across the street from the milk house and cow barn.

"It's going to be the store and sales office, Mrs. Malin. You shouldn't have any problem having customers. Of course, Pauli and Trant were going to hire someone to run the station, but if you think you and your husband can do it, I'm sure they'd be glad to reconsider."

Mr. Gorman hadn't shown the farm to anyone else, he told them. In retrospect, Emilie thought Mr. Gorman must have sensed Friederich had already made up his mind to buy it. From Mr. Gorman's point of view, he told himself, if I just get him to think it might be gone before he can buy it, then the sale could be made that much sooner. The Malins found out later, Mr. Gorman hadn't actually gotten such a favorable report from his conversations with Pauli and Trant. They actually wanted to be sure someone was living on the farm first, then the gas station would be built. If they had the station built sooner, they would have had to hire someone to manage it, apart from the farm. They didn't think there were too many farmers who would also want to operate a gas station! It would be too much for any single family to manage. Mr. Gorman, however, told Pauli and Trant he thought he could find a buyer who would have both the interest and the man power to do both. What Pauli and Trant had really told him was "If you think you have someone like that, Ted, then go ahead and sell it. If you find such a person, we'll extend the financing to him. All we want is one third down and we'll carry the rest in a twenty year mortgage."

Mr. Gorman knew he could arrange for some kind of a sale. It was just a matter of convincing this German about what a prize he would have if he bought this farm. He must have thought to himself, he may not know anything about farming, but then that's his problem. All I have to do is stress the potential of the place and he'll buy it! And stress it he did!

"Fred, if you sell your house and business on South Ave, you'll have more than enough to make the one third down payment. The owners are good men. Mr. Pauli has his own farm and he knows how hard it is to work a farm. You'll get a lot of understanding from him. Mr. Trant grew up on a farm and, while he's been a banker most of his life, you'll find him sympathetic and interested in helping you get started in farming."

What Mr. Gorman also told these two owners was that Frederick Malin had never farmed before. Neither in Germany, nor in America.

"If he can't make a go of it," he told Pauli and Trant, "You'll have your farm back again on a foreclosure! You really have nothing to worry about. In the meantime, you'll have someone living there and working the farm. It'll be like collecting rent. If Malin can't pay anymore, the farm's still yours."

Pauli and Trant must have liked this suggestion from their realtor. It was for this reason they decided to extend the sweetener to the Malins about owner financing. When Mr. Gorman said the owners would be willing to hold the mortgage, Friederich took up the offer. He told Mr. Gorman "I think I'll be selling my house within the next month. In the meantime, I'll put down five hundred dollars towards the one third down payment that the Mr. Pauli and Mr.Trant require."

Mr. Gorman seemed pleased Friederich had reached this decision.

"Fred, you won't regret it. You've got yourself a beautiful place. Isn't that right Mrs. Malin?"

She agreed. "It is a very nice farm, Mr. Gorman. But it's so big! Do you think we can swing it, Papa?"

Then, as if to answer her own question, she said thoughtfully, "I suppose if the Haussmanns go into it with us, we should be able to do it. But if they aren't willing to work with us, I don't think we can do it alone. It's an awful lot of money and it's a long time to pay it off. If we buy it, we won't be able to leave it any more, Papa. There aren't too many people who can afford such an expensive farm."

Mr. Gorman sensed she still had cold feet. He started in again with his litany.

"Think of all of the advantages there are on this farm. Why just in the gas station alone, Mrs. Malin, there'll be enough money to support your family once it opens! And then there's the tourist business. People go by here every day on their way to Albany or New York. It's the most heavily traveled road in upstate New York. They're bound to stop here over night.There aren't any hotels around here! You'll have all the guests you can handle! Look at those barns! There aren't any better around here. That silo is the biggest in the entire county! Look at those fields over there (he pointed down to the fields beyond the barns). There's enough land there to support a large dairy. You can raise ducks, chickens, geese, whatever you want! You can do it right here!"

"Do you remember the place by DeRuyter Lake, Papa? We looked at it just before winter? It was one of the last places we saw together before the baby was born. Volkmar and Inge enjoyed playing down by the lake. Remember how you liked that place? But you didn't think we could afford it. It was even nicer and newer than this farm with the lake right in our back yard. You said it was too expensive and you had your doubts about whether or not we could pay for it. Now you want to buy this farm. I'm just asking, Papa, what's the difference between that farm and this one?"

Emilie could tell Friederich was getting angry.

"The Haussmanns and Karl have seen this place and were as impressed with it as much as I am. They didn't see the one at DeRuyter! This farm is located on a major highway and that one was in the hinterland. This farm has a lot more buildings on it and has potential, with the new gas station, which the other farm didn't have. There may have been a lake behind it, but this one has one of the best views I've ever seen from the top of the hill! You can see Oneida Lake off to the north. You have a commanding view of the entire countryside. This farm is also about ten acres larger, with a much bigger wood lot. All in all," he concluded, "This farm's advantages out weigh those of any of the others I've seen!"

Emilie had to agree. It was an impressive farm. Without anymore discussion, Friederich told Mr. Gorman

"We'll buy "Valley Farm". Here's five hundred dollars down as my first payment. I'll give you the rest in three months."

"All right, it's deal."

Mr. Gorman gave Friederich a receipt for the five hundred dollars as his first down payment.

"You'll have to pay the other four thousand five hundred in three months."

Friederich was confident he would have the house on South Ave sold by then. He wanted to move out to the farm as soon as possible. Emilie said to Friederich "Mr. Gorman never mentioned the one hundred dollars you gave him last December, Papa"

"That's past," Friederich said angrily in German. "I asked him to hold the farm and he did. That's just part of business!"

"Is there a problem, Fred?" Mr. Gorman asked.

"No," Friederich responded. "The farm's ours."

Mr. Gorman took them back to South Avenue. None of them said much in the car. When they arrived, Mr. Gorman said, "It's been a pleasure to have met you, Mrs. Malin. I'm sure you'll be very happy on your "Valley Farm."

After he left, Friederich felt he had to straighten Emilie out. "I gave him the one hundred dollars to guarantee he wouldn't sell it to anyone else. He might have sold it. Then where would we have been?"

Ted Gorman got his full commission and Friederich got his farm. No one else knew about the private arrangement between them.

"I don't want you to tell anyone else about it, either," Friederich told Emilie.

Emilie and Friederich now had something to look forward to again. It was to be another move. Emilie hoped this one would be her last, at least, for some time. They had lived in five different homes since they left Germany! Now, with the baby, she wanted some place where she could put down her roots for a while. She felt the security of a fixed residence would work wonders, both for the children and for her. She knew it probably didn't matter to Friederich. But for her, it would bring the stability and continuity again to her life she had missed since leaving Germany. Volkmar, in particular, made friends very easily wherever they lived. Emilie did notice, however, it was becoming more and more difficult for him each time they moved. She spent hours explaining where they were moving, and why. He often cried in his sleep, especially after they had moved. She sensed these moves were harder for him than for her and Friederich. She hoped, with the Haussmanns moving out to the farm, Volkmar wouldn't mind the move so much this time.

That evening, as Friederich took Grandmother back to Haussmanns again, she said "So Friederich, I'm very glad you bought the farm. Emilie may think it cost too much, but you'll be able to afford it!"

Grandmother was responding to Emilie's uneasiness. Emilie had told her,

"Grandmother, it costs so much. I hope we can afford it!"

"It's a beautiful farm, Emilie. No matter what happens, you have all that land and all those buildings. Not everyone has so many possibilities from what they buy."

Emilie had to agree. It was a very unusual farm. She just couldn't quite believe they could do everything such a big farm required.

When they arrived, Haussmanns were just finishing supper. Friederich and his mother sat down with them for coffee and kuchen. He explained to them what he had just done and they were also pleased.

"As soon as it's spring, we'll move to the farm," they all agreed. It was tentatively decided they would move around the first of April. Friederich told them

"Emilie and I will move out there around the end of March. This should be enough time for me to sell my house and business. I've got to start looking around for some farm machinery. I want to be all ready for the spring planting. Mr. Gorman told me the few pieces of equipment that are on the farm belong to a Mr. Daniels and Mr. Borzewski. They live in Mycenae."

Before Friederich was finished, Karl stopped by. As he listened to Friederich, he said, "The best place to buy machinery, from what I've heard, is at farm auctions. The next time I see one advertised in the paper, Fritz, we'll go take a look and see what farm machinery costs."

Friederich had several prospective buyers stop and look at the house and business. The man who had raised the question about starting a towing service was the one who paid Friederich's price. He got seven thousand dollars for the house and business. This gave him more than enough to pay off the note on the house, make the down payment on the farm, and still have money left to buy some farm machinery.

"You can stay here until April 1st. I won't be moving in until then," the buyer told Emilie and Friederich.

"That's fine," Emilie told him. "That's okay, isn't it, Papa?"

"Yes. It'll give us time to pack our things for the move to the farm."

Chapter V

The First Year on the Farm

Between taking care of the baby and packing, Emilie had more than enough to do. It meant taking the children out of school and getting them enrolled in another district. It meant washing their clothes and the baby's diapers daily so everything would be clean and mended for the move. It meant she had to pack the clothing and dishes, all of the other household items, plus meet the daily needs of the family for food and sustenance. Friederich collected boxes and helped her with the packing. But with looking after the baby, in addition to packing, Emilie felt she had never worked so hard in her life! They had a lot to do to get everything done for the big move to the farm.

Friederich hired a mover to come to South Avenue on the 29th of March. Grandmother came almost every day to look after the children. After two weeks they were prepared for the move. Friederich picked up Grandmother each morning and took her back to Haussmanns each evening. She not only looked after the baby and the two older children, she often cooked for them while Friederich and Emilie sorted through their things and got them packed. Each afternoon, Friederich drove out to the farm and sorted through those things Mr. Gorman said went with the farm. He threw out many items, or put them in the garage behind the main house.

"Once I have some horses and a wagon, I'll haul all the junk down to the woods. But for now, it's at least out of the house. There'll be plenty of room for all of our things and the Haussmanns when we move in."

On March 29th, the mover came. Friederich and Emilie had finished packing the day before. The movers packed their furniture and other belongings on their truck only to discover they couldn't take everything on one load. They had to return for a second trip. All of the furniture, beds, dishes, books, everything they had purchased from Mr. Cambridge had to be transported. Emilie stayed at South Avenue until the second trip. Friederich went out to the farm to show the movers where to put the furniture and other items. He came back with them and after loading the rest of their things, Friederich and Emilie drove over to Haussmanns to pick up the baby, Volkmar, Inge, and Grandmother for the drive out to the farm. The children were very excited. They could hardly wait to see their new home.

Grandmother had told them everything that was on the farm; about the big house and the little one; where they would live; about the barns; the cabins; the fields; the garden. They kept asking her,

"Are there any other children nearby, Grandmother?"

"I kept telling them, pretty soon your cousins will be there and you'll have lots of company. They kept asking me over and over again, 'when are we going to go to the farm?'" Grandmother told Friederich and Emilie.

"They're just so excited to go to the farm, Grandmother. They haven't seen it yet," Emilie told her.

"I told them not only are their cousins from Syracuse coming to live on the farm, but their other little cousin, Waltraude, is coming from Germany. You'll have lots of company," Grandmother related.

Volkmar remembered Waltraude. Inge barely remembered her name. She was only four years old when they left Germany.

When they arrived on the farm, Volkmar and Inge were overjoyed with their new house. It wasn't as big as their place on South Avenue, but it was surrounded by large trees. The garden, with its open spaces, reminded them of Elmwood park. Friederich and Emilie showed them their rooms and helped them carry their things up the stairs. Grandmother then took them out to the garden so Friederich and Emilie could unpack and set up the beds and dressers without having them constantly under foot. They unpacked all of their things in the little house. Emilie even washed the dishes so they could eat their first meal there that evening. Grandmother was given the bed in the baby's room downstairs. It was fortunate she could stay with them until they were settled in. She was a big help caring for the baby.

Friederich and Emilie finished getting the house ready. Emilie asked Friederich "Papa, could you take me to the Mycenae so I can enroll Volke and Inge in school?"

"Yes. We better take care of that right now."

Friederich drove the half mile to the school. Volkmar was finishing his second year in Elmwood. They both wanted him to continue to keep up with his class. He had learned English very well and was getting marks in the nineties. His teacher said his grades were excellent. She also advised he shouldn't miss any more school after Emilie took him out of Elmwood.

"Mrs. Malin, Volkmar is about the smartest boy I have in my class. You really shouldn't keep him out of school too long. He needs the stimulation of other children. He does exceptionally well when he's competing whether its in arithmetic, spelling or reading. He likes to be the best."

Emilie was very pleased with this report from Miss Brennhofer. She knew Volkmar was very intelligent. And his English was without accent.

When Friederich and Emilie took the children to the Mycenae school, they were very surprised. It was a one-room school house with grades one through eight. The teacher was a very pleasant elderly lady.

"Well that's nice," she said, as Emilie introduced the children to her.

"I can easily fit in another second grader. But your little daughter will have to wait until fall because we don't have a kindergarten. She'll be able to start first grade then. She really needs to start at the beginning of the school year and since she's already had some kindergarten, she shouldn't have any problem making the adjustment. Volkmar has already been in school so it's no problem for him to continue."

"Our niece is going to move to the farm soon, Mrs. Doerr. Can I enroll her too? Her name is Margaret Haussmann and she's in the seventh grade. She should really be in the eighth, but the principal kept her back a year so she could first learn English," Emilie told her.

"That's no problem. There are still some seats available, Mrs. Malin."

Volkmar and Grete walked to and from the Mycenae school together that first spring. The whole family all had to get used to each other again. The Haussmanns hadn't had any farming experience either, so everyone had to make adjustments. Not only did they have to decide who would do what on the farm, but how to do the farm work.

The Haussmanns moved to the farm on April 1. Richard was assured by the Easy Washer Company he could return at any time. Gretel also asked her employers if she might return in case something didn't work out on the farm. They also assured her they would be pleased to have her back anytime she wanted. Riche didn't want to move to the farm because he was in high school and wanted to complete the year. His parents arranged for him to continue to live at home on Knaul Street and each evening he went to his aunt Bertha's for dinner. The Kesselrings lived just around the corner on Highland street. This arrangement worked out well for the Haussmanns. They were relieved Riche was well cared for. It also meant someone would continue to live in their house. They had toyed with the idea of renting it, but when Riche objected to transferring to another high school, they decided he should stay. There were too many uncertainties in this venture on the farm. What would they do if they had to return sooner than they anticipated? Subsequently, they left a door open to escape from the farm should it prove necessary.

Moving into the big house was a lot of fun for the Haussmanns and Grandmother Malin. Grandmother picked the bedroom towards the back of the upstairs. The window looked out into the garden and the afternoon sun shone brightly into her room. She was at the top of the stairs and easily went up and down as needed to work in the kitchen.

Gretel and Richard picked out the large upstairs bedroom towards the west end of the house. This way they could save the best bedrooms downstairs and in the eastern part of the upstairs, for the tourists. They could also look out of the windows towards the smaller house of the Malins across the garden. Gretel and Emilie often called to each other, if necessary, to get the other's attention. They, then, met halfway in the garden to exchange information, or answer each other's questions. When Gretel and Emilie weren't too busy, they came back and forth to each other's house to help out, or just visit.

The Haussmanns hadn't brought too many things to the farm. They only had enough beds and items for the kitchen, plus the dining room, that they would need for the tourist business. The extra beds and dressers, which the Malins had purchased from Mr. Cambridge, were set up in the spare bedrooms for the tourists. Even then, there were a few empty rooms for lack of furnishings.

Friederich and Richard went to an auction near Jamesville shortly after they moved in. They bought a complete household, plus most of the farm machinery and three horses. They both felt they needed everything they could buy and since it seemed so cheap, they out bid many of the other farmers.They drove two of the horses back to the farm hitched to the wagon they had bought and loaded it with all sorts of things for the house. The third horse was tied to the rear of the wagon. While Richard drove the horses, Friederich drove along behind in his Willys-Knight. It took them more than four hours to make the trip. They had to go back and forth with the horses and wagon for the next three days to bring all of the items they had bought. Neither Friederich nor Richard had ever driven horses before. They were, indeed, pleased they drove as well as they did. Two of the horses were blind and Friederich remembered the auctioneer said,

"There's nothing easier than driving a blind horse!"

The horse that wasn't blind was the one that walked behind the wagon. Since each of the horses already had a name Friederich and Richard continued to use the same ones. The female was called "Lady" and was blind. The other blind horse was called "Dick". Both of them were strong and proved to be faithful workers throughout their years on the farm. The other horse, named "Tom", was by far the strongest of the three. He not only could see, but he seemed to know when someone was coming to get him for work. He was a whitish, gray Belgian. Once he was put out to pasture, he was almost impossible to catch. He soon became known as "Tom the Farter". Whenever he was hooked up to a load, whether a wagon, a machine, or just a log, he invariably farted and continued to do so during his efforts in harness. Anyone who had to work behind "Tom", and there was no other way to drive a horse, had a constant aroma of horseshit in his nostrils. After a few weeks of chasing "Tom" through the pasture and finally cornering him near the barn each time they wanted to harness him, Friederich learned, if he wanted "Tom" to do any work, he had to tie him up. Otherwise, they could spend hours trying to corner him. It was an art to capture "Tom". He allowed someone to come within an arm's length of him. He then turned and ran away. His tail flew out behind him and he farted continuously as he ran. Friederich and Richard had to make a choice. They could either tether "Tom" to a tree, to an old wagon wheel in the pasture, or continue to chase him. Friederich elected to use an old wagon wheel because he could move it from place to place. When "Tom" had cropped the grass, Friederich moved it to a spot where it was more abundant. "Tom" was such a strong horse, he usually pulled the wheel around to find his own best grass. In this way Friederich could use him when he needed him, and the rest of the time "Tom" found his own sustenance pretty easily. He even pulled the wheel to a nearby water hole to drink as needed.

At the auction, Friederich and Richard bought two wagons, a drag, sulky plows, a harrow, cultivators, a mowing machine, dump rack, lots of tools and wrenches, drills, jacks, saws, hammers, nails, fence posts, wire, virtually everything the farmer had collected through forty years of farming. Friederich learned at the auction the farmer was selling out because he was getting too old to do the work anymore. He was going to move to the city in his retirement. While the equipment was old, it was still in good shape. With some of the pieces of equipment that were left on the farm, Friederich and Richard thought they had more than enough to start farming that spring.

Emilie was busy with the baby. Gretel and Grandmother had to care for the big house and the tourists. Grete had the job of tending the new gas station after school. It was already put in by the time the Malins arrived on the farm. Each day, after she came home from school, Grete pumped gas and minded the little store. Riche helped her on weekends and over the summer. Unfortunately, however, there wasn't much tourist business that season. Gretel estimated they had no more than two dozen tourists from May through September. Grandmother had the job of making breakfast for the overnight guests. Gretel showed them the rooms and did the wash after each use. She also set the prices. It cost seventy-five cents for a single bed and one dollar for a couple in a double bed. If the guests wished to have breakfast, another twenty-five cents was added to the single guest's cost and fifty cents for a couple. Since two of the bedrooms were large and had double beds, they were reserved for families. The cost for these rooms was two dollars for a family of four which included breakfast. Often weeks went by between tourists. If Gretel stayed up late enough (until twelve), she would have at least one or two guests. She only discovered this fact by accident. One night she had left the light shining on the tourist sign after eleven, her usual dead line. She got up when the doorbell rang and showed two different couples to their rooms. She really didn't want to stay up that late. She also helped with the field work and in the garden after the house work was finished. It was hard work raking hay or hoeing potatoes even after a good night's sleep. Not leaving the light on after eleven o'clock became the cause of another one of those arguments between Friederich and Gretel which so often occurred. Gretel much preferred to go to bed by eleven and not be awakened by a customer.

"Why don't you leave the light on longer! You won't get the late guests if there's no light on! No wonder there are so few tourists," Friederich told her angrily.

"I'm in charge of the tourists! You take care of the farming! I don't tell you what you ought to do!"

Gretel also had her doubts about the toilet facilities. She noticed that potential guests left rather than having to find their way to the out house behind the garage.

The tourists who lived in the cities, especially, wanted similar facilities available to them as they had at home. When the tourists inquired about the toilet and washing facilities, she often heard, "No thanks, we think we'll drive a little further."

When tourists did decide to stay, Gretel scurried to get the water for the tourists to wash themselves. She had to go to the pump behind the house, carry the water into the kitchen, and pour it into a huge kettle. She had to heat the water over a wood stove. It was then placed in a pitcher in each guest's room next to a wash basin. After the guests had washed themselves, they could either pour it down the drain, or open a window to dump the water. Throwing the water out of the windows did wonders for the flower beds around the house. The water poured down the drain splashed into the cellar and eventually found its way to a pipe leading from the cellar to the roadside ditch. If the facilities seemed primitive to the city dwellers, they seemed luxurious for those who had come over from the old country. While these types of conditions were taken for granted by Friederich, Gretel kept telling him "This tourist business isn't going to work, Friederich, unless you put in improved bathing and toilet facilities! I don't blame the people for not wanting to wander out to the outhouse at night! If they don't have a flashlight, what are they supposed to do? Look at the bathroom! I have to heat the water for people who want to take a bath. If there are two people who want to bathe, they don't want to use the same bath water over again! They have to wait until I've heated another kettle of water for them!"

"They can take a bath at home. They at least have water to wash. That's enough for tourists!" Friederich said stubbornly.

"It's no wonder we don't have much business!" Gretel countered. "They take one look at what's offered and go on! Why should I stay up late at night for none takers?"

Friederich wasn't interested in spending any money updating the bathrooms. Either people accepted what was offered, or they could go elsewhere. Besides, it would cost him a fortune to make such improvements. He no longer had any Reichsmarks in reserve. He had spent everything he had buying the farm, equipment, and cows.

Nevertheless, since Gretel was in charge of the tourist business, she had to provide not only the hot water, but the use of their bathtub, if someone wanted to take a bath. She charged an extra dollar a night for this convenience. There was only one bathroom with a copper lined bathtub for the Haussmanns' use as well as for all of the tourists. Gretel wasn't very keen on having just anyone use her bathtub. When guests asked for this convenience she had already made up her mind whether or not she would indicate a bath was available. If they looked clean and drove an expensive car, she would say a bath was available at extra cost. This issue was another one of those over which she and Friederich quarreled

"Your just too lazy to heat the water for each person," he taunted her.

"I'm not going to have just anyone's dirt and disease in my tub! I'll be the judge of who I let in and who I don't!" she fired back.

Gretel slept in, if she had had to get up to let someone in, or had stayed up late to encourage business with the lighted sign. Each evening she left a note for her mother telling her when she should be awakened, or how many people she should expect for breakfast. Since Grandmother spoke no English, breakfast proved to be an interesting experience for the overnight guests. On one occasion when the guests asked for oatmeal, she made fried eggs. When the guests again asked for oatmeal, she said "Ja, i mach's" and went into the kitchen and made more fried eggs!

The guests didn't say anymore. They ate the double helping of eggs and went on their way. Gretel found out what had happened from Grete. The tourists stopped at the gas station to have the tank filled. They told her about the double order of eggs they had been served. They were pleased they didn't have to pay any more for the extra breakfast!

The usual breakfast Grandmother made was coffee and rolls (which she baked); plus jellies, bread, and either soft-boiled, or fried eggs. It was only after Grete told her mother about the double breakfast that Grandmother offered oatmeal instead of fried eggs. It was still possible to have both soft-boiled eggs with oatmeal, but not fried eggs.

"Mother, why don't you make both oatmeal and soft-boiled eggs?" Gretel suggested.

"Was? Es gibt doch so viel ueberrich! Es ist doch ein Schand das weck zu schmeizen!" (What? There's so much left over! It's a shame to throw it away!) she said angrily. She couldn't believe people would eat both oatmeal and soft boiled eggs at the same meal. She disliked throwing anything away!

At the end of April, Karl went to New York again for the third time to get more of his relatives. This time it was his Aunt Katharine, and his sister, Elise and her daughter, Waltraude. Aunt Katharine had sold her house. They booked passage on the very next ship out of Bremerhaven for New York. Karl was again the translator and expediter for their things from the ship to Chittenango, New York. He arranged for them to have their things shipped by railway freight to Chittenango Station. Friederich, then, picked up their things with a rented truck for transport to the farm.

The families were very glad to see them again. The new comers were also pleased with the large farm house into which they moved. Friederich had originally thought all three would move into the farm house with the Haussmanns and Grandmother Malin. Karl, however, told them he was planning on finishing his house before winter. During the train ride to Syracuse, he asked Aunt Katharine

"Would you be interested in moving in with us? I'll have a brand new house by winter. Anne works in a restaurant full time and we need someone to look after Wilhelmle."

"Yes, That's possible, Karl. But I'd like to spend the summer months on the farm and help out wherever I'm needed. Your Mother wrote me there's lots to do."

In spite of her seventy years, she was still capable of doing all of the housework and especially enjoyed working in the garden. Elise also worked on the farm. Her job was to help with the haying and milking. Friederich and Richard had bought twenty cows and since they had to be milked every day, Elise was the logical one to help with these chores. Waltraude, who was only two weeks older than Volkmar, spent most of her time playing with him and Inge.

With neither Friederich nor Richard having had any farming experience, they appreciated any help they could get. A neighbor, two farms up the road towards Mycenae, thought he better stop by and get acquainted with this newcomer. He was one of the oldest farmers still actively engaged in farming in the area. He wanted to be sure his new neighbor knew which fence lines were his in order to keep them in good repair.

Frank May drove to "Valley Farm" in his new Model A Ford and paid Friederich a visit. He had heard from Henry Borzewski this man from Germany couldn't talk right.

"There's something wrong with his throat," Henry told him. "He has a scar along the bottom of his left cheek. He must have had an operation or something. He can't speak very loudly. I can hardly understand him."

Henry had worked the Mabie farm for Pauli and Trant. He was the first person from the area who had met Friederich. Mr. Borzewski's grandparents had come from Poland in the 1880's. Henry had long forgotten the old language and the ways of his parents. He considered himself a solid American citizen now and didn't know how this new foreigner was going to get along among his new neighbors.

"As far as I can make out," he told Frank, "It's a large German family that's moved in, but none of them knows a thing about farming!"

This comment intrigued Frank May even more. He couldn't see how anyone could be a farmer and not know anything about farming! He not only wanted to get acquainted with this new family, but he thought he ought to go down there and see if they were getting along all right. Frank's two sons had their own farms and he halfway thought maybe this family, if there were so many of them, might someday want to buy some more land. He might consider selling his farm at some future date. He was getting on in years at seventy-two. His wife had died two years previously and farming alone wasn't much fun for him anymore.

Frank May was a very tall, dignified looking gentleman. He wore rimless glasses and had a well manicured mustache. At his age, both his hair and mustache were white. He reminded Emilie of one of her college professors at the Froebel Institute. He also spoke very softly with a friendly, disarming smile. When he walked into the horse barn where Friederich and Richard were cleaning out the stables, he introduced himself.

"Hi. I'm Frank May. I live just down the road towards Mycenae. I heard you had moved in and want to get acquainted."

Friederich extended his hand and shook it heartily.

"How do you do. My name's Fred. This is my brother-in-law, Richard Haussmann."

Friederich liked Frank May almost immediately. He appreciated the fact that he was the first of his neighbors who had taken the time to come and introduce himself. This is the way it would have been done in Germany, Friederich thought. As he looked over his old neighbor, he couldn't help but think he must be old enough to be my father. He treated him with respect. Frank listened very carefully as Friederich spoke to him in broken English. He was surprised he could understand him, after what Henry Borzewski had told him.

"Have you had a farm before?"

"No, this is the first one I've ever had."

'Why did you buy the farm?"

"I've had my own businesses both in Germany and here. People have a hard time understanding me when I speak. I thought if I could buy a farm, I'd be left alone. I wouldn't have to bother with other people."

"I know what you mean, Fred. People have always thought I can't hear because I speak so softly. They think I'm deaf! I can't help it. Ever since I've been a boy, I've spoken quietly, so people think I must be hard of hearing."

Friederich was gratified with this new neighbor. Here is a man who really understands what it's been like for me all of these years, he said to himself. They talked at some length about their families.

"Let me introduce you to the rest of the family, Mr. May."

He brought him over to his house, first, and introduced him to Emilie.

"Emilie, this is Mr. May. He's a neighbor who lives towards Mycenae."

"How do you do, Mr. May. I'm very glad to meet you."

"Hello, Mrs. Malin. I've just had a nice visit with your husband."

"I'd like to introduce our children to you, Mr. May. This is Volkmar and Inge. We call her Ingele."

Mr. May shook hands with Volkmar. When he wanted to shake Inge's hand she hid behind her mother's skirt.

"You're a little shy, aren't you? I don't blame you. I'm just an old old man to you," he chuckled.

"Let's go over to the big house and meet the rest of my family and Richard's," Friederich suggested. He took him to the main house where Gretel invited him to stay for the morning "Veschber" (mid-morning snack) of coffee and kuchen. Mr. May did so gladly.

"My wife died two years ago," he said slowly. "It's pretty lonely living alone in an empty house."

"You can stop by any time and have something to eat with us," Friederich volunteered.

Mr. May had sat down and had a cup of coffee and a piece of Grandmother's kuchen.

"What are you going to plant this spring, Fred?"

"Probably some oats and corn, and lots of potatoes."

"That sounds good. If you ever need any help, Fred, you can call on me. We like to help our neighbors around here. You'll find this a pretty good place to live."

Friederich thanked him. From that time onward, whenever he wasn't sure about a crop, or when to plant it, he visited Frank to get advice before proceeding. Frank taught him how to broadcast seed since Friederich didn't have a grain drill.

"You want to plow and harrow your fields first, Fred. Then, when the lumps are all broken up into fairly small, smooth pieces, begin by walking about ten yards from the edge of the harrowed field to an identical spot across the field. So that you'll know where to cross the field the next time, Fred, hang a cloth on a tree, or fence post. Each time you cross the field spreading the seed, you'll know where you've been. You don't want to do the same part of the field twice," he laughed. "You'll only waste your seed. There should be about ten yards between where you finished coming across the field, and the next time you go across spreading the seed. I'll give you a sack I use to put in the seed. You take the sack, fill it with seed and hang it around your neck and shoulder. You then take your right hand and reach into the sack, get a hand full of seed and spread it with a right to left swing of your hand. You'll cover about ten yards in each sweep as you walk towards your flag across the field. That's called broadcasting seed. Move the cloth another ten yards along the side of the field each time until you've covered the whole field. After you're through spreading the seed, take your horses and drag and run over the seed so it's lightly covered with soil."

Mr. May also taught him how to plant corn with the newly purchased hand corn planters Friederich had acquired at the auction. Friederich, Elise and Richard planted corn that first spring using Mr. May's method. He gave Friederich a yard stick to mark the corn rows thirty inches apart.

"Use the same cloth guides when you go from one side of the field to the other, Fred. That way you won't cross your rows if you keep your eyes straight ahead and always walk towards the cloth. Since there are three of you using the hand planters, you should mark out the thirty inch rows ahead of time with stones. Once you're on the other side of the field, mark your next row with the yard stick and put your cloth the same distance on the next tree or fence. Then return to the previously marked spot and walk back across the field with the corn planter. Don't forget to check your planter after each crossing. Otherwise you'll have to go back over the rows that didn't have any seed!"

They learned their lessons well. There were no gaps in their corn rows that year.

Mr. May also told Friederich how to tell which part of a fence line was his to repair in America.

"What you have to do, Fred, is stand along each fence line on the edge of your fields and face north. On the left hand side of a field the first half of a fence line is your responsibility. On the right hand side, you have to repair the second half of the fence separating you from your neighbor. This makes good neighbors, Fred, and everyone knows right away which half of the fence is his to keep repaired."

Friederich hadn't known this before and it sounded like a good way of settling otherwise troublesome disputes. Another neighbor, who noticed his own part of the fence was the poorest, told his son, "I'm going to put one over on that immigrant! He won't even know the difference."

"Fred, when you face north, the first half of the common fence line on the right is yours to repair. I'll repair the second half. That's the way we do things here in America!"

This was the exact opposite from what Mr. May had told him.

"That's not true! It's just the other way around! Your part of the fence is the first half on this right hand side. Mine is the last half! If you're going to lie to me, you can go to hell!" Friederich said vehemently.

Unfortunately, this first encounter with Jack Henson was not a good one. Friederich was immediately suspicious of this neighbor. It was the start of many years of problems which he was to have with him. He had been an immigrant too, but from Great Britain. Friederich thought, aha, here's another example of why we had to fight against them in the war! Each spring this neighbor stopped by and said, "Fred, you've got to fix your fence! I'm going to let my heifers out and if they go over to your property, it'll just be too bad for you!"

When this man had come over at the turn of the century, he spoke English, but with as pronounced an accent as Friederich's; but a cockney accent. Each of them had difficulty understanding the other. Jack was a big man in size and his loud voice was intimidating to those who did not know him. The only time he ever stopped to see Friederich was to complain about something. He didn't like Germans, and often said so. His family in Britain always spoke of them as the "Huns", he told Friederich on one occasion. Jack had had two cousins killed on the Western Front fighting the Germans. This didn't endear the Germans to him, either. He really couldn't care less about this new neighbor. He hoped he would fail in farming and go away. He was surprised Friederich knew the rules about fences. The fact that this "Hun" had told him which fences were his and which ones weren't, took him aback. Everyone else had always tried to please Jack when he was upset with them. He never forgot nor forgave Friederich for "straightening him out" about something he should have known better than to try to put over on him.

The first summer making hay was also a new adventure for the family. They had seen how other farmers were cutting hay with their horses and mowing machines. They also saw how the hay was raked into long even rows with side delivery rakes and then picked up by a hay loader attached to a wagon. Since Friederich had neither of these two pieces of equipment, he and Richard used the dump rake they had purchased at the auction to rake the hay in more or less even rows. They then went over the rows, vertically, and made rough piles which they pitched up on the hay wagons.

Friederich mowed the hay with the old mowing machine he found in the horse barn. He hitched "Lady" and "Dick" to the mower and made sure to oil the machine frequently. Mr. May had told him "That's one of the best ways to keep a machine running for a long time; frequent oiling."

The first field he cut was on top of the hill just behind where he and Richard had planted potatoes. Frank had also told him to make sure the hay was dry before putting it in the barn.

"If you put the hay in green in the haymow, there's danger of spontaneous combustion."

"What's that?" Friederich asked.

"It means if the hay is wet and is put into the haymow (where you store the hay), it can catch fire because when the wet hay becomes too hot, it ignites when its piled on top of itself," Frank explained patiently. "That's what we mean by spontaneous combustion. It happens very suddenly. You don't expect it to happen, but it does. You better wait until the second day after the hay is cut to rake it and put it in the barn."

Friederich waited until the second day. He then took the horses and the dump rake to the newly cut hay field and raked the hay into long rows. He then went vertically up these rows and made piles of hay to be pitched on the hay wagon. After the hay was dry, Friederich drove the horses hitched to the hay wagon, with Richard, Gretel and Elise on board to the top of the hill.

"Oh my God, look at the size of those piles!" Gretel exclaimed. "Who's going to pick those up?"

"I'll make them smaller next time," Friederich assured them.

Friederich and Richard picked up the piles with their pitch forks; Elise had the job of tramping the hay down on the wagon; and Gretel raked the loose hay together into new piles. After the men loaded the hay as high as they could reach, Richard said "Fritz, I think the wagon's full enough."

"Ja."

Friederich drove the horses and hay wagon down the road to the barn. Since neither he nor Richard had ever made hay before, the loads were rather loosely piled on the wagon. Elise couldn't always put the piles into the center of the wagon and tramp them down. She sometimes left them exactly where they had been thrown by her brother, or brother-in-law. Subsequently, the very first load of hay shifted dramatically, as they proceeded down the dirt road. Richard, Elise and Gretel walked along the downhill side of the load with their pitchforks holding the hay on the wagon. It was not an easy task because they had very little room between the wagon and the trees lining the edge of the steep embankment. Friederich drove the horses very slowly. They barely arrived in the barn before the whole load collapsed on the floor. It took them three more fields of hay until they learned how to load the wagons correctly. Friederich and Richard had to reload two wagons which collapsed all over the bumpy dirt road leading into the barn. The rocks bumped the wheels continuously. The hay shifted from side to side, and if the load was not piled correctly, inevitably, it collapsed.

It was a busy summer for everyone in 1929. The garden grew lots of vegetables and fruit. Richard even bought himself some chickens and ducks. He enjoyed going into the chicken coop each morning to collect the eggs. He had a mixture of leghorns, New Hampshire and Rhode Island reds, plus a few Plymouth barred rock. He had built them their own yard so they were fenced in. He had originally taken Friederich's advice. "Richard, why don't you just let the chickens run loose around the yard. They can find their own food and water that way."

After a couple of his chickens were run over by cars as they tried to get to the barns across the road, Richard bought chicken wire and put up a fence in which he kept both his chickens and a few ducks, he had also bought. This meant, however, he had to feed and water them twice a day. He dug a pit in the chicken yard into which he placed a metal washer tub. He kept it filled with water for his ducks. They all ate from the same metal feeders every day and Grandmother and her sister brought them scraps regularly from the kitchen. Having chickens and ducks around meant there was always plenty of meat and eggs for their households. Grandmother Malin and Aunt Katharine were used to beheading the ducks and chickens. It was no problem for them to clean these fowl. They had done this in Germany where they also had raised their own.

As the heat rose in July and August, Karl came out on weekends with Anne and Billy. He took the children swimming in nearby Green Lake. It was a beautiful natural lake which had been formed from the remains of a water fall after the last of the ice ages. It was designated a state park, but hadn't been completely taken over by the state. People went swimming at their own risk. Sand had been hauled in to make a beach. It was a safe place for children so long as they didn't go out in the water too far. Emilie liked to go there, too, with the baby. She usually sat on the beach or went wading, while he slept. It was fun for Volkmar, Inge, Waltraude and Billy, too. Volkmar learned to swim on these outings and enjoyed going with his uncles and father into the deep part of the lake. The state had erected a water slide towards the end of the shallow part of the wading area. The children could only make it out to the slide with an adult since the water was over their heads. The families went almost every Sunday on hot days. It was a refreshing break from the heat and hot work on the farm. There were days when Richard asked himself which was hotter; working in the machine shop at Easy Washer, or forking hay into the mow after it had been pulled up and dropped into the loft by the hay fork? He had never had to sweat as much in the shop as he did in the haymow!

As September approached, Gretel asked Richard, "Daddy, what do you think? Has the experiment of working on the farm gone well this summer? When we came last April, we shared all expenses and income. But I don't think there's enough business for two families. We better tell Friederich, it's not going to work."

"Ja. I guess there's just not enough income for both of us."

Gretel and Richard walked over to the Malins and found them sitting at their dinner table. Emilie had just made coffee and was cutting up a cake she had baked that morning.

"Ah, Gretel and Richard! Come on in. You're just in time," Emilie said.

"I'll just take a cup of coffee, Emilie," Gretel said.

"How about you, Richard? You'll take some cake too, won't you?" Emilie asked.

"Yes. I'll take coffee and cake. Maybe a little milk in the coffee, too, if you have it."

"Friederich, we've come to talk with you," Gretel began. "There's not enough income for two families. We've tried working here over the summer and the tourist business has fluctuated, at best. If we don't have running water and an indoor toilet, people are not going to stay here. They want the same as they have at home. We can't expect them to use that stinking, old out house! That's just too primitive for them! I've taken in fifty dollars for the whole summer. That's not even enough for one family, let alone three! I thought there might be a chance of increasing our income from the camp ground, but we still have the water and toilet problem there, too. I don't think Richard will ever earn as much here as he can in the factory! The only profitable part of the operation for us, is the gas station. It's doing well, especially since it's only been in operation for a few months."

Friederich sat still, as if thunderstruck! He stopped drinking his coffee and looked sharply at his sister.

"I'm afraid Gretel's right, Fritz," Richard chimed in. "The only area where there's potential income in the future is from the gas station. The rest of the work that we've done, hasn't really shown much promise for higher income. The amount of work that we're doing is not paying off."

"There are more and more cars on the road and with some additional items in the store, it might be enough for one family, but certainly not for two!" Gretel began again. "The price of milk isn't likely to increase either."

"We could buy more cows," Friederich suggested. "This would increase our monthly milk check!"

"What good would that do? With more cows we also have more work!" Gretel countered. "If the price of milk isn't going to increase, we would actually be making less money for more work!"

Friederich really felt himself in a quandary. He had used up his profits from the sale of his two houses and businesses when he bought the farm, cows, and equipment. He and Karl had bought an old Fordson tractor and some additional farm machinery, earlier in the summer, at another auction. That had largely used up the rest of his Reichsmarks.

"If the farm's going to earn money, it has to do it now. I don't have anything else to fall back on anymore!" Friederich replied angrily.

"It should certainly get better next year," Emilie suggested. "We've only just started, Gretel. With the increasing numbers of cars on the road, the gas station should pick up even more next spring."

Friederich was getting angrier by the minute with his sister and brother-in-law.

"You're not thinking of leaving the farm, are you?" he asked. "No one has worked anymore than anyone else! We've all done our fair share. No one can say he or she did more work than anyone else!" he went on. "Look at how hard the two old ladies have been working! Do you hear them complaining about the work? Everyone has enough to eat!"

"Friederich, we're just trying to decide what we should do. We haven't gone yet," Richard assured him. "We just thought we ought to tell you what we've been thinking."

When the Haussmanns returned to their house, Friederich was beside himself.

"How can they even think of leaving? I can't milk all of those cows alone and I can't afford a milking machine! If they leave, Emilie, you'll have to help me in the barn and around the farm. There are twenty cows that have to be milked twice a day! I don't know how we can keep the gas station going! I'm not going to pump gas! No one can understand me anyway and, besides, I much prefer farm work to working on cars!"

The more he thought about the discussion with his sister and brother-in-law, the angrier he became.

"She can go to hell, as far as I'm concerned, if that's the way she feels! But it leaves us holding the bag. We'll have to get along without them!"

The more enraged he became, the more upset Emilie was by this prospect of being alone on the farm without the Haussmanns.

"How in the world can we continue to farm all by ourselves, Papa?" she sobbed.

"You're a very hard worker, Papa, but even you can't do everything yourself!"

Friederich went over to the cow barn to milk the cows. Emilie gradually stopped crying. I've got to talk to Gretel, she said to herself. We can't possibly do all of this work ourselves!

"Volke, I've got to go over to talk with Aunt Gretel. You stay here with the girls. If the baby cries, come over and get me, okay?"

Emilie hurried through the garden to the Haussmanns. Grandmother and Aunt Katharine were weeding the carrots and beets.

"Where are you going in such a hurry, Emilie?" Grandmother asked.

Emilie started crying again. She didn't say anything and kept on going.

"There's something wrong, Katharine. I'd better go inside and find out what's happening."

"Gretel, how in the world can Friederich and I do all of the work on the farm, plus the tourists, and the gas station? It's simply not possible!" Emilie exclaimed.

"We can't do everything ourselves! You've got to continue to work with us!" she sobbed.

"What's this?" Grandmother asked. "Who said anything about leaving?"

"I'm sorry, Emilie. But we can't stay here anymore. There's just not enough income for all of us."

"We should continue to work together. I don't have to be paid for the work I do. I like what I'm doing. We've got a big operation going here. It's not possible for anyone of us to do alone," Grandmother said. "But together we can do it! Why do you want to go back to the city, Gretel?"

"Because the children have to go back to school. We can't stay here! Richard doesn't even drive. The only way we can go anywhere is either take the bus, which comes by twice a day, or depend on Friederich to take us anywhere! We haven't been able to save hardly anything since we came out here last April. It's just not possible!" Gretel said adamantly.

Elise listened to the discussion, but said nothing. As she reflected on these past months working on the farm, she realized she wasn't making much progress learning English. Maybe if we lived in the city, she said to herself, both Waltraut and I could improve our English. I haven't received anything from either my brother or brother-in-law since we arrived on the farm from Germany. How can I ever become self-sufficient if I don't get some sort of a paying job? she told herself. I won't say anything yet. I'll wait and see if the Haussmanns leave.

The issue which finally made the Haussmanns decide to return to Syracuse was due to their daughter, Grete. She was a very pretty girl and there were entirely too many suitors to please her parents. Not only were the Olin boys always coming around to visit her, but also the Thayer boy from Chittenango. They all seemed too wild for Gretel and Richard. They felt she should have a better sort of young men with whom to come in contact. These were nothing more than country bumpkins; not very intelligent; poor farmers' sons; who used very poor English. Grete was dating a lot and even though her father and mother finally forbid her to go out anymore, if she went to school again in Mycenae, these boys would be there. They were afraid she might get pregnant by one of them unless they moved back to the city. When the boys brought Grete home in their cars, they let her out in front of the Malins house. This way, they wouldn't run the risk of confronting Gretel or Richard. Grete asked her aunt and uncle not to tell her parents about her dates.

"They'll only get upset, Tante Emilie."

"I won't tell them, Grete, unless they ask. Then I'll have to tell them," she told her.

On the first of October, Gretel came over to the Malins' house.

"I'm sorry, Emilie, but we just can't stay here any longer. Grete needs to get away from here. Those Olin boys are just too crude and sloppy. They're nothing but trash and we don't want her associating with these types of people."

Friederich flew into a rage. He said something to her for which she never forgave him.

"Look who's talking about other people being trash! How long did it take you to get married? How many children did you have before Richard finally married you? That's nothing more than an excuse to leave! You don't want to stay here anymore and you know it! You've already made up your mind and now you're looking for some excuse to make it sound justifiable!"

"You hypocrite! Who are you to talk about the behavior of others? Who raped us when we were little girls? Who tried to force me to do it repeatedly while I lived at home with Riche and Grete? Who's making those remarks even now to Grete about helping her become a woman? You're nothing more than a brutal bastard, just like your father!" she screamed at him.

Emilie couldn't believe what she heard. Friederich did that to her and Elise?

"That's not possible, Gretel!" Emilie retorted. "He'd never do anything like that!"

"I'm sorry for you, Emilie, but I had to tell him like it is! He's a lot different than you, or anyone else thinks. He's a dangerous man and has been all of his life. He gives the impression that he's the victim of circumstance! Ha! That's about the cruelest hoax there is. Be careful, Emilie. He'll make victims of others before he'll ever be a victim himself!"

Emilie was so shocked, she had to sit down.

"No, no that just can't be true!" Emilie shouted. And really started to cry.

That was just too much for Friederich. He was about to hit Gretel when Richard came into the kitchen.

"Friederich stop! You can't hit my wife! If you touch her, we're leaving right now!"

Friederich stopped in his tracks. He spun around and stormed out of the house slamming the door so hard, the lock fell off. He knew it was all over with the Haussmanns. It just wasn't going to work anymore. He went over to the cow barn and sat looking out the back door.

"I'm afraid it's finally over, Emilie," Richard said thoughtfully. "I didn't want it to come down to this, but it has. We're going to leave tomorrow on the bus. Karl and I'll come out next weekend and get the rest of our stuff."

"I'm sorry you heard what I said to Friederich, Emilie," Gretel said sheepishly.

"But he just raised my hackles higher than they've ever been raised! He's a son-of-a-bitch! I hate to tell you this, since you're married to him, but he just can't leave girls alone! Just be careful. I wouldn't be at all surprised if he were to get interested in your own daughter! He has a real weakness for young girls. It's more like a sickness with him!"

Emilie couldn't stop crying. Between sobs she said, "Gretel, I don't want to stay out here all alone with just Friederich and the children! What'll we do? We can't do all of the work ourselves!"

She still couldn't believe what Gretel said about Friederich.

"But he's such a good man, Gretel! He'd never do anything like that!"

"You don't want to believe it, Emilie, and I don't blame you. I wouldn't want to know that about my husband either! But it's the truth. It'll take some time for that fact to sink into your consciousness. You may even try to suppress it. But I hope you don't forget what I've told you! You're too good a person to have to suffer through anything like that! Good bye, Emilie."

They hugged each other as they both cried. Richard also hugged Emilie and told her "You're always welcome to come to our house, Emilie. If things get too bad for you out here on the farm, you and the children can come anytime."

After they left, Emilie became afraid for Friederich. Where in the world did he go? she asked herself. She told Volkmar and Inge to look after Fritzle.

"I've got to find Papa."

She walked over to the barn hoping she might find him there. She had noticed whenever he was upset with anything, he often went into the cow barn and sat down beside the door looking out over the fields. She walked through the horse barn first, but didn't find him. When she entered the cow barn, she saw him sitting at the back door holding his head in his hands.

"Papa, what's the matter? You're white as a sheet."

"Don't bother me! The Haussmanns are quitting!"

"I know! What are we going to do, Papa? How can we keep on going without them? You're still learning how to farm and we've got all of these cows to milk and look after. Oh God, how can we keep going?" she asked almost in a wail.

Friederich got up and walked around and around in the barn. He kept cursing and hitting his fist in his hand, over and over again. Emilie wasn't sure which angered him the most; what Gretel had said to him, or what they had decided to do! She could understand how he clearly felt betrayed. She felt the same way! Here he had bought the farm with such high expectations of founding a family enterprise. He had hoped by working together, they could expand the scope and size of the farm, eventually buying some additional land. Now that he had spent everything, he had bought the farm, the cows, and the equipment, it was all coming to an end! He was bitter towards his sister. Not only at what she had said in comparing him to his father, but he held her responsible for the family breakup. Quitting the farm was, for him, an unforgivable act. It never occurred to him to feel sorry for what he had said to her. He honestly felt certain what he had said to her was true.

"She just wanted some excuse to leave the farm and she used Grete to do it! Well, by God, she's going to regret it! We're going to stay here and make a go of it, if it's the last thing I ever do!"

Emilie didn't say anymore. She kept crying to herself. She still hadn't been able to grasp everything Gretel had said about Friederich. She knew he would never bring up the subject again. She was afraid to raise it herself. He looked as though he could kill someone right now!

The Haussmanns started packing that same day. When Grandmother Malin came into the house and saw Gretel putting her things in the boxes which she had saved, she asked, "Gretel, what are you doing?"

"I'm getting our things together. We're going back to the city! Friederich's impossible to work with! He can just do the work himself, as far as I'm concerned!"

"Why? What happened?" Grandmother asked.

"Oh, you wouldn't understand! It's just something that involves us. But we're not going to stay here any longer! We can't make a living here anyway, so it's better we go back to Syracuse. Richard can go back to work at Easy Washer and I'll go back to Gales. We just can't get along with Friederich."

Grandmother couldn't believe what she was hearing. She knew that Richard, in spite of the heat of the hay mow, liked working and living on the farm. He spent every morning feeding his chickens and ducks after breakfast. He very much enjoyed gathering the eggs each morning. He even sang on occasion which she hadn't heard him do since she first came to America.

"Is Richard in agreement with this return? Does he really want to go back to work in the factory?" Grandmother asked.

Gretel became irritated with this line of questioning by her mother and said curtly, "He'll do what I ask him to do!"

She didn't respond any further to her mother's questions. But she did ask, "Are you going with us, or are you going to stay here?"

Grandmother hadn't anticipated leaving the farm.

"I'll have to talk it over with Elise and my sister, but we'll probably stay."

Gretel had forgotten about her sister and aunt. She had talked earlier in the summer with Elise about what she ought to do. But because there was so much work on the farm, they had never come back to the subject again until now. The discussion with Grandmother had jogged her memory of the earlier conversation. In spite of herself, she hoped, for Emilie's sake, Elise would decide to stay. She couldn't imagine Emilie doing the work Elise was doing in the barn. Besides, Emilie still had the baby to look after! Maybe when he was a little older, Emilie could do more work around the farm, she told herself, but not yet. Gretel decided she would talk with Elise, too. Maybe she could persuade her to stay on at least through the coming winter. Her Aunt Katharine, she knew, was slated to go to the

Karl Malins in Lyncourt soon. Karl had finished the interior of the house enough to move his family in that summer. He had also fixed up a room for her. Gretel knew Karl and Anne depended on Aunt Katharine to look after Billy. Anne was working steadily. Billy was staying most of the time with Anne's sister next door. Anne's sister, however, wasn't interested in taking care of her nephew any longer. She had had a job offer and suggested Anne take care of her son herself. Now that Aunt Katharine was going to move into Karl's new house, there was no way she could remain on the farm. Anne was opposed to the idea of Aunt Katharine staying on the farm even when Karl mentioned, earlier in September, "The Haussmanns might return to Knaul street."

Anne had said, Gretel recalled Karl telling her, "If the Haussmanns come back to the city, then Friederich and Emilie will have to come back, too. They can't do all of that work on the farm alone! Aunt Katharine returning to the farm, is out of the question. She stays with us. We need her just as much as Friederich does! He can't afford to pay her, so she'll just stay here with us!"

Karl never raised the question again. He had already learned if Anne became angry with him, she wouldn't let him touch her for weeks. Karl didn't want to agonize over the prospects of having no sex life. He enjoyed it very much, even if Anne didn't. Having it only once a week was at least better than not having it at all, he told himself. He reminded himself of one other time when she had gotten angry with him. He had had to wait three months before she felt in the mood for it again! No, he told himself, he can't reconsider having Aunt Katharine stay on the farm any longer. Even when she asked him "How will Friederich and Emilie get along without the Haussmanns' help?" he couldn't do it.

Elise and her mother decided to stay through the winter and make the decision the following year about whether or not to move to Syracuse. Gretel was surprised at this decision. She had half-way assumed both of them would decide to move with them back to the city. She felt relieved she didn't have to try to persuade them to stay. Friederich and Emilie were going to have a hard enough time as it was. At least there will be two more women to help even if Richard and I do leave. No, Gretel thought. It will be better for her brother and sister-in-law if they stayed. She felt genuinely sorry for Emilie. Not only would she now have to do farm work and take care of the baby, but, as she told her earlier, "You still have to live with my brother!"

Gretel didn't know which was worse. "Emilie, I don't know what will be the worst for you. Having to work on the farm, or having to put up with Friederich! I don't know how you can live with him! I couldn't!"

Gretel wrote Karl and asked him to come and get them that next Saturday. Karl drove out to the farm and helped them move their things back to the city. He drove a truck he had rented. He still couldn't believe it was happening.

"Who's doing all of the milking?" he asked incredulously after he arrived.

Gretel told him the whole story. Karl listened quietly and agreed it would probably be best.

"Well, I don't think they can do all of the farm work themselves. They'll have to come back to the city, too, before too long."

After loading the truck, Richard and Karl went over to the cow barn to say good bye to Friederich. He was milking the cows. It was difficult for all of them.

"I enjoyed the farm, Fritz. It's a really nice place, but there's just not enough money in it for all of us. You can keep my chickens and ducks. I can't take them with me to the city. I'm sorry we couldn't make a go of it. Good bye. I hope to see you again before too long."

Friederich didn't say anything. He kept on milking. He didn't even bother getting up to shake hands. Karl and Richard left. They came over to say good bye to Emilie. It was a very tearful farewell for her. Richard apologized again for having to leave.

"It's all for the best that we're leaving. There just wasn't enough income for us to stay any longer, Emilie. I certainly hope everything goes well for you and the children."

Volkmar and Inge were also crying as they shook hands with their uncles.

"Who are we going to visit now?" Volkmar asked. "If you're not over there, we won't see you anymore!"

"Your Grandmother, Aunt Elise and cousin Waltraut will still be there. You can go over and visit them every day!" Uncle Richard told him.

"Who'll take me to school in Mycenae if Grete isn't here anymore?"

"You're a big boy now. You have to take care of your little sister and cousin. You'll have to take them to school each day and make sure they get back home again, just like Grete did for you!" Uncle Richard answered.

"I'll still miss Grete. We'll have to walk home from school instead of riding home with the Olin boys." He already seemed to sense without his older cousin along, the older boys wouldn't be interested in giving them a ride home after school anymore.

"Who's going to scoop out the ice cream cones at the gas station?" Inge asked. "Grete gave us a cone almost every day." Both children remembered they had had their daily treats there when she was in charge.

Amidst their tears, the children and Emilie waived good bye as Uncle Karl and Uncle Richard left in the truck carrying the Haussmanns' things. Emilie stood in front of the little house while the children ran along the side of the hill to the end of the property, waving and waving until the truck disappeared around the curve by Frank May's barn. Grandmother Malin, Elise and Waltraut also stood in front of the big house and waved good bye. They, too, wiped their eyes with their handkerchiefs. They also really hated to see them go.

Friederich stayed in the barn and continued milking. He hadn't bothered to say adieu to his brother and brother-in-law. He was absorbed in his own thoughts; embittered and enraged at his sister; and wondering how he was going to be able to do all of the work on the farm by himself. When Karl stuck his head in the barn one more time to say good bye after the truck was loaded, Friederich just nodded to him. Richard came by one last time before getting into the truck and called out,

"Aufwiedersehen, Friederich!"

Friederich still didn't answer. Richard took one last look at him sitting there milking all alone.

"It probably would have ended at some time at any rate, Karl. But I really wish it hadn't ended like this! I really feel sorry for him and actually feel guilty leaving him with all of the work on the farm to do by himself."

As he got into the truck he said to Elise "You better go over and give your brother a hand with the milking. At least you know how and that'll be a big help to him."

After drying their eyes, Elise, her mother and Waltraut went over to the barn to help Friederich milk the cows. He still didn't say anything when they came in. They asked him which ones hadn't been milked and he nodded towards the row by the silo.

"These?" Grandmother asked.

Friederich nodded his head again without looking up. Grandmother and Elise sat down to finish the milking. There were only four more to milk since Friederich was a fast milker. Each of them milked only one cow by the time he had milked the last two. After turning the cows out to pasture for the night, they left the barn and went their separate ways. No one said much. Each one seemed to know it wasn't the same anymore. The Haussmanns were the catalysts in the family. There were always the jokes and good humor of Richard; and the spirited repartee of Gretel which would be sorely missed by all of them. Friederich had grown accustomed to working with Richard. He appreciated his wit and help on the farm. No, Friederich thought, it's Gretel who caused this break up. I could have gotten along fine with Richard, but Gretel . . . !

Towards the end of October, with the Stock Market crash, the price of milk began its downward spiral. It had been two dollars for one hundred pounds of milk; by early 1930, it was down to one dollar and falling month by month. That next summer, it was down to fifty cents per hundred weight. There were fewer cars on the road, it seemed, and hardly any tourists anymore. Grandmother, Elise and Waltraut spent their first winter in the big house. They closed off most of the rooms, sleeping in one of the bedrooms just off the kitchen. It was just too hard to heat the upstairs bedrooms. There was a wood stove and the kitchen stove by which they kept themselves warm throughout the winter. Friederich and Emilie had much smaller quarters. Their wood stove kept the house warm enough throughout all of the rooms. Even the bedrooms seemed to have at least a little heat in them. Elise had taken over running the gas station. Her English was still rather limited, but she had the help of Volkmar after school.

"Volke, when you come back from school, go over to the gas station and help Aunt Elise," Friederich said. "She still can't speak much English so if she has trouble understanding what people want, you can tell her."

After school each day, he and Inge went with Waltraut to the big house. Aunt Elise called him if she needed him. He went over to translate what people wanted. As the depression wore on, there was less and less need for him to translate. With fewer and fewer cars on the road, there was less call for gas. With less call for gas, the station, itself, became a losing proposition. Emilie went into the barn more and more to help while Grandmother looked after Fritzle. At first, Grandmother tried to pitch the hay down for the cows and tried to clean the barn, but Friederich saw the work was way too heavy a job for her.

"She's just not as strong as she used to be," he told Emilie.

"It takes her way too long to milk even one cow, let alone several. Why don't you let her take care of Fritzle and you can help me in the barn? You can learn to milk cows if my sister can."

Thus began Emilie's entry into active chores on the farm which were not to end for the next twenty years. She had never had to work so hard in her life. She pulled the cows teats with verve and even seemed to make a great effort in pumping out the milk. Friederich tried to show her how to pull more evenly and steadily so the milk would flow out almost by itself. It took time, however, for her hands and arms to become toughened enough to squirt the milk into the pail. Her pumping efforts usually meant the milk splashed down the outside of the pail.

"You're squirting the milk right down the side of the pail!" Friederich said angrily.

"I can't help it! If I don't pump like this, nothing comes out!"

He kept coaching her from day to day. As the first days went by, she felt her muscles tightening in her forearms. They got so sore, she could hardly hold anything in her hands! They just wouldn't close. She couldn't even change the baby's diapers because she couldn't press the pins to open or close.

"Emilie, don't try to change his diapers! There's too big a risk you won't close the pins correctly once you get them open," Grandmother said. "Let Friederich change his diapers before you put him to bed at night."

Emilie told Friederich what his mother said. He agreed. He changed Fritzle's diapers each evening thereafter. She just couldn't do it anymore! Her arms hurt so much those first few weeks of milking, she often cried out in her sleep.

"What's the matter, Emilie?" Friederich asked.

She didn't respond. He knew she was crying in her sleep.

"You were crying in your sleep last night," he told her the next morning.

Emilie was amazed. She didn't know she had cried out.

"It felt like someone was walking on my hands and arms."

"You'll have to keep milking, Emilie," Friederich said. "Your hands and arms will gradually get used to it and then they won't hurt anymore. I had the same problem when I first started milking."

Surprisingly, her ability did, indeed, increase. Shortly after she thought the pain had gone away, she milked six cows. But that was the limit. She almost screamed out from the pain as she began the seventh cow.

"Papa, I can't get my hands to close anymore! It hurts too much!"

She felt she was going to faint.

"Well, then let it go. Just milk these six cows and I'll do the rest. At least I have six fewer cows to milk."

It took Emilie another month before she was able to milk without pain. She could milk almost as fast as Friederich, but he wasn't sure how thoroughly she had milked them. He sat down and made sure there was no more milk left in the udder. After a few days of such "testing," he was satisfied she was doing almost as well as he in milking the cows. The old red cow was one she always left for him to milk. Try as she might, she couldn't get the milk to come out. Even Friederich had difficulty milking her. He had to use the strip method which meant he essentially had to use his thumbs and forefingers to strip down the teats of the cow from the udder to their ends. Had she not been such a good producer, he was tempted to sell her.

Emilie learned farming very quickly. She was much bigger and stronger than either her mother-in-law or sister-in-law. Friederich noticed she didn't seem to mind carrying sacks of grain. She could lift almost as much as he. He thought since she was such a good worker, she should also learn how to drive the team of horses.

"You know, Emilie, if you could drive the team, I could use the tractor," Friederich said one morning.

Since it was early spring and time to do the plowing and planting, Friederich thought it was time to teach her how to harness the horses. He didn't share her concern about being afraid of them. She didn't want them to step on her feet. In order to put a harness on a horse, a person has to stand close to the horse to throw the harness over its back. She didn't want to stand any closer than was absolutely necessary. Subsequently, she never threw the harness high enough to attach it on both sides of the horse. Friederich got very angry with her over her timidity and inability to harness the horses.

"Emilie, you're strong enough to harness the horses! Stand closer to them as you throw the harness over their backs!"

"I can't. What if they kick me?"

Friederich grabbed the harness and threw it over Lady without any problem.

"Here! Now you try it!"

She stood about three feet away and let the harness fly. It landed pretty much as it did before; right on the floor next to Lady. Friederich got angrier with each attempt.

"How can you be so dumb! Get up next to her before you throw the harness!"

"I'm afraid of horses, Papa! I can't work with them, if I'm afraid of them! Don't you understand?" she said sobbing.

Friederich picked up the harness and threw it over the horse without any problem.

"All right!" he yelled. "Then you're going to learn how to drive the tractor! I can't see why a big, strong woman like you should be afraid of horses!"

On May first, behind the cow barn, Friederich tried to teach her how to drive the Willys-Knight. It proved to be a big mistake which he admitted years later.

"I should have used the tractor to teach her how to drive. It would have been slower and easier to use than the car!"

He drove the car with her down the lane behind the barn and explained how to use the clutch and shifting lever.

"Here, you and I change places. You get in the driver's seat and I'll sit next to you on the passenger side."

Emilie moved into the driver's seat as Friederich got in on the passenger side.

"Push in the clutch and pull the shifting lever into first gear."

She did as she was told. After putting the lever in first gear, she let the clutch out too quickly. The car leaped forward and stalled.

"Put the shifting lever into neutral again, and I'll get out and crank the motor. This time, give it lots of gas with the throttle lever so it doesn't stall."

The motor started running again. After Friederich got in, she pushed in the clutch, and pulled the shifting lever into first gear. She pushed on the throttle and the gas pedal at the same time, and let the clutch out very fast. The car not only lurched forward, but tore down the lane.

"How do I stop it?" she yelled as she pushed the excelerator to the floor.

"Take your foot off the gas pedal!" Friederich yelled as loudly as he could.

She wrenched the steering wheel from right to left. The car weaved sharply from side to side.

"Take your foot off the gas, by God!"

He grabbed the throttle levers and pulled them way down. The car came to a dead stop. He was boiling mad. "That's not the way to drive! You don't have to keep turning the steering wheel from side to side! That won't slow it down! You just let the car find its straight course by itself! You only have to make a slight correction as it starts so it'll go where you want it to go! And don't let the clutch out so fast! Try to let it out a little at a time as you push on the gas. When you set the throttle levers, you should need very little additional gas from the pedal!"

He got out and cranked it several times until it finally started again. This time Emilie tried to do everything he told her. The car still lurched forward a couple of jerks as she pushed the clutch in and out.

"For God's sake, leave the clutch out!" he yelled.

She did and the car raced down the lane. She tried to let the car go where it wanted. But this time, instead of making the necessary steering corrections, she let the car go where it was headed.

"Turn! Turn!" Friederich yelled.

It was too late. She turned the steering wheel hard to the left and the car went into the fence! It came to a complete stop when it struck a large fence post. She cried and cried.

"I'm sorry, Papa, but I don't think I can learn how to drive! It's no use! I can't do all of those things you told me to do all at the same time! You told me to let the car go by itself and I did! But look where it went?"

Friederich was seething with anger. "You're too dumb to learn! I can see that already! Forget it! We're lucky we still have a car!"

That was the end of his big plan to have her learn how to drive. She not only never learned how to drive a car, but he was afraid to have her try the tractor. He never asked her to try it again, nor to work with the horses. If anyone had to do it, he'd have to do it himself.

As the summer wore on, and unemployment began to grow in the cities, two men, whom Friederich had known since they first moved in with the Haussmanns, came and asked if they could cut logs on shares. The Booher Lumber Company was looking for logs. They heard from the Haussmanns there were a lot of big trees in the woods.

"We'll cut the trees on shares. Fifty percent for you, Herr Malin, and fifty percent for ourselves. We'll take care of selling the logs and we'll cut up the tops of the trees for firewood. You won't have to do anything. We'll use our own equipment, too."

Friederich thought this was fair enough since he had more than enough to do with farming. He couldn't work in the woods, too. The two men were also from Germany. They had arrived in the early twenties and still had very heavy accents. They spoke with each other in German and were glad Friederich spoke it. They had tried to interest other farmers in a similar proposition, but were not able to reach any agreement.

"Other farmers don't trust us. They don't want to have anything to do with us because we're German," Hermann Finkbeiner said.

"Yes, that's probably right," Friederich agreed. "They could still be prejudiced against you because of the war."

Both men had been drafted into the German army in 1918. Unfortunately, Friederich sympathized with them too much. He didn't bother to set any conditions on how they should cut the trees, nor what size they should cut, nor what they should, or shouldn't cut.

"Booher wants all kinds of timber. It doesn't matter whether it's hardwood or softwood," Finkbeiner told Friederich.

Friederich showed them the boundary lines to the farm on the north side of Route Five. The next day, they drove out in the same model A Ford which they used both for hauling their equipment, and later, for power to run their buzz saw. They drove down the lane to the wood lot taking a tent with them. They set it up beside the creek and lived there throughout the summer. They started along the fence line on the Madison County side and cut trees irrespective of size. Friederich used the wood lot as a pasture into which the cows wandered from time to time. After more than a week had gone by, Friederich walked down to the wood lot to see how they were doing. He couldn't believe his eyes! They had literally cut down every tree from the very largest, to the very smallest. He was dumb-founded by this clear-cutting! When he finally found them, he asked "What in hell are you doing to my wood lot? You're not supposed to cut everything that's standing! Cut down only the big trees! You shouldn't be cutting anything smaller than twenty millimeters in width! What you've done is a tremendous waste and if you do any more of this, you're all through cutting any more trees in my woods!"

"But, Herr Malin, we told you we're going to make firewood, too! We thought you knew we'd cut everything!" they pleaded.

"If you only want us to cut down the bigger trees, we'll only do that! We won't cut anything smaller than twenty millimeters. I'm sorry if we cut down too many trees!" Finkbeiner apologized.

"It's too late now! But don't ever let me catch you cutting down any more little trees!" Friederich warned.

He turned around and walked back towards the barn. On the edge of the wood lot, he turned around and looked back from the edge where they had started. It looked almost like his pasture had continued on into where the trees had stood. The only difference was the vast number of stumps in every direction! It'll just be a matter of time before the grass grows, he thought, and I'll have more pasture for my cows. It was very swampy land. He realized it wouldn't make very good pasture. In the meantime, it was one vast open space where the trees had once stood. The trees were all on the ground cut into logs and the tops were cut and piled into six foot lengths for the buzz saw. How dumb can people be, he thought to himself! It'll take years before there will ever be trees here again!

X   X   X

The first summer of making hay by himself, with only women to help, proved to be very hard on both Emilie and Friederich. She went into the fields each day with him and Elise to help load the hay wagon. Friederich made huge piles again, as he had the year before. But this year, he had Emilie to help pitch the hay on the wagon. It usually took her several pitch forks full until she had each pile on the wagon. Elise had learned how to stack the hay somewhat better than in the year before. Only one load collapsed during the entire summer! Friederich drove the horses and the hay wagon between the long rows of hay piles. He sorely missed Richard. It took much longer to pitch a load of hay. Instead of putting five hay loads into the barn each day, they were only able to manage three. Everyone was working just as hard as ever. But, it took Emilie much longer to load and mow away the hay

107

than it had taken Richard. She was completely exhausted by the end of the day. It was hard enough work to pitch the hay piles on the wagon, but mowing away the hay in the hayloft was almost more than she could take! Each time a big fork full of hay was drawn up into the barn, she had to mow it away into the back corners of the loft in order to make room for the next fork full. Elise led the horses pulling the rope attached to the pulleys and hay fork which pulled the hay into the loft. She couldn't help Emilie. After each load of hay was mowed away, Emilie barely had the strength to climb down the ladder to the floor of the barn. Fortunately, Friederich took pity on her.

"Emmy, you'd better rest a while."

She lay down on a pile of hay for a few minutes while Friederich climbed up into the loft to finish mowing the hay into its furthest corners. The hay also had to be tramped down in these corners in order to make more room for each succeeding load. For someone who had never done anything like this before, Friederich was pleased Emilie could work so hard. Even Grandmother and Elise complimented her.

"I would never have thought a woman who was a teacher could be so strong and work so hard!" Grandmother said one evening. "I'll bet you never knew you had such muscles before, did you Emilie?"

Especially when they hurt so much after mowing the hay back into the loft!" Elise joked. "You really have to be a strong woman do such hard work!"

Emilie was glad to hear they thought she was so strong. But to herself she wondered, can I do this for the rest of my life?

The Willys-Knight was giving Friederich problems. Not only did the radiator leak from its encounter with the fence-post, but each time he drove to Chittenango, he had to add a quart of oil to the engine. The gas station was handy in this regard. Whenever he went anywhere, he checked the oil level and usually took a couple of quarts with him. The car needed new rings. Karl offered to help him take it apart and fix it, but Friederich wasn't interested.

"It'll take too much time and I can't spare it now. I've got too many cows to take care of."

The cheese factory in Chittenango bought the milk which was produced on the farm. Even before the Malins bought the farm, the previous farmer had also shipped his milk to the plant. A truck was sent around each morning to pick up the milk in forty quart cans. Because of the drop in cheese prices in the markets and grocery stores, the management of the factory put all of their dairy farm suppliers on notice they could no longer afford to pick up their milk each morning. The farmers would have to bring the milk to the plant themselves. Friederich had thought of buying a truck anyway. He thought this would be a good time to buy one. He found an old, used Model T truck at a car and truck agency in Chittenango. He paid one hundred dollars for it. It took his very last cache of money from the Reichsmarks which he had been saving as souvenirs, if for nothing else! He had to deliver his milk, so saving these Reichsmarks was out of the question. He needed a truck now. He left his Willys-knight in Chittenango and drove the truck home. He thought the next time Karl comes to the farm, I'll have him drive me down to Chittenango to pick it up.

The truck was ten years old with very worn tires. They had been patched several times. The salesman assured him the truck should last at least another ten years. Friederich hauled the milk to the cheese factory every day and was pleased he had bought the truck. Two weeks later, however, he began having flat tires, either in driving to the factory, or returning from it. He became quite expert in repairing them, but soon realized it was taking him most of the morning to make this daily two mile run to Chittenango and back. There was nothing he could do about it. He had to drive back and forth. He didn't think he could afford to buy new tires! One cold November, Saturday morning, Friederich and Volkmar were riding together in the cab of the truck delivering the milk to the plant. As they drove past George Murray's farm, they suddenly saw a tire and wheel go whizzing past them. It was almost at the same time they noticed the truck was shaking tremendously and literally bouncing down the road. Friederich pulled over to the side of the road and noticed the wheel which had gone past them, was his own left rear wheel! Fortunately, the milk cans hadn't spilled since he had tied them to the cab. The entire wheel and tire had come off. Friederich and Volkmar walked up the road looking for the wheel. They found it about one hundred yards ahead on the opposite side of the road. The wheel had continued on across the road and only stopped because it had fallen into a culvert. The bolts, which held the rim to the spokes of the wheel, were no where to be found. Friederich couldn't drive any further unless he had another rim and tire. As he was looking over the situation and cursing his bad luck, George Murray came out of his barn and saw him standing next to his truck. George wandered over.

"What happened? Did you have an accident?"

"No, the wheel came off and I don't have another to put on the truck," Friederich said. "The one that was on it is no good anymore."

"We don't have a spare," Volkmar said.

George looked at the truck and the wheel. "That certainly won't work anymore, will it? Where are you from?" he asked.

"We're just down the road on the next farm over the county line. I bought the Mabie farm.

"Ah, so you're the German family that's bought the farm over the county line! I've heard about you from Jack Henson and it wasn't very good."

He laughed as he said it.

"I don't like Jack either. What's your name?"

"I'm Fred Malin and this is my son, Volkmar."

"I'm George Murray, your next door neighbor." He extended his hand. After shaking hands, he said, "Why don't you come with me over to my workshop. I may have another wheel that'll fit your truck. I have a Model T, too."

Friederich and Volkmar went with him to his workshop. Friederich was amazed at what he saw. There was every tool imaginable in George's workshop. George looked behind the garage among some old tires and wheels and finally picked one out that looked about the right size.

"Here's one that'll do," George said. "Take this one with you and when you get a replacement for yours, you can bring it back. I won't be needing it for a while."

Friederich thanked George. "If there's ever anything I can do for you, George just let me know. I'll be glad to help."

Friederich appreciated this gesture of helpfulness. He would really have been stuck had George not offered him his wheel and tire. Friederich put the wheel on after jacking up the left rear side of the truck. Luckily, George also had the nuts and bolts to reattach the rim to the spokes. Friederich and Volkmar, then, delivered the milk. When they returned, Volkmar ran into the house and told Emilie all about their new neighbor they had met along the road to Chittenango. Friederich confirmed what Volkmar related about this nice new neighbor they had met quite by accident.

"He must also have had some problem with Jack Henson, too," he told Emilie. "George said he's of Scotch-Irish descent and he also served in the war. But he doesn't mind that we're German. We all make mistakes, George said. Maybe even getting into the war in the first place," Friederich recounted. "He's another neighbor we can trust, like Mr. May."

It was the start of a good neighborly relationship that would continue for as long as George lived

Now that the summer was over and the fall was rapidly approaching, Elise thought it was time for her to call it quits on the farm.

"Mother, I think by November at the latest, Waltraute and I will be moving to the city. Why don't you come along? There's no sense in staying on the farm. We had practically no tourists this past summer and the gas business was hardly better. I'm barely making enough to buy groceries each month. I want to look for a better job. The gas station and the tourist business just don't pay enough."

"What? You want to leave the farm, too? That'll mean Friederich and Emilie will be here all alone working the farm. What'll they do? They can't do the work all by themselves!"

Grandmother asked herself this question almost as much as she asked her daughter. The Haussmanns had written to her and asked her to come back to them on Knaul Street. They offered her ten dollars a month, plus room and board, if she would come back. They needed someone to look after their daughter, Grete. She was home alone much of the time. Riche was in the College of Forestry now. He had finished North High School the previous June and was spending most of his time at the University. With both she and Richard working, Grete was spending much, too much, time home alone, Gretel wrote her mother. In a previous letter, she had written they were concerned with Grete's cousin, Peter Kesselring, who lived just around the corner on Highland Street. He was spending a lot of time at their house since they had come back from the farm the year before. They liked Peter, but they weren't sure he came just to visit them. Gretel had spoken to her sister, Bertha, about Peter's constant visits.

"He just likes to talk with you, Gretel," Bertha said. She pooh poohed the idea there was anything more than that in his frequent visits.

Gretel wasn't so sure. She didn't think he came just to talk to her. Peter was sixteen and had dropped out of high school to go to work in a new factory that had opened not far from the Easy Washer Company. He had gotten a job as an apprentice tool-maker and was in the midst of learning the trade. Each afternoon he stopped at the Haussmanns to visit and drink coffee. Since Grete had also dropped out of school and hadn't found a job yet, she was always home when Peter came to visit. If you were in the house, Gretel wrote her mother, then nothing would happen between the two cousins. But if you're not here, I'm not so sure.

As Grandmother Malin thought over the request and offer, she felt maybe Friederich and Emilie could get along on the farm by ourselves. She wasn't so sure about her two grandchildren, Grete and Peter. She decided she would take the Haussmanns up on their offer. She recalled it was the Haussmanns who had provided the means for her to come to America. She could stay with them at no cost to herself. With the offer of ten dollars a week, it would even be possible to save a little money. It was just the incentive she needed to make the decision to leave the farm.

For Elise, the decision to leave was not only prompted by the little income she was able to garner working with the tourists and in the gas station. She also had to contend with Friederich's suggestions if she ever felt the need for sex, all she had to do was let him know. The more she thought about it, the more revolted she was by his suggestion. He had forced her when she was eleven and he was almost twenty. She had never told anyone about it until Gretel talked with her about their older brother.

"He's a mean and horrible man," Gretel told her. "He did it to me when I was only ten the first time. I thought it was kind of fun, but when he kept coming back for more and more, I got really scared. I knew how babies were made and I didn't want to have any yet. I did it a few more times with him because it was fun. But when he demanded it, I told him I'd never do it with him again! This made him so angry, I always made sure someone else was around when he was there. I was afraid to be alone with him!"

Elise recalled it had started quite similarly with her. "He told me the first time he wanted to show me; something that was a lot of fun," she told Gretel. "There was no one home at our grandparents house that day and Friederich took me upstairs to his bedroom. He told me to undress first and then he would, too. He then took my hand and put it on his penis which was gradually getting hard. He then put his hand on my leg and ran it up to my crotch and gently rubbed it. I liked the sensation. He told me I should lie down on the bed, and I did. He kept rubbing me. He told me to spread my legs as wide as possible. I did and he put it into me. He shoved so hard, I almost screamed with pain! He put his hand over my mouth and forced me down on the bed. I tried to move away from him because it had hurt so much. He told me to be quiet and relax. It wouldn't hurt so much. He eased up a little at that point and rubbed some more. It really felt good in spite of the pain. He started to do it to me again. It didn't hurt anymore and it felt good in spite of how it had felt earlier. Then all of a sudden, he moved it in and out several times in rapid succession. I felt like I had never felt before. As much as I hate to admit it, Gretel, I relaxed as he kept going back and forth. I'll never forget when he thrust it in all the way. He kept groaning. I thought something hurt him! Only in thinking back on it years later, did I realize it was nothing more than his orgasm! He told me not to tell anyone and he would buy me a present when he went to Stuttgart the next time. You know, Gretel, I actually kept quiet. I haven't told anyone about it until you, just now. The more I think about it, the more repugnant it is. I was really lucky not to have gotten pregnant. He used me for his own satisfaction, that son-of-a-bitch! It didn't stop until I was fourteen! Our grandparents were away and he suggested we go up to his bedroom. I refused. He knew there was no one at home. He had grabbed my arm and twisted it behind my back and forced me to go upstairs. This time he simply pulled my pants down and forced me on his bed. He raped me. He had the nerve to tell me since I had refused to do it, he wasn't going to bring me a present! 'I'll only bring you a present when you let me do it.' Can you imagine, Gretel, I actually let him do it when I was a little girl! I thought the presents were very nice!"

"Anyone who would do such a thing to his own sister must be sick, Elise. I don't know how you can even stand to be around him!"

"You're right, Gretel. I probably should have told someone right after it happened. But I was too ashamed to tell anyone. I did what you did. I made sure I was never alone with him again!"

She shuddered when she thought back upon that last time.

"Gretel, you probably won't believe this, but he tried to do it again this past summer. Emilie had gone down from the loft to rest before going out for the next load of hay. While he and I mowed the rest of the hay back he tried to drag me down into the hay. If I hadn't had the pitch fork in my hands and threatened to use it on him, he probably would done it to me again right there!

"Oh my God, Elise. And you're still wondering if you should stay on the farm?"

"No, I guess you're right. It isn't getting any better with Friederich! Even if he is married to Emilie, he still seems to think he can have it with whomever he pleases! He reminds me of my former husband. He, too, thought he could run around and do it with whomever he pleased. The sexual sickness in men is almost beyond belief, isn't it?

"I'm amazed you've stayed on the farm as long as you have, Elise. Some men are just horrible that way. I'm certainly glad my Richard isn't like that!"

"No, Gretel. You're really lucky to have someone like Richard. He'd never think of doing anything like Friederich! I've wondered sometimes whether or not I should tell Emilie what kind of a man her husband is. But I've never been able to do it."

"I've as much as told her, Elise. I don't think it registers with her! She heard me yell at Friederich when I told him what I thought of him for what he did to us as girls! I don't know what it takes, but I don't think Emilie is capable of grasping the kind of man he is! It's almost as if 'her Papa' is some kind of icon that can't be destroyed no matter what he does! In her eyes, he's not only her husband, but her surrogate father, too! I like Emilie. Don't get me wrong," Gretel went on. "But she shuts out anything that conflicts in anyway with what she wants to think and believe. She can't begin to think critically of him! He's her all in all! You and I know what kind of a man he really is, but she seems incapable of accepting it!"

"Well, I've sort of decided since she married him, that's her problem, not mine," Elise said. "If she didn't know what kind of a man he was before she married him, I'm certainly not going to tell her now! I've never said anything at all about what I've just told you, Gretel. If you've told her what he did to us as little girls and she still stays with him, then I don't think telling her even more sordid tales is going to have any effect on her. She's in her own little cocoon. I just hope, for her sake, and the sake of other little girls, it's only her security of silence. I'd hate to think she would participate in a conspiracy of silence! But you know, Gretel, what other alternative does she have? She can't leave him. What would she do all by herself with three small children to raise? It's been hard enough for me with just one child. If I hadn't been able to come back home to Mother, I wouldn't have known what to do, either."

Chapter VI

Going It Alone

The winter of 1930 was a long and lonesome one for the Malins on the farm. Emilie, especially, felt very lonely. She often cried to herself as she cooked or washed. Here we are, she thought to herself, stuck on the farm after all the relatives had been so enthusiastic about our buying it! They all said they were going to help us work it! Now there's no one here but us . . . How can we ever do all of the work next year all by ourselves? she kept asking herself. Who'll plow, plant and make hay this next spring and summer? And the garden . . . She cried even harder. The first summer it was such a good one! The potatoes were such large ones. They had been hoed and hilled, just like Grandmother said they should be and they turned out wonderfully. Even this past summer, if it hadn't been for Grandmother working several hours each day in the garden, it would have been overwhelmed with weeds. And next year . . . ? What's going to happen then? The more she thought about the future, the more upset she became. She had no idea how she and Friederich could continue to do all of the work required on the farm!

It was a very snowy, cold winter. Since there was no one in the big house, Friederich said they should move into it. It would be much closer to the barns and

"We won't have to walk so far each morning to do the milking."

Emilie was reluctant to leave the little house. They had already had people inquiring whether or not they could rent the big house. Friederich didn't want to rent it, but might consider renting the little one. The big house was right in the middle of the entire farm operation whereas the little house was off by itself on the edge of the farm. Again, because Friederich wanted to do something, they did it. They made the move relatively easily from the little house to the big one. Emilie was amazed with the size of the rooms.

"Could we just use the rooms at the rear of the house, Papa? They would be the closest to the kitchen, the bathroom, and the toilet."

Friederich agreed. "We might be able to rent different parts of the house to others if we use only the back rooms."

It just so happened that a middle aged couple had noticed the big house looked empty. They stopped at the little house as the Malins were in the midst of moving.

"Who owns the big house?" Mrs. Spencer asked. "We're looking for a place near Mycenae. All of my brothers and sister live there. My husband works in Manlius. He's always wanted to move out into the country. I'm also tired of living in the city. With my relatives living nearby, we've often driven past the farm and noticed there was no one in the big house."

It was only by chance they stopped at the little house. They saw the horses and wagon pulled up to the rear door of the big house where Friederich was unloading items. They decided to stop and ask. Emilie invited them in. Her English had gotten much better. She understood almost everything they said. Volkmar and Inge were also helpful if she didn't know what a word meant. They told her the word in German.

"Who owns the house next door?" Mr. Spencer asked.

"We do." Emilie answered.

"Isn't there anyone living in it now?" Mrs. Spencer asked

"No," the children and Emilie answered almost simultaneously.

"My mother-in-law and sister-in-law have just moved out and my husband wants to move into it."

"Well, if you move into the big house, what are you going to do with this one?" Mrs. Spencer asked.

"My husband hasn't decided yet, but we might rent it."

"If you're going to rent it, we might even be interested in buying it," Mrs. Spencer said.

"I have two brothers in Mycenae. One is Herman and the other is Jake Bus. They've both worked on this farm for several years. They're very familiar with it and if your husband ever needs any help, he can call on them. I also have a sister, Mrs. Steltzner, who lives just on the edge of Mycenae. She has two daughters. They're probably about the same age as your son, I'd say. How old are you young man?"

"I'm already ten, and my sister is going to be eight this year," Volkmar told Mrs. Spencer proudly.

"You're getting to be a big boy, aren't you? What's your sister's name?"

"Her name's Ingetraude, but we call her, Inge. She's only in the third grade, but I'm in the fifth grade."

"Well, you are a smart young man. How did you get so far ahead so quickly? Isn't he pretty young to be in the fifth grade already, Mrs. Malin?"

"I've been moved ahead of my class. I should really be in the fourth grade, but my teacher, Mrs. Doerr, said I belong in the fifth grade. She said I was too smart for fourth grade!" Volkmar volunteered.

"So that's why you're so far ahead," Mrs. Spencer laughed.

Emilie was very pleased with her older son. "He's a very smart boy. He can do almost everything already and helps us on the farm."

Since Friederich hadn't returned yet from the big house, the Spencers left. Before going Mrs. Spencer reminded her "If you want to rent either of the two houses, please let us know. We'll be back this spring when it's warmer! We're not in any hurry yet, but if you want to rent one of them, we're very interested."

"Could you give me your address so I can write you and tell you what my husband wants to do with this house?"

"Certainly. Do you have a piece of paper, Mrs. Malin?"

"I have one Mrs. Spencer."

Volkmar took one out of his tablet and Mrs. Spencer wrote down their address. She wrote, Mr. and Mrs. Edward Spencer, 135 Pleasant Street, Manlius, New York.

"Here you are, Mrs. Malin. Please let us know what you decide to do with either this house or the big one. We'd be very interested in either one."

"Thank you very much for the visit, Mr. and Mrs. Spencer. I'll let you know what my husband decides to do about the house."

They're such nice people, Emilie thought. And for the first time, she had met people who addressed her as Mrs. Malin instead of Emilie. All of the others had immediately called her by her first name. She couldn't help but think, they treated me like people in Germany would treat me; with respect. She appreciated that. That's what she really missed since coming to America.

When Friederich returned with the horses and wagon for the next load, she told him about the visitors.

"Papa, guess what? A Mr. and Mrs. Spencer were just here and they'd like to rent one of our houses. I told them we were just moving into the big house and this one would be empty. They want us to rent it to them next spring. They might even be interested in buying it."

"Excellent! We can't take care of two houses anyway. And next spring the tourists will start traveling again and we'll need the rooms in the big house for them."

"They don't want the house right now, Papa. They want to move in next spring. Mrs. Spencer wrote down their address. She wants me to let them know what you decide to do with either house. Should I write and tell them that we'll consider selling this house?"

"Yes. Tell them to stop by next spring and we'll talk about selling this place."

Emilie wrote to Mr. and Mrs. Spencer the next day. They were surprised but pleased with how quickly their offer appeared to be accepted. The little house stood empty that winter. Emilie went over occasionally to make sure everything was all right. Friederich didn't want to be bothered with it anymore.

"I don't have time to go over there. If the Spencers want to buy it, then they'll have to take it, as is."

Emilie didn't say anything. She simply went over after the children came home from school and cleaned the house a couple of times that winter.

Spring arrived earlier than usual. Friederich started plowing in the third week of March. The weather had become unusually mild and the wind was warm and drying. Since there was no longer any snow on the field next to Jack Henson, Friederich decided this year he would put in some corn and make ensilage for his cows for the following winter. He had heard it helped increase milk production and he wanted to see if, indeed, it would make a difference. He had thirty cows now.Some of them were producing well and some not so well. The hay was mostly what Mr. May called, horse hay; lots of timothy and orchard grass.

"There's very little alfalfa left in the fields," he told Friederich. "You need to reseed some of the fields into alfalfa and clover, Fred. You'll notice a big difference in your milk production if you have that kind of hay. You'll have even better results if you plant corn and make ensilage next fall."

Friederich decided this was the year to plant corn on the lower part of the farm. He'd try some oats and alfalfa on the hill top. He took his tractor down through the lane to the lower field by Henson's and began to plow. He didn't really have a tractor plow, but the old sulky plow had an interchangeable connecting bar for a tractor, or for horses. He thought he'd use the tractor for plowing since Karl told him it would go a lot faster than with the horses. The tractor was the same old Fordson he and Karl had bought at an auction in Chittenango the year before. Friederich had driven it along the roadside to the farm since it was on steel wheels. It made quite a bit of noise but ran well. It was on steel with slant lugs on each of the back wheels. These lugs gave it more traction and kept the wheels from slipping if he drove over rough ground or through mud. He liked the tractor and noticed it was able to plow easily in second gear. He plowed about four of the ten acres of the field that morning. When it was time to take a break for lunch, he thought about driving home but decided against it because it would only use up gas. Instead, he left it at the end of the furrow going north and shut off the engine. As he walked back to the house, he told himself, I'll be able to finish most of the field when I come back this afternoon.

After dinner and his usual ten minute nap, he walked back down to the field to continue plowing. As he came near the tractor, he noticed the spark plug wires were dangling unhooked from the plugs. He thought, that's strange, I hadn't taken them off before I left. When he got to the tractor, he saw water had spilled in the furrow underneath the tractor. He couldn't imagine how this could have occurred. There wasn't any water on the top of the hill where he had left the tractor. As he put the wires back on the spark plugs, and was about to turn the crank, he saw a site that sickened him. The radiator had big holes stuck through it as if someone had taken an ice-pick or had driven a spike through it several times. He looked around, but didn't see anyone. Who in the world could have done this, he asked himself? As he looked over towards Jack Henson's fields, he saw a man plowing with horses and went over to talk to him. Here's the man who probably did it . . . Friederich thought to himself. But he couldn't be sure. There wasn't anyone else around. It must have been he. As he came closer, the man saw him and called out, "How's the plowing coming along?"

Friederich thought to himself, aha, he already knows there's something wrong, otherwise he wouldn't have asked such a question! And yet, he wasn't sure.

"I'm Fred Malin and I own the farm over there. Did you see anyone walking around my tractor?"

"No, I didn't see anyone. I've been plowing here with these horses. They're not as fast as a tractor."

"What's your name?"

"Leonard Young. I work for Jack Henson. I live right up the road from you in Madison County."

"You're sure you didn't see anyone around my tractor?"

"No," he replied. "Why? What's the matter?"

"Somebody's ruined my tractor! There are holes in the radiator and I can't use it anymore!" Friederich responded angrily.

"That's too bad. It looks like you'll have to finish plowing with your horses." He smiled as he said it. Friederich felt like pulling him off his plow and hitting him, but thought better of it. It might just be a coincidence that he was down here plowing at the same time I was. But he certainly looks like he could have done it, Friederich thought to himself . . . and he works for Jack Henson, too. Friederich glared at him as if he could kill him and spun around and went back to his tractor. He couldn't move it the way it was. He unhooked the plow and pushed it back away from the tractor.

"God dammit," he cursed to himself. "Now I'll have to go back to the barn and get the horses!"

He had to leave the tractor where it was. The next time Karl comes, we'll take it apart and put in a new radiator, he told himself.

"That bastard over there! I'd almost swear he ruined my tractor!"

While Friederich was down in the field with his tractor, Mr. and Mrs. Heaton came by to ask if any of the rooms in the big house would be available to rent.

"We don't want the whole house, Mrs. Malin. We'd just like to rent one or two rooms at most," Mr. Heaton said. "We liked it so much last summer as tourists, we thought you might be interested in renting us a couple of your rooms for the summer."

"Oh, that would be nice," Emilie smiled.

"Let me talk it over with my husband. Could you give me your address so I can write you his answer?"

"Tell you what, Mrs. Malin. We'll drive out this next Saturday and you can tell us then. Is that okay with you?"

"That would be fine. I'm sure he'll make a decision very soon. I certainly hope he says yes, Mr. and Mrs. Heaton. I'd very much like to have you as neighbors."

When Friederich came back from the fields that afternoon to get the horses, he was furious! He came over to the house before harnessing the horses for a cup of coffee.

"My tractor's ruined! Someone put several holes in the radiator! That bastard over at Henson's. I'm almost sure he did it! He denies knowing anything about it. But he's the only one that was even near it!"

"Oh, Papa. What are you going to do?" Emilie asked bewildered.

"I'd like to shoot the bastard!"

"Oh, you can't do that. You don't know for sure he was the one who did it!"

"Who else was down there? He's in the next field plowing with horses. He says he works for Jack Henson!"

"Here's your coffee and kuchen, Papa. I've just baked it. Maybe someone else did that to the tractor. Can't you fix it?"

"Yes, but it takes time. I don't have any money for a new one! I'd just like to get a hold of the one who did it! He wouldn't do anything like that again!"

"At least you have the horses, Papa. You can finish plowing with them, can't you?"

"Yes. But it'll take me an extra day. The tractor was going so well, too."

Emilie decided she wouldn't say anything to him about the Heatons' visit yet. He was much too angry, she thought, to be interested. She didn't want him to make a rash judgment before considering their request carefully.

Friederich finished his coffee and cake. He went across the road to the barn and caught Dick. Tom was already in the barn. Only Dick and Lady wandered in and out. He kept Tom in the barn because he was almost impossible to catch in the field. Since Tom could see, he trotted off as soon as he saw Friederich coming towards him. Hence, Tom was consigned to the barn until later in the spring. Friederich tied him to a wagon wheel to drag around while he found his own grass to eat. After harnessing Tom and Dick, Friederich put the horse Tee on the wagon. He had to switch from the tractor drawbar to the horse Tee in order to finish plowing the field. He then hitched them to the wagon and rode down to the field where he had left the tractor and plow. He took off the tractor bar and put the horse Tee on the plow. He then hitched up "Tom" and "Dick" to the plow. He put "Tom" on the right side so he could walk in the previous furrow. When "Dick" was on the right side, he kept stumbling over the sod each time Friederich turned them to go back down the next furrow. Fortunately, Friederich had at least one horse that could see where he was going. He stayed on the plow until five o'clock. The horses were working well, but even with "Tom" on the team, they were still slower than the tractor.

Before he quit for the day, he had only plowed half the field. Had he continued with the tractor, he said to himself, I could have finished this field today!

After driving the horses back to the barn, he led them to the water tank for a drink. He tied "Tom" up in his stall. He let "Dick" wander (he never ran away when Friederich approached him in the field or barnyard), but before letting him loose, Friederich took him to his stall so he would eat his oats and hay before wandering off into the barnyard. "You boys need some oats today," Friederich told them. "That's hard work pulling the plow!"

He left the door open to the horse barn. "Dick" and "Lady", then, could go out to the pasture themselves. There wasn't much grass yet, but as soon as "Lady" smelled the oats, she came into the horse barn and wanted some oats, too. She pushed her way into "Dick's" stall and started eating with him. Friederich put her in her own stall.

"No, no, you didn't do any work today. Get over where you belong."

He tied her up so she couldn't come back into "Dick's" stall. Friederich didn't worry about "Tom". Whenever "Lady" tried to enter his stall, he kicked at her and bit her so she backed out of his stall very quickly.

Friederich then went over to the cow barn and fed the cows grain and hay before going across the road to the house. He wanted to get something to drink before starting to milk. When Emilie saw him she said "Papa, guess what? Do you remember Mr. and Mrs. Heaton who stayed with us for a few days last summer? They stopped in this afternoon."

"Vaguely. What do they want?"

"They want to rent one or two rooms from us for the summer. They liked it so much last year, they want to stay here all summer with us!"

"That might be arranged. Do they want to eat here, too?"

"I didn't ask them that and they didn't say anything. We could rent them the big front room with the little toilet attached, Papa. If they want to eat with us one or even two meals a day, I think I could prepare that, too."

"That's certainly the nicest room in the house. Isn't that the room they had last summer?"

"Yes, it is. They didn't ask for that room, but I'm sure they'd be pleased to rent it again. They'll stop by on Saturday to find out what you think of the idea."

"I think that would be an excellent idea. We'd have permanent tourists for the summer in at least one of our rooms."

Emilie was very pleased he agreed. She'd have someone to talk to on occasion and wouldn't feel so lonely over the summer. With all of the relatives gone, she had no one to talk to except Friederich and the children. When he was in one of his moods, he often didn't talk to her for weeks at a time.

Mr. and Mrs. Heaton came by early Saturday morning. The Malins had just finished breakfast when there was a knock at the door. Emilie went to open it and there they were.

"Ah, good morning, Mr. and Mrs. Heaton. Do come in. My husband and I have just finished breakfast. What you like a cup of coffee or tea?"

"I'd prefer tea, if you don't mind, Mrs. Malin," Mrs. Heaton said. "My husband, too. We're tea drinkers for breakfast."

"Mr. Malin, how nice to see you again," Mr. Heaton said as he shook hands and introduced his wife. "You remember my wife, don't you? We stayed with you last summer for a few days. We liked it so much we'd like to stay longer this summer, if it's convenient for you and your wife," Mr. Heaton continued.

Friederich bowed slightly as he shook Mrs. Heaton's hand.

"Yes, I remember you."

"What a charming husband you have Mrs. Malin. He's a real gentleman. It's not everyone these days who bows when he shakes hands with a woman! Does he greet all of the ladies that way, Mrs. Malin?"

Emilie laughed. "He's very much a gentleman, Mrs. Heaton."

"You're interested in renting one or two rooms from us for the summer?" Friederich asked as they drank their tea.

"Yes," Mr. Heaton answered. "Actually, any two rooms would be okay with us. But we really liked the big front room that we had last summer."

"Would you want to eat your meals here, too?" Friederich asked.

"If we could have breakfast each day, it would be nice. Or if we could use your kitchen so we could make our own meals when you're not using it. We'd really appreciate it."

"Tell you what," Friederich said. "We'll let you have the big front room with the little toilet attached, plus breakfast, for fifteen dollars a month. You can use the kitchen for lunch at one o'clock each day. How does that sound to you?"

"Great! We'll take it. I'll write you a check right now for the first month's rent, if that's okay with you, Mr. Malin?"

Emilie was overjoyed. Now, at least, there'll be someone else in the house, she thought. The Heaton's moved on the first of May.

"What would you think, Emilie, if we ran an ad in the newspaper to rent the gas station?" Friederich asked. "You don't have time to run that, too. You've got to help me full-time on the farm. You're already helping milk the cows. You're going to have to help me plant corn this spring."

"That's an excellent idea, Papa. I was really wondering how I was ever going to be able to continue running the gas station with the tourist season coming soon. I don't think I can stay up as long as Gretel did to wait for tourists. Getting up at five a.m. to milk the cows, getting breakfast for us and the children, and now for the Heatons, too, it's going to be a full time job. I thought you might want to shut it down altogether."

"That's why I thought we should put an in the paper. We've already put a sign in the station window. If someone is interested, we could use the extra income."

Friederich had only recently hung a sign in the station stating "Open from 9 to 4". Friederich had lost his patience with the customers coming over to the cow barn in the morning wanting their tanks filled. The Haussmanns had opened at 7 a.m. and the customers wondered why there was no one there that early anymore.

Two days after the ad was in the newspaper, a man stopped and asked what Friederich wanted for rent.

"A dollar a day," Friederich replied.

"That's a lot of money." the prospective renter said.

"Take it or leave," Friederich stated abruptly.

"I'll try it for two months, and see how things go. If it doesn't pay, it's all off. Is that okay with you?"

"Yes, that's fair enough."

Friederich was very pleased with how things were working out.

"We've got enough to cover our mortgage payments, Emilie. If we can rent the little house to the Spencers, then whatever we make on the farm is pure profit."

The milk price had fallen to fifty cents for a hundred pounds and Emilie didn't think they were going to be able to meet all of their expenses. She wasn't at all as optimistic as Friederich about covering their costs. In addition to her other work, she also kept track of their accounts. She usually did this after the children had gone to bed and was waiting for tourists. She had a much better idea of how much money was available than Friederich and how much was still lacking. She had learned almost from the beginning of their marriage Friederich wanted to make all of the big decisions concerning expenditures. She had only been able to prevail upon him to talk these decisions over with her first, at least, before he went ahead and made them. He usually disagreed with her assessment, but he did hear her out when it entailed spending money. When she wrote her mother she was now keeping track of the books, her mother was very pleased. She sent her a large account book similar to the one she had used to keep their accounts in Germany years ago. While Emilie often had trouble staying awake at night, this task was inevitably the last one of the day; to make the daily entries of debits and credits in her accounts journal. With all of the work Emilie had to do, her annual spring cleaning was one of her most extensive ones. While she helped Friederich do all of the farm work, he did not help her in these household chores. She had a real problem of what to do with their youngest son, Fritzle. He was now a toddler. When she washed the floors, she didn't want him to walk through the rooms until they had dried. She likewise didn't want him climbing her ladder when she washed the windows. She decided to take one of her long clotheslines and tie him to one of the trees in the front yard. With Volkmar and Inge in school, she felt she had no alternative. She had tried, at first, to let him run loose in the yard. It only took one tooting of a car horn to change her mind. She found him in the middle of the road, on his way over to the barn when a passing motorist blew his horn repeatedly until she came outside to see what was wrong. The driver yelled out of the car, "You can't let a little baby run loose here lady. There are just too many cars on the road! If I hadn't seen him coming across in time, I would have hit him!"

She apologized profusely to the driver and thanked him for stopping. She picked up Fritzle and carried him into the house.

"Don't you ever go out in the road again, Fritzle. Do you understand? You can get run over by a car, if you go out into the street!" she scolded. He seemed to understand, but that's when she started using the clothesline. When Friederich came back up from working in the fields, he found Fritzle tied to one of the chestnut trees on the front lawn. He was upset with Emilie for doing this to their youngest son.

"I don't like the idea of tying him to a tree, Emilie! That's just plain cruel!"

"Do you want to take him down into the fields with you?" she asked perplexed "I can't do all of my housework and look after him, too! Who's going to clean the floors and windows for the tourists, if I don't do it? We can't just let him run loose anymore. We were lucky the last time he went into the road!"

In spite of his misgivings, Friederich decided he would take Fritzle with him when he went down to the fields. It was fine when he used a wagon to haul seed or wood. But when he tried to plow with Fritzle on his lap, the first time, he gave up by noon.

"I can't take him along when I'm plowing! It's just too dangerous to have him sit on my lap. There's just not enough room on the seat for both of us. I have to stop, put him down, reset the plow, turn the horses around, then stop again to pick him up. I'm just not getting anything done that way!"

Friederich was pretty worn out after a morning of Fritzle on his lap. After lunch and a rest, he told Emilie "You'll just have to keep him here. I can't do any plowing with him sitting on my lap. If I were plowing with the tractor, it would be different, but with the horses, it's simply impossible!"

Fritzle, at two and a half, had become a real favorite of his father. Whenever Friederich drove the horses down into the woods to get a load of firewood, he always took him along on the wagon. He wanted to go wherever his father went. Friederich even agreed to have him share his bed, particularly in the winter, in order to keep the little fellow warm.

Fritzle delighted in riding either "Dick" or "Lady". After Friederich harnessed the horses, he put him on one of them and told him to hang on to the two harness knobs. They were brass and looked similar to door knobs. He let Fritzle ride on one of the horses from the barn to the wagon or machine he was going to use for the day. When he took him off again, Emilie had to take him with her back into the house. Fritzle cried when his father took him off the horses before he was ready to come down. But there was nothing that could be done about it.

"I'll be back this afternoon, Fritzle, then you can ride on "Lady" again," his father assured him.

Fritzle was the name everyone used around the family. He was simply a little edition of his father. Since he had the same middle name as Friederich, it seemed appropriate. Whenever Emilie had to go with Friederich to plant corn or potatoes that first spring alone on the farm, they had to take Fritzle with them. There was no one to look after him at the house. With his brother and sister in school, Emilie took a blanket along. When Fritzle got tired, she spread it out on the grass under the wagon where he could sleep. The horses were unhitched from the wagon and allowed to graze nearby along the edges of the field. They were some distance away from where he was sleeping. She took along a container of water for Fritzle and herself. Friederich had his cider. During their lunch break, they ate the sandwiches she had prepared earlier that morning.

Planting corn was an arduous task. Friederich marked off the corn rows, thirty inches apart, with white strips of clothe tied to the trees like Mr. May had shown him two years previously. The hand corn planters were those he had bought at an early auction with Richard in Jamesville and then used by him, Richard and Elise that first spring. Friederich and Emilie had to fill them with corn from the sack of seed on the wagon after every pass across the field. Emilie started at the field's edge and pushed the beak of the planter into the freshly harrowed ground. The spring at the bottom of the planter caused the jaws to open and drop the seed down into the newly opened slot in the ground. It was then covered as the planter was raised to be put into the ground again for the next seed to fall from the planter. With each step, she put the planter down into the ground going across the field, back and forth. When they had gone about fifty yards from where the wagon stood, Friederich came back with the horses and moved the wagon closer to where they were planting. It took them all day to plant a field in this manner. They planted three fields of corn in their first spring alone. Friederich wanted to make ensilage that next fall and, therefore, that many fields had to be planted in order to fill the silo. Mr. May had promised him, if he got his corn planted, he would see to it Friederich's silo would be filled in the fall. Frank had a corn binder. George Murray had an ensilage chopper and tractor to do the job. He had been assured with enough neighbors, silo filling was easily done.

The routine on the farm had become pretty steady. Each morning, Friederich and Emilie got up at five a.m. and went to the barn to milk the cows. There were times when she was so tired, Friederich had to yell, "Wake up! You're sound asleep again!"

On one occasion, after milking a cow at one end of the barn, he didn't hear any milk splashing into the pail at the other end. He walked down to see what was wrong. He found her seated next to the bull with her hands on his scrotum, her head against his stomach, sound asleep.

"So? You're trying to milk the bull? I wondered why I didn't hear any milk splashing into your pail!"

Emilie got up very embarrassed.

"Oh, excuse me, Papa! I wondered why there wasn't any milk coming out and then I must have fallen asleep," she said sheepishly.

Friederich laughed and made a joke of it. "You'll have a hard time getting milk out of a bull!"

By seven a. m. they were usually finished with the milking. Emilie returned to the house to make breakfast. She awakened Volkmar and Inge and got them ready for school. They got themselves washed and dressed, while she helped Fritzle get dressed. After Friederich fed the cows, he came over and they all had breakfast together. Volkmar and Inge then went off to school. It was a mile hike for them since there was no school bus. Emilie washed the dishes while she and Friederich talked about what they were going to do that day. It was a big decision trying to decide what Friederich should do so Fritzle could go along. If he couldn't go, he had to stay with Emilie. When she didn't go into the fields, she knew Friederich wanted to eat his dinner promptly at twelve o'clock. She usually made something hot such as soup and noodles, with meat and gravy. They also always had a salad. She knew Friederich had to have some liquid with his food in order to swallow it easier. Occasionally, however, when he wasn't careful, or in a hurry, food would go down his windpipe. He often choked and seemed unable to breathe. She watched in horror as he ran to the kitchen sink and threw up most of what he had swallowed trying to get the piece of food out of his windpipe. When he returned to the table, he was white as a sheet from the effort. He rarely wanted to eat anymore after one of these choking spells. He drank his tea and took a nap. He gradually felt better again and worked until four o'clock in the afternoon. It was then time for coffee and kuchen of some sort.

Volkmar and Inge came home from school each afternoon between four and four-thirty. Emilie prepared a supper of soup again for the children and warmed up leftovers. Friederich and Emilie ate cold cuts, bread and butter, with coffee. Volkmar went with his father into the barn and took his little brother along. After they fed the cows, Friederich and Emilie did the milking. Inge washed dishes or dried them depending upon when her mother came back from the barn. Both of the older children liked to read after their chores and did so until bedtime. Occasionally, one or the other would read to their little brother. In this way, he too was exposed to English. During the day he spoke only German with his father and mother. This was their preferred language. They spoke only German at home. It meant all three of the children learned both languages.

"You know, Papa, since the relatives have all gone, Volke and Inge are speaking to us mostly in English."

"We get our English practice that way," Friederich said.

Only Fritzle preferred to speak German even when his brother and sister spoke to him in English.

"Why don't you speak English, Fritzle? When you go to school you'll have to speak it all the time," Volkmar told him.

"I don't want to. Papa and Mama don't speak it. I like German better."

Frank May had told Friederich two years earlier, "Fred, you'll need to replant your hay fields into alfalfa again. It's thinning out way too much. It's best to do it in a mixture of oats, or some other grain with the alfalfa seed."

Friederich decided this was the year to replant the entire hill top in alfalfa. He was short of cash, and when he told Karl what he wanted to do, Karl offered,

"I'll buy the seed for you and help you plant it. You can pay me back when you've saved some money."

"Thanks Karl. You'll get it back."

Friederich plowed, harrowed, and dragged the fields until the ground was prepared. Karl bought the seed at the Eberling's Seed Company in Syracuse. The salesman told him, "It's the best we've got. It should give you a good stand of alfalfa for several years once it's taken root."

Friederich and Karl spent an entire Saturday planting the two fields on the top of the hill with the broadcast method. Friederich gave Karl instructions of how to do it and both were satisfied they had done a good job. Friederich, then, dragged the field again to make sure the seed was covered. He thought with such big fields of alfalfa, he would have plenty of hay for his cows the next year. He wasn't sure what he was going to do with the oats they had planted with it.

"I'll probably cut it for hay instead of threshing it. Frank May told me threshing and silo filling were usually done by all of the farmers going from one farm to another to help each other. If I'm going to have ensilage put into my silo this fall, I don't think I can expect my neighbors to come and help me thresh oats, too. It would be too much to expect in one year," he told Karl.

Tourists stopped to enquire whether or not there were any accommodations available. The 'Tourists' sign was still in front of the big house. Since Emilie and Friederich had decided to move from the little house to the big house the previous fall, they had not taken all of their furniture with them. Friederich made several trips with his model T truck to haul the rest of their things from the little house. Emmy helped him load these items on the truck at the little house. The furniture was so heavy, she felt she couldn't carry them anymore.She helped Friederich carry one of the dressers out the back door and lost her grip. The dresser fell in a heap.

"What are you doing?" Friederich yelled.

"I couldn't hold it any longer, Papa! I had it until I had to go down the steps. Then it slipped out of my hands!"

"Look at the leg! It's broken off!"

"I'm sorry, but I can't carry such a heavy dresser, Papa!"

Friederich stormed out of the house and picked up the dresser himself. He loaded it on the truck and put a block under the broken leg to keep it upright. As he put some smaller chairs and boxes on the truck, Emilie suggested, "Maybe Mr. Heaton could help you, Papa. Shall I ask him?"

Friederich waved his hand as if to say don't bother me. Emilie hurried through the garden and knocked on the Heaton's door.

Mr. Heaton came to the door. "Ah, Mrs. Malin, come in."

"Excuse me, Mr. Heaton. But could you help my husband load and unload the truck with the furniture from our other house? I tried to help, but the dressers are just too heavy for me."

"Why of course, Mrs. Malin. I'm surprised you even tried to lift such heavy furniture. I'll go right over and give your husband a hand."

She took him through the garden to the little house.

"My, you've certainly got a big garden, Mrs. Malin! Who takes care of it? Surely you don't do all of this work yourself?"

"It's not going to be easy this year, Mr. Heaton. Unfortunately, our relatives aren't here anymore. I guess I'll have to do it myself. My husband plows it and then he helps me plant the potatoes. The rest of the vegetables I plant myself."

"I'm amazed, Mrs. Malin, how much work you have to do. You help your husband milk the cows too, don't you?"

"I just milk a few. My husband does most of the milking. I have to make breakfast and get the children off to school. Once they're a little older they'll be a big help to us on the farm."

Friederich was just coming out of the house with another dresser when they arrived.

"Here, let me help you Mr. Malin. Don't strain yourself. You'll get a hernia from lifting this furniture all alone!"

Mr. Heaton grabbed one end of the dresser and together, they quickly loaded it on the truck. It took them three more trips and the furniture was all moved into the big house.

Emilie made some lemonade and tea for the men. She also invited Mrs. Heaton to come and join them in the kitchen. She put bread and jelly on the table in case someone wanted something to eat.

"I'm sorry I don't have anything baked yet. I usually bake on Saturdays."

"That's all right, Mrs. Malin. You've got more than enough to do as it is," Mrs. Heaton told her. "My husband was glad to help, weren't you Harry?"

"Yes. Your jelly is very good, Mrs. Malin, Did you make this yourself?"

"No. That's some my mother-in-law made last summer."

"Oh yes. That was the lady who couldn't speak English, wasn't it? She's the one that cooked breakfast for all of the tourists." he laughed. "She knew how to fry good eggs, Mr. Malin! That was your mother, wasn't it?"

"Yes. It's too bad she's not going to be with us this year."

"Didn't she want to stay on the farm?" Mrs. Heaton asked.

"She has to look after her grandchildren in Syracuse. My husband's sister and her husband both work and there's no one home to look after the children. So she felt she had to go back to the city with them," Emilie volunteered.

"It makes a lot more work for you, doesn't it, Mrs. Malin?" Mr. Heaton asked.

"I'll manage. I like being at home. Besides, I have a little baby to take care of, too. My husband does most of the work on the farm. I just work around the house mostly," Emilie said self-deprecatingly.

The Heatons had seen all of the work Emilie was doing. Evangeline Heaton told Harry later. "I don't see how Mrs. Malin can do all of the things she does. She has a toddler to look after; she helps with the milking; she gets her two older children off to school each morning; she does the cooking and cleaning for us and her family; she stays up at night and waits for the tourists; she does the bookkeeping for the farm; and, in the summer, she takes care of her garden and helps with the planting and haying. I don't see how she does it all, Harry!"

Before going back to their rooms, Friederich gave Mr. Heaton a bottle of wine for his help.

"Thank you very much, Mr. Malin," Mr. Heaton said. "I'm sure my wife and I will like the wine."

They were very pleased with the gift. It was a bottle Richard had given Friederich the year before from his own grapes.

"I wouldn't mind trying that wine again, Mr. Malin," Mr. Heaton told him a few days later. "It was excellent. My wife and I finished it in just two days!"

The big house was a real treat for the children. With the tourist season in full swing, Friederich and Emilie decided to use only the lower bedrooms for themselves. They saved the upstairs bedrooms for the tourists. The Heatons were using the best room with the adjacent privy downstairs. This meant Emilie and Inge slept in one bed just off the kitchen. Volkmar and Fritzle slept in the other bed. Friederich took the big front room on the lower west end of the house for his bedroom. It gave him a good view of the barns across the road. It was the same room his mother had used as her second dining room for the tourists. There were big white painted doors which ran on an iron track at the bottom. They could be opened or closed as needed. As Friederich's bedroom, these doors were kept closed. Fritzle usually slept with his father, but not during the summers. It was just too hot.

"It'll be all right again next winter, but not for the summer," Friederich told Emilie. They both agreed it was best for someone to sleep with Fritzle. He awoke in the middle of the night and had to go to the bathroom. Someone had to turn on the light and hold up the chamber pot into which he could urinate. He couldn't do it by himself.

The bedroom Emilie shared with the children, was directly under a copper roof. Every time it rained, it sounded as if the roof were going to come down; the stronger the rain, the louder the noise. When it hailed, it was loud enough to prevent any conversation at all. Since the four of them slept in this bedroom, Emilie waited until the children were asleep before she undressed. She slipped off the upper part of her dress and brassiere, put on a night shirt over her head which covered her body. She then took off the rest of my clothes under her night shirt. Fritzle often awoke when the light was turned on. He watched through partly opened eyelids as she took off her brassiere. She was somewhat surprised when he asked her one day "Why are your breasts so large and Inge's so small?"

She laughed. "Have you been peeking again, Fritzle? You're supposed to keep your eyes closed when we undress," she scolded.

Inge followed the same procedure in undressing for bed. Emilie reminded Volkmar, "Now when Inge and I get undressed, you keep your eyes closed."

She never mentioned it to Fritzle. He usually was sound asleep when they went to bed. It didn't seem necessary to tell him. Besides, Emilie reminded herself, he was still just a little boy.

It was a long hot summer for Emilie in the big house that first year "alone." Not only did she now have a lot more house to clean, she also had to stay up late each evening in case tourists came by looking for a room. She sat at the dining room table reading the newspaper or a book. It was usually eleven o'clock before she turned off the light and went to bed. By ten o'clock, she was often asleep at the table with her head on whatever she was reading. One evening Friederich awoke and saw the light on in the dining room. He got up and as he came into the room he said "Emilie! Wake up! There's no use sitting here at the table! You couldn't hear the doorbell ring anyway if some one wanted a room! Go to bed!"

Emilie was very embarrassed. "Oh, Papa, I didn't know I was asleep. I can't seem to keep my eyes open any longer!"

After two weeks of these late hours, Friederich decided ten o'clock was late enough for her to wait up for tourists. Even Friederich conceded with getting up early in the morning to milk the cows, and then working with haying, it was simply too much for her. She was very glad he was so understanding. It was a lot of work.

"Take a nap after dinner for fifteen minutes, Emilie. You'll feel a lot better and perk up for the afternoon's work," he told her.

She did as he suggested. She was surprised how much those naps helped. They seemed to revive her for the rest of the day. She never had a problem falling asleep. As soon as her head touched the pillow, she was completely out. If Friederich wanted sex, she hardly knew what was going on. He made the trip to her bed and was so quick about it, he didn't even awaken Inge. She never objected to his inclinations. But she never pursued them herself. Once she lay down, she was out. She couldn't begin to think about sex anymore. She was simply too tired. Besides, after Elise and Grandmother left the farm, there was no way she had either the time nor the energy to raise another child. Therefore, before the end of these nocturnal cohabitations, Friederich knew he had to withdraw in order to prevent another pregnancy. She hardly ever had an orgasm. She was too afraid to let herself go for fear she would try to keep him from withdrawing at the crucial moment. It was no longer a pleasant experience for her. Rather, it became one of those wifely duties she had to perform. None of the children woke up during the night to go to the toilet, other than Fritzle. They pretty well knew when that would be. Emilie felt secure in having Friederich come during the night whenever he wanted sex. It was quiet, short, and obviously necessary for him.

X   X   X

As the depression wore on, the Malins noticed a sharp increase in the number of men wandering the road looking for work, or something to eat. Almost daily, Emilie answered a knock at the back door and would find a man standing there asking

"Is there any job I might do for you for something to eat?"

"Go out to the garage where you'll find a big pile of firewood. Take the ax and after you've split six blocks of wood, come back and I'll have something for you to eat," she told him.

She gave these unemployed men a meat sandwich of some sort; beef, pork or liverwurst on thick, homemade slices of bread and a glass of milk. If she happened to bake that day, she gave them a cookie for dessert. The sandwich was served on a plate.

"When you're through eating," she told them, "Leave the plate and glass on the porch."

She washed the plate and glass with the rest of their dishes after dinner. It was rare that any of the men went first to the pump outside the garage to wash up before eating. They were much too hungry to take the time to wash. After a couple of wanderers asked for seconds, Emilie decided she wouldn't ask them to do anymore work before eating. She told them, "Wait here on the porch. I'll fix you something to eat."

Fixing sandwiches was the quickest meal she could give them. She felt rather uncomfortable having them around too long. She had to call the children to come into the house. They had been fascinated watching how fast some of the men wolfed down the sandwiches and milk.

"Why do they eat so fast?" Inge asked her mother.

"They're very hungry. They probably haven't eaten anything in a long time. That's why I don't want you out there watching them. They don't need an audience. It might embarrass them. Besides, we don't know who these men are. It's just better to let them eat alone!"

The next time a man stopped, Emilie was glad Volkmar took Inge and Fritzle into another part of the yard until he had finished. She noticed when the children stood around watching the men eat, some of them asked the children, "Could you ask your mother for another sandwich and glass of milk?"

"Did they ask you to ask me for another sandwich?" she asked Volkmar, somewhat perplexed. Three men had stopped together and sat on the porch waiting for something to eat. With the request for another sandwich for each one, she used up most of the bread she had baked for the family that day. By giving each of the men two sandwiches a piece, plus two glasses of milk, she quickly learned if the children weren't around the men as they ate, they were not likely to ask for seconds. Each time, thereafter, she told the children in German "Now you stay here in the house until they've finished. You don't have to go out and talk with them. They're hungry!"

She never had anyone ask for seconds after that one time.

X X X

Emilie's youngest sister, Mariele, came to the United States in 1931 to marry her boyhood sweetheart, Karl Fleckhammer. He had come a year earlier and had started his own grinding and surgical instrument sharpening business in New York City. It was a good place for such a trade. There were very few such skilled craftsmen in the area.

Frau Bartholomae didn't want Mariele to marry Karl. As with each of her other daughters, she didn't think Karl was from an appropriate family. She forbade Mariele to marry Karl before he left for America. She could no longer do anything about her objection now that Maria was twenty-one and determined to go through with the marriage. Karl sent her the money to pay for the trip. She booked passage the very next day.

Mariele wrote Emilie and invited her and Friederich to come to New York for her wedding. It was to be on the same day as Emilie's and Friederich's anniversary. Maria thought it might be nice for them to come to New York, not only to celebrate her arrival, but to attend her wedding. After Emilie read her letter to Friederich, he laughed.

"Who does she think we are, some rich relatives or something? No, we're not going and if they want a present from us, they'll have to come and get it!" he said emphatically.

Emilie was sorry the wedding would have to take place without them. She knew Friederich was right. They could neither afford to go to New York, nor take the time off from their chores to make the trip. Obviously, Maria had no idea what kind of life they were living on their farm in upstate New York. Emilie even wondered how they were going to able to buy them a wedding present! She didn't like Friederich's comment

"I'll be glad to give her the biggest present she's ever had!"

Emilie knew exactly what he meant. He didn't have to explain it to her. He had told her on several occasions, "Your little sister is like ripe fruit; a voluptuous young girl; just waiting to be "plucked"!

She didn't want to believe what Mariele told her once while they were still in Germany.

"Emilie, your husband looks at me all the time. It's not hard to guess what he's thinking! Do you know what happened to me when you and the children were out shopping one morning? I had gone to visit you and found Friederich upstairs alone eating his mid morning snack. He invited me in and told me to sit down next to him. I didn't want to so he started after me. I ran to the open window and said "If you come any closer, I'm going to jump out this window! I yelled at him, I'm not going to be one of your conquests!"

Emilie still shuddered when she thought of what might have happened! Fortunately, Friederich took her seriously and made no move towards her. He didn't want to be held responsible for her injury or death.

Before Emilie wrote her, she asked Friederich "Can I invite her and her husband to come and visit us, Papa? They only have an apartment in the city. It would be a nice break for them to drive up here and pay us a visit. It would be a nice break for us, too. We don't have many visitors these days, other than Karl and his family," she said remorsefully.

Emilie wasn't sure, exactly, why no on else came to visit them anymore. She knew Friederich felt betrayed and deserted by the rest of his family. She also knew he was still steaming from what Gretel had said to him that last day on the farm. But Emilie felt more hurt, than angered by the rest of his family. She enjoyed the visits and the chance to talk with someone else for a change. If Mariele and her new husband could come to visit, she could find out about the rest of her family. She hadn't seen any of them since they left in 1927. She was pleased one of her sisters had come to the United States. Maybe, she thought to herself, we'll be able to see each other occasionally.

"Okay," Friederich said. "You can invite them to come this summer."

Emilie wrote to Maria and explained they couldn't come. There was simply too much work to do on the farm. There was no one else who could milk the cows and they have to be milked twice a day. Besides, who would look after the children? Grandmother Malin works for the Haussmanns. I would love to come, Maria, she wrote. But we really can't leave the farm. Why don't you and Karl come and visit us this summer? We've got lots of room and it's really beautiful here in the summer time. I've got flowers planted around the house and the garden is full of vegetables that time of year. You'd really have a very nice time if you could come and visit us.

Emilie was overjoyed when she received a letter from Maria the next week. She and Karl were very sorry they couldn't come. They had thought maybe they had help on the farm and didn't know the Haussmanns were no longer there. In concluding her brief note she wrote, Karl and I will come for a week's visit the second week in August. That's when Karl shuts down his shop for the summer vacation.

After reading Maria's letter outloud, Friederich told her he knew Karl Fleckhammer. "I used to see them together when she was still in school. One of my apprentices told me she and Karl had a wrestling match to see who was the stronger and Karl accidentally broke her arm. Don't you remember? You and your mother thought she had fallen going down the steps to the Enz? That's what she told you, but he actually broke it. He should have wrung her neck," Friederich said.

"I didn't know that, Papa. Why didn't you tell us that when it happened?" Emilie asked somewhat perplexed.

"I didn't want to get the boy in trouble. I knew how your mother felt about him. What do you think she would have done if she knew he had broken her arm? It would have been the last time she would ever have been allowed her out of the house! I thought it was a pretty good excuse she made up. You know how narrow that little alley way is behind your mother's house. It's been used for hundreds of years as a trysting place for couples," he laughed.

Emilie remembered the alley way. It was built in the middle ages as a tunnel out to the countryside during a siege of the town. You couldn't tell there was anyone in the tunnel unless you stood at the entrance and looked very carefully. Otherwise, the darkness only allowed you to distinguish figures in the tunnel, but not who it might be. The stairway was also an ideal place to sit in the dark. No one would disturb you unless they were coming through the tunnel.

"But how did she break it?" she asked.

"You know how athletic she always claims to be. She wanted to prove to him she was stronger than he. They put their hands together and each tried to bend the others back. They struggled for a few minutes and as she attempted to press his hands back, she felt something snap. Her right arm went limb. It hurt so badly she let out a yell and Karl quit bending her hands back. He had broken her right forearm just behind the wrist. Your mother was very upset. She refused to let Mariele see Karl again until her arm had mended even though she had said she fell on the steps."

"That's right," Emilie said. "Maria was confined to the house and Karl could only call up to her from the street."

"Yes, and these daily long distance visits were an embarrassment to your mother. Do you remember?" Friederich continued. "Her neighbors chided her about the conversations Mariele was having with her boyfriend. The whole neighborhood heard what they talked about."

"Poor mother. She meant well, but none of us followed her advice," Emilie replied thoughtfully.

"Yes. She finally had to allow her out of the house. Mother couldn't do anything about Karl's long range visits. She tried to talk to Karl's mother, but she couldn't do anything either," Friederich concluded.

"And now they're getting married. Mama still can't do anything about it! At least I'll be able to see someone from my family again, Papa."

"I wonder if she's still as sexy as she was when she was a girl?" Friederich said out loud. "As I recall, Karl's sterile. He had an accident in his uncle's carpenter shop when he was a boy. The rumor around the shop was he wouldn't be able to have any children because of it."

"What? I never heard that!" Emilie exclaimed.

"Supposedly, he only has one testicle. He fell down a stairs and one of his testicles receded."

"Oh, poor Maria. Although she once told me she didn't want any children. Maybe it's just as well if they don't have any."

The Fleckhammers arrived late on a Saturday evening in the middle of August. It had taken them fourteen hours to make the trip because of breakdowns with the car. It was an old Chevrolet, with worn tires. Karl had to patch two of the tires four times during the trip. He also had carburetor trouble. By the time they found a gas station that was still open, it was after mid-night before they arrived. Emilie thought she had misunderstood the date of their arrival. She went to bed after eleven o'clock. When the Fleckhammers finally arrived and knocked on the door, Emilie was very glad to see them.

"My, you've grown into quite a pretty young woman, Maria!" Emilie exclaimed. "You're so slender and trim. I've started putting on weight. Ever since I've started working on the farm, I've been putting on the pounds."

"Emilie this is my husband, Karl Fleckhammer. He's Luise's husband's cousin."

"Oh yes, I remember. You used to visit Maria when she was still in school, didn't you? Mama didn't like it one bit as I remember," Emilie laughed.

"Yes. We've known each other a long time," Karl said.

"Emilie, we haven't had anything to eat since we left New York!" Maria said.

"I'll make some tea and heat up the soup I made. I've also baked some bread."

Emilie went into the kitchen with the Fleckhammers following behind. She put an old newspaper into the kitchen stove and placed kindling wood on top of it and lit a match. The stove was soon giving off heat and Emilie heated the soup and water for tea.

"Tell me, how is Mama? Is she getting along all right?" Emilie asked.

"Yes. She's doing well. She gave me some money before I left so we could buy a new bedroom set. It was our wedding present from her," Maria said proudly.

"That was very nice of her. What did you get from Lina?"

"She bought me my wedding dress. Karl's parents gave us five thousand Reichsmarks. They wanted each of their sons to have the same and that's what they gave each of the other two as well."

Emilie poured the soup into two bowls and placed the bread and butter on the table. The Maria and Karl helped themselves.

"This is very good bread, Emilie. Did you bake it?" Karl asked.

"Yes. I try and bake every three days. It's a lot cheaper than buying it in the store."

Emilie watched as they ate their soup and bread.

"Emilie, you've got to forgive Maria," Karl said.

"She's done nothing but talk about what she's received. How are things going on the farm?"

"Okay," she said slowly. "We've had to work very hard since Friederich's relatives left the farm. That's why he's not up. He's dead tired at the end of the day. I didn't want to wake him. You'll see him tomorrow. Let me show you to your room."

She took them upstairs to the west end of the house. It was one of the larger rooms and directly above where Friederich had his bedroom.

"Why don't you both sleep as long as you want tomorrow. I'll make breakfast for you when you get up."

Maria and Karl slept until ten a.m. They probably would have slept longer except Fritzle called up the stairs to them before Emilie could tell him to be quiet. She had seen that evening they were exhausted. She felt there was no need to awaken them earlier. Friederich didn't see them until that afternoon. He was raking hay in the back lot next to the Frank May farm when Karl walked down to see him. Friederich wondered who was coming since he didn't recognize him. Karl had put on some weight since the last time he had seen him. He finally recognized who it was when Karl called out, "Wie geht's Fritz?" (How are you, Fritz?)

Friederich stopped the horses. He got off the rake and shook his hand. They talked about the trip and Karl told him all of the trouble they had had getting there.

"My wife's still tired and exhausted, not from the work, but from worrying during the trip. She kept saying, maybe we should go back home. Maybe we shouldn't go this time."

Friederich laughed. "That's the way I've always known her. She was worried about the least little thing. Now you're stuck with her, Karl. She'll worry about whatever you do."

"It's really not that bad. I'm getting used to it. I'll manage."

Friederich wondered, to himself, whether or not Karl could manage his wife. He didn't pursue the subject any further.

"Can I help with the haying?" Karl offered.

"Not yet. When I'm finished making these rows into piles, you can help me load the wagon and we'll take the hay to the barn to unload."

Friederich was glad Karl was willing to help. He could use all of the help he could get. During that brief week's stay, Friederich and Emilie finished their haying for the summer. They had finished all but the last two big fields themselves. They were very glad for the help.

The Fleckhammers took the family swimming at Green Lake that first Sunday. After the work in the fields was finished, on two other late afternoons, they took Volkmar and Inge there again. Since Friederich and Emilie had to milk the cows, they couldn't go. Fritzle wanted to go, too, but Maria didn't want to have to take the responsibility for him.

"He's too small to swim," she told her sister.

Fritzle cried and cried, but to no avail. The four of them went off to swim in Green Lake by themselves and didn't come back until almost dark. After they came back, Fritzle said, "You can go home now. You've been here long enough!" Karl laughed, but Maria thought he had been put up to it by his father. She asked Fritzle, "Did your father tell you to say that?"

Fritzle didn't answer. Emilie protested. "No! Papa wouldn't say anything like that, Mariele. Don't be so sensitive! Fritzle's just angry because you didn't take him along to Green Lake!"

Friederich laughed. "You really think I put him up to saying that? Well, you can think what you like, but if I wouldn't want you here, I don't have to have a child do the talking for me! You can stay longer, or leave. That's entirely up to you."

"Well, we've been here a week already and I've got to get back to work next Monday," Karl replied. "I can't keep my shop closed too much longer. We'll leave tomorrow."

Volkmar and Inge wanted them to stay longer but they really couldn't. "We'll come again next summer, if our car can make it," Maria assured them. "But if we have the same amount of trouble we had this time, we won't be able to afford it. We'll have to stay home."

That was the first of many visits of the Fleckhammers to "Valley Farm" each summer.

X   X   X

At the beginning of September, the days were already getting rather crisp and chilly. Frank May had filled his silo and asked Friederich if he were ready to have his filled. Friederich said he was. Frank May came with his horses and corn binder and began cutting the corn. Frank alerted George Murray who came with his tractor and silo filler. George's hired man began to put up the pipes on the side of the silo to the top little window through which the chopped corn was to be blown. George set up the ensilage chopper at the base of the silo. He had an old McCormick-Deering tractor which he used to drive the belt to the ensilage chopper. The air from the chopper blew the ensilage into the silo. By noon, the neighborhood crew was assembled. It consisted of George Murray and his hired man, Floyd Cloud; Frank's son, Roy May; Fred Holtz; Jake and Herman Bus; the Olin brothers; and Roy Brentlinger. Each man brought a team of horses and a wagon. They began to load up the corn shucks which Frank had cut. Once each wagon was full, it was taken to the silo filler where George made sure the bundles were fed into the chopper properly. The crew worked until five o'clock that first day. The next day they came again and finished the job. Friederich learned what it meant to have good neighbors who put thirty acres of corn into his silo for the winter.

Emilie had the job of cooking for the harvest crew that second day. She made a big roast beef dinner with spaetzle, gravy, potato salad and extra noodles, in case the men didn't like the spaetzle, plus a green salad. For dessert she made a variety of kuchen with either tea or coffee, whichever the men preferred. She also made bread which, she heard from Mrs. Spencer, practically all of the men ate with their meal. They washed up at the well behind the house where Emilie had provided them with wash basins, soap and towels. Only George and Frank washed up in the kitchen. Emilie kept making more noodles and spaetzle since it was apparent the appetites of the men were greater than she expected. It was a good group of men, she thought. They all had worked together before so everyone knew each other. Friederich and Emilie heard all kinds of stories about the neighborhood which they had not known before. It was an educational meal for them, as well as one of good fellowship. They learned there had been many parties held in the big house. George told of the time when the whole downstairs had been used as one big ballroom.

"Georgine Kelly and the Florence Tremper were great granddaughters of old Colonel Ambrose Mabie. They enjoyed spending as much of the family's money as possible," George chuckled. "At least that's what the neighbors thought. This farm's always been owned by people with money, Fred. You must be one of those, too, since you own the farm now."

"I'm not a rich man, George. We were just here at the right time to buy this farm. I had a machine shop and sold bicycles and motorcycles in Germany before we came over here. With what I made in Germany from selling my business and a couple of other properties here in Syracuse, we were able to buy the farm. My wife comes from a rich family, but I don't."

Frank May then told a story he had heard for years about the big house. "Old Colonel Mabie was a very rich man. He liked to invest in gold and jewels. All of his daughters and granddaughters wore very expensive necklaces and bracelets. They carried rings with large diamonds and jade set in gold. I remember seeing some of them.They were the biggest I'd ever seen!" Frank continued. "There was always rumor going around, Fred, that just before he died, old Ambrose had a secret chamber and vault built in the house somewhere. He kept many of the most expensive items he had collected in this vault. He only brought them out on special occasions. No one has ever been able to find the secret chamber. It must still be here, somewhere, Fred. If you ever find yourself with nothing to do, you might dig around and see if you can find it!"

The men all laughed heartily with Frank. Friederich didn't know whether Frank was serious, or not, especially when everyone laughed right along with Frank. Friederich poured the cider for the men from the barrels he had in the cellar. Some of the cider had been there from the previous year and was very hard. Only Fred Holtz seemed to like it and had several glasses with the meal. The rest of the men only drank one glass, then water with the meal. Drinking water with a meal was also something new for Friederich and Emilie. They had never encountered people who had done that with their meals. Cold water was always assumed, in Germany, to be bad for the stomach.

"No one ever drank cold water there," Friederich said.

"I'm used to drinking water with my meals," Jake Bus said. "I've always done it! My daddy did it! And my grand daddy did, too. I don't know any further back than that."

"Mrs. Malin, could I have some water, too, please?" Roy Brentlinger asked.

The others then asked if they might have water, too. Friederich went to the pump and got a pail of water. To Friederich's astonishment, the men drank the whole pail. He had to get a second one before the dinner was over.

After an hour had passed, Frank May said, "We'd better be getting back to work. We could sit here and eat all day, but it's not going to get the silo filled. If we want to finish today, we'd better get back to work. Probably most of you, with the exception of George, don't know this. But Fred's silo is the biggest in the county!"

The men took their teams and wagons down to the field and continued bringing load after load to the ensilage chopper. Friederich had the job of tramping down the ensilage in the silo. George climbed up the ladder periodically to check on how he was doing.

"Fred, be sure to keep the ensilage spread evenly across the entire silo and keep treading on it to pack it down. You don't want any air pockets in it. It'll only spoil if it's not packed down tightly enough."

George rigged an extender pipe into the silo window with a rope on it so Friederich could direct the ensilage as far around the hexagon as possible. Because the silo was so large, Friederich had to shovel much of the ensilage from the center to the edges. In spite of his best efforts, George had to wait a few minutes between loads so he could finish tramping down the ensilage which he had spread.

After chopping up another load, George came up to help him. He tramped down around the edges several times causing the ensilage to sink a few inches.

"If there's any space in between the loads, Fred, the ensilage could spoil. The cows won't eat spoiled ensilage no matter how hungry they get. You have to be real careful."

By the end of the second day, the thirty acres of corn had been put in the silo as ensilage. The silo was only three quarters full.

"You'll have to plant more corn next year, Fred," George told him. "What you've got in here now should last you a good part of the winter even if you feed the cows twice a day."

Before he left that evening, Frank reminded Friederich "It's your turn, Fred, to help some of the other farmers who've helped you. My son, Roy, is going to start filling his silo tomorrow."

The next morning, he took his team of "Dick" and "Tom" over to Roy May's farm and helped him, together with the others, to fill his silo. He then went to Fred Holtz's farm to help him as well. He spent the better part of a week helping these two farmers fill their silos as they had helped him. This is a good system, he thought. This way, everyone benefits by helping one another do what he can't do very easily alone.

X X X

On January 2, 1932, Volkmar was eleven years old and already helping with the chores around the farm. He liked to take his little brother with him when he went across the road to the cow barn. Volkmar had the job of shoveling the ensilage down from the silo while Friederich and Emilie did the milking. Without fail, Emilie always told Volkmar ("Fall nett!") "Don't fall!"

Inge stayed in the house while the rest of the family was in the cow barn. Fritzle was old enough to take along because he liked to sit and watch his father and mother milk the cows. He moved his stool from one cow to the next, just like his father.

He sat across the gutter from where Friederich was milking to watch how he did it. Fritzle liked the smell of the ensilage Volkmar threw down the chute from the silo. Friederich had learned from Frank May if he mixed the ensilage with grain, the cows would not leave any of it. Fritzle liked to sit on the bags of grain next to the silo while the cows were fed after milking. Since there was no electricity in the barn, Friederich and Emilie used kerosene lanterns for light in doing the milking. One lantern stood across the gutter where Friederich was milking and another stood near Emilie. Volkmar originally had one which he took with him up and down the ladder into the silo. However, Friederich watched, on one occasion, when he almost let the lantern slip out of his hand as he climbed to the top. His father then decided it would be better if Volkmar threw down the ensilage right after getting home from school while there was still enough day light by which to see inside the silo. It also lessened the chance of a fire occurring from a tipped-over lantern. Friederich and Emilie were acutely fearful of fire. The fire, which burned off the roof of their home in Germany while they slept, was a very close call for them. In a barn, with so much combustible material everywhere, they were especially careful. Whenever wandering men stopped by to ask if they might sleep in the hay loft over night, Friederich granted their wish, but insisted they not smoke in the barn. He was especially concerned with the horse barn virtually on the roadside. There was no way he could prevent someone from getting into the barn if he really tried. He kept the front door locked along the road side, but it was still possible for someone to get in from the large sliding door in the rear of the barn. The threat of fire was always at the back of his mind. He thought if he allowed men to sleep in the barn overnight, they would not be so likely to set fire to it, either deliberately or accidentally. What Friederich didn't take into account was something he also learned from Frank May three years earlier, but had forgotten.

Frank happened to stop by one day just as Friederich and Emilie were putting hay into the horse barn. Frank looked at the hay and said, "Fred, this hay is still pretty green. You really should leave it out in the fields until it's completely dry. Even some green clumps of hay can produce spontaneous combustion."

"I wanted to get it in before it rains," Friederich told Frank.

"Well, you've got to be careful about green hay. It can catch fire quicker than you think. I put some green hay into my barn once, and the next winter, when I was pitching it down to my cows, I discovered a pile of ashes right in the middle of the mow. It must have been so hot the hay ignited inside the pile. I was just lucky my barn didn't burn!"

Friederich had never heard of spontaneous combustion before Frank May told him about it. This was, again, something new for him to learn about farming.

"You better spread as much salt on the hay as possible. It helps make the hay sweat and the moisture may prevent the hay from catching fire," Frank suggested.

"Emilie, go over to the house and get some salt. I'll unload the hay until you come back."

Emilie looked for salt in the kitchen cupboard but the only container she found was the iodized salt she used for cooking. She brought it over to the hay barn and Friederich spread it over the greenest parts of the hay they had put in the hay loft. Frank watched as Friederich spread it over the hay. The salt container was soon empty.

"Do we have anymore?"

"No, Papa. That was the last one I had."

"The next time you go shopping, get plenty of salt, Mrs. Malin. You may want to spread even more salt on this hay, Fred. But you'd better do it soon. You don't want to put such green hay into the hay loft. I suppose what you've put on it is better than nothing. It might help to make the hay sweat and the moisture might prevent it from catching fire until it's dried out. It's still risky, but it'll be better than nothing," Frank concluded.

On a cold, February evening, around six o'clock in the evening, Volkmar had just taken Fritzle over to the barn to watch his parents milk the cows. On his way back to the house, he saw smoke coming out of the hayloft over the horse barn. That previous night, two men had slept in the loft and left the next morning. Volkmar ran back to the barn and told his parents, "There's smoke coming out of the horse barn haymow! What should we do?"

"We've got to let the horses out into the pasture!" Friederich said. He and Volkmar ran to the horse barn and let the three horses out. Volkmar drove them down the lane to put distance between them and the barn. After climbing up into the mow, Friederich saw the flames starting up the side of the wall next to the road. He climbed down again and ran to the cow barn.

"Emilie, get to a telephone and call the fire department. The hayloft over the horse barn's on fire!" he yelled. "Volkmar, take Fritzle over to the house and then come back and help me let the cows out."

Friederich began untying the calves and drove them out into the snow. Emilie ran down to the county line store to call the Chittenango Fire Department. The Fire Department had already been alerted by some motorists. They had driven past and had seen the fire shooting out of the roof of the horse barn. Emilie ran back to the barn to see what else she could do. Friederich and Volkmar had already chased all of the cows out of the barn and driven them down the lane towards the horses. Friederich carried pails of water from the well into the mow. The fire had spread so quickly, as soon as he reached the top of the ladder and threw the water on the fire, it broke out out below him. He had to scramble down the ladder in order to get away from the fire. He threw some tools lying on the floor of the garage out the door. He then ran back to the cow barn to see if there was anything else he could use to fight the fire. When he got to the cow barn, he found the fire department spraying water on the cow barn to keep it wet.

"Are all of the animals out of the barns?" The fire captain asked.

"Yes. We just got them all out," Friederich assured him.

"Why aren't you spraying water on the horse barn? That's where the fire is!" Friederich told him.

"You'll be lucky if we can save your house. There's no use spraying water on the fire. The fire's too hot! The water evaporates as soon as it hits the fire! There's probably not much sense in spraying the cow barn, either. The only reason we're even doing that is to try to dampen down the heat a little. The cow barn's just too close to the horse barn. We're going to start spraying your house, too, to try to keep it from catching fire. I've sent for another tanker to come so we don't run out of water right away. It looks like you're going to lose all of your barns on this side of the road. I just hope the fire doesn't get so big that it sets off your gas station! If that blows, then there'll be nothing left of the place!"

Friederich felt sick when he heard what the captain told him. He's going to be lucky if they can save the house he asked himself? He still couldn't accept it. In as loud a whisper as he could muster, he yelled at the captain, "Why don't you continue spraying the cow barn?"

The captain directed the hose man to spray the cow barn roof once more just as the fire started on the peak nearest the horse barn. The jet of water burst through the roof and sent the fireball fire ball hurtling into the haymow. The whole west side of the cow barn seemed to ignite spontaneously. The hose man then redirected the spray from the cow barn to the north side of the house facing the barns across the road. The house literally steamed from the combination of heat and water during the height of the fire. The Chittenango firemen placed themselves between the burning barns across the road and the house and gas station, as if to provide a human heat shield to protect the buildings on the south side of the road. When the tanker truck from Kirkville arrived, the Chittenango captain directed the men to spray the gas station and the garage next to the big house. He didn't think it was necessary to spray the little house to the west since it hadn't caught fire even at the height of the blaze in the horse barn. The main house had a ladder placed on the rear side and a human chain of buckets from the well to the roof continued wetting down the roof on the front side until the fire in the two barns had subsided. The firemen also sprayed the huge elm tree whose branches hung over the big house and road towards the horse barn. They thought, if the fire got hot enough, it might ignite the limbs and then the house. Emilie went back into the house and began packing clothes, feather beds, and what she thought were other essentials into boxes in order to move out quickly if it should prove necessary. She kept going to the front door and looked out across the road at the fire. She couldn't stop crying. She kept wiping her eyes repeatedly. She came every few minutes to the front door and looked out at the fire with the three children. The flames had enveloped not only the horse barn, but the cow barn and the silo. She kept saying "Oh God! All of our summer's hard work making hay, planting corn, and filling the silo has been lost!"

"Where are we going to put the cows?" Volkmar asked. "Will we have to buy hay for them now?"

Emilie continued quietly crying. She finally said, "We'll have to wait and see what Papa says. We'll have to do something!" she answered with some exasperation.

The neighbors from miles around had seen the flames lighting the night skies and came to see the fire. There were cars and trucks of all makes, shapes and sizes standing along the side of the road. The firemen and policemen wouldn't let anyone go past the burning barns. It was too dangerous. The police had already set up detours at Mycenae and on Tuscarora road. Anyone who needed to go on Route 5 was forced to take one of these detours on the west or east. Charley Nesbitt lived on the hilltop just across from George Murray's farm. He had seen the fire from his kitchen window and came down immediately. He sought out Friederich from among the multitudes who had assembled watching the fire. He had met him while helping George Murray fill his silo. His barn was empty of cows since he had sold all of them the previous fall. But his barn was full of hay from last summer's haying. When he saw Friederich standing next to the firemen spraying the fire, he asked, "Fred, would you like to use my barn until you decide what you're going to do? You'll have to put your cows somewhere. They can't stay outside in weather like this for too long."

"Oh, that would be very helpful, Mr. Nesbitt. I'll pay you rent until I decide what I can do."

"Don't worry about that now, Fred. The first thing we have to do is get these cows and calves inside my barn so they don't freeze."

Friederich was overwhelmed by the generosity of his neighbors. Not only had Mr. Nesbitt offered sanctuary for his calves and cows, but Charley organized the neighbors to drive the cows to his farm. Several men got ropes out of their trucks and tied them around the necks of those cows Friederich designated as leaders. They led them while the others drove the rest of the cows behind in a long line the half mile to Nesbitt's cow barn.

The twenty cows and five calves fit snugly into the Nesbitt's barn. These same neighbors fed the cows before going back to the fire. The three horses were taken by Frank May and his son, Roy, to the Meagher farm where there were three empty stalls available. Charley didn't have any room for them since he had kept his own horses to continue to raise crops on his farm.

The next morning was like a nightmare to the Malin family. The smoke was still rising from the smoldering hay and ensilage. The firemen had decided to let the fire burn itself out.

"There's no need to keep pouring water on the smoldering hay and ensilage," the captain said. "It's just a waste of water."

There was nothing left of the wood structures of the barns and silo. There were a few beams on the ground that were almost consumed, but the captain didn't think they'd pose any problems.

"You'll probably see smoke rising from the ruins for the rest of the week. But it shouldn't catch anything else on fire. There's nothing left to burn!" he said with a chuckle.

As Friederich and Emilie walked up to the Nesbitt barn to milk the cows that first morning, she asked, "Should we move back to the city, now, Papa? We don't have any money to rebuild the barns. The insurance will be given to Mr. Pauli and Mr. Trant. We won't get any of it!"

Friederich didn't say anything. He was angry and frustrated. He thought how unfair it was that the insurance on the buildings should be given to the mortgage holders! They had nothing invested in it; they hadn't made all of the hay or filled the silo; they hadn't lost twenty sacks of grain, or the hay forks, the ropes, the pulleys, the harnesses, and most of the tools! They're only going to reap what they didn't sow, he thought bitterly to himself. The more he thought about it, the angrier he became. He finally said, "I don't know yet what we're going to do! But one thing I know. We're not leaving the farm! I wouldn't think of giving them the satisfaction of retaking what they don't deserve to own!"

They walked the rest of the way in silence. Emilie knew when Friederich spoke that bitterly, it was best not to pursue the question for the time being. She would have to raise it again, she told herself. But later. They had to do something. They couldn't go on like this.

Friederich and Emilie hadn't thought of what they would need that first morning after the fire. Mr. Nesbitt had said the night before they could use his equipment including his milk pails and cans. He didn't need them for the time being. They were very glad he was so generous and didn't say anything about rent. It didn't take them very long to milk the cows that morning; first, the cows didn't have much milk due to their nocturnal journey; and second, they hadn't gotten used to their new surroundings yet. Emilie had only milked five cows when Friederich told her, "You better go home and see that Volke and Inge get off to school. I'll come back when I've finished milking and fed the cows."

Fortunately, it was a relatively mild winter so far with very little snow on the ground. It wasn't a problem walking back and forth between the two farms. It just took time. Since Mr. Nesbitt had said he was in no hurry to have him decide what to do, Friederich thought he would have time to think over his options. What he really wanted to do was rebuild his barns, but he knew this was impossible. He didn't have any money for such a project. They simply couldn't afford it. He thought of other things they might do. He felt he could cut wood. Finkbeiner and Schultz had cut a lot of trees but there were still plenty left. He thought he could ask them to increase the amount they were cutting and set some aside for his own use as timber should he decide to rebuild in the next few years. Yes, the more he thought about this option, the more he felt this was the only one he really had. In the meantime, he would keep on milking his cows at Nesbitt's, and pay him for the hay they were consuming.

After a week had gone by, Friederich asked Mr. Nesbitt, "What do you think I should pay you for rent and for the feed my cows are consuming?"

"I'm in no hurry for any payment, Fred. But whenever you think you can start, I thought maybe ninety dollars a month would be all right."

Friederich was floored by this amount. This was almost half of what he was making on his milk check at seventy-five cents per hundred weight! Friederich had thought two dollars a day would be a good price. But not three dollars a day!

"Is this your best offer?"

"Yes."

"Then I'm going to have to sell my cows as soon as I can. Can you wait until I sell them to settle up with you what I owe?"

"Sure," Charley answered. "But you don't have to sell your cows, Fred. You can keep using my barn."

"At three dollars a day for rent! I'm not making enough to keep them!"

Three weeks later, Friederich had arranged with an auctioneer to come to Charley's barn for the sale of the cows and calves. He sold all but three of his cows and one heifer. He wanted to keep them since they were his best milkers. He felt they could be the basis for rebuilding his herd in the future. He was appalled with the prices he got for his twenty-six cows and three calves. He got an average of forty dollars per cow and three dollars for each calf. He had paid sixty-five dollars each for most of the cows just three years earlier. He couldn't believe they weren't worth at least that much today! Emilie couldn't bear to watch. She stayed for the auctioning of three cows. When she saw what each cow brought, she went home again. She couldn't see how they were going to make anything on the auction. Once all of the cows were sold, Friederich settled up with the auctioneer and with Charley Nesbitt. He took home eight hundred fifty-five dollars. He felt the auctioneer didn't do a very good job talking up the value of the cows, either. He noticed when Jack Henson bought a couple of his cows, he laughed at some joke the auctioneer had told him. It was obvious to Friederich the auctioneer and Jack were friends. He wondered if the friendship had something to do with the low prices his cows were bringing. He appreciated the fact that George Murray bought three of his cows and had paid the highest price of anyone for each cow. One of the cows George bought was a real hard milker. Friederich told George "She's a good cow, but very hard to milk."

"That's okay, I've got a milking machine. I won't have to milk her by hand, Fred."

Friederich took the three cows and heifer which were left back to the farm and put them in the garage next to the house. Fortunately, he had put hay in the loft that summer so he had plenty of hay ready to feed them. He had already decided to dig out the basement under the garage and make it over into a make-shift cow barn. He had been working on it even while the cows were at Nesbitt's. He had also erected a lean-to shed behind the garage so he could bring his horses back to the farm. They had been in the old Meagher barn, now owned by John Kelly. This meant he had to go there each day to feed and water the horses. The benefit from this arrangement was he didn't have to pay any rent. Mr. Kelly had wanted the old hay in the barn eaten up anyway, so it didn't matter if Friederich's horses ate all the hay. The stalls were similar to those in which they had been kept on the farm. They seemed relatively content in this new horse barn. Only "Tom" seemed nervous and didn't seem to make the transition very well. Each time Friederich approached him, he had to talk to him as he went past so he wouldn't kick.

Six weeks after the fire, the whole family came down with the flu. Only Volkmar was able to get up. He had to look after the animals. He had no difficulty feeding and watering the cows. Friederich got up long enough to milk his three cows. He felt so weak, he told Volkmar "You'd better go over and feed and water the horses, Volke. I don't think I can make it."

Volkmar went over to Kellys to feed and water the three horses. It seemed a long time until he returned.

"Has Volke returned?" Friederich asked Emilie.

"No. he's not back yet. Do you think he had trouble with them?"

"I don't know. I should have told him to be careful around Tom. He's very nervous in this new barn. He likes to kick."

When Volkmar returned, Friederich asked him, "Did you have trouble with the horses? What took you so long?"

He was very pale and couldn't remember if he had been there or not.

"I think I was over there, Papa, but I don't remember. I don't feel very well. I think I'm going to throw up."

Emilie quickly got the chamber pot and placed it in front of him just in time. He started vomiting and said, "I don't feel so good."

"Did Tom kick you?" Friederich asked.

"I don't remember."

"You'd better go back to bed, Volke," Emilie said. "Where did you get this bump on your forehead? How did you get all of this horse manure on you? Your clothes are all dirty!"

"I don't remember. I think I went over to the horses, but I don't remember anything else."

He spent a fitful night. Emilie had to get up with him on two different occasions because he thought he had to vomit. She prepared hot tea and toast for him and he gradually fell asleep. The next day, he felt a little better, but still had a severe headache.

"I think Volkmar should stay home today, Papa. He still doesn't feel very well."

"Ja, that's a good idea. Maybe a day in bed will help him."

The next day she wondered if she should keep him home again. She decided to send him to school. When he still complained of a headache several days later,

Emilie went over to Mrs. Spencer and asked, "Mrs. Spencer could you take Volkmar and me to the doctor? I think he may have been kicked by our horse. He still has a headache and it was three days ago."

"Certainly, Mrs. Malin. I'll be right over."

Emilie walked back through the garden and got Volkmar ready. Mrs. Spencer took them to see Dr. Boyd in Chittenango. Dr. Boyd sent them to the Canastota hospital for an x-ray of Volkmar's head. He then examined the results and told Emilie

"He must have had a concussion, Mrs. Malin. I think your husband might be right. Your horse must have kicked him in the head. There's a swelling on the right front side of his brain. It should gradually go down. You can give him a couple of aspirin to ease the pain every four hours. Just make sure he doesn't get hit in the head again. He should be okay in another day or two."

While the family was ill, the children got into bed with Emilie and Friederich. Friederich had decided from the very beginning of their stay on the farm, he and Emilie would not sleep together.

"I like to sleep alone. I sleep a lot better if I have the bed to myself."

The only exception was when he agreed Fritzle could sleep with him in the winter. During their illness, the older children also climbed in bed with Friederich and Emilie. It was much warmer in their parents' beds. Their fevers seemed to drop when they slept with Friederich and Emilie. When Inge slept with Friederich, he stroked her head until she finally fell asleep. After a while she awoke because of a strange sensation she had never felt before. His hand was stroking her all over. She liked the feeling, but was bewildered by it at the same time. She wasn't sure why he was doing it to her. She didn't move and he continued to rub her until she felt she couldn't stand it anymore. She moved away from him.

"Where are you going?" he asked.

"I'm going to get in bed with Mom."

"No you're not. You're staying here with me."

Fritzle had crawled into bed with Emilie. Volkmar was sleeping in his own bed. Inge had usually slept with her mother, but had only gotten into bed with her father when he suggested it might be nice to sleep with him for a change. After Friederich told Inge to stay with him, she didn't get out of his bed. He stopped rubbing her and she fell asleep again. She awoke next morning when she felt him stroking her again. This time she got up and climbed into her own bed. Friederich didn't say anything. She thought he must be asleep. Inge wondered why he had done that to her. Her mother had never done anything like that to her, nor had anyone else. She couldn't understand it. And yet it felt good. It left her wondering what it meant and why he had done it to her . . .

X   X   X

The Spencers had moved into the little house renting it that previous spring.

When they paid the rent in April, Mrs. Spencer told Emilie, "Mrs. Malin, we really like it here. Would you be interested in selling the house and four acres with it?"

"Let me ask my husband, Mrs. Spencer. I think he might be interested in selling it to you. Could you come back this evening? He's down in the woods right now."

"All right. My husband will be home from work then, too. We'll come over after supper."

"Fine. We'll look forward to seeing you this evening, Mrs. Spencer."

Friederich came back up from the wood lot at four o'clock. Emilie had dinner ready for him and the children. As they were eating, Emilie said, "Papa, Mr. and Mrs. Spencer want to talk to you about buying the little house and four acres. I told them to come by this evening. Would that be all right with you?"

"Ja, that's okay. Let's hear what they have in mind."

As Emilie and Inge were washing the evening dishes, Mr. and Mrs. Spencer came over to talk about buying the little house.

"Good evening Mrs. Malin, Mrs. Spencer said as Emilie opened the kitchen door.

"Good evening Mrs. Spencer. Come in. My husband is waiting for you."

"Hello Mrs. Malin," Mr. Spencer said. "Hello Mr. Malin," he said as he turned towards Friederich. He had gotten up to shake hands with the Spencers.

"Good evening," Friederich said as he extend ed his hand to each of them. "My wife tells me you're interested in buying my little house and some land with it?"

"Yes, That's right. We like the location and it's not far from my relatives and not far from Ed's job in Manlius," Mrs. Spencer answered.

"The house is worth a lot of money," Friederich told them. "But I'll sell it to you very cheaply because you're such good neighbors."

"We'd also like to buy about four acres with the house, Mr. Malin. Ed wants to have a garden and raise his own vegetables and fruits."

"You can have the land from the corner of our garden straight up the hill to the fence line on top of the hill and then over to Kelly's line. That's about four acres all together," Friederich proposed.

"What are you asking for the house and four acres?" Mr. Spencer asked.

"I think five thousand dollars would be a fair price."

"That's way too much, Mr. Malin" Mr. and Mrs. Spencer said in unison.

"We'll give you four thousand five hundred for it. We can't afford any more."

"I'll take it," Friederich said. "You've both been very good neighbors. I'm sure you'll pay us off when your note comes due."

"You won't have to worry about that, Mr. Malin. We've already made arrangements to take out a loan with our bank. We'll have the money ready for you by the first of next month," Mrs. Spencer replied.

They had already arranged to take out a bank loan to cover the mortgage. They didn't want Friederich to hold it. They felt it would be better having to pay a bank than their neighbor. They had privately thought Friederich's asking price would be around five thousand dollars. It was this amount they arranged to borrow from their bank in Manlius. Buying it for five hundred dollars less, they congratulated themselves for saving so much money. Emilie was pleased the Spencers had bought the house. It not only meant they would continue to have good neighbors, but they would also have some money with which to live while deciding what they were going to do next. She hoped Friederich would decide to leave the farm. Without cows, they no longer had a monthly milk check. How else can we live, she kept asking herself?

After the sale of the little house, Friederich told Emilie "Why don't you write your mother and ask her for a five thousand Reichsmark loan so we can rebuild our cow barn?"

Emilie was floored by this request. "How can we rebuild even if she would loan us the money? What will we do in the meantime? Until it's built and we buy more cows, we don't have any income?" she asked incredulously.

Friederich didn't like this response at all. "You're always opposed to whatever I propose, aren't you? You want me to give up the farm? Well, I'll tell you for the last time! We're not going to give up the farm! We're staying here and that's that! Now write your mother and ask her to loan us some money!" He stormed.

"But Papa," she pleaded. "What are we going to live on until it's built? Our truck doesn't run anymore. The car hasn't been driven in over two years! We can't count on the tourist business making any money! The price of milk is supposed to go down even more this spring. Even if we buy more cows, we'll be getting less for our milk than we did before the fire! How can we live on that?"

Friederich really got angry with her after these questions. "You're always harping about how little we have! Well, where I came from, we never had very much to begin with! So everything I see here on the farm is worth a lot more than I ever had or will have! Get used to the idea, Emilie! You're married to me and not to some rich man like your father! You're going to have to make do with what we have! You ought to learn how to get along on a lot less than you do. You're spending way too much on groceries, as it is! Do more baking and less buying and you'll see how much more you can save!"

"But I don't buy too much!" she protested. "I even save a little from what we give out each week for the groceries! I only spent two dollars and fifty cents last week on groceries!"

"That's too much. You shouldn't be spending more than two dollars a week!" He stormed out of the house slamming the back door so hard the house shook.

The digging under the garage was going more slowly than Friederich had thought. It was a lot harder to make much progress by himself. While getting their mail out at their mail boxes one morning, Emilie talked with Mrs. Spencer. She told her what Friederich was doing.

"My two brothers aren't busy at the moment, Mrs. Malin. Why doesn't your husband talk to them about helping him dig out the space under the garage?"

"Thank you Mrs. Spencer. I'll tell my husband what you suggested."

After returning to the house, Emilie said "Papa, Mrs. Spencer thinks her two brothers might be able to help you dig out the foundation for the new cow barn. She said they aren't doing anything just now and would like a job."

Friederich thought that was a good idea and walked up to Mycenae to talk with Herman and Jake Bus.

"Yeah, we can help you, Fred. We'll take three dollars a day for work like that."

"I can only afford to pay you two dollars a day," Friederich replied.

"That's a lot of work for two dollars a day," Herman said.

"Yeah, but it's a job Herman. We ain't worked for the last two months," Jake drawled.

"Yeah, I guess you're right, Jake. Having a job is better than none. Okay, Fred. We'll work for two dollars a day. What sort of hours are you talking about? Sun up to sun down?"

"No. You won't have to come that early. It'll be from seven in the morning until six at night with a half hour off for lunch. Bring your own tools, too. Do you have a wheelbarrow?"

"Yeah, we've got one," Jake said. "We've got shovels and pickaxes, too."

"All right. I'll expect you to start tomorrow morning."

The next morning, Herman and Jake Bus arrived in their model T truck with their tools loaded in the truck bed.

"Good morning," Friederich said.

"Good morning," they both answered.

"It's a pretty nice day, ain't it, Fred?" Jake said.

Friederich nodded. He took them through the little door into the area where he had already started the excavation. It was already standing room high. They didn't have to stoop to continue the digging.

"What I want you to do, is continue to dig out the dirt and wheel it to the west side of the building. I want you to make a ramp so I can drive my horses and a wagon into the upstairs. It's going to be my cow barn when it's finished."

There was already a ramp there, but he wanted to lower the second floor of the barn in order to have more room for hay in the mow area. The barn floor under which they were excavating was the previous ground floor. The second level was approximately through the center of the building. He wanted to remove this floor and keep the ground floor where it was. The excavation was taking place beneath this ground floor for his new cow barn. Once the excavation was completed, he planned on taking out the second floor planks entirely. He wanted to drive into the hayloft like he had done in the barns across the road. There were two big doors on the west side of the garage. The southern door would make an ideal entrance into the hayloft for his horses and wagon.

Herman and Jake worked on the project for the next two months. Once the excavation was finished, Friederich looked over the basement. It was completely empty of dirt under the entire basement of the barn.

"That's a good job," he told the Bus brothers. "Now what I'd like to have you do is put in a concrete floor and gutters for the cows. I'll build the stanchions the while."

"Yeh, we can do that," Herman said. "But you only asked us to excavate the basement for two dollars a day. Concrete work is a lot harder. We'll have to have four dollars a day for that kind of work!"

"I'll give you an extra dollar a day," Friederich countered.

"Nope, that's not enough," Herman said. "It's four dollars a day. And you'll have to buy the cement. But we'll use our team and wagon to go down to the creek side and use your gravel," Jake volunteered.

Friederich was in a bind. He knew he couldn't do the job himself. It would take too long. Both Herman and Jake had been good workers, he thought. The only time they really stopped working was to put new plugs of tobacco into their mouths. Friederich reluctantly agreed. He'd try, somehow, to raise the money. He hoped to hear from his mother-in-law that she would loan him the money.

"All right," Friederich said. "But you've got to be here at seven in the morning with your team and wagon!"

Friederich and Emilie had a row over how much kuchen and cider she should take out to the Bus brothers during their work hours. At the beginning, she had taken out a jug of cider and kuchen twice a day; once at mid morning and once in the mid afternoon. This is what would have been done in Germany, she thought.

"Once a day is enough, Emilie! If you go out there twice a day, they'll take too much time off from the job!"

"But they're doing a good job, Papa."

"I don't care! I'm losing at least half an hour a day while they drink my cider and eat your kuchen!"

Emilie didn't argue. She took out cider and kuchen in the morning and only cider in the afternoon, if Friederich was around. They usually helped themselves to water from the pump in addition to these repasts she brought. Occasionally, when Friederich wasn't around the barn, she also brought out kuchen with cider in the afternoon.

"This is good cake, Mrs. Malin," Jake said. "I could eat this all the time."

After the barns burned, Friederich told his tenant in the gas station, "As of the first of May, I'm going to take over the gas station myself."

Originally, he had not wanted to pump gas, but with no further milk checks coming in, he thought the station would give him more income, if he ran it himself. The amount of rent was simply too small to make a profit. When Herman Bus found out Friederich was going to run the gas station himself, he talked with him about hiring his daughter to look after the station.

"How would ten cents an hour be, Fred, if she worked all day?"

"That's out of the question. If she'd like to work, I'll give her twenty five cents for a ten hour day. She can't take any time off for lunch. She'll have to be on call all during that time."

"I don't think that's enough, Fred," Herman replied. Jake spoke up and said to his brother, "She'll at least have a job, Herman. She ain't doin' nothin' now and it ain't likely she'll get another job anyhow."

Reluctantly, Herman agreed. The next day he brought his daughter, Dorothy, to pump gas. There weren't many cars on the road in the spring, but Friederich hoped there would be more in the summer. He didn't want to have to pay her if there was no business. There was an average of four cars a day stopping to fill up with gas. The customers spent a few more cents, occasionally, on candy bars, ice cream or soda pop. Friederich realized a three dollar a day clear profit after expenses from his gas station. He felt he was making enough to keep it open.

Chapter VII

The Struggle to Survive

Emilie not only wrote to her mother, but to the Haussmanns and the Malins. Friederich hadn't told her to write them. She had simply gone ahead on her own. She thought they would certainly want to know the barns had burned and that they had had to sell their cattle. As soon as they received her letters, the Haussmanns and Malins decided to drive out to the farm the next Saturday. Friederich was surprised to see them, and not very pleased. He still bristled because they had all left so abruptly three years previously.

"Friederich, why didn't you write to us right away? We would have come out sooner! What are you going to do now? You can't stay here any longer. You don't have any income! You might better come back to the city. Maybe you could even get your old job back at Easy Washer," Gretel stated.

Richard agreed. Even Karl said, "That's right, Friederich. You can move in with us until you get settled and find a place of your own."

Friederich didn't like this mode of questioning. He took umbrage that anyone would even suggest he leave his farm! Especially, from these relatives of his who had left him in the lurch three years ago! Even his mother asked him, "What are you going to do, Friederich?"

"I'm going to stay right here! I've still got the land, the woods, three cows and a heifer. I've still got my horses and most of my machinery. There's no reason why I can't continue. We've got the gas station, too, and this summer, we'll go on with our tourist business. I just don't have my cows anymore, or my barns. But I'm not finished yet! This is a lot better than working in a factory!"

Emilie tried to use the alliance she felt with his relatives by suggesting,

"But maybe you could work in the shop for a while until we rebuild. Then we can always come back to the farm!"

The work had been hard on Emilie. Not only had she been helping Friederich do all of the farm work before the fire, but If we stay, she thought to herself, I'll have to continue to do so, and even more. Friederich was already telling her, "Emilie, keep an eye on the gas station. Dorothy Bus needs supervision. And don't forget to collect the receipts every couple of hours."

Emilie also had to look after the tourist business. True, there were not many tourists. Most of them asked if they had a flush toilet. When she said they didn't, they usually drove on. Every now and then, they had had a full house. With the Heatons still living there, Emilie had to do their weekly washing and cleaning, in addition to her own. The Heatons often ate with them so Emilie had to cook on an average of one meal a day for them, in addition to breakfast. This was an additional burden on her since she never felt she could cook anything less than a major dinner. She liked the Heatons. They weren't a bother to her. It was just that she knew she had to make an extra effort to take care of their needs, in addition to those of her own family. While Friederich worked hard cutting wood, plowing, or planting crops, he only had one thing to do at a time. Emilie, on the other hand, had to take care of several things simultaneously. She wouldn't have minded moving back to the city at all! She wouldn't have to empty the privy pail each day for the Heatons, either! She did have to take care of her children, including a three year old. But she enjoyed doing this. It was just that she had to do so much in addition to raising her family! When Friederich realized what Emilie had done in trying to use his family as allies against his plans for staying on the farm, he blew up.

"Quiet! I'll make the decisions in this family!"

He turned to his sister, "If you came out here to torment me about moving back to the city, forget it! You can all just get back in the car and go back home! We're staying here, and that's final!"

Emilie apologized.

"Papa, I didn't mean to offend you. I just thought it might help to have someone else's point of view. Let's have some coffee and kuchen and talk about something else."

The Haussmanns, Karl and his mother stayed for coffee. They dropped their line of questioning about leaving the farm. Each of them saw it was useless carrying on the conversation any further with Friederich. Grandmother Malin said "As soon as it's summer, I'm going to come out for a few weeks when Gretel has vacation. I can help out in the garden. Emilie won't have to do so much weeding and she'll have time to help Friederich make hay."

"I'll come out as much as possible on my vacation, too, Fritz. Anne is working full time now, but mostly in the evenings," Karl promised.

Richard also offered to come out during his vacation.

"I'd like to gather wild grapes and try to make some wine from them."

Before they left, each one seemed to feel better for having come. While they couldn't talk Friederich into leaving the farm, at least they thought he could use some help in spite of the kind of man he was! They all were willing to do what they could for his family, if not for him . . .

The summer of 1932 was similar to that of 1929. The relatives came out to help on the farm. Not only was the new make-shift cow barn under the garage completed, but Richard, Karl and Friederich finished putting up the lean-to shed behind the garage in which the horses could be kept. They would no longer have to be left for the winter in Kelly's barn. Friederich could also use them more frequently, as needed, to haul wood from the woods, or manure out to the fields. The garden grew so well that summer, especially potatoes, the Haussmanns and the Malins took several bushels with them back to Syracuse. The field east of the garage produced such a surplus of potatoes and cabbage there was more than enough for the entire winter. Unfortunately, the alfalfa, which Karl and Friederich had planted on the hill top fields, never grew. There were only a few stalks springing up here and there. Friederich talked to Frank May about the problem and Frank came to take a look.

"Did you use any pesticide on your seed, Fred?"

"No, I didn't."

"Well that's what's wrong with it, Fred. Any field that's not had alfalfa on it for several years, or where you're trying to plant a new crop of alfalfa, you have to inoculate the seed. Otherwise, it'll just rot in the ground before it can grow. The seed might have been old, too, Fred. It may not have been of good germinating quality. But if you didn't inoculate it, the seed store won't give you any credit for it. You have to use all of the steps they require to ensure it'll grow. They won't give you a refund if you didn't inoculate the seed. Did you use any fertilizer, Fred?"

"No. I didn't think it was necessary."

"It's a real shame, Fred. You spent all that money and nothing grows, but that happened to me once, too. I tried planting fifty acres of corn one time without fertilizer and I only had a very spotty field. It almost wasn't worth cutting. I learned one thing, Fred. If a man is going to spend much time and money on anything, it better pay off. I don't do any planting anymore without fertilizer. It's just not worth it. It's too bad, but maybe you've learned something the hard way from this."

Friederich could only think about how much it had cost him. Actually, it was his brother who had bought the seed. They had planted it together last year with the oats. Friederich thought this year would be an excellent hay crop for his dairy. He no longer needed the hay so badly now that he didn't have his herd, but it was a real loss, nevertheless.

"You don't have to pay me back, Friederich. It's my loss," Karl told him.

Friederich didn't like being beholden to anyone, even if it was his brother. He would pay him back, he told himself, when he had some extra money. But he couldn't afford it now.

The conversations over the dinner table were always interesting when Gretel and Richard were there. Richard told stories and gave the impression that he was easily offended, for emphasis. The rest of the table roared with laughter. His self-deprecating humor was infectious and made others feel good. When he had a little too much to drink, his antics were even funnier. He once told them how Gretel wanted him to sleep in the bed upstairs so she wouldn't get pregnant again. He told it in such a way that it was obvious he didn't like the idea.

"But what can I do about it?"

Everyone laughed at his predicament. They were all doing exactly the same thing . . . Sleeping in separate beds, if not separate rooms, so the women wouldn't get pregnant. Only Karl and Anne were experimenting with condoms and, of course, this brought outbursts of laughter and ridicule whenever Anne's name was mentioned. It was common knowledge she only allowed Karl a sexual visit once every two weeks. She couldn't be careful enough and, besides, as she always said "Sex is dirty and men shouldn't be such animals in wanting it so much!"

Of all of the relatives, only Friederich, it seems, had sex when and how often he wanted. He and Emilie simply made sure his orgasm took place outside of her vagina. It was never really satisfying, but they didn't have any more children. They knew about Karl and Anne and their experimentation with condoms. They had concluded, however, first, they were too expensive; and second, they would interfere with the real feel of flesh on flesh. Friederich liked that feeling and didn't want any interference with this aspect of sex.

Grandmother Malin didn't like these conversations which her children had.

"Stop talking about sex, so much!" she scolded. "It's not a subject to talk about!"

She left the table when Richard or Gretel made some pointed remark about sex, or the need to control the number of children a couple should have. According to Grandmother Malin, "Children come from God! If he wants people to have children, they'll have them irrespective of what they do, or don't do."

She disapproved of Karl's and Anne's reluctance to have children. She told Anne on many occasions, "You need to have more children! Wilhelmle should have company growing up. If he doesn't have brothers and sisters, he's going to grow up to be a spoiled brat!"

She also berated her daughter-in-law for spending too little time at home with her family. "You'll regret it someday, Anne."

She didn't say why she would regret it. She took it for granted Anne would know. Grandmother also took Karl to task. "Karl, you need more children. You can't raise a little boy all by himself. He needs at least one brother or a sister! It's not normal to have only one child."

"Mother, I agree. But what can I do about it? I can't have children by myself! I'd like to have more, but Anne's against it. She didn't even want Wilhelmle, but I didn't pull out in time and she got pregnant. She's still never forgiven me for that. That's why I have to use rubbers. That's the only way I can have any sex with her at all!"

The rest of the family felt sorry for Karl, especially Friederich. His dislike for his sister-in-law intensified when he first heard this lament of his brother.

"She ought to be raped," he said to those who talked about her. "Then she'd know what he should be doing! She should be taking care of kids, instead of working!"

The conversation came to a momentary halt.

"No, Friederich, that shouldn't be done! You can't go around raping whomever you please! Men just don't do that!" Gretel said indignantly.

"And why not? When a woman is stubborn and ornery, why shouldn't she be shown what she has to do? To hell with such cold women! It's their job to be responsive to the male. Just look at the way animals do it! Have you ever seen a chicken that really wants to do it? Of course not! The rooster has to pursue her until she quits and he gets on top of her. He lets her have it whether she wants it or not! Don't tell me how to treat women!"

It was obvious to those who were listening, there were two conversations going on at the same time. The one Gretel was referring to, and the one Friederich had undertaken. Gretel meant men can't go around raping whomever they pleased. Friederich, on the other hand, was referring to what he observed in nature and never once did it occur to him she meant him and his past actions towards her and other women.

"Human beings are different from animals!" Gretel said emphatically. "We're not chickens! We're not cows! We're not sheep! We're women and we have a right to express what we want, or don't want, and from whom and when! So don't tell us that we're not!" she said heatedly.

Friederich responded with his peculiar and cynical grin.

"Yeah, you're all alike. You only want it on your own terms! That's not for me! If a man is able to pay enough, he can get whomever he wants. Well, I'm going to get it and not have to pay for it!"

Gretel then turned to Emilie. "Emilie, I feel sorry for you! How can you live with this man?"

"Oh, he's really not that bad. I like it, too, and he certainly knows how to do it!"

And with that, she stroked his arm and smiled at him. He smiled at her but drew back. He didn't like any expressions of touching or loving gestures. That just wasn't for him. You have to take what you can get and that's the only way to do it, he thought to himself.

"No one ever did anything for me! Why should I do anything for someone else?" Friederich asked.

What Gretel was talking about was alien to him and his experience.

"You ought to go to church! Maybe then you'd learn how to be a human being!" Gretel chided.

Her ire was rising and Richard recognized some sort of joke was necessary otherwise these two would be fighting again. He proposed a toast.

"Here's to another good harvest of potatoes and grapes!" and raised his glass amid the laughter. Everyone raised his glass to the toast and forgot what had initiated the discussion in the first place.

X X X

1933 was the last year the Heatons lived on the farm. Emilie had gotten used to the weekly drives to Chittenango with them to go grocery shopping. She liked to go to Mr. Bailey's Red and White store because he was such a nice, friendly man. He knew who she was and where she lived. He always greeted her with, "Hello, Mrs. Malin. How are you today?"

"I'm fine, thank you, and how are you, Mr. Bailey?"

"Fine. And what will it be today? Do you need any flour or yeast?"

She always did. Her grocery bill came within a few cents each week of two dollars and fifty cents. She felt this was all she could afford to spend. The Heatons were amazed. Their purchases of fruits, cookies, and breads amounted to more than Emilie's.

"And we're only two people, Harry!" Mrs. Heaton exclaimed when they talked over the shopping trip upon their return to the farm.

Emilie had to plan for five people. Before going with the Heatons, she put on her best dress, stockings and coat. She felt she had to look her best whenever she went into town.

Mr. Heaton came into the kitchen one day as Emilie was preparing dinner.

"Mrs. Malin, I hate to tell you this, but my wife and I have decided we're moving back to Syracuse next month. We thought it best to tell you now so you can plan to use our room for your tourists this summer."

Emilie was visibly upset.

"Don't you want to stay at least over the summer? You really don't have to worry about the rent. We'll have tourists this summer again, so there won't be such a need for rent from you?"

"Well, we'll think it over again. Maybe we could stay one more summer."

The Heaton's had already talked it over, however. They were planning to move to Florida next winter. He was getting tired of the cold winter months and they both wanted to see what it was like to live in the south.

"Thank you for telling me, Mr. Heaton. I'm very sorry you're going to leave us. We'll miss you both very much!"

She genuinely liked the Heatons. They were both very friendly and helpful to her. They even looked after little Fritzle on occasion when she had to go the city and Friederich couldn't take him along to the woods or fields. She wondered what she would do when they were gone. They also came over everyday for dinner at noon. Emilie enjoyed talking with them during the meal. It gave her practice with her English and even Friederich seemed to like them. He was even a little embarrassed on one occasion when Mrs. Heaton was seated at the table eating dinner. Fritzle stood near her and watched her very closely for a long time. He then lay across his father's lap while Friederich was eating. As he lay there, he looked up at Mrs. Heaton and also down her legs. He got off of his father's lap and went over to Mrs. Heaton. He took hold of her dress and before she realized what he was doing, he had lifted it up over her thighs and looked at them. She gave a surprised laugh.

"You little scamp! Don't lift up my dress!"

She pulled her dress down quickly and both she and Friederich laughed.

"Fritzle, we don't do that! You have to leave Mrs.Heaton's dress down," he told him.

Fritzle didn't say anything. He went back to his father and lay across his lap again while he resumed eating.

"You certainly have an active little boy, Mr. Malin! I'll bet he takes right after his father!" Mrs. Heaton joked.

Everyone laughed at this comment, including Friederich. He couldn't imagine where Fritzle had gotten such an idea. He certainly had never told him to do it, he thought to himself. But she does have nice legs. After hearing what had happened, when Emilie came back from the kitchen, she apologized. "I'm sorry, Mrs. Heaton, he lifted your dress. I hope he doesn't do that again."

As the Heatons returned to their room, both of them said, "Don't worry about it. He's too young to understand what he did. He just wanted to see what was under my dress, that's all. If he were older, it would be a more serious matter. But he's only four years old!"

After the Heatons left, Friederich asked Emilie, "Where do you suppose Fritzle got the idea to lift up her dress?"

"I don't know, but it certainly was embarrassing."

Friederich joked, "He's certainly learning early there's something nice under a woman's skirt!"

Emilie smiled. She was pleased Friederich liked what she had for him under her skirts.Whenever they sat at the table, she was very close to his right hand and he often let it go up her leg to her thigh. He stroked and patted it. Fritzle watched and occasionally did the same to her with their approval. When there was no one around, she reciprocated Friederich's touches. She used her left hand on his thigh and worked it up his leg. He liked that. He just didn't like it when she stroked his arm or hand when someone was present. He hated to have anyone think he was gentle or loving in any way. It was only to be done in private, not for public display.

While Volkmar and Inge were in school, Friederich came in for his"Vesper" (snack) each morning. He and Emilie sat together at the table while he drank his milk or coffee and ate slices of bread and cheese. His right hand roamed up her thighs and under her skirt or dress, whatever she had on that day. The dress rose to the tops of her thighs and he rubbed them and stroked them. Fritzle liked to watch and came over from his place at the table. He liked to stroke her thighs, too. He rubbed his face against her knee while patting her thighs all the way to the top of her legs. He caressed them and loved to put his face next to them. He put his arms around the bigness and softness of one while Friederich continued to rub the other. Fritzle did to her one thigh what his father did to the other. Emilie would get so aroused from both of them stroking her two thighs, she had to get up and walk around a bit before she could sit down again. They then started all over. Friederich thought this was funny and was amused his little son was so enamored with his wife's thighs and legs.He often told her, "Sit down so Fritzle can rub your thighs!"

He got a kick out of seeing his son overjoyed to rub his mother's legs, especially her thighs. Fritzle often wanted to hug them and kiss them. He ran his little hands up her legs to the very tops of them and even got in under her panties. This was too much of an arousal for Emilie and she gently took his hands out and held them together.

"Only to the tops of the thighs, Fritzle." She put his hands back down on her knees. The same movements would begin again. Friederich smiled and laughed at the way his wife and son seemed to play with each other. He got as much of a kick out of watching them, as he he did doing it himself. It got a little disconcerting for Emilie, however, when later in the day Fritzle said, "Sit down, Mama. I want to play with your thighs again!"

She would do this occasionally, but only if she really wanted to sit down to rest from whatever she was doing. He would then lift her dress and start stroking her thighs just as he had seen his father do. He then hugged and kissed them. He liked their silky whiteness.

"They're just like milk, Mama!"

A few months later, she told Friederich, "I don't think I can do this much longer. Fritzle always wants me to sit down and the first thing he does is lift my dress and stroke my thighs! This "game", as you call it, has gone far enough. I also think you shouldn't rub my thighs at the table anymore while he's around. Haven't you noticed? Recently, when he was stroking them, his little penis was stiffening. He might begin to think what he is doing to me might have something to do with that! I don't think we should encourage him anymore than he's already been."

"I don't think it's all that bad. But use your own judgment on what you should do."

Emilie sat down less and less upon request, and then not at all. When she did sit down one day and he began his familiar caressing of her thighs, she said,

"Fritzle, you can't do that anymore. You'll have to wait until you're grown up and have your own wife to do that to. Then you'll be able to do it as much as you want."

Fritzle didn't understand what she meant. He felt, somehow, cheated. He had enjoyed stroking her thighs very much and looked forward to it as often as possible. He couldn't understand why it suddenly was not possible anymore.

"Don't you like it?" he asked in a plaintive voice. "Don't you always kiss me on top of my head when I hug on your thighs? Why can't I do it again?" he wailed.

The first few times after she rebuffed his advances, he cried. It just didn't seem fair, he thought to himself. He almost couldn't cope with the termination and asked in sobs, "Don't you love me anymore?"

"Of course I do. You just can't lift up my skirts all of the time, Fritzle! As people get older, they can't do what they did as babies. You're a bigger boy now, aren't you? You want to be more grown up, don't you?"

"Yes," he sobbed.

"Then you can't get under my skirt anymore. Volkmar and Inge don't do that, do they?"

"No," he choked.

And beg as he did, to have her let him just look at her thighs and feel them, she didn't allow him to lift her dress or skirt again. He could only look from afar and whenever she sat down, his eyes were always on her legs to see if he could see her beautiful thighs that he was never to touch again! Whenever the opportunity came about, he was glad, at least, to look at them. He would think about them and remember how nice they felt to squeeze, caress, and kiss.

It at last dawned on Emilie. "Papa, I think I know where Fritzle got the idea to look under Mrs. Heaton's dress."

"Yes? Where?"

"You know every time I sat down with you at the table and he was around?"

"Yes. What does that have to do with it?"

"What did he like to do when you rubbed my thighs?"

Friederich laughed. "Yes, that could be. I never thought much about it. But that could be where he got the idea. There's nothing like getting an early start."

Emily didn't reply. She just hoped these caresses hadn't gone so far as to make Fritzle sexually aroused whenever he saw a woman's thighs! What she feared did, indeed, continue for the rest of his life!

X   X   X

Friederich cut wood every day when he wasn't doing some other farm work. He enjoyed being in the woods even if cutting down trees was very hard work. He liked being alone. He had only the horses with him and then he often let them graze while he sawed or chopped down trees. He hired another team of two wood cutters to cut down the biggest trees. They were to saw them into twelve foot lengths. He kept half of them and they kept the other half. They also had to use their own team of horses to skid the logs out of the woods. Friederich made sure from each tree there was the correct distribution. He didn't want only the soft woods. He wanted the same number of logs from each species as they took for themselves. "Tom" and "Dick" pulled out the logs he claimed as his and put them in a separate part of the wood lot. He told the two loggers "Those logs next to the lane are mine. I'm going to have them sawed into planks and boards for my new cow barn. The rest of the logs that I don't need, I'll put with yours to sell to the sawmill."

He put his initials with chalk on all of his logs which were sold for lumber. When several truck loads were ready, the loggers hired a trucker to take the logs to the sawmill. Friederich made sure each of the piles was appropriately scaled so each of them would be paid accordingly. He earned enough money from this logging operation to buy himself a buzz saw. He still had the old model A Ford from Finkbeiner to use as the power source for the saw. Finkbeiner had decided he didn't need the car any more and left it on the farm. The motor still ran. Friederich jacked up the rear wheels of the car, put the car into second gear, and the left rear wheel, with the tire on it, drove the belt to the buzz saw. Second gear worked best. He tried it in first gear, but the momentum was not enough to saw through the wood. He sawed up the branches and some of the smaller blocks of wood by himself. On Saturdays and over the summer, when he wasn't making hay, Volkmar helped him cut up the huge piles of firewood he had gathered where the barns once stood. The piles were in sections six to twelve feet in length. They sawed these piles into twelve, eighteen and twenty-four inch lengths. After cutting up large piles of assorted lengths, Volkmar had the job of piling them into cords according to the measurements laid out by Friederich. Each pile represented a face cord of wood. By far, the most popular lengths were the twelve inch variety because people used this length in their wood stoves, or coal furnaces. The longer lengths were for people who had fireplaces. Friederich charged anywhere from two dollars a face cord, to six dollars, depending upon the type of wood and the length. He learned from the requests made by his buyers that those people who had fireplaces wanted not only a good quality of firewood, but were willing to pay more for it than ordinary stove wood. He much preferred cutting the longer lengths.

X   X   X

Among the summer tourists that year, were a mother and her daughter from Queens. The mother was in her forties, the daughter in her late twenties. They enjoyed their stay so much they invited Inge to go with them to New York City. Both women gave the appearance of some affluence driving a large, new Buick. Friederich was very impressed with the two women. They seemed to have plenty of money. When the younger of the two suggested they would like to take Inge with them so she could see the big city, Friederich thought it was a good idea. She was only ten years old, but he thought anyone who was as rich as these two women, must be trustworthy.

"Papa, maybe at some time in the future, Inge might be able to make the trip. I really don't think she's old enough yet to make such a long trip by herself," Emilie suggested.

"She'll be with these two ladies on the way down to New York. She won't be alone then. On the way back, they can put her on the Greyhound bus and she won't have to get off until she's back in Chittenango. It would be a great trip for her," Friederich countered.

To Emilie's dismay and misgivings, Friederich over ruled her objections. Inge accompanied the two women to the big city. Emilie wrote to Maria almost

immediately to tell her that Inge was in New York and gave her the address which
the women had given her. She stressed to her sister, she was giving her the address
of these two ladies just in case something might come up, she would know where
Inge was. Before Inge left with the ladies, Emilie told, out of hearing of the two
ladies, "If there's anything you don't like, or if you're having any problem with the
ladies, be sure and call your Tante Maria. Here's her telephone number and street
address. She should come and get you, if you're having any problems. Okay?"

"Don't worry, Mama. I'll be all right."

Emilie wasn't as trusting of the two women as Friederich seemed to be. She
didn't like the flirtatiousness of the younger woman. She put her arm around
Friederich when she asked him if Inge could come with them to New York. She
was a rather attractive woman, Emilie thought. Why isn't she married, she asked
herself? She felt very uncomfortable packing Inge's things in the little suitcase they
had brought over from Germany. Inge was thrilled with the idea and was very eager
to go. When everything was ready, she gave her mother a hug and a kiss and literally
ran into the car's back seat. She had never ridden in such a splendid car before. By
the time they got to New York, Inge was asleep and saw very little of the city. The
next day her two hosts took her around the city and bought her ice cream and candy.
She had no appetite for the hamburger and French fries which they offered her for
supper. The newly completed Empire State building was a fantastic experience for
her. She had never been so high before. That evening, the younger woman told
her she was going to take her to meet some of her friends. They drove to a night
club where the woman's friends had gathered. They insisted Inge have something
to drink with them and she did. She thought it had a funny flavor, but drank it,
and had some more. She was soon asleep and the woman's boyfriend carried her
out to the car. He also went along to carry her into the house since Inge couldn't
stand, nor did she wake up. They put her to bed. The next morning she felt sick
to her stomach. The younger of the two women told her "You'd better stay in bed
this morning. When you feel better this afternoon, we'll go for a ride."

Inge stayed in bed and slept the entire morning. In the afternoon, Wilda
Braunstein, the younger of the two women, asked "Inge, would you like to take a
ride around Manhattan?"

"Oh yes! I've heard so much about it. I'd love to see it!"

After a few hours of riding around in the car, Inge couldn't keep her eyes open
any more and fell asleep. She slept all the way back to Queens.

That evening, Wilda told her, "I want you to go with me this evening again.
You could be very helpful to me."

"Sure, I'll go with you. Isn't your mother going along?"

"No. She's going to stay home this evening. She'll probably have a guest or two
stop by later herself. So she has to stay home to be here when they come."

Inge wondered what it was that she could do to help Wilda. She thought about
it again when Wilda drove up to a big, fancy, house with large pillars in front.

"Inge" Wilda said, "Go to the front door and after you ring the doorbell a man will come to the door. Tell him Miss Teller is in the car. He'll know who it is. Then come back and get in the back seat of the car."

Inge did as she was told. The man soon came out and got into the car. Wilda drove some distance to another big house with high steps in the front. All of the houses looked exactly the same. Inge couldn't tell one house from another. Wilda said

"Inge, now you be a good girl and wait here in the car. I'll be out in a little while."

She and the man went up the steps into the large front door and continued upstairs. Inge couldn't see where they had gone but waited for what seemed a very long time in the back seat of the car. Wilda finally came out with the same man and drove him back to the fancy house where she had picked him up. She then drove to another part of the city where Wilda again said, "Inge, go up to the door and tell the man who answers Miss Teller is waiting for him in the car. He'll know what to do."

Inge, again, went to the front door, rang the doorbell, conveyed her message, and returned to the car. The man came out very quickly. Wilda drove the car with him to the same place she had driven before with the previous man. Wilda then told Inge

"Wait here in the car until we return."

Inge made four trips to the front doors of four different houses that evening. Each time telling the man who came to the door, "Miss Teller is waiting for you in the car."

After the second of these long appointments, she fell asleep in the car. As Wilda drove from one house to another she told her, "As soon as I'm through with my appointments, we'll go out to another night club and get something to eat. I imagine you're getting pretty hungry by now, aren't you?"

"No, I'm not too hungry, yet. I like to sleep in this car. It's really comfortable."

After the fourth appointment, Wilda didn't bother to awaken Inge until she had returned the man to his residence. Then she said, "Wake up, Inge! We're going out to get something to eat."

Wilda took her to a very expensive restaurant and night club. She ordered two large dinners, two cocktails, and a bottle of wine for the two of them. Inge didn't remember much of that evening. She remembered falling asleep even before she had finished her dinner. Wilda got her out to the car with some difficulty. She had to carry her upstairs when they got home. During the night, Inge got very sick and vomited everything she had eaten and drunk that evening. Wilda was upset with her.

"Look at this mess you've made! Here's a pail, a mop, and soap. Clean it up! And don't forget to wipe off the sink and bowl in the toilet! I've never seen such a mess!"

After she cleaned up the rooms, she told Wilda "I'm finished."

While Wilda looked over the rooms and disinfected them, Inge called her aunt.

"Tante Maria? Could you come and get me? I was very sick and threw up all over the apartment. Miss Braunstein is finishing cleaning it up. I don't want to go back to bed."

"Don't go back to bed. We'll come and get you. Why didn't you call earlier? What made you sick? You can tell us after we come and get you!"

About an hour later, Maria and Karl arrived to take Inge home with them.

"Inge's no problem!" Wilda protested. "She just got a little sick this evening, that's all! I just wanted her to help me clean up after she got sick!"

"What do you expect when you give a ten year old girl whiskey and wine to drink!" Maria said reproachfully. "You don't do that to a little girl!"

"We had such a good time with her," Mrs. Braunstein protested. "Didn't we, Inge? Wilda and I took her all over Manhattan! We went up the Empire State building; we took the boat across to Staten Island; we saw the Statute of Liberty. Whatever she wanted to do, we did," Wilda added.

Maria and Karl were adamant. "She's coming with us! I have a letter from her mother," Maria said. "She told me if Inge calls, I should go over and get her right away! It's her way of saying she didn't want to stay with you any longer. Isn't that right, Inge?"

She was on the spot. "Yes, I'd like to go with my aunt and uncle. I've had a good time, but I want to go now. Thank you for taking me around New York."

Maria turned to Mrs. Braunstein and her daughter.

"That settles it! She's going with us right now!"

With those parting words, the Fleckhammers took Inge with them to their apartment in Jamaica. She spent the next two days resting and recovering from her stay at the Braunsteins. When she told her aunt and uncle what she had done and seen, they couldn't believe the Braunsteins could have done such a thing to a little girl. "You mean she sent you up to those houses to tell the men she was waiting for them in her car?" Maria asked incredulously.

"Yes, Tante Maria. Mrs. Braunstein had her appointments at her apartment, Wilda told me, so she had to go somewhere else."

"And your father gave you permission to go with those two women to New York?"

"Yes. He said it would be a good experience for me to see the big city.".

"It was an experience, but far from anything good!" Maria said in disgust.

Maria and Karl took Inge with them to Jones Beach and to the local amusement park for the rest of the week. They bought her new clothes and dolls. When the week was up, Karl and Maria drove her home to Chittenango. Upon arriving at the farm, Maria and Karl told Friederich, "You should never have let your daughter go with those women to New York! Do you know what kind of women they were?

They were nothing more than prostitutes! If we hadn't gone there to get her, she would have had to do more than just ring door bells!"

"That's nonsense! Those were two rich ladies who took a liking to Inge. You're just making up stories about them because you didn't like them! You wanted her to stay with you and not with strangers. The women were too rich to be mere prostitutes!"

Maria was livid. "Karl, I'm not going to stay in this house if Friederich thinks I'm just making this up! He doesn't believe he put his daughter in danger with these two prostitutes!"

Emilie tried to calm her sister down. "Friederich didn't mean to offend you, Maria. It's just hard for him to believe the ladies were what you think they were."

Maria got upset even more with her sister. "You don't know anything about New York! You don't know how easy it is to buy whatever you want, including women! That's the way little girls are brought into the city everyday and before long, they become prostitutes themselves! You're just so naive, Emmy, it's pathetic!"

Whenever Maria became upset, she started to cry and kept dabbing at her eyes with her handkerchief. She couldn't bear to look at Friederich directly. She looked at him from out of the corners of her eyes. Friederich laughed.

"It's an experience Inge won't forget. It wasn't as bad as you're making it out to be. She saw a lot more than most girls her age. At least she'll remember her first trip to New York."

Karl and Maria left early the next morning. Maria refused to shake hands with Friederich or to say good bye to him. Karl tried to make light of it. "We'll see you next year, Fritz. It'll all be over by then and she won't remember why she was upset. She'll want to come back for a visit by next summer!"

"No, I'm not! Not this time! He's trying to make me out to be a liar! Well, I'm not! I'm telling him the truth! He just doesn't want to hear the truth! I won't come again!"

X   X   X

Volkmar had become twelve years old that year. He was eligible for Boy Scouts. Jerry Mabie told his Scout Master "Mr. Hossbein, Volkmar Malin would make a good scout. He's very smart and old enough to join. He'd be a good member for our troop. After the Scout meeting, Art Hossbein drove over to visit the Malins. He parked his Model A Ford in the yard and went around to the front of the house. After ringing the doorbell. Emilie went to the front door. She thought a tourist was coming.

"Hi, I'm Art Hossbein," he said as he introduced himself. "I'm the Scout Master over in Kirkville. I heard from one of our members that your son is old enough to become a scout."

"Oh, Mr. Hossbein, come in. Let me take you to my husband. I'm sure he'd like to meet you, too."

She escorted him through the hallway to the back kitchen where Friederich was seated reading the newspaper.

"This is Mr. Hossbein, Papa. He's the Boy Scout Master in Kirkville. He wants to talk to us about Volkmar joining the Boy Scouts

"Hello, Mr. Malin. I'm Art Hossbein."

"How do you do. Have a seat. You want Volkmar to join the Boy Scouts?"

"Yes. Jerry Mabie told me about your son. He thinks he'd make a very good scout. I just came from our weekly scout meeting. We meet every Monday evening for an hour, or an hour and a half at most. Then there are special meetings occasionally and over-night camping trips. But those don't happen until the second year of scouting."

"Well, I'm not so sure he can join. He's very busy with his school work and with chores he has to do around the farm. Besides, scouting costs money and we don't have any. I don't think we can afford it."

"It's not that expensive, Mr. Malin. It'll cost ten cents a week. If you can't afford it, I'll take care of it myself. But I really think he should join. We've got a great group of boys. He already knows most of them from school."

"Papa, it would be good for Volkmar to make friends with boys his own age. I could make some of the things he might need. We don't have any money for a uniform or equipment, Mr. Hossbein. But if someone tells me how to do it, I could make a tent for him to use," Emilie volunteered.

"That's great, Mrs. Malin. I'll tell you how to make a tent. But you won't have to worry about that until next year. In his second year is when he goes camping with the boys."

Friederich saw it was important to Emilie. "Mr. Hossbein, so long as you know Volkmar's first responsibilities are to his school work and chores, I'll let him join."

"You won't regret it, Mr. Malin. He'll make a very good scout and you'll be real proud of what he can do."

Volkmar joined the Boy Scouts and walked the three miles to Kirkville and back each Monday evening. Mr. Hossbein brought him home if the meetings went later than expected, or if the weather was bad. Emilie made a tent for him and water-proofed it following Mr. Hossbein's directions. She made it from flour sacks which she dyed a dark green. She sewed them together with a large flap in the front almost as high as Volkmar. It was like an Indian teepee in style. The ends were stretched out and staked to the ground while the front had to be attached to a tree or high pole at the front. The opening flap could then be closed relatively easily from inside with string and large buttons. These were sewn into the lining of the flap. When the tent was closed from the inside, no one could tell whether or not anyone was in the tent.

Volkmar made his own back-pack with instructions from Mr. Hossbein. Emilie saved a few pennies each week from the grocery money and bought him the rope necessary to tie his tent and other items to his pack. He was very proud of his new tent and back-pack. Some of the boys in the troop made fun of his "homemade" equipment, but it didn't bother him, especially when Mr. Hossbein complimented him for his diligence and workmanship in making what he needed for scouting. The Haussmanns provided him with the scout pants and shirts they had left over from the days when Riche was a Boy Scout. His uncle Karl bought him a Scout hat and Aunt Bertha bought him a pair of shoes. Mr. Hossbein gave him other jobs to do around his house so he could earn the money he needed to complete his outfit.

After three months, Volkmar returned home with his first merit badge. He was so proud of himself, Friederich and Emilie couldn't help but be impressed with how good this experience was for him. He had obtained his merit badge faster than any of the other boys in the troop. Friederich still didn't like the drill exercises Volkmar told him about at each week's meeting. It reminded him too much of the army. Such regimentation was okay for soldiers, he thought, but do Boy Scouts have to learn how to march and parade? It became obvious to Friederich, Volkmar didn't mind this regimentation at all. In fact, he seemed to like it. When Mr. Hossbein brought him home one rainy night, he stopped in to see Friederich and Emilie.

"Mr. and Mrs. Malin, you should be real proud of your son. He learns things so easily and enjoys what he's doing. He's about the best scout I've ever had!"

"Thank you very much, Mr. Hossbein. He looks forward to going to Boy Scouts every week. He really would be lost if he couldn't go to the meetings. He does his chores very quickly, but well. We trust him to complete what he undertakes and then he works on his scouting projects. We're very glad he's doing so well, Mr. Hossbein," Emilie said.

X   X   X

Friederich and Emilie thought it would be well for Fritzle to go to school, too. He was five years old in December and since he was with his brother and sister each day before and after school, he should have learned enough English to have no language problem. In early January 1933, Emilie took him to the kindergarten in Fayetteville on the Syracuse-Utica Bus. The bus went by every two hours. After arriving in Fayetteville there was still a ten block walk to the school. It was outside the village limits of Fayetteville. It was about a fifteen minute walk from the bus stop on Route Five to the school. Emilie told Fritzle "I'm going to take you to school, today, Fritzle. You'll be in the same school Volke and Inge attend."

He wasn't sure he wanted to go.

"You're, old enough now to go to school. Let's go and see how you like it."

When they arrived at the kindergarten, Miss Fowler welcomed him warmly.

"So you're Donald. I heard about you from your brother. I'm glad you're starting school with us. There are lots of boys and girls in our class. I'm sure you'll get to know them very soon."

Everything was strange to him. He never left his mother's side. She thought she would stay a short time and then leave. But he kept hold of her hand. The boys and girls played with toys he had never seen before. When she said "I have to leave now."

He started to cry.

"You don't have to cry, Fritzle. Volke will come and get you after school this afternoon. You'll ride home with him and Inge on the school bus."

Try as she might, she could not get him to release her hand. He held on to it with both hands and continued to cry. Miss Fowler tried to calm him, but to no avail. After almost half an hour of non-stop crying, during which the other children asked Miss Fowler "Why is he crying? Is something wrong with him?"

She said, "Mrs. Malin, I think you better take him home again. There's really no use in forcing him to stay. It'll only upset him even more. He may become frantic and even hysterical if you leave him. There's no sense to that. He should enjoy being here. He'll be all right by next fall when the new school year begins."

Emilie agreed. "Yes. I think it's just too soon for him to go to school. I thought he would like it, but apparently not."

She helped him put on his coat and hat and they walked back down to the bus stop in Fayetteville. After waiting a few minutes, the bus came and took them home again. Fritzle was so happy his mother had taken him back home. He asked her,

"Mama, what can I do to help you in the kitchen?"

"You could get me some firewood for the cooking stove."

He had gotten a brand-new little wheel-barrow made out of wood for his fifth birthday from his Uncle Richard. It was hand-made and Fritzle was very proud of it. Even the wheel was hand-made with a hard rubber tire over the wooden wheel. He took his new wheel-barrow and brought in enough split wood to fill both of Emilie's two baskets next to the stove. It was hard work to push the wheel-barrow through the snow into the kitchen. But he didn't mind. It was far better, he thought, than staying with all of those strange boys and girls in the school!

When Friederich came home from working in the woods, he was amazed to see Fritzle still at home.

"Didn't you take him to school this morning?"

"He cried so hard and long, Papa, the teacher told me to take him back home again. She said I should bring him back next fall when he's ready to come to school. He seemed so afraid of the other boys and girls. I really couldn't leave him there. I've never seen him act like that before!"

Friederich laughed. "Then you'll just have to stay with us and work on the farm, Fritzle."

"Yes, that's what I want to do!" he replied almost immediately. He ran to his father and gave him a big hug and kiss.

"See, Papa," Emilie said. "I didn't write to tell my mother to tell her he was our sunshine for nothing!"

They were both pleased Fritzle was still at home. Emilie had felt uneasy about whether or not he was ready for school. She wasn't sure she really wanted to stay home alone during the day. If Fritzle went to school, there would be no one at home with her. She felt she would really be lonely, if he were in school, too. She often felt lonely. Friederich was in the woods most of the day. There would be no one to talk to if all three children were in school. No, she told herself. He's still a little boy. It would be too long a day for him. The school bus comes at seven forty-five each morning and doesn't return until four fifteen in the late afternoon. It's really too long a time for such a little boy to have to stay in school, she thought. I wish he could have gone to kindergarten in Vaihingen like Volkmar had done. It was only for a half day and then the children came home again, she reminded herself. It would be much better for little Fritzle. As she thought about it, she started to cry. So much has happened since we left Germany! We've moved so many times and now we have this farm! If only the barns hadn't burned down! At least we'd have a steady income from the milk check! How are we going to be able to pay the interest on our mortgage, to say nothing about the principal, she asked herself? We rarely have any money anymore. Papa sells an occasional cord of wood and that's it. The more she thought about their circumstances the more she cried. Her cry was not loud. She just couldn't stop the tears from flowing. She repeatedly had to blow her nose. If it weren't for the garden and the three cows they kept, they wouldn't have had much at all to eat! At least we're not starving, she consoled herself. She started crying again when she thought of her mother's letter. Friederich had asked her to write to her mother to request a loan in order to rebuild their cow barn. She had not wanted to ask her mother for money, but Friederich had insisted. He made her read her letter to her mother to make sure she had put in the request for a loan. He thought with about five thousand Reichsmarks, they would be able to rebuild and maybe even have a little left over to buy a few more cows. When she read her mother's response she cried even more. She wasn't embarrassed this time when Friederich saw her crying. She just couldn't help it! Her mother really couldn't believe they were so hard pressed for money. Emilie read the letter aloud to Friederich.

My Dear Loved Ones!

Thank you very much for your latest letter which I received yesterday. I'm glad you've decided to keep Fritzle home from school until this next school year begins. It's probably a lot better for him. If you don't have a kindergarten near you, it would be much too long to keep him in school all day. After all, he is only just five years old! I can well imagine, he is your sunshine! I miss not seeing him and I miss not seeing dear little Ingele and also Volke! I'm glad they are both doing so well in school. They are very smart children. If they were here in Germany, they would be heading for the Latein school to prepare them for the university. I hope they will be able to do that in America.

I'm truly sorry to hear about the fire which burned off your barns! Didn't you have any insurance on them? Surely, you should be able to recoup your losses from the insurance. I can't imagine anyone not having insurance, especially on a farm. When I worked for your Grandfather, he always told me he had to make sure the local farmers were all insured. There were simply too many hazards not to carry any!

As I recall, Friederich sold his mother's garden, his house, and his business before he left Germany for a big profit. From what you wrote to me, I remember he also bought and sold two houses in Syracuse and made a handsome profit each time! Why doesn't he take out a loan from a bank to rebuild? Why is it necessary to ask me for money which I don't have anymore? If you're not making any money on the farm, why doesn't Friederich go back to work in a factory as a tool-maker? Times are very bad here in Germany. Violence and strikes occur daily throughout the country; the unemployment rate is over twenty-five percent and banks are failing left and right. I may not even be able to keep my job at the Savings bank if this economic crisis continues! We have just had new elections and we now have a new chancellor. His name is Adolph Hitler. We're expecting great things from him! If anyone can bring order out of chaos, he can.

You probably won't like this letter, but I can't afford to lend you any money. I barely have enough for myself these days.

With best wishes to you and lots of hugs and kisses to each of the grand children, I remain your beloved mother and mother-in-law,

Grandmother Bartholomae.

After reading the letter to Friederich, he got extremely angry. He shouted,

"What kind of a response is this? She has the money! She just doesn't want to let any of it go! I thought you were so rich? Everyone in Vaihingen years ago said that Friederich Bartholomae was one of the richest men in town! It certainly couldn't have all disappeared!"

"But Papa," Emilie pleaded. "You seem to have forgotten the inflation of 1923! You were in Brazil at the time. Mama lost almost everything my father had invested! And all of the bonds she bought during the war were worthless! All of her savings were only worth one tenth of their former value! When she writes she doesn't have any more money, I believe her!"

Friederich flew into a rage and stormed out of the house slamming the door behind him. Emilie was now very upset. First, she was disappointed she had even asked her mother for help. And second, she knew, now that the unfavorable answer had come, it would be several days before Friederich would speak to her again! When he was in one of these moods, it was terrible. She would speak to him or ask him questions, but he refused to answer or say anything. She asked him repeatedly, "Papa, what are we going to do? How are we going to rebuild our barn? How are we going to pay our mortgage? If we don't pay Mr. Pauli and Mr. Trant, we might even lose the farm!"

Still, there was no answer from Friederich. He really didn't have any answer. How did he know what he was going to do? He continued to brood to himself and spoke only to the children. He didn't answer Emilie. He held her responsible for her mother's intransigence. She must not have written their need strongly enough to her mother! Emilie didn't want to face the same scene she had witnessed the year before with Mr. Pauli and Mr. Trant. They had come to the farm with the expectation of foreclosure.

"Mr. Malin, we've come to collect our money for this year. Since you've not paid anything yet, we're afraid we're going to have to take back the farm."

Friederich had gotten so livid, he slammed his fist on the table and shouted at them as loudly as he could. "If you dare to try to take this farm away from me, I'll kill you both! You can depend on that!"

Emilie became so frightened she said, "But Papa, you don't have to get so violent!"

He turned on her and almost hit her as he told her, "Shut up!"

He turned to the two men. They became very pale as he slammed his fist down on the table next to them again. "Just remember what I said."

The whole table shook. They were very frightened what he might do next.

"Don't worry, Fred," Bill Pauli said. "We won't do it if you can pay us the interest each year."

"You can pay us back the principal after you've rebuilt your barn," Trant added.

"Make no mistake about what I've said. If you ever try to take this place away from me, it'll be the last thing you both ever do!"

"Can you pay us the interest, Fred?" they both asked almost simultaneously.

"Yes I can. You'll have your money next week!" he answered quickly.

Both men left, after the promise from Friederich, apparently glad to be alive. They never came back even that next week when Friederich said he would pay the interest. Trant's son-in-law came to pick up the money. He didn't leave the car after he drove into the yard. He blew the car horn until Emilie came out to see who it was.

"I'm Leonard Markert, Mr. Trant's son-in-law. Are you Mrs. Malin?"

"Yes."

"I've come to pick up your interest payment for Mr. Trant and Mr. Pauli. I'll wait here in the car."

"How do you do, Mr. Markert. I'll go and get the money for your father-in-law."

Emilie went into the house and told Friederich who was outside.

"So the two cowards couldn't come themselves, could they? They had to send someone else to do it!" he said scornfully.

He gave Emilie the two hundred dollars in an envelope and she took it out to Mr. Markert.

"Here you are, Mr. Markert."

Without so much as a thank you, he took the envelope, opened it, and counted the money. It was all in one dollar bills. It took him a few minutes to count the entire amount. Emilie waited patiently beside the car until he had finished.

"Yes, it's all there. Good bye."

"Good bye, Mr. Markert."

Emilie never found out where Friederich had gotten the money. He had gotten up one morning and told her he had to go to the city. He got dressed in his suit and took the Syracuse-Utica bus to Syracuse. When he returned that evening, she thought he was in an exceptionally good mood. He didn't say where he had been.

"I visited some of my relatives," was all he said.

Chapter VIII

How Could You Do Such A Thing?

August was usually the month the Fleckhammers came for their annual vacation on the farm. New York City was depressing in the summers; hot and steamy, with the sunshine reflecting from the buildings and pavement producing temperatures in the high eighties and nineties. With the onset of spring in 1933, however, Maria longed to get away from the city even earlier. Emilie had written how beautiful the fruit trees were in full bloom. The lilacs had also blossomed behind the house. The red, yellow and stripped, red gold tulips had also pushed through the soil and the woods were filled with trilliums.

"Karl, can't we go to the farm now?"

The warmth of the early May sun shone on their little apartment over the workshop.

"Why don't we close up for a spring vacation? I don't want to stay here in the city all of the time!"

It had been a very depressing winter for Maria and Karl. The depression was at its full height. The banks had been closed for several weeks. The Fleckhammers' customers had been few and far between. Karl knew winter was the slack time of the year, but this year was even worse than usual.

"I want to go somewhere else and see something besides these four walls every day! I'll go crazy if I have to stay here much longer!"

Karl was very understanding of his wife. He hardly ever denied her every wish. If she wanted to go somewhere, he'd either take her himself, or he would arrange for her to go with someone else. Her mood swings were often a problem. He noticed in Germany she was not only a very headstrong woman, but a very emotional one as well. The least little argument would produce a rush of tears and

"You don't love me anymore! You want me to stay here and lose my mind, don't you Karl?"

"Maybe we can go to the farm earlier this year, Maria, but I can't go right now. The customers are starting to bring their lawn mowers in for sharpening. The grass is starting to grow again."

"Why can't I go now? There's nothing for me to do here, Karl. We hardly have any customers in the store. I just sit here day after day waiting for someone to come in!"

173

They had bought a small grinder's workshop with a store out front, a two bedroom apartment overhead, and a small backyard on one of the major east-west roadways out of New York city to Long Island. Karl had come to the United States earlier than Maria and had gotten himself a job as a master grinder for a large medical instrument company. He had rented a room with a German family and saved every penny he made so he could send for her to come to America. He had wanted to marry her in Germany, but her mother wouldn't hear of it.

"You get yourself a job first, then we'll see about marrying my daughter!"

Frau Bartholomae didn't want Maria to marry Karl. He was another one of those tradesman like her two sons-in-law. Why can't she marry someone who has stature in Vaihingen, she asked herself? She had forgotten Maria wanted to become a physical education teacher. Instead, her mother made her leave school after the ninth grade because she felt she couldn't afford to send her to the Latein Schule. Maria spent two years working for her Grandmother Meyer and Uncle Otto on their farm in Gerabronn. Grandmother Meyer was a very difficult woman to please. If she told Maria to wash the windows, they were never clean enough.

"What? You call that window clean? Look at all the streaks you've left along the side of the glass! You've got to do them over again. I can't have my house looking that sloppy!"

If Maria cooked the potatoes too long, Grandmother scolded. "You can't leave the potatoes in the water that long! They'll get soft and I can't afford to throw them out to make a new batch just so you can learn how to boil them correctly! Now do your work right!"

It had been a very hard time for Maria. She often cried herself to sleep after a hard day's work in her Grandmother's house. Grandmother Meyer wrote to Maria's mother,

"She's a sniveler! She cries at the least little criticism. How can she learn to become a housewife if she lets every little thing upset her? She's got to learn that life is hard! Maybe she better work for your brother, Otto. I can't have her around me day after day. I can't stand a woman that cries over everything!"

Frau Bartholomae wrote and asked her brother, Otto, if he would mind having Mariele live with them on the farm so she could learn how to cook and run a household. He agreed and Maria stayed in the country for the rest of her two year practicum to become a housewife. In spite of her misgivings and antipathy towards housework, she did learn how to cook, clean, and sew from her Aunt Matilde. Her aunt was a very tolerant and understanding woman. If Maria made a mistake, she told her "Mariele, you have to wet one window at a time, then use a clothe to wipe it clean. With a second clothe, you have to rub the window until it shines. And before you know it, the window's clean. Here, let me show you."

Aunt Matilde used the demonstration effect each time she taught Mariele something new. She did it first and then watched as she imitated her. If Mariele made a mistake, Aunt Matilde demonstrated again what she was supposed to do.

In spite of the lessons she received, she wanted to stay as far away from cleaning, cooking, and sewing as possible. She appreciated her aunt's help and liked her, but she didn't want to spend the rest of her life being a "Haus Frau!"

When Maria first met Karl, it was at the Vaihingen swimming pool along the Enz. She was a tall, statuesque young woman of sixteen with long blonde hair in two braids, bright blue eyes, and exceptionally well shaped legs and figure. She and Karl often went for walks with Emilie and the children. Maria's mother didn't know she came and asked Emilie "Would you mind if I came over Sundays and met Karl here? Mama doesn't want me to see him, but I want to. He's a real nice guy. She thinks he's just another apprentice! She wants me to marry someone who's rich and comes from a good family. I don't care about that at all! I just want someone who loves me!"

Maria started to cry and dabbed at her nose with her handkerchief. "You don't have to cry, Mariele. I'm sure Friederich won't mind. He likes you. I'll talk to him about it. But as far as I'm concerned, you can come over any time even when you're not working for me."

"Thank you, Emilie. I wish Mama were as understanding as you are!"

Friederich liked having Maria around. She had become even more beautiful than when he first met her. She was now "a real woman" as he told her. She still blushed whenever he complimented her.

"Any time you really want to learn how to become "a real woman", Mariele, just let me know. I'll be glad to show you."

She was already beginning to suspect what Friederich meant. Since she was so athletic, she was pleased to put on a show for the children.

"Show us how you can walk on your hands, Tante Mariele?" Volkmar asked.

She did and was able to walk from room to room on her hands. Friederich seemed to enjoy these athletic feats almost as much as the children.

"Friederich thinks you're the best girl in your class at the Turnverein, Mariele," Emilie told her.

"I should be. I got the prize for somersaults at last year's competition. But I like to do hand stands the best. I wish there were competition in doing that."

Karl came each Sunday afternoon. Maria told her mother she was going to go for a walk with Emilie and the children. Her mother knew Emilie liked to go for long walks as often as possible. It never occurred to her that Maria went to visit her sister in order to meet her boy friend. As Maria and Karl went off together into the nearby fields, Emilie couldn't help but remember Luise and Hermann. It's strange, isn't it, she thought to herself? First, Mama objected to my marrying Friederich. Then she objected to Luise marrying Hermann. And now she doesn't like Karl. She probably won't want her to marry him, either, if it ever gets that far. It had gotten that far. Her mother did object and made it mandatory for Karl to go to America alone before she allowed Maria to follow him. She also had to wait until she was eighteen and Karl could send for her to join him. They both knew they wouldn't have any children. Karl had had an accident at his uncle's carpentry shop. Maria had been told by her doctor her ovaries hadn't developed enough to have any children.

Karl decided to let Maria visit the Malins. Maybe the change from the city to the country would do her some good, he thought.

"Okay, Maria. If you want to go visit your sister for a few weeks, I won't mind."

"Thank you Karl. You're a real sweetheart!"

She bought a round-trip Greyhound bus ticket from New York to Chittenango. Karl took her to the Queens bus station before he opened his shop. It took almost ten hours to make the trip because of all of the stops en route. When the bus stopped in front of the Malins late in the afternoon, Inge ran into the house and called out to her mother

"Mama, someone's coming! The bus is stopping in front of our house!"

Emilie went out with Inge to the road. Volkmar was already there helping Maria carry her bags up the side walk.

"Well, what a surprise this is, Maria! Why didn't you write and tell me you were coming?"

"I wanted to take you by surprise, Emmy. Your letter about how beautiful it is in the spring time made me think it was like Vaihingen. The city is so dirty and gray after the winter. I wanted to see the green grass and flowers again. Ja, Inge how are you? You're getting to be so big. And Volke is already taller than you are, Emmy!"

"Yes, the children are growing. Wait until you see Fritzle. He's down the woods with Friederich. They should be coming back any time now. Come on in. I'll make some coffee and we'll have some kuchen. I just baked some this morning. How's Karl? Didn't he want to come, too?"

"Actually, he's getting pretty busy sharpening lawn mowers right now. But we don't have much business in the store. He said I should come and visit you a while. Is that okay with you Emmy?"

"Of course it is! Friederich will be surprised. But I'm sure he won't mind. You can sleep in one of our guest rooms upstairs. The tourist season doesn't begin for another month or so. We have plenty of room."

"It's so beautiful, here, Emmy. The apple and pear blossoms smell so sweet! Just like Vaihingen!"

"Let me show you our orchard, Tante Mariele."

Inge took Maria's hand and led her, with Volkmar, out to the garden behind the house.

"See all of the flowers and blossoms, Tante Maria? Aren't they beautiful?" they both asked. The blossoms were at their peak. The blended fragrance of combined apple, pear, plum and lilac blossoms was almost overwhelming.

"Oh, that smells so sweet! It almost makes you want to eat the blossoms!" Maria said.

Emilie came out of the kitchen. "You can come in now. The coffee is ready. Friederich and Fritzle are across the road. As soon as the horses are fed and watered, they'll come in too."

Emilie had gone out to the barn and told Friederich who was here.

"Papa, Mariele came to visit us. She said Karl told her to come and get away from the city for a while. You don't mind, do you?"

"Well, she's already here. I guess we can put up with her for a while. Why did she come? Did she and Karl have a fight?"

"No, I don't think so. She just wanted to get away from the city for a while and he told her she could come."

"I don't see how he could do that. If he's grinding lawn mowers every day, he's got to have someone in the store. He can't do everything himself."

"Maybe they've got someone helping them. I don't know. She didn't tell me there was anyone else."

Friederich and Fritzle came into the kitchen from the horse barn.

"Hello, Friederich. I see you come right into the kitchen with your boots on," Maria said.

"Hello, Mariele. So, what if I do? This is my house. I can do what I want in it."

"Think of how your wife must feel when you come into the house with your dirty boots on."

"You can think what you want! But I'll do what I want! If you don't like it, you can go back home again."

"I didn't mean to get you upset, Friederich. I just thought it might be nice for your wife if you took off your boots before you came into the house."

"It's all right, Mariele. I don't mind. I can clean the floor very easily," Emilie said soothingly as she frowned towards her sister. "Papa works hard."

"Karl takes off his shoes before he comes upstairs from the workshop. I see Fritzle does just like his father. He keeps his boots on, too."

"Let's drink our coffee and cake, Maria. Have you heard from Luise lately. We got a letter from her for Inge's birthday, but we've not heard from her since."

"She wrote me for my birthday, too. They seem to be getting along quite well. Hermann is very busy overseeing the construction of stores and hotels in Rio de Janiero. They moved from Juiz de Fora three years ago. There wasn't enough work for him in such a small town. They also lost another little girl to tropical sickness. She was just two years old. Marianne seems to be thriving. She speaks fluent Portuguese and gets very good grades in the German school in Rio."

"That's what Mama wrote us about them. They've lost two children so far since they've been in Brazil. It must be hard for Luise," Emilie said. "I don't think I'd like it in such a hot climate day after day. They sent us pictures they had taken on the beach at Rio. They seemed to look healthy enough."

"I wouldn't want to be there," Friederich volunteered. "It's too hot in the summer time! It's ideal in winter, but the summers are unbearable."

"Do you go to school, Fritzle?" Mariele asked. "You're five now, aren't you?"

"He's going next September. He's was only just five in December," Emilie answered for him. "We tried it in January, but even the teacher said he wasn't ready for it yet. She told me to take him home again until next fall."

"And how do you like school, Volkmar?"

"I love it. It's great. I'm reading all kinds of books and the teachers call on me when no one else can answer a question in class."

"You must be really smart, Volke." He beamed as did Emilie.

"How are you doing Inge?"

"I love math. That's my favorite subject. I'm a lot faster than any of the other kids in class when the teacher asks a math question."

"Well, you and Friederich can be real proud of your children. You know that we can't have any children, don't you?"

"Mama wrote something to us one time about it, Maria. But just what is the reason?"

"Dr. Bauer told Mama that I'd never have any children because my ovaries haven't really developed. He didn't think I'd ever have to worry about becoming pregnant. Karl had an accident in his uncle Luipold's shop when he was a boy. He fell down a ladder and lost one of his testicles. Dr. Bauer told him he'd never have any children."

"I'm sorry, Maria. I didn't know why, but I thought maybe it wasn't true when Mama wrote us about it."

"That makes it pretty easy for you and Karl," Friederich commented. "You don't have to take any precautions."

"Well, I'd like to have a son or daughter like Volkmar or Inge. I don't think I'd want more than one, though. Children are so expensive these days."

"Nonsense. They can work, too. You don't have to buy them everything they want," Friederich answered.

"Maybe you don't care, but I do. I would want my child to have nice things. I don't see how people can have so many children, especially when they can't afford them!" Maria replied.

Friederich had already moved away from the table. He didn't think the conversation was going anywhere.

"Emmy, I don't see how you can live with that man! He's opinionated; selfish; and stingy. Why doesn't he fix up this place?"

"We can't afford to do that. We just barely get by with what we grow in the garden and what Papa makes from selling firewood. We don't have anything left over."

"Then why don't you leave the farm? He can get a good job in the city!"

Emilie tried to push back her tears. She blew her nose several times. But the tears came out anyway. She told Volkmar and Inge to go outside. She and Tante Mariele wanted to talk.

"He won't leave the farm. I've suggested it to him occasionally ever since the fire. But he becomes very angry and tells me he would rather die than go back to work for someone else!"

"I feel sorry for you, Emmy. You've had a good education. You were a teacher with a lot of status in Vaihingen. You play piano beautifully, and now you've come down to this; a farmer's wife!"

Emilie couldn't keep back her tears any longer. She knew her sister was right. But there was nothing she could do about it now.

"He had me write Mama and ask her for a loan to rebuild our barns. I didn't want to do it, but I had to. He insisted on it. He just about went wild when she turned us down. She couldn't believe we didn't have any insurance."

"What? You asked Mama for money? How could you? You should have known she wouldn't do that. She only gave me a thousand Reichsmarks for my wedding. Karl had to pay for practically everything. She could afford it, Emmy. She just didn't want to do it."

"That's what Papa said. He couldn't believe she didn't have the money. He thought we were so rich in Vaihingen."

Emilie and her sister talked long into the night about Vaihingen and the family's circumstances. Friederich and the children had gone to bed when Emilie looked at the clock.

"Well, I've got to get up tomorrow morning, Maria, and get the children off to school. You can sleep in if you want. Papa will be down in the woods and Fritzle stays with me. You shouldn't have anyone bother you so you can sleep as long as you like."

At around nine thirty the next morning, Emilie was in the garden with Fritzle when Friederich came back from the woods with the horses. He came out to the garden.

"Emmy, you and Fritzle have to go to the city. I need a new link for my log chain. Grants is the only one that has the right size. If you hurry, you can still, catch the ten o'clock bus."

"What about Maria? She isn't up yet."

"Do you think I'm going to wait until she gets up to go to work? Get yourselves ready. You don't have much time as it is!"

"Okay, Papa. Come along Fritzle. We'll have to change and get right out there for the bus."

Just as they went across the road, the bus came. As they got on, Maria had gone to the window to see why the bus was stopping. She couldn't believe it. She saw Fritzle and Emilie getting on the bus. She waved frantically out the window, but the bus continued on. She threw a robe around herself and raced downstairs. Friederich was just getting himself something to eat and drink when she came into the kitchen.

"Where have Emmy and Fritzle gone?"

"They've gone to the city to buy a link for my log chain."

"Why didn't she wait for me? We could have gone together and done some shopping!"

"The hell! You certainly don't expect me to wait until you get up to go to work?"

"She could have at least told me where she was going!"

"Don't be ridiculous. She only had just enough time to catch the bus as it was. If she had awakened you, she'd still be here! No way! I need the link as soon as possible!"

"You old goat! You never let her do anything!"

She sprang at Friederich and seized him around the neck. She began choking him. After his momentary surprise at the vehemence with which she grabbed hold of him, he lifted his arms through hers and broke her hold. He grabbed her robe and pulled it off. Since she always slept in the nude, she had nothing on underneath. She grabbed his right arm and tried to throw him to the floor. He was too strong for her. He picked up and carried her into the bedroom just off the kitchen. He threw her on it and jumped on top of her. She struggled and fought as hard as she could but she couldn't throw him off. He unbuttoned his pants and raped her. As he was climaxing he said "I've wanted to do this to you ever since you were a little girl. You've got an even more beautiful body than your sister."

Maria began crying. She couldn't believe he had done this to her. In spite of herself, she stopped resisting as he forced himself on her.

"How could you do such a thing? I'm a married woman!"

"Karl's a pretty lucky guy to have you. And you can't get pregnant. I don't see anything wrong with my doing it to you, too. You women all want it, and you know it!"

Friederich finished wiping himself with his handkerchief and offered it to her. She took it and wiped herself as she kept on crying quietly.

"Now let's have something to eat," Friederich said as he returned to the kitchen.

He got the cheese, butter and wurst out of the ice box. He went down cellar and got a bottle of wine. He set two plates, two knives, two forks, and two glasses on the table. The bread was already there. He sliced himself some cheese, wurst and bread, smeared a bit of butter on it, poured two glasses of wine and proceeded to use his fork and knife to eat his snack. Maria came slowly out to the kitchen. She was still crying silently to herself. She reached for her robe and sat down at the table. She was very hungry. She hadn't eaten since the previous evening.

Friederich reached over and patted her thigh. She drew back from him.

"You have the same round thighs like your sister. Actually, you've got even nicer legs than she does."

Maria, drank slowly from her glass of wine. She cut a slice of bread and a piece of wurst and ate it. She looked reproachfully at Friederich.

"How could you have done such a thing to me?"

"Who tried to choke me? Who tried to throw me to the floor?"

"But you didn't have to rape me!"

"Come on, now. You enjoyed it as much as I did! Besides, you're always walking around here with practically nothing on and you do somersaults and hand springs even with a dress on. You know darn well, you wanted it!"

He filled her glass again. She ate more determinedly. She cut another slice of bread and wurst. They ate silently. As she finished her third glass of wine, he reached over to her and patted her thigh. She didn't move away this time. He ran his hand up her right leg and she opened her legs wider. He gave her another glass which she drank without stopping to sip it. He ran his hands over her breasts and she leaned back in her chair.

"Let's go to bed again, Maria."

She didn't pull away when he took her hand and half led and half carried her into the bedroom again. He helped her lie down on the bed. Rubbed his moustache over her nipples and ran his hands up her thighs. She didn't reject his advances. She lay there as he mounted her again. She fell asleep as he had his second orgasm.

"Mariele, get up. You'd better go to your own bedroom."

She was sound asleep. She didn't even stir when he pulled her toward him. He picked her up and carried her upstairs to her bedroom. He put her to bed and she didn't wake up again until that evening when she heard Emilie calling.

"Maria? Do want any supper?"

She woke up and looked at her watch.

What? It's five o'clock she asked herself? She quickly got dressed and as she went downstairs, she gradually recalled the events of the day. Her head felt as though she had been hit with something heavy. I drank too much wine, she told herself. And then she remembered what Friederich had done to her. She shook her head in disbelief. How could he have done such a thing to me, she asked herself?

She shook involuntarily as she walked into the kitchen. How could she have let him do it to her, she thought? I can't tell Emmy. She probably wouldn't believe me if I did.

"So, did you sleep off the effects of last night, Mariele?"

"Yes. I've slept way too long. Where did you go this morning, Emmy? Why didn't you take me with you?"

"Papa needed a link for his log chain. I had to leave before I could tell you where Fritzle and I were going. We couldn't have done anything else anyway. We had to come back on the very next bus. We just had time to go to Grants, buy the links, and return to wait for the afternoon bus. We couldn't even visit anyone in the city."

"When does the next bus go back to New York, Emmy?"

"What? You've only just come, Mariele! There's no bus until this next weekend. You don't want to go home already, do you?"

"I think I better, Karl's all alone in the shop and if someone comes into the store, he'll have to come out and see what they want. He needs me in the store."

Friederich laughed. "I told you you shouldn't have left him."

Maria gave him an angry look, but said nothing.

"Why do you have to leave so soon, Tante Mariele," Volkmar and Inge asked almost together. "We haven't showed you around the farm yet. We could take a walk down to the woods and pick some trilliums and leeks. Leeks are good to eat," Inge volunteered.

"I think I'd better get home. Your Uncle needs me in the store."

"We can at least take a walk down to the tulip tree and the ravine after we come home from school tomorrow, Tante. It would be a shame not to see the beautiful flowers all over the woods."

"All right. We'll go after you come home from school tomorrow."

Maria and Emilie played games with the children after they had done their homework. She had brought "Snip-Snap" for them from New York. There was a German export-import store just three blocks from their own cutlery store. They had all kinds of games, books and toys some of which were from Germany. In this card game, each person took ten cards which had large numbers on them on the top and bottom of each card. As each person turns over the card from his stack, whoever said "snap" first in like numbered cards held by each of the players, gathers in all of the like numbered cards from the other players. The object of the game is to collect all of the cards in this fashion. As each card is turned over by the player he/she says "snip" until the card comes up which is the same as the card held by someone else. Then the first person who says "snap" collects all of the other cards that are the same. They played this game and rummy each evening Aunt Maria was there.

When Saturday arrived, Maria had all of her bags packed and Volkmar helped her carry them to the roadside. Maria, Emilie, Volkmar, Inge and Fritzle waited for the bus to come at nine o'clock. Friederich shook hands with her in the house. She looked at him rather strangely, Emilie thought. She simply said good-bye. She didn't say thank you to him or say anything about coming again when he told her

"Anytime you want to come again, I'll be here. Best regards to Karl."

"When are you coming again, Tante Maria?" Inge asked.

"I don't think I'll come again this year. Maybe some time in the future."

"We'd like to have you come again this summer, Tante. Wouldn't Uncle Karl like to visit the farm again, too?" Volkmar asked.

"We'll see," was all she said.

As the Greyhound bus came to a stop, Maria and Emilie were really crying. Each one was blowing her nose and the children began to have tears in their eyes as well. The bus driver got out and opened the baggage compartment in which he put her bags. The two sisters hugged each other. They didn't say anything. They were too overcome. The children hugged Aunt Maria, too.

"Best regards to Uncle Karl, Tante Mariele," Inge said through her tears.

"We'll really miss you and all the fun we've had, Tante Maria," Volkmar said.

Maria gave the driver her ticket to New York; turned once more to say good bye to Emilie and the children, and took her seat directly behind the driver. As the bus drove off, Inge said

"I wish I could live in New York with Tante Mariele and Uncle Karl! There's a lot more to do there than there is here!"

Chapter IX

The Beginning of Recovery

1934 was the fifth year on the farm for Emilie and Friederich. They had been able to hang on even after the devastating fire, much to the surprise of their relatives and neighbors. Frank May watched from his farm one day as Friederich was cleaning out a fence line with an axe. He strolled down to where Friederich was working and said, "There isn't much you can't do with an axe, is there Fred?"

"No, there isn't. It wastes an enormous amount of wood, but it's a lot quicker than trying to do it with a saw."

Frank May agreed.

"You're real handy with that axe, Fred. Don't worry about the loss of wood from the chips. There are plenty of trees in these woods. I can't chop so much anymore. I have to use a saw and it's a lot slower. I wish I could do what you can do with your axe."

"I have to cut as much wood as I can, Mr. May. I can cut down a tree in less than one quarter the time it would take me to use a saw. I don't like doing it that way, but I don't have a choice. I have to sell wood to make a living."

"Why don't you talk with Harold Coon over in Kirkville? He has a sawmill and he could saw up logs for you into planks and boards to build a new cow barn."

Friederich had been saving some of the best logs of the trees he had cut down.

"If you cut the ends off with a saw, you'll be able to have him saw up your logs pretty easily," Mr. May suggested.

"That's a good idea. Thanks Mr. May."

When Friederich returned to the house from clearing the fence line, he told Emilie "Mr. May thinks we can get Harold Coon to come and saw up my logs for me. Write him a card and ask him to stop in and see us as soon as he can. I've got a business proposition to offer him."

Emilie wrote the card to the address Mr. May had given Friederich. Harold Coon came the very next week. He drove into the yard and found Friederich across the road stacking cord wood. He went over to him and introduced himself.

"Hi. I'm Harold Coon. You wanted me to stop by and talk about a joint business of some kind. What do you have in mind?"

Friederich shook hands with him.

"I understand you've got a sawmill?"

"Yes, that's right."

"How about cutting logs on shares," Friederich began. "I've got lots of logs cut already. You could move your mill over here and saw the best logs on shares. The ones you think aren't good enough to sell, you could saw up for me into inch boards, two-by-fours, sixes, eights, tens and twelves."

"Let me see your log pile?"

Friederich showed him approximately two hundred logs scattered around the field just behind where the old cow barn had stood. There was a mixture of mostly basswood, hemlock, ash, cherry and oak. Friederich had pulled these logs up from the woods with his horses. Because he worked by himself, the logs lay where the horses had pulled them. Harold was impressed with what he saw. He thought he could make a good profit from Friederich's offer.

"There are a lot more logs already cut, still in the woods. As soon as I can, I'll pull them up here with my team."

"You've got a nice bunch of logs, Fred. I'll bring my sawmill over as soon as I can," Harold promised. "I've just finished another farmer's wood lot and was looking for some other place to relocate. Your offer came just at the right time."

Harold Coon moved his sawmill, tractor and equipment truck to a spot almost in the middle of Friederich's log pile. He wanted to have easy access to them.

"If I put the mill in the middle of the log pile, it'll be easier to move them on the skids to the saw. You won't have to pile them up. You can keep your team dragging up enough logs each day so my hired man and I can roll them on the skids ourselves. I'll let you know how many logs we need."

Harold Coon told Friederich which logs to separate into piles he wanted to sell to Booher Lumber.

"There can't be any knots or bad spots in them. Booher wants only the best." By making the selection of which logs he wanted to sell, Coon had the best of the logs from which to choose. Friederich, on the other hand, gained from having Coon saw up logs with knots or other blemishes which the lumber company didn't want. He was pleased how each day his pile of specified lengths was being cut and stacked in neat rows to dry out.

"You can keep the slab wood, too, Fred. I don't want to bother with that."

Friederich cut up the slab piles into firewood and kindling for himself and for his customers. For the next two years, Friederich's former barn yard was filled with stacked cord wood, kindling, planks and boards. Each Saturday Friederich and Volkmar sawed up the slab wood. This gave Friederich plenty of wood to stack in cords of firewood while Coon sawed up the log pile.

X   X   X

Due to an outbreak of tuberculosis among cattle that year, all of the cows in the Syracuse area had to be tested for the disease. The State Department of Agriculture sent around a veterinarian to test all of the cows, county by county, throughout the state. Friederich's three cows and heifer were also tested. Only the heifer was found to be free of the disease.

"The only reason she's free of TB is due to your having kept her separated from the three cows. If she had been in the row with the others, she'd have it, too," the veterinarian told Friederich.

Practically all of the Malin neighbors also had some cows found to be tubercular. The State Agriculture Department decided to round up all of the infected cows and calves at one time in four regions into which each county was divided. The farmers in the eastern part of Onondaga county were instructed to drive their cattle into Madison county to the Chittenango station railway siding where special holding pens were constructed prior to hauling the cattle by train to the designated slaughter houses. Friederich drove his cows out of the barn as the Department employees came by driving the collected herd ahead of them along the side of the road. His three cows joined dozens of other farmers' cows on the drive to the collection depot. Each farmer was given a flat sum of fifty dollars per cow and ten dollars for each calf that had to be destroyed. For the majority of Friederich's neighbors, the poorest cows were found to have been infected. With the money his neighbors received, they rebuilt their herds from healthy, newly purchased animals. For Friederich, however, it meant his best producers were lost and only an unbred heifer remained from the foundation of cows he had kept to rebuild his herd. He was glad he had at least received some payment for his loss. Friederich was told by the veterinarian, "Be sure to disinfect your barn before you put anymore cows into the stanchions. Here's some Lysol. You have to scrub the floor, the mow from which the cows ate, and the gutters over which they stood. Be sure you clean anything your cows touched. Otherwise, the next animals you put in the barn will get infected."

Because he had only a few cows in his barn, Friederich had constructed a chicken coop in one corner. The chickens wandered in and out all day long. After the TB epidemic, however, he kept them in the outside coop which Richard had built five years earlier. He didn't want them to become carriers of the disease to his remaining heifer.

Due to the discovery of tuberculosis among the cows of Onondaga County, all of the school children were also checked to see if any had contracted TB. Fortunately, none of them had. The school nurse felt, as a precaution, some of the poorer children should be given cod liver oil to give them additional resistance to the disease. Volkmar, Inge and Fritzle (now called Donald when he went to school) were supposed to take their dosages once a week for a month in her office. Donald took his only once. He couldn't swallow it a second time. When the nurse tried to give him a tablespoon the second week, he threw up. Miss Wagger, the nurse, decided she wasn't going to go through that episode again! She never again tried to force him to drink it.

On March 30, Inge became eleven years old. Her mother told her the evening before, "Inge, I'm going to take you with me to the city tomorrow. I have to go to the dentist, but you can come along because it's your birthday."

"Can I really go? I'd like that. Maybe we could go to a movie while we're in the city."

"Well, I don't know if we can do that. It's pretty expensive to go there. No, maybe we can visit the Haussmanns while we're there and then come back home."

Emilie hadn't mentioned any of her plans to Friederich. He knew she had a dental appointment. He didn't know what she had made out with Inge. When Inge decided to stay home from school that day, he asked her "Why aren't you going to school?"

"I'm not feeling well so I thought I'd stay home."

After the school bus came and only Volkmar and Donald got on, Emilie told her "Inge, get dressed. You're going with me to the city today."

This was the first Friederich had heard of the idea. He angrily told Emilie

"Nothing doing! If she's not well enough to go to school, then she's certainly not well enough to go to the city!"

He turned to Inge. "Go back to bed! You stay in your room today!"

Inge started crying and continued to do so even after he told her a few times to stop.

"Please let me go with Mama to the city, Papa! It's my birthday! Mama said I could go with her!" she sobbed.

"Anyone who's too sick to go to school certainly isn't fit to go to the city!" he reminded her.

"I'm sorry, Inge," her mother apologized. "But Papa says you can't go. You'll have to stay home today. Maybe you go another time."

"But I want to go now, Mama!" she cried.

She kept on crying and pleading so much Friederich finally hit her a couple of times with his open hand. She cried even harder. When she still didn't go back to her room, he dragged her back and put a chair against the door so she couldn't open it. Emilie felt very badly about what had happened. There was nothing she could do. She had to go to the dentist to have her teeth extracted. The appointment had been made over a month ago.

"I'll have a surprise for you when I come back home," she promised Inge.

"Stop your crying, Inge. There's nothing you can do about it."

It was too late to go to school now. The bus had already come and gone. Neither Friederich nor Emilie would have thought to have her catch the Syracuse-Utica bus to go to school. That would cost too much. Besides, she had deliberately not gotten dressed in time so she missed the school bus. She really had no other option but to stay home and go to school again the next day.

Emilie went out of the house and across the road to catch the bus. As the bus stopped, Inge heard it and ran to the window to watch as her mother got on. Oh how I wish I were getting on it, too, she sighed to herself through her tears. I could have been allowed to miss school this one time, she said to herself! I hardly ever miss it! My report card is almost as good as Volkmar's. It's just not fair!

After the bus had gone, Friederich went out to the chicken coop to gather the eggs and feed the chickens. It was almost time for his morning Veschber anyway, so he came back into the house. He washed his hands and, before making himself something to eat, he went to the bedroom door where he had placed the chair to keep Inge in her room.

"Do you want something to eat?"

"No! I just want to go to the city!"

Friederich's temper flared up again. "So, you still want to go to the city, do you? Well that's no way to talk to me. I told you, you should have gone to school today, didn't I?"

"Yes. But today's my birthday! Mama said I could go with her and then you kept me here instead!"

She started crying all over again.

"Stop your crying! It's not going to help you at all!"

Inge was still in her nightgown. It was a little big for her. She stood there with her arms folded and looked right at him in an accusatory manner. Friederich saw her breasts were already bulging slightly over her folded arms. He could also see her figure outlined under the night gown. She was really a very attractive girl, he thought. She has a slender but definitely good figure, even for her age. Her legs are attractive already, he thought to himself. She's going to become a very pretty woman. Her long braids hung down her back. As she looked at him, she reminded him of his younger sisters, especially Gretel. She was about the same age as Inge, he mused. He remembered the first time he had experimented with her. It was a great feeling getting into his little sister. The more he looked at Inge, the more he remembered Gretel and how he had done it with her for the first time. He started towards Inge. He was about to reach out to her when she bolted away from him. She didn't like the look in his eye. She became frightened as he came toward her again.

"You don't have to be afraid. All you have to do is get back in bed."

"No! I don't want to . . ."

He started towards her again. This time she ran around the other side of the bed so that it was between them. She was even more frightened now.

"What are you going to do?"

"Come here," he said quietly. "It won't hurt. It'll feel good."

He reached across the bed and caught her by the arm before she could get away. He was very strong. She struggled as much as she could, but he pulled her down on the bed. She felt very weak and started to cry again. She stopped struggling because he had lifted her nightgown over her head. He looked at her naked body and unbuttoned his pants. She's even prettier than I thought, he said to himself. There was just the faintest outline of pubic hairs growing around her labia. Her breasts stood out like ripe strawberries before him. She hoped whatever he was going to do, wouldn't hurt. She started sobbing again.

"It won't help you a bit. No one can hear you."

"But I can't breathe!"

He pulled the nightgown down from her head and got on top of her at the same time. He attempted to force her, but it didn't go very far. He withdrew from his attempt. She stopped crying and lay very quietly on the bed. He was still on top of her. He stroked her clitoris. She didn't move. It made her feel very excited. The more he rubbed, the more she moved against his hand and came closer to him. He tried copulating again, but still didn't get very far. He then put his finger into her vagina at the same time as he rubbed her clitoris. This time his finger went in as far as his hand. The opening seemed to be getting wider. He tried once more to penetrate. This time he succeeded. He pushed back and forth a few times until he ejaculated. She felt the wetness almost at the same time as she felt a big release. She was still frightened. She hoped nothing more serious was going to happen to her. Friederich got off and wiped himself and her with his handkerchief. He told her "Don't say anything to anyone about this. This is our little secret."

She didn't say anything. She just looked at him as he wiped himself and looked away. She couldn't look him in the eye anymore. She heaved a few more sighs from her previous sobs and was very glad it was over.She hoped it would never happen again. After he had cleaned himself, he went over to her and hugged her. She lay there very limp. She didn't know what to do. She was afraid he was going to do it again. Instead, he said, "Inge, you're my little girl."

She didn't want to be his little girl. She wanted to be left alone. She was very glad when he went out of the room. She crawled under the covers and cried herself to sleep. She only awoke when she heard her mother calling her to come to dinner.

X   X   X

Mr. Grossmann often came out to the farm for a visit on Sunday afternoons. On one occasion when he had taken Elise and Waltraude with him, he asked Friederich

"Would you and your wife like to take a ride up to Lake Ontario with us?"

"Thanks, Mr. Grossmann, but Sundays are the only day I have to catch up on my sleep. I better stay home."

"Mr. Grossmann, since Papa can't go, could the children go along?" Emilie asked.

Mr. Grossmann thought it over.

"You know, Mr. Grossmann," Elise added, "Waltraude doesn't have anyone her own age to play with. It would be nice if her cousins could go along. I'll keep the children quiet. They don't get much of a chance to go anywhere."

"How old is your son?" he asked Emilie.

"He's almost thirteen and Inge is just two years younger. Fritzle is just six."

"The youngest one can't go. That's out of the question. I don't want him getting car sick and throwing up all over my new car! If the others start getting car sick, you'll have to tell me. I don't want to get my car all dirty. I'd never get the smell out of my car!"

As they climbed in the car, Fritzle said, "I want to go, too!"

He clung to his mother. "No, you can't go this time, Fritzle. There's not enough room in the car for all of us."

He started to cry and hung on to her hand.

"Fritzle, the next time I drive the horses and wagon down to the woods, I'll take you along," Friederich told him as he picked him up.

As Mr. Grossmann started the car and drove off, Friederich said "He'll be all right," he assured Emilie. "Wave goodbye, Fritzle."

Friederich put Fritzle down and went into the house to sleep. Fritzle played with his little trucks among the hollyhocks along the side of the garage. He drove all through his mother's flower beds. Only the hollyhocks were too big to drive over! As he made ruts with the wheels of his toy truck tires, the little kittens came out from under the garage. They played in his newly made tracks.

"Get out of there! You're ruining my tracks!"

The kittens continued to run back and forth between his tracks and safety under the garage. He caught one of the kittens and put it in the rain barrel which was half full of water. It had been a large fifty-five gallon wooden wine barrel for years. One end of it had broken. Emilie used it as a rain water collector with which to water her flowers. There were pieces of wood floating in the water. Fritzle put the kitten in the barrel and it sank to the bottom before coming up again. It clung to the pieces of wood and cried as loudly as it could. The other kittens continued to play in Fritzle's truck tracks. He angrily proceeded to catch each one and put them into the rain barrel, too. All five kittens were desperately clinging to whatever pieces of wood they could. When the mother cat returned from hunting, and heard all of the cries of her kittens emanating from the rain barrel, she jumped up to the top. She meowed loudly to her kittens. Fritzle pushed her in, too. The mother cat let out a loud cry as Fritzle laughed. He thought the kittens and their mother were really funny struggling to stay afloat. He couldn't reach them because the sides of the barrel were too high. He used a stick to push the pieces of wood down into the water so the kittens and their mother kept getting wet. After the second dunking of the mother cat, she succeeded in climbing out of the barrel and clung to the side letting out a howl of meows so loudly Friederich heard her. He came out of the house and saw what Fritzle was doing.

"Na, na, don't do that! Cats don't like water!"

He reached down into the barrel and brought them out one by one. Two of them had already drowned. The other three were barely alive by the time he fished them out. The mother cat quickly took the three survivors back under the garage. Friederich sent Fritzle into the house. "You've probably saved me the trouble of drowning them, but we might have found someone who might have wanted them. You shouldn't have done that, Fritzle."

Friederich carried the two drowned kittens on a shovel out behind the barn and buried them. When Emilie returned with Mr. Grossmann, Elise, Waltraude, Volkmar and Inge, the first words Friederich said to them was "Guess what happened to two of the kittens today?"

"What?" Emilie asked.

"Fritzle tried to see if they could swim! He saved me the trouble of getting rid of two of them, but there are still three that survived."

"What did he do?" Volkmar and Inge asked almost in unison.

"He put them in the rain barrel."

"What? You drowned two kittens? How could you do such a thing, Fritzle? The kittens wanted to live, too," Emilie said reproachfully.

Volkmar and Inge ran over to the garage to see which of the kittens were still alive. The very ones they wanted to keep for themselves were drowned.

"You just wait," Volkmar threatened. "You drowned the one I liked best!"

"I was going to pick one of those for myself!" Inge cried. "And now it's dead!"

Friederich had promised they could each pick out one kitten for their own. The rest would have to go. They didn't like the three survivors. They weren't as pretty as the two drowned ones. Volkmar made a move to hit Fritzle for drowning his kitten.

"Leave him alone! I've already scolded him for doing that!" Friederich told him.

Emilie felt sorry for Volkmar and Inge. It was another instance where Friederich never hit his youngest son. Volkmar and Inge often received corporal punishment if they did something far less mischievous than this. Fritzle stayed close to his father for the rest of the evening. He didn't want to receive any punishment from his brother, if he could help it. Volkmar growled at him under his breath, "You just wait! I'll get even with you!"

Inge rarely hit him. She yelled at him if he did something she didn't like. Occasionally, she slapped him across the face if she were angry enough at him. Volkmar, on the other hand, often took it upon himself to lay Fritzle across his lap and wallop him hard on his bottom. Fritzle knew it hurt and didn't like it one bit. He was afraid of his big brother.

Mr. Grossmann unloaded the box of stones from the trunk of his car. Volkmar and Inge showed Friederich what they had collected. There were all types of stone; striated ones with quartz and granite; pure granite; sandstones; some with black spots embedded in them, and all of them smoothly rounded. The stones were around the farm house for years. The children had also collected pieces of driftwood which Emilie and Friederich used as door stoppers.

Before Friederich went down to the woods the next day, he left instructions for Volkmar to repair some of the shingles on the garage roof.

"Tell Volke he should take a look at the leak over the stairs in the garage. If the shingles have rotted, he should cut a piece of tar paper and fit it underneath the upper shingles so that the hole in the roof is covered. He can then take a few roofing nails to nail down the tar paper patch and a can of tar to seal the nail holes. He should be able to do that by himself."

"Do you think he can do that alone, Papa?"

"He should be able to do that. If the hole is too big, tell him to wait and I'll help him cover it with the tar paper when I come back tonight."

"Okay. I'll tell him."

When Volkmar got up, Emilie said "Volkmar, after breakfast, Papa wants you to take a look at the garage roof. He thinks maybe you can fix it yourself. If the hole's too big, wait and he'll help you put a roll of tar paper over it when he comes up from the woods tonight."

Volkmar climbed out of the second story window on the copper roof over the back bedroom. From there he climbed up the side of the house to the next level of the roof which covered the attic to the annex of the house. He then walked along the ridge of the annex to the garage roof where he let himself down to look for the hole his father had said he should fix. While he was looking for the hole, he saw Fritzle on the ground looking up at him.

"Fritzle, come up here. I need your help. You can get me the nails I'll need to repair the roof."

Fritzle dutifully climbed up on the roof just as his brother had done. Volkmar waited until his little brother had climbed to the top of the ridge of the annex. He then dropped down to the copper roof and came over to Fritzle below where he sat.

"Now I've got you! You can't get down until I say so!"

"What are you going to do?" Fritzle asked anxiously. "I want to get down now! It's too high for me!" he cried.

"Did you give the kittens a chance to get out of the rain barrel? You stay right there until I tell you, you can get down! If you try to get down before I tell you, you'll be lucky if you can make it!"

Volkmar went back to work. Fritzle sat there sobbing until he couldn't cry any more. His mother heard him crying and came out to see what was wrong. "What's the matter? Why are you crying?"

"Volkmar won't let me down again!"

"He's going to have to wait until I'm through," Volkmar volunteered.

"Volkmar, why don't you help him down now. He's afraid to be up so high."

"I can't now. I've got to finish the roof first. If he wants to go down now, he can. Otherwise, he'll have to stay up here with me until I'm finished."

"Just wait until Volkmar is finished, Fritzle. He'll help you down. You don't have to be afraid," his mother assured him.

"But he said he wouldn't! He said he's going to push me off the roof!" he cried.

Emilie ignored his protest. As she went back into the house she said once more, "You don't have to be afraid. He won't hurt you."

It's obviously a case of a little boy being afraid of the height, she said to herself.

Volkmar laughed at Fritzle as he said quietly, "Just you wait! I'll get even with you for drowning my kitten!"

Volkmar enjoyed tormenting his little brother. I'll scare him, he said to himself. After all, he didn't take pity on the little kittens yesterday!

After he had finished repairing not one, but three holes in the garage roof, Volkmar picked up his hammer, nails and tin of tar and walked back along the ridge of the garage roof to the annex roof. He climbed up the annex roof which led to the top of the tee of the annex to the roof of the main house. Fritzle sat still on this roof. As Volkmar passed he said "Well, get up and come along!"

"No! I'm afraid! I can't get down!"

Volkmar laughed. "Well, then I guess you'll have to stay up here!"

He continued to walk down the ridge to the main section of the house. He then walked along the edge of the annex roof which abutted the main part of the house. He held on to the roof of the main house until he had descended to the edge of the annex roof. He sat down and let himself drop slightly to the lean-to copper roof and went back through the open window into the second story.

"Are you coming, or not?" He called to his little brother. "If you're not coming, I'm going to close the window. The only way you'll be able to get down then is to jump to the ground!"

Fritzle started crying all over again. He crawled on all fours along the top ridge of the annex roof to the main house.

"I can't go any further!" he sobbed. "Help me get down! I don't want to stay up here!"

Volkmar waved to him from inside the house. He pretended not to hear him. He took the hammer, nails, and can of tar back to the garage. After he put the tools away he came out again and looked up at his brother. He was still sitting there, but sobbing so loudly his mother came out again to see what was the matter.

"What's wrong?" she asked Fritzle.

"Volke left me up here and I can't get down!"

"Volkmar!" she called out.

There was no answer.

"Volkmar!" she called out again. Emilie became concerned. "If Papa comes home and finds Fritzle crying up there, he'll get very angry with you! He'll, no doubt, give you a beating for not getting him down again!"

Still no answer.

"Volkmar! You'd better come out wherever you are. I'll tell Papa and you know what he'll do to you!"

Volkmar came out, reluctantly, from hiding in the garage.

"You'd better go back up and get Fritzle down!"

He climbed through the upstairs window again unto the copper roof of the lean to, held on the side of the main house roof and climbed up on the annex roof to the top of the ridge where Fritzle was sitting. He had stopped crying and looked at his brother apprehensively. Hadn't he said he was going to get even for drowning his kitten, he thought to himself?

"Follow me down the ridge to the main house."

Fritzle followed. When Volkmar reached the roof of the main house, he said

"Now lean on this roof and let yourself down to the edge of the annex roof. Sit down and let yourself drop to the copper roof."

"I'll slip!" Fritzle protested.

Volkmar grabbed him by the arm and pulled him towards the main house roof.

"Don't pull! I'll come!"

As soon as Volkmar let go of him, he climbed back up to the annex roof ridge.

"I can't go any further!"

Volkmar had already let himself down to the copper roof and stood waiting for his brother.

"Come on! If you don't come down, I'll come up and hit you!"

Fritzle started crying again. "It's too dangerous! I'll fall!"

He continued to sit there. Volkmar got angry with him. He climbed back up on the annex roof and slapped Fritzle across the top of his head. He grabbed him again.

"You're coming with me this time and no excuses!"

He pulled his brother behind him until he got to the edge of the annex roof. He let go of Fritzle so he could let himself down to the copper roof. Fritzle quickly clamored back up to the annex ridge again.

"I can't come down!" Fritzle wailed. "I'll fall!"

Volkmar got so exasperated with him, he climbed back up to ridge of the annex roof and hit him several times on his head and arms as he tried to shield himself from his brother's blows. Volkmar got hold of his brother's wrist and dragged him across the roof. He hung on to him as he let himself drop down to the copper roof. Since he held on to Fritzle, Fritzle came right behind him. Volkmar almost lost his footing on the very edge of the copper roof. He was really angry with his brother now. Fritzle had almost pushed him off the roof.

"Okay! Now you're going to have to jump off the roof to the ground!"

The copper roof of the lean-to section of the house was approximately eight or nine feet above the ground.

"I can't jump from here! It's too high!"

"Jump!" Volkmar threatened. "If you haven't jumped by the time I count to six, I'll push you off!"

He started counting. With each number, he moved closer to Fritzle. Fritzle cried and cried. Emilie came out of the house just in time to see him land in the tall grass. She ran over to where he landed.

"What happened? Are you all right?" she asked solicitously.

He pointed to Volkmar on the roof. Volkmar laughed.

"Come down here this instant! I'm going to tell Papa what you did! He could have caught himself on the clothes line on the way down! Did you push him?"

"I didn't push him! He jumped!"

"You don't make a little boy do something like that!" she scolded. "What if he had gotten hurt?"

"I only told him to jump. I knew he wouldn't hurt himself, and he didn't. He's okay."

Fritzle stopped crying. He wasn't sure whether he was glad Volkmar was going to be punished, or felt sorry for what would happen to him. He spent the rest of the afternoon thinking about what had happened. He was both astounded he had jumped off the roof, and yet pleased he had done so.

When Friederich returned from the woods, Emilie told him "Can you imagine? The boys got in such an argument this afternoon, Volkmar forced Fritzle to jump off the back bedroom roof! He could have hurt himself!"

Friederich got very angry and grabbed Volkmar by the arm. He was about to slap him when Fritzle said "I jumped off the roof! He didn't push me!"

Friederich stopped almost in mid-air from striking Volkmar. He still held him by the arm and shook his finger in his face.

"Don't you ever scare him like that again! He's only a little boy!"

"Yes, but he drowned our little kittens!" Volkmar replied almost under his breath.

"Never mind that! He didn't know what he was doing! You'll have to be satisfied with another kitten!"

X   X   X

Karl was just closing up shop when Maria called from the bus station.

"Karl. I'm home. Can you come and get me at the bus station?"

"What? You're home already? I thought you going to stay the whole month of May?"

"No. I thought you might need my help in the store. Besides, it's not fair for me to take a vacation when you have to work."

195

"Okay. I'll be right over to pick you up."

Maria came back to work. Karl was actually glad she did. There were altogether too many interruptions during the day. He had had to spend nights working in his workshop because of the customers who wandered in. Even though Maria covered the store, Karl still spent a few hours each evening, after supper, working in his workshop to complete the sharpening of lawn mowers and surgical instruments promised for the next day.

In early July, Maria complained to Karl about not feeling well in the morning. After a week of feeling nauseous, he finally convinced her to see the local doctor. He had also emigrated from Germany. Dr. Schuster examined her and gave her a pregnancy test. As he suspected, she was pregnant.

"Frau Fleckhammer, there's nothing wrong with you except you're pregnant. Hadn't you noticed you had missed your period?"

"Yes, but I thought maybe it was something else. How can I be pregnant? Dr. Bauer in Germany told me I'd never have children. My ovaries weren't developed. And besides, my husband is infertile. He had an accident when he was a child. I can't be pregnant, Dr. Schuster!"

"Whoever told you you couldn't get pregnant, didn't know what he was talking about! You're probably in your second month."

Maria didn't quite know what to make of this news. She thought back to the scene on the farm with Friederich. She remembered he had raped her. She hadn't told Karl anything about it. She didn't want him to get upset, nor bring any more hardship on her sister. She kept quiet about what happened. She did notice she seemed to have a much greater appetite for sex ever since she came back. Sometimes Karl was up to it and sometimes he was just too tired. What will Karl say when I tell him what Dr. Schuster said, she asked herself? It'll be a shock to him. Dr. Bauer told him he'd never be a father!

She walked the three blocks home from Dr. Schuster's office a little apprehensively. She wondered how she should tell Karl about the pregnancy. I'll just tell him I'm pregnant and that's why I haven't been feeling so well in the mornings. Dr. Schuster says, it's called morning sickness. Yes, I'll tell him and see what happens. I can't hid it anymore.

As she came in the door, Karl was there to meet her. "Well, what do you have? The flu?" he asked.

"You'll never guess what he said, Karl."

"Why? Is there something seriously wrong with you?"

"I'm pregnant!"

Karl's mouth dropped open. He looked at her for what seemed several minutes. He finally said, "So much for what the doctors know in Germany! Well, that's certainly going to change our life style, Maria. I never thought we'd have a child. Tell you what, as soon as the baby comes, I'm going to have myself castrated. We don't need more than one. With this business, we'll have more than enough to do with you taking care of the baby, too!"

"Then you're not disappointed, Karl?"

"No. But it sure is going to be a surprise to my parents when I write them they're going to have an American grandchild!"

Maria and Karl stayed near the city that summer. At the end of July, Karl suggested "Let's shut down the business for two weeks in August and go up to visit your sister and her family in Chittenango."

"No, I don't want to go there again this year, Karl. I was just there in May. Why don't we go up to the Catskills for a vacation? I've read it's a beautiful place. We could rent a cottage and relax for a week or two. You hardly ever have any time off and you wouldn't have to drive so far, either."

"Would you really prefer to go there instead of the farm?"

"Yes. Do you remember the last time we went there, Karl? You helped with the haying. You don't need to do that heavy work. We've got to make plans of how we're going to hire someone to help us in the store when the baby arrives. I won't be able to be in the store as much, Karl. I want to breast feed the baby. Emmy used to give the breast to each of her children on demand. From what I've heard from Luise, she did the same."

"Okay. We'll go up to the Catskills this year."

"Will you still love me, Karl, even after I've had the baby? You know my figure won't be the same anymore."

"Of course I'll still love you, Maria! You're still number one with me!"

She loved to hear him say it. She had quietly started to cry. She had never even thought of becoming pregnant. What a surprise, indeed. Her whole life was about to change.

"I don't want you to tell anyone, Karl, until after the baby arrives. Okay? Let's just keep it a secret between us for now. Once the baby comes it'll be early enough to tell everyone."

"Okay, okay, whatever you say! You're the baby bearer. Don't you even want your mother to know about it?"

"No. I'd rather take them all by surprise. Everyone thinks I can't have a child. It'll be shock enough to them when the baby is here. I just don't want to take any chances of some disappointment."

On February 24th little "Booby" arrived. Maria and Karl had just received a letter from Brazil saying Luise and Hermann had also just had a little boy on the 14th of February. When Karl wrote his parents and Maria's mother about their baby, they thought there was some mix up. They thought he was referring to Luise's and Hermann's baby. It was only after Maria wrote to tell her mother the name of the baby that her mother recognized she had two new grandsons, not just one. The Fleckhammers named him Karl Friederich Fleckhammer. Junior for short or, "Booby", the preferred name Maria gave her son until he was out of kindergarten.

Emilie and Friederich were astonished at the news. When Friederich came up from the woods, she read him the letter she had received from Maria.

Dear Emmy and family,

You'll never guess what we have in the Fleckhammer family.

"Probably a new dog!" Friederich said sarcastically.

He arrived on February 24 at four a.m. in the local hospital where Karl had taken me. We have a son! His name is Karl Friederich Fleckhammer.

Friederich raised his eyebrows and looked surprised at Emilie.

"Did you know she was pregnant?"

"No Papa. I didn't know anything about it. They did pick out a couple of good names, though."

Friederich was quiet while she continued with the letter.

He sleeps about two hours at a time and then he's hungry. I let him have the breast whenever he wants it, just like you did, Emmy.

"I thought she couldn't have any children?" Friederich asked as much to himself as to Emilie.

"That's what we were told while we were still in Germany, Papa. The doctors don't know everything, do they?"

Emilie continued reading.

We'll try and come visit you this summer. Until then. Best wishes to all of you.

Your affectionate sister,
Maria and Karl

Chapter X

A Surprise Visit

It was more then two years since the Haussmanns had visited the farm. Karl asked them repeatedly "Do you want to take a drive out to the farm?"

Gretel wasn't interested. She bristled each time she thought back to their last conversation with Friederich. But her mother kept after her.

"Don't you want to see how they're getting along without the cows?"

"I'm not interested in what that man does. If he's that stupid to keep on farming without any barns or animals, that's his problem!"

When Karl stopped by and casually asked if they wanted to go, Grandmother Malin said "As soon as Gretel goes with us. Richard would like to go. He'd like to see the farm again."

Richard wanted to go out to the farm very much. He wondered what had happened to his ducks.

"Don't you want to see Emmy and the children?" he asked his wife.

Gretel didn't respond. Her mother repeated the question.

"Aren't you interested in Friederich's family?"

Gretel knew she would have to go, even though she hated the prospect of doing so. It had been more than two years since their last visit. She really thought Friederich and Emilie would have come back to the city before now. She kept asking Richard "What are you going to say when Friederich wants to come and live with us again? I don't want him here!"

"I don't think he'll leave the farm. If he hasn't come back after two years, he's not coming back at all."

"What can he do out there all alone? He doesn't have any cows anymore. They've got to live on something!"

Gretel wrote Emilie and asked her if she wanted to come back to live with them. As much as Gretel hated the thought of it, she believed she had no other choice than to offer to take them in. Each time Emilie wrote, we're getting along fine. We've got lots of room, our garden produced a lot of vegetables and fruit this year and we buy Jersey milk from our neighbors. Papa is cutting wood every day and he's selling a lot of firewood. He and Volkmar cut the wood up each week end on our new buzz saw. Friederich had bought one the very next spring after the fire. He had gotten Finkbeiner's old car running again and used it to drive the belt to the saw.

Gretel finally relented in the summer of 1934. She wanted to invite the Malins to Grete's wedding.

It was a hot July day when Karl brought his family, together with Grandmother Malin and the Haussmanns out to the farm in his Maxwell. He had put the top down and the wind was a refreshing relief from the heat of the day. Grandmother Malin wrapped her scarf around her head to keep her hat on. Gretel let her hair flow in the wind. Karl, Billy and Richard sat in front. The three women sat in the back seat. Karl still wore the same fisherman's cap he had bought on the boat coming over. Billy wore his sailor's cap which he carried with him wherever he went. Richard wore the same trainman's cap he wore to work every day. The sun shone brightly with very few clouds in the sky. It was the perfect day for a convertible ride.

As they came past the Kelly barn and twin silos on the left, Gretel exclaimed

"Oh, oh. Isn't that a shame? That's where the barns used to be and the big silo. Well look at that! Look at all the wood that's piled up!"

In place of the two barns, the yard was filled with stacked cord wood of various lengths. The buzz saw sat in the middle between the stacked wood and the huge pile of limb tops and small sections of the upper parts of trees. The old car sat approximately twenty feet away from the saw facing in the opposite direction.

"That's Finkbeiner's old car," Karl exclaimed. "Fritz must be using it for power to run the saw."

"The milk house is still there," Grandmother pointed out.

"The elm tree next to the horse barn is still alive," Richard said. "I didn't think it would live."

"There's not much of it that's green anymore," Gretel said. "Look at how the entire east side of it is dead!"

Karl drove slowly up to the house. Their eyes were all across the road.

"How sad," Grandmother said. "And to think there were two large barns here before the fire."

"Yes, but look at all of those logs that are over there behind the stacks of cord wood! Friederich much have been cutting down trees everyday to have that many logs!" Karl said in astonishment.

As Karl drove in the yard, Fritzle ran into the house and shouted "They're here!"

"Who's here?" Friederich asked.

"Uncle Karl and the Haussmanns!"

He quickly ran outside with his brother and sister to greet their aunts and uncles. They gave each of the children a hug and a kiss. Grandmother Malin opened her purse and took out three Hershey's chocolate bars, one for each of the children.

"Thank you very much Grandmother," Volkmar said as he opened his bar to begin eating it.

"Yes, thank you Grandmother," Inge repeated.

Fritzle held on to his. He didn't know what to do with it. He watched as his brother and sister opened theirs and began eating them. He handed his to his mother.

"You can eat some of it, Fritzle. Here, I'll break a piece off for you." Emilie broke the end piece off and gave some to Billy, too.

"No, he doesn't need anymore, Emmy. Wilhelmle has chocolate every day," his mother stated. "That's for Fritzle. He doesn't have much candy, does he?"

"Sometimes, when his Grandmother sends some from Germany. But that's around Christmas each year."

Billy gave his piece back to Fritzle at his mother's insistence.

Friederich came out the door slowly. The children were running up to the chicken coop and the barn showing their cousin all around.

As Friederich came out the kitchen door, Richard caught sight of him and called out, "Gruess Gott, Fritz! Wie geht's?" (Hello Fritz. How are you?)

He extended his hand to his brother-in-law and shook it warmly. Friederich shook each one's hand. Even Gretel, begrudgingly, extended hers.

"So, you've decided to come out and see us again." Friederich said mockingly. "We're still here."

"You must be working really hard, Friederich, to have so much wood cut across the road," Grandmother said solicitously.

"We're managing. I've got plenty of work to do in the woods. As soon as I'm through with the haying, I'll be cutting more trees."

"Yes, Papa has only one more field of hay left to do and then we're through with haying for this year," Emilie volunteered. "Come on in. I'll have the coffee ready very shortly and I've got lots of kuchen and pies."

Emilie led the way into the kitchen. They sat around the big table and began their Sunday discussions of international and domestic politics.

"Have you read where Hitler wants to take Germany out of the League of Nations? He doesn't think the League is interested in anything other than what the French and British want," Karl stated.

"It's about time. I don't see how Germany has stayed in as long as they have. They've gotten nothing but a swindling ever since the Versailles Treaty! The Allies have whittled away at Germany's territory! I don't see how Hitler can do anything other than say to hell with the League of Nations!"

Friederich wrapped his knuckles on the table for emphasis. "Mark my words, there's going to be war over the Polish corridor if the Poles think they can keep German territory! Look what the Allies have done to Danzig! An international city! The very idea. It's as German as any other city in Germany. There's nothing international about it!"

Friederich was practically shouting at this point. He had to reach deep within himself in order to give some volume to his words.

"Before you get all hot and bothered about the war again, Friederich, we want to tell you about Grete," Gretel began.

"What about, Grete?" Friederich asked.

"She's going to get married!"

"Married? To whom? We didn't even know she had a boyfriend!"

Richard chimed in. "His name's Billy Weiss. She met him recently at the Arion Club. He's a real nice boy."

"Thank God she's met someone nice. Do you know what her cousin, Peter asked me the other day?" Gretel said incensed. Friederich shook his head.

"He asked me if he could marry her! I told him to get out of my house before I took the broom to him! The very idea! Doesn't he know first cousins can't marry each other? People just don't do that! That's incest! Think of the imbeciles they might have produced!"

"Maybe not," Friederich said. "They might have had brilliant children. Just because they're related doesn't mean the children wouldn't have been exceptional. In fact, they could have been even more intelligent than their parents! Just look at the British royal family. Queen Victoria and Albert were first cousins and look at all of the children they had!"

Gretel didn't know what to make of her brother. He says some of the darndest things sometimes, she thought. Is he really serious about cousins marrying? She repeated her earlier statement. "I don't know about the British royal family but everyone knows incest breeds imbecility! How can you say such a thing, Friederich? Would you want your daughter marrying one of her cousins? At any rate, Peter is not to enter my house again until Grete is married. Then he can come to visit again."

Friederich, in his usual cynical tone of voice asked, "You're sure she's not pregnant?"

He was a little surprised the wedding was going to take place that next month.

"Of course not!" Gretel retorted. "That's why we don't want Peter to come around anymore. He was like a lovesick puppy! Anyway, the wedding is going to be held in the Mt. Tabor Church and Pastor Schedding is going to conduct it. We'd like to have you come."

Friederich still couldn't believe Grete wasn't pregnant. Why would they rush into this marriage, he thought to himself? There must be a reason for such an early marriage. This was the first time we've even heard of this young man, he told himself. Well, if that's who she wants to marry, then that's who she'll marry! But I'd be very suspicious if my daughter wanted to get married this quickly, he told himself.

"Billy's parents don't speak German so Pastor Schedding is going to conduct the service in both languages," Gretel continued.

The Malins remembered the church on Butternut Street very well. Emilie had taken the children there when they lived on Butternut Street. They also knew Pastor

Schedding. He conducted services twice a month in German because so many of his parishioners were only fluent in German.

"I'm not sure I can come, but maybe Emmy can go. I've got to stay home and look after my animals," Friederich said. The speed of the wedding still bothered him.

"How long has she known this Billy?"

"She's known him for three weeks," Gretel replied.

"And she's going to marry him this next month?" he asked incredulously. He followed up his own question with another one. "So how long has she been pregnant?"

Gretel was upset with this line of questioning. She didn't quite know how to respond. Everyone was looking at her. She had to say something.

"All right, I'll tell you! But you don't have to spread it around the neighborhood!" she said dejectedly. "No one else has to know! She's not quite in her second month, but she's already way past her period."

Friederich smiled knowingly. "And you're going to have a church wedding? Isn't that being hypocritical now that she's pregnant?"

"That's what I've been trying to tell her for the past week. I want her to get married at home. Gretel wants her to be married in the church because she never had a church wedding herself. I can't talk her out of it," Richard continued. "It would be so much simpler and easier if she got married at home."

Grandmother Malin agreed with Friederich and Richard.

"A person only gets married in the church if she's a virgin! If she's pregnant, she's no virgin!"

Gretel started to cry. Now her mother, brothers and husband were all against her! She felt let down. She had always dreamed of a beautiful church wedding. She had never had one herself because with two children, the church didn't allow it in Germany.

"Here in America, it shouldn't make a difference! She can still get married in the church!" Gretel said defensively.

The rest of the family kept making fun of her attempt to legitimatize the forthcoming marriage by having it sanctified with a church wedding. What can I do, she thought to herself. They're all against me! When Richard raised the issue of how much a church wedding might cost, she relented.

"Okay," she said very dejectedly. "We'll have it in our living room."

Friederich prided himself in having talked his sister into some common sense.

"I can't make it, but we'll see if Emmy can. We'll send something along for Grete. I've always liked her. She's really my favorite niece."

Grete had also been very fond of her Uncle Friederich. He had given her gifts as a little girl when she, her brother, and mother lived in Vaihingen with him and his mother. He remembered how she liked to sit on his lap when she was a little girl and allowed him to put his hand under her dress. She didn't seem to mind at all whenever he held her and played with her. She seemed to like it almost as much as he did. Her mother told her once "Grete, you don't have to sit on your Uncle Friederich's lap all the time! Leave him alone! He doesn't want you hugging and kissing him over and over, either!"

She got off his lap whenever her mother was around. But as soon as she was gone, she'd climb on again and hug and kiss him. He was the only man she knew as a little girl. Her parents weren't married and she seldom saw her father in those days. He was in the army. She knew no other model of a man than the one she saw and experienced everyday. She thought this was the way all little girls and men must behave. She couldn't understand why her mother was so against her doing what she enjoyed so much.

Grete married Billy at home. After an overnight hotel honeymoon paid by her Uncle Karl, they returned to live with her parents until the birth of their first daughter. Riche had moved out earlier in the year having married Margaret Sherman. Unfortunately for Gretel, this marriage was another one of those that shouldn't have happened. Neither she nor Richard took too kindly to this girl their son had brought home and introduced as his future wife. Gretel felt he hadn't chosen someone who was up to his intellectual level. As she explained it to her brothers and sisters,

"This is one of those cases where Riche should have picked out a college girl. Margaret is okay, but Riche is a graduate of the College of Forestry! Why didn't he choose someone who studied at the university like he did? Margaret didn't even finish high school! She dropped out when she was sixteen! Riche has such a good education," her lament continued. "He has a very good job with the government. I just know she married him because she knows he's going places! It's so sad to think he doesn't know how important it is to marry someone at least on his own level. I wish he had waited a few years before marrying her!"

Richard, Jr. got a job with the U.S. Forest Service following graduation. After their wedding, they moved directly to their first location in Pennsylvania. It also meant the upstairs was now vacant. Since neither Grete nor Billy had any money with which to rent an apartment of their own, the Haussmanns invited them to move into the upstairs bedroom. It wasn't the most private arrangement for a newly married couple, but at least it gave them a place to live.

Gretel was thankful her daughter and nephew hadn't gone any further than they had . . . Billy also worked at New Process Gear, just like Pete Kesselring, but they barely knew each other. Since they worked in separate parts of the factory, their paths never crossed. All of the relatives had been invited to the wedding, except for the Kesselrings. Gretel still couldn't get over the way Pete had tried to interest Grete in marrying him. She wasn't about to spoil her daughter's wedding by inviting a former suitor and his family! Bertha was very disappointed. She liked her younger sister and her family. She also thought very highly of Grete. She felt

Gretel had over reacted to Peter's interest in her daughter. After Bertha found out from Pete what had happened to him, she went to see her sister.

"Gretel, did you tell Peter he should never come to visit you anymore? Doesn't he have the right to visit his Grandmother, or you, and your family? He likes all of you very much. If you hadn't gotten so violent towards him and let him keep coming, I'm sure his love affair with Grete would have ended by itself."

"How do you know what it was like having him around all of the time? He didn't come to see his Grandmother, nor any of the rest of us! He just wanted to see Grete! He asked me if he could marry her! What should I have said? If I hadn't told him to get out and never come back, he might have gotten her pregnant just as surely as I'm talking to you! You know darn well cousins shouldn't marry! They'd have nothing but idiots and imbeciles for offspring! I don't want to hear anymore about it! I didn't ask him to come! And I'm not going to listen to you lecture me on what I should have done! You've got problems of your own! Mind your own business, and I'll tend to mine!"

"What do you mean, I've got problems of my own?" Bertha replied vehemently.

"I had to move out! I couldn't live with Gustav any longer! He was always drunk! That's not fair, Gretel! Peter never had a chance to learn how to behave. He was always being beaten by his father! He just fell in love with all of you because for the first time in his life, he was treated like a real person! You can't blame him for that! I guess it's no use talking to you anymore! You've never had to confront the brutality and viciousness of a drunken father and husband like we've had!"

With these bitter words, Bertha left.

"Bertha," her mother said. "Why don't you stay for some coffee and kuchen. It's all ready."

"No! Goodbye Mother. I can't take anymore."

Bertha had had to find another place to live with her two children. She had given Gustav an ultimatum. "Either you stop your drinking, or the children and I are leaving!"

He didn't stop drinking. When she came home from the grocery store late one afternoon, she found he had not only been drinking, but was in bed with their daughter. She packed their things and took both of the children with her to the family where she had worked as a housekeeper for several years. Mrs. Tholens had always told her "Bertha, you can move in with us anytime. We don't have any children so yours would be a lot of fun to have in the house."

With Bertha siding with her son, she wasn't invited to Grete's wedding, either. Only the Haussmanns, the Weisses, Grandmother Malin and her sister, Karl and his family, Elise and Waltraude were in attendance. Emilie didn't go. She had asked Friederich if she might go but noticed he wasn't very pleased when she asked him. "Why don't you save the bus and trolley fares and buy Grete something they can use? It would make a lot more sense to save the money you'd spend on a new dress and give it to them than try to do both."

"Yes, you're right, Papa. Can I send them a check for ten dollars as a wedding present?"

"That's way too much. Make it six dollars and that's still a lot for us."

Emilie wrote their regrets and enclosed the check as the Malins' wedding present to Grete and her new husband.

X   X   X

What had started as an attempt to provide security for Emilie through her silence, became a conspiracy of silence. Not only was it safer for her not to reveal what she had learned about her husband, but she remained in denial that he could do such things to his family and relatives. Their bifurcated life style continued as if nothing untoward had ever happened. She continued to find solace in her children, her garden, her piano playing, and church attendance. Friederich continued to work on the farm until called to employment as a tool maker on the eve of World War II. His sexual proclivities continued to be expressed in unsanctioned ways.

For those persons who wonder why no one did anything to obstruct or hinder these proclivities of Friederich, we should remember the historical period was one more closely related to the Victorian era than to the late twentieth century. He was a product of an era long gone. This is not to say these things do not happen today. The difference is that now such behavior would no longer be kept silent and, nor would these crimes be left unpunished.

Chapter XI

A New Horse, Or A New Tractor?

It was January 1935 when Friederich decided he had to buy another horse or a tractor. He wasn't sure which he should do. The previous summer, "Tom" had choked himself to death. He had gotten the wagon wheel, to which Friederich had him tied, caught between a tree and a large rock. In his struggles, "Tom" had pulled and pulled only to tighten the rope around his neck. Ordinarily, the rope wouldn't have choked him, but it had rained that night. The rope was wet and became gnarled and twisted from "Tom's" efforts to free himself. Volkmar and Fritzle found "Tom" the next morning stretched out next to the rock as if he were asleep. Friederich sent them down to see why "Tom" wasn't getting up. Friederich wanted to use him, together with "Dick", to cut hay. Volkmar and Fritzle ran back and told him "Papa, "Tom's" dead! He's cold to the touch. He must have died during the night" Volkmar said.

It was a blow to Friederich. His strongest horse was dead. Only "Lady" and "Dick" were left. "Dick" was strong enough, but since he, too, like "Lady", was blind, they were unsure of their steps. Hence, Friederich knew they were hesitant to put their full strength into a task. "Tom" always pulled ahead on any load to which he and "Dick" were attached. "Dick" had to do the same simply to keep up with him. Together, they had made a very powerful team. Friederich quickly noticed when he hitched "Lady" and "Dick" to pull "Tom's" body down to the swamp, neither horse seemed sure of itself. No, he thought, I'll have to get another horse that can see. These two simply aren't good enough by themselves.

He went to see Frank May to ask him where he might buy a good horse.

"Mr. May, my strong white horse is dead. Would you know where I could buy another one as strong as he?"

"You mean that big white horse of yours is dead?"

"My boys found him in the field this morning. I had him tied to an old wagon wheel and he dragged it between a rock and a tree. The rope that I had around his neck was all twisted and gnarled. It must have choked him to death when he tried to get loose."

"That's too bad, Fred. He was a strong worker. He sort of led the other horses around, didn't he? Wasn't he the one that could see?"

"Yes. That's the one."

"I could tell you where you might buy another one, but maybe you ought to buy another tractor, Fred. You had one before, didn't you? A tractor can do a lot more than a horse. You can run your buzz saw with a tractor. You wouldn't have to worry about the old car starting. Naw, Fred, you don't want to buy another horse. Get yourself a tractor instead."

Friederich hadn't thought too much about a tractor. He still hadn't gotten the old Fordson fixed from the vandalism. It was just too costly to repair.

"Isn't it a lot more expensive than a horse?" he asked.

"It depends on what kind you buy. If you buy a great big one, sure it's going to cost you a lot of money. If you buy a smaller one, one that will do the jobs you want it to do, then it won't cost too much. If I were you, Fred, I'd buy a tractor before I bought another horse. There's a dealer up in Cazenovia you ought to talk to. He's got good tractors and all different sizes. His name's Stanley Bitner."

Friederich thought over what Frank May said. So he'd buy a tractor before he'd buy another horse? Maybe that's not a bad idea. The more he thought about it, the more he thought maybe that's what he should do. He remembered something else Frank May told him, "Don't forget, Fred, you have to feed and water a horse all the time whether you use him or not. A tractor just needs some oil, gas, grease and repairs now and then. The rest of the time, it just sits there. You don't have to feed it or anything, and it goes a lot faster than a horse."

Yes, Friederich told himself, I guess I better look for a tractor. He thanked Frank for his advice and after writing down Mr. Bitner's telephone number he returned home. After telling Emilie what Mr. May had suggested, he told her

"Go over to Kellys and call Mr. Bitner. I want him to stop in and tell us about the tractors he has."

Emilie had gotten used to going over to Kellys to use their telephone. They didn't have one themselves, nor did many of the other neighbors. She knew the people that lived across the county line had one, but she didn't know them very well. Besides, she knew the Kellys ever since they had quartered their horses in their horse barn after the fire.

Mr. Bitner was the local John Deere dealer in Cazenovia. He was only too glad to stop at the Malins to talk about buying a tractor. It was mid winter, with lots of snow on the ground. Hardly the time, he thought, for anyone to come to his agency to look at tractors.

"I'd be pleased to come by, Mrs. Malin. How would it be if I came next Monday?"

"That would be fine, Mr. Bitner. We'll expect you next Monday."

When he arrived, he came to the front door and rang the doorbell. Emilie went to the door.

"Hello. I'm Stanley Bitner. You wanted me to stop and talk to you about buying a tractor? Are you Mrs. Malin?"

"Oh yes, Mr. Bitner. How do you do. We're expecting you. Come in. My husband is in the living room."

She led the way into the living room and introduced him to Friederich.

"Papa, this is Mr. Bitner. He's the one that sells tractors in Cazenovia."

Mr. Bitner extended his hand to Friederich. Mr. Bitner spoke a few words of German he still remembered from his grandparents.

"They came from Germany, too," he said. "Some place called Frankfurt."

"Ah, so you're a Hessen," Friederich replied.

Mr. Bitner didn't know for sure if that was what they were. "If you say so, Mr. Malin. If that's the place they came from in Germany, then that's also where the Hessens were recruited to serve in the British army to fight the Americans in the Revolutionary War."

"It probably was," Friederich said. "The present English King's family came from Germany, too, and is related to our last Kaiser. In fact, he's a cousin of his."

Mr. Bitner was duly impressed with the knowledge Friederich exhibited. While they made other comparisons of family origins, Emilie asked Mr. Bitner,

"Would you like a cup of tea?"

"Why yes, Mrs. Malin. That would be very good on this cold, wintry day."

She prepared the tea and brought out cookies she had baked the previous Saturday. They drank the tea as they discussed what kind of tractor to buy.

"It sounds like you want a Model B tractor, Mr. Malin. I only have a Model A right now, but I should have a Model B and a Model D John Deere next week. I'll leave some brochures with you to look through and when the others come in, I'll come pick you up and take you to my show room so you can see them for yourself."

He gave them several brochures of the different kinds and models of tractors John Deere produced. They also had the prices in them for each of the models.

"I'm sure you'll find the right tractor for you in these brochures. After they come in, I'll call you and find out when I can take you to my showroom."

"I'm sorry Mr. Bitner, but we don't have a telephone."

"That's a all right, Mrs. Malin. I'll stop by and take you to my showroom after they come in. Thank you, for the tea and cookies."

With these words he took his leave after shaking hands with both of them.

No sooner had he left, Friederich and Emilie poured over the brochures. The prices were high for most of the models.

"The models A and D are out of the question for us. We don't have that much money," Friederich said.

He then looked further and found one that cost only three hundred dollars.

"It's called a Waterloo Boy," Friederich said. "It's made in Waterloo, Iowa. We might be able to buy that one."

"But Papa, how could we ever pay for it? We can barely make our interest payments now. A tractor for this amount would be impossible to buy except on credit," she said reproachfully.

She knew Friederich didn't like to buy anything on credit after the disastrous experience he had had extending credit in Germany.

"We'll have to think of some way to do it. I could sell some of my logs that I was saving to rebuild our barn. I could also sell my oats that I've been feeding the chickens and horses. We should be able to get most of the money together."

Mr. Bitner came to pick up Friederich and Emilie that next week. The new models had just come in and there was a new Model B and a Model D tractor in the show room with the older Model A. They didn't even look at the other models. They went straight to the new Model B tractor. It was a bright green and yellow color, on steel with lugs on the rear wheels.

"The Model A would really be better for you, Mr. Malin. It's on rubber and you could use it on the road," Mr. Bitner said.

Friederich discounted the suggestion with the comment,

"It would never hold up in the woods. I don't want to have a flat tire all the time!"

"Oh you wouldn't have a flat tire, Mr. Malin. The rubber's too thick for that."

Even more to the point, however, was the fact both he and Emilie had agreed, the Model A cost one hundred dollars more than the Model B.

"No," Friederich said. "I don't want a rubber tired tractor. I only use it on my own farm anyway. I'm not going to be using it on the highway."

Mr. Bitner realized Friederich had already made up his mind. He couldn't get him to reconsider. It was now a matter of trying to reach agreement on a price for the Waterloo Boy.

"What do you have to have for this tractor, Mr. Bitner?" Friederich asked.

"The price is three hundred dollars, Mr. Malin."

"I don't have that much right now. Would you be willing to take my oats and some logs towards the price?"

"How many tons of oats do you have?"

"I think there must be at least twenty tons. I'll add fifty of my best logs that you can select from my log pile."

"Do you have anything else, like a tractor, or a car that I could take on a trade?"

"I have an old Fordson tractor, but it needs a new radiator. Some one put holes through it while it was down in the fields."

"Someone must not like you, Mr. Malin, if they did something like that to your tractor!"

"I have an idea who did it, but I can't prove it."

"Well, tell you what, Mr. Malin. I'll take a look at your oats, logs, and tractor. You're sure you don't want the bigger Model A?"

"No. I'm sure. We can't afford one that big."

Mr. Bitner drove Friederich and Emilie back to the farm and looked over the oats, logs, and tractor Friederich offered to trade towards the new Model B.

He liked Friederich.

"How did you lose your voice, Mr. Malin?"

"I was in the German army during the war and a doctor cut the nerves to my vocal cords."

"Were you wounded in the throat?"

"No. I had some polyps growing in my throat that made it hard to swallow my food. The doctor cut them out and cut the nerves."

"Did you get any disability from it, Mr. Malin?"

"No. The army gave me a discharge. I didn't have to return to the trenches."

"You were lucky, Mr. Malin. You could have been killed, if they hadn't released you."

Friederich waved his hand. "When you can't talk, or have people understand you, it would be better to be dead."

"I wouldn't say that, Mr. Malin. You've got your health. You've got a nice family. And you own a big farm. I know some men who didn't come back from the war. I doubt they'd feel the same way."

Friederich didn't say anything. It's easy for you to say, he thought to himself. You don't know what it's like not to be understood. People look at me as if I'm a freak of some sort.

When they arrived at the farm, Friederich took Mr. Bitner across the road to look at the logs. The snow had melted somewhat so most of them were clearly visible.

"Did you cut all of these logs yourself, Mr. Malin? There are some pretty big ones here."

"Most of them. I had a couple men cut some logs last summer. I'm going to have a sawmill brought in this spring to saw up these logs into lumber. I want to rebuild my cow barn as soon as possible."

"You're not going to use cherry and maple for your barn, are you? They're too valuable for that."

"No. I'm going to sell the hardwoods to Booher Lumber."

"I'm glad of that. It would be a waste of good trees to cut up for a barn. How many logs do you have here?"

"About four hundred."

"Where is the oats you were going to show me? Let's take a look at that."

Friederich took Mr. Bitner over to the barn. He had closed off one end of the upstairs to make a granary. One quarter of the upstairs of the barn was filled with oats.

"That's nice looking oats, Mr. Malin. I'd say you have at least thirty tons here. Tell you what I'll do. I'll take fifty of your best hardwood logs and twenty tons of your oats for one hundred seven-five dollars towards the Model B. How would that be with you?"

"That's not enough, Mr. Bitner. I've got to have at least two hundred dollars, or I can't buy the tractor."

Mr. Bitner took out his note pad and did some figuring. After a few minutes of calculating, he said "You said something about a Fordson tractor that you had. Where is it?"

"It's out behind the barn. I pulled it there with my horses."

"Let's take a look at it."

Friederich took him behind the barn and showed him the tractor. The holes in the radiator were clearly visible.

"Is that all that's wrong with the tractor?"

"Yes. I just haven't had the time or money to repair it."

Mr. Bitner looked over the engine and the spark plugs.

"Someone broke off the top of this plug, Mr. Malin. Didn't you see that?"

"No. I hadn't noticed. I just saw what they did to the radiator. I didn't bother to look it over any further."

"Tell you what, Mr. Malin. I'll take the fifty logs, twenty tons of oats and this tractor for two hundred dollars. But that's my final price. It's going to cost me money to have your logs and grain shipped up to my mill. And this tractor is going to cost me money to get running again. How would that be with you?"

"Can you wait until December 31st to receive the final one hundred dollars?"

"You're a hard man to deal with, Mr. Malin! Okay. Pay me the final one hundred dollars at the end of the year."

Friederich felt very pleased with himself. He not only got a new tractor, but he got an extension until the end of the year for the final payment. If worst came to worst, he thought he could borrow one hundred dollars from his brother. He didn't think it would be necessary, but it did give him a fall back position should he need it by the end of the year.

On a cold, snow covered, sunny February afternoon, Mr. Bitner delivered the new John Deere Model B tractor. It sat out in the yard next to the garage when the children came home from school. Volkmar and Inge looked at the tractor briefly on their way into the house for hot chocolate. Donald, however, climbed up on the tractor seat and pretended to steer it. There was a big glob of paint on the inside of the steering wheel which he tried to bite off. The metal was very cold. As he put his mouth against the steel inside of the steering wheel, his mouth and tongue froze to the metal. He tried to pull back from the steel. As he did so, part of his tongue and lips stayed on the metal. His tongue and lips started to bleed. He didn't want anyone to know what he had done. He climbed down from the tractor and put snow in his mouth. It soothed the pain and stopped the bleeding. He put more and more snow on his lips until the bleeding had entirely stopped. He then went into the house making sure no one looked at him directly.

"Fritzle, did you see the new tractor?" Emilie asked.

"Yes. I even climbed on the seat and sat on it."

He didn't say anything about his lips or tongue. Overnight it had healed enough to create a scab on his lips.

"What happened to your lips, Fritzle?" his mother asked the next morning.

"When I climbed on the tractor yesterday, I put my tongue and lips on the steering wheel and they stuck to it."

"You can't do that. You always have to keep your skin away from something that's that cold in the winter. Otherwise you'll stick to the metal and it can really hurt you," she said as she looked at his lips. She dabbed a little Vaseline on them and said

"Leave the scab on it. It'll come off by itself. Otherwise, it's going to bleed again."

Chapter XII

Elise and Waltraude

Elise felt very fortunate in having such a good job working as Mr. Grossmann's house keeper. She had had to impress him with the fact that her daughter, Waltraude, would be well behaved and wouldn't be too noisy in his presence. He had thought he didn't want a house keeper with any small children when he first put the ad in the newspaper. But when he saw Waltraude with her mother, he was impressed with her beauty.

"Is she a quiet girl, or will she make a lot of noise?"

"Oh no, Mr. Grossmann! She's a very quiet girl. If I tell her to do something, she'll do it. You don't have to worry about her!"

"Well, I'm used to having my peace and quiet around the house. If I want to have any children around, I go out to the country and visit my son and his family in Chittenango. I can't stand more than a day around them. That's why I'm still living here in Syracuse."

"I'm sure you won't have any trouble with Waltraut, Mr. Grossmann."

"Okay. You can start right away. You can use the upstairs bedroom across from the bathroom as your room. Your daughter can sleep in the adjoining bedroom."

"Oh thank you very much Mr. Grossmann! I'll do my best to see you're completely satisfied in taking me on as your house keeper."

As they moved into Mr. Grossmann's house about two blocks up towards Butternut Street from the Haussmanns on Knaul Street, Elise told Waltraude

"When Mr. Grossmann tells you to do something, Waltraut, be a good girl and do whatever he asks. Okay? We're lucky to be able to live in such a nice house and you don't have far to go to school."

"Yes, Mama. I'll be real good."

For the first few weeks, Waltraude did exactly as she was told. She was always quiet around Mr. Grossmann and sat next to him after her mother gave her hot chocolate and cookies upon her return from school. She took her little doll with her before she climbed on the couch and sat next to him. After a few days of sitting together, Mr. Grossmann pulled her closer to him and began to stroke her hair.

Elise happened to see this on one occasion and thought, well isn't that nice. He seems to like her, she thought to herself.

After several weeks went by, Elise noticed Waltraude wasn't eating her food very well and couldn't seem to wait to leave for school. She wanted to leave as soon as she had her breakfast.

"You've got another half hour before you have to leave Waltraut. You'll make it in plenty of time."

"But I want to go now!"

"Why? Don't you like to play with your dolls before school?"

"Yes. But I want to go to school, now."

"No. There's no reason for you to leave this early. You stay in your room and I'll call you when it's time to go to school."

"But I want to leave before Mr. Grossmann wakes up," she pleaded.

"What?" her mother asked in astonishment. "You want to leave before Mr. Grossmann gets up? Why? What does that have to do with you going to school so early?" she asked in surprise.

"I don't want to have to sit next to him all of the time!"

Elise couldn't believe what she heard. "Why not?"

"Because he always puts his hands all over me!"

Elise was quiet for a long time, lost in her own thoughts. Waltraude brought her back from her reverie by asking, "Why does he put his hands all over me?"

"Probably because he likes you," she tried to explain to her little daughter.

Elise didn't really believe what she was trying to tell Waltraude. She was concerned maybe things had gone too far between Mr. Grossmann and her daughter. She remembered what she had herself seen on Sunday afternoons as they drove out into the country. Mr. Grossmann always insisted Waltraut sit between them on the front seat of his new Franklin. She saw how he let his hand rest on her knees and thighs after shifting. She hadn't thought too much about it until then. They liked their rides into the country, she thought to herself. Waltraut liked to go to Green Lake and walk along the edge of the lake and throw stones into the water. But when Waltraut wanted to sit in the big back seat by herself, after returning to the car, one day, Mr. Grossmann had gotten very angry with her.

"You sit up front with your mother and me! None of this, I want to sit in the back seat business with me!"

Elise decided she would watch very closely what went on between the two of them after Waltraude came home from school that afternoon. But she didn't come right home.

"I'm going to have to look for Waltraude, Mr. Grossmann. She should have been home from school by now. I can't understand why she isn't home!"

"Yes, you'd better go and find her. She should have been back a long time ago. I've missed her, too."

Elise walked quickly up Knaul to Butternut Street and then to the Garfield school. She found Waltraude in the school yard with two other little girls playing in the sand box. Elise was very cross with Waltraude and scolded her.

"Why didn't you come right home after school, Waltraut? I was concerned about you and even Mr. Grossmann wondered where you were! You can't just stay here after school! You are to come home as soon as possible!"

"I wanted to play with my friends. They live right next door. I didn't think anything about it. They asked me if I wanted to stay and play and I said yes."

"Well from now on, you are to come home right after school. Do you understand?"

"Yes Mama, but I don't want to have to sit next to Mr. Grossmann all the time. I don't like it when he puts his hands all over me!"

Elise took her daughter by the hand and pulled her along home. She wondered again what she was going to do. The job she had with Mr. Grossmann was a well paying one. They had a very nice place to live. If only he'd keep his hands off of her, she thought to herself.

After two more weeks of wanting to go to school earlier and earlier, Waltraude still came home late from school more often than on time. Elise spanked her on a couple of occasions because she was so late coming home. Mr. Grossmann was very cross when she didn't come home directly after school. He even threatened to go and get her in his car, if she didn't come home right away. Her mother threatened, "You don't want Mr. Grossmann to come and get you, do you?"

Waltraude didn't say anything. She told her mother that evening as she was putting her to bed "Mama, I don't like Mr. Grossmann. I'm afraid of him. I don't want to stay here any longer."

So that's it, Elise thought to herself. He must be doing something pretty bad if Waltraut feels that way! Well, I guess I'll have to tell him we can't stay here any longer. The next morning, after Waltraude went to school, she informed him

"Mr. Grossmann, I've enjoyed working here, but I'm going to look for another job. I need to find someplace where there are other children with whom Waltraut can play. It's just too dangerous for her to have to walk all of the way to Garfield School just to play with girls her own age."

"What? You want to quit a good job and a nice place to live just so your daughter has some friends to play with? I think that's absolutely silly. She should learn to be on her own!"

"I'm sorry Mr. Grossmann, but I'm afraid we'll have to leave. It's really important for a child to have other playmates her own age. I've enjoyed working here. I don't think you'll have any trouble finding a new housekeeper. We'll stay until the end of the month, Mr. Grossmann."

He was almost beside himself. He liked Elise and her daughter. The meals were excellent. He always had company in the house with him. And Elise did an even better job of washing and ironing his clothes than his late wife had done.

"I can't understand how you can throw away such a good job and place to live, Frau Brendel. I can give you another ten dollars a week if you need more money?"

"No, Mr. Grossmann. I really have to go somewhere else. It's not the money. Waltraut needs friends of her own. I divorced my husband before we had any more children. It's very important for her to be in contact with children her own age. Since she's an only child, I have to be careful she doesn't become spoiled from being around adults all of the time."

Mr. Grossmann was not one to plead his case. If anyone crossed him, he cast him off without further consideration. "If you're going to be that stupid and turn down lifetime employment, then there's no need for you to stay after this week!"

"I'm sorry you feel that way, Mr. Grossmann. I wouldn't mind finishing this month."

"No. That won't be necessary. The sooner you leave the better it'll be for both of us!"

Elise walked up the street to her sister's house and talked with her mother.

"Mother, do you think we could move in with the Haussmanns until I find another job? I've got to leave Mr. Grossmann. Waltraut's afraid of him and I told him she needs other children to play with. He can't understand how I can throw away such a good job and place to live so my daughter can have playmates her own age! I didn't want to tell him the real reason."

"Why? What's the real reason?"

"He puts his hands all over her. She doesn't like that. I don't blame her. He wants her to sit next to him as soon as she comes home from school. I can't watch him all the time. I have my work to do."

"Why that old goat! Of course you can move back here. I don't think Gretel will object."

Elise returned to the Grossmann house and started packing their things. She had only four suitcases into which she quickly put their clothes, Waltraut's toys, books and pictures she had brought from Germany. She thought she could ask Karl to take her things to Haussmanns the next time she saw him.

As soon as Gretel came home from Gale's, Grandmother told her of the visit from Elise. "You wouldn't mind, would you, if Elise and Waltraut came back to stay with us until Elise finds a new job?"

"Of course not. What happened at Grossmanns?"

"Mr. Grossmann is putting his hands all over Waltraut and Elise is afraid he may do something worse."

"Well that sounds familiar. What is this about all these men? Do they think the whole world revolves around them and their weird inclinations? I've often wondered why he doesn't live with his son in Chittenango. He probably isn't welcome there, either!"

"But Mr. Grossmann is a rich man, Gretel. He can go wherever he wants. It's too bad. I always liked him."

"You don't know what he's like, Mother. Maybe he does have a lot of money. But that doesn't give him the right to molest little girls!"

Elise saw Karl the next day while visiting her mother.

"Karl could you pick up my bags for me from Mr. Grossmann's house and bring them over here?"

"Sure. What's the matter? Aren't you staying there any longer?"

"No. I'm going to look for another job. Mr. Grossmann's getting too familiar with Waltraut. I don't want to take a chance something worse might happen to her."

"So. The old goat's getting horny, is he?"

"He's probably been that way for a long time. I just hadn't noticed it before. Waltraut doesn't want to stay there any longer."

"I don't blame her. It must be hard for little girls when there are so many men out there who want sex with them. Do you want to go over now and get your things?"

"Okay. Mr. Grossmann usually takes a nap at this time of day. He may not even wake up when we come."

Karl drove Elise over in his new model A Ford coupe with the rumble seat. He backed into the driveway and parked it while Elise went into the house.

Mr. Grossmann awoke when he heard the car backing in and looked out the window.

"Who's that?" he asked Elise.

"That's my brother, Karl. He's coming to pick up my things, Mr. Grossmann."

"You won't reconsider? I'll give you an extra ten dollars a week, Frau Brendel."

"No thanks, Mr. Grossmann. I've already made plans to move back in with my sister, Frau Haussmann. Besides, as soon as Waltraude comes home, we'll be leaving. In the meantime, my brother is taking my things over to her house."

"Hello, Mr. Grossmann. I'm Karl Malin. I met you at my sister, Gretel's house, a couple of years ago. I don't know if you remember me or not."

"Yes. I remember you. Your mother's sister works for you, doesn't she?"

"Yes. She looks after our son while my wife and I work."

"That's convenient. I don't have any relatives over here of my wife's. My sister has her own family to look after. Can't you talk your sister into staying? I've offered her an extra ten dollars week."

"That's her decision, Mr. Grossmann. I can't tell her what she should do. Where are your things, Elise?"

"There are two bags in my room and two bags in Waltraut's room."

"Okay. I'll take these two out first."

He took the two bags and put them in the trunk of the car. They barely fit because of their size. He then came back for the other two and put them in the rumble seat. When he finished, he returned to the house and said good bye to Mr. Grossmann.

"Herr Grossmann, good bye. Why don't you go to Florida this winter? A lot of older people are going there these days. You might even like it better than here."

"It's too far to drive. And I don't want to take the train. I wouldn't have my car down there. No. I'll stay here. Besides, my son lives out by Chittenango."

"He does? My brother lives out there, too."

"Yes, I know him. I've been there a few times."

"Why don't you live with your son?"

"I don't get along very well with my daughter-in-law. And besides, they've got small children. I can only take them for short periods of time and then they get on my nerves!"

"Well, good luck in finding a new house keeper."

"You go ahead, Karl," Elise said. "I'll wait for Waltraut and then we'll walk over to Gretel's."

It was only a few minutes later when Waltraude arrived. Elise wanted to say good bye to Mr. Grossmann but he refused to come out of his bedroom when she called out to him.

"Herr Grossmann, Waltraut and I are leaving now! Good bye."

There was no response.

"Isn't Mr. Grossmann going to say good bye to us, Mama?"

"I guess not. Maybe he's fallen asleep again."

As Elise and Waltraude walked the two blocks to the Haussmann's, Elise told her "Now we'll be staying with Grandmother, Tante Gretel and Uncle Richard. I don't know how long it'll be, but as soon as I find another job, we'll be moving again. At least you'll be safe, Waltraut. Grandmother will always be around."

"I like my Aunt and Uncle, Mama. Grandmother is very strict. But I'll try and get along with her, too."

Hardly a week had passed before Elise landed another job as a house keeper for another German gentleman. Mr. Jacob Nicky, the Director of the "Turnverein", was looking for a house keeper. His wife had also recently died. While he was a proficient cook, he hated washing dishes, clothes and house cleaning.

"That's a woman's job!" He told Friederich in his best Prussian high German shortly after Elise started to work for him. Elise and Waltraude had similar rooms to those which they had at Mr. Grossmann's. He occupied the downstairs bedroom and they used the two upstairs bedrooms. Mr. Nicky was a no nonsense sort of a person. He left the house early in the morning and went to his office at the Turnverein (Gymnasium). He came home for dinner at noon and then returned to his office until five o'clock each day. After supper three evenings a week, he returned to the gymnasium to give gymnastic lessons to young boys and girls who wished to become proficient in tumbling, the parallel bar, the balance horse, and a variety of acrobatic rings. Mr. Nicky had opened the Turnverein gymnasium at the request of many of the German immigrants who wished to have their children learn the same physical fitness routines they had learned in Germany. Mr. Nicky was a certified Master Gymnastics teacher from the Hanover Gymnastics Institute. Prior to immigrating to the United States, he had retired from teaching. He wanted to live closer to his sister who lived in Syracuse. Since he and his wife had no children, they wanted to spend more time with his sister and her family. His wife had been an only child and had only distant relatives in Germany. When Mr. Nicky proposed immigrating to the United States, she had no objection. It was difficult for him during the war since he wasn't a citizen.

"I didn't say much in public or at the Turnverein. Fortunately, I was surrounded by fellow German immigrants like myself. We all wished the war hadn't occurred," he told Friederich when he met him for the first time.

X   X   X

As for the Malins, they lived through the early 1930s making do with what little they had. Friederich's wood cutting and sale of firewood, was the only income they had. A gallon of milk purchased from the Kelly's Jersey dairy cost twenty-five cents. The flour, yeast, salt, pepper, corn flakes, and sugar with an occasional banana for each member of the family, cost no more than two dollars and fifty cents per week. On Sunday mornings Emilie was able to offer Wheaties for breakfast. She sometimes had a special treat for the family on holidays. She bought canned, sliced pineapple and give each one two slices in a bowl.

Friederich spread the horse and chicken manure on the garden each spring before plowing it under. The vegetables grew abundantly. Food, other than canned goods, cereals and condiments, Emilie raised on the farm. She had brood hens sit on eggs which she placed in bushel baskets. She placed another basket over the top to protect the brooding hens from rats and foxes. She had an annual supply of newly hatched chicks from this process each year which supplied the family with plenty of eggs and chicken as their major sources of protein. Karl and Anne brought oranges and grapes whenever they came to visit. There were also plenty of apples, wild grapes, cherries and strawberries on the farm which Emilie canned for the winters. She made grape jelly and jams of all kinds to smear on the weekly bread she baked. She also made her own butter from the cream which she took off the top of the gallon of Jersey milk which Volkmar bought at the Kellys. There was never a time of famine in the Malin household. If there were too many eggs to use on a daily basis, or for baking, Emilie placed them in cold storage in the cellar. Even during the winters, she had plenty of eggs to draw upon for cooking and baking.

One of the unusual luxuries they afforded themselves was having a daily newspaper delivered for three cents a day. Friederich wanted to keep abreast of what was happening in the world. They had neither a radio nor a telephone. Their only avenue to the outside world was through the Syracuse Herald-Journal. They had many books to read which they had brought from Germany plus those they had purchased from Mr. Cambridge. Volkmar and Inge read book after book from this library each evening after their homework was finished.

On weekends, the family played a variety of games such as checkers, Chinese checkers, world travel, pinochle and rummy; most of these games they had also brought over from Germany. The sun rose and set day after day as the children grew and the Malins became more proficient in learning how to cultivate the land and harvest whatever the forests and fields had to offer. Subsistence was a way of life for many American families in those early days of the depression. The Malins were no exception. They were more fortunate than many others who did not have a farm to exploit or land upon which to raise whatever they needed. Clothing came from the Haussmanns, the Kesselrings, the Karl Malins and the Fleckhammers in the form of "hand me downs". Whatever was of no interest to them any longer, or was "getting old", was taken out to the farm.

"Emmy, maybe you can use this dress of mine. I've just gotten a new one," Gretel told her when Billy Weiss brought them to the farm for a visit. The same rational was used for the children, except Volkmar grew larger than any of his cousins. He inherited a jacket from his Uncle Richard who was his size. Aunt Maria bought him a new pair of shoes to go to school. His feet grew so much larger than anyone else's in the family, none of their shoes fit him! Inge inherited dresses from Grete, Norma and even Waltraut as Elise accumulated enough money with which to clothe her daughter in new clothes at the beginning of each school year. Donald received all of his cousin Billy's clothes including shoes each year. Billy was viewed as the rich cousin in the family. Donald was very glad to have his things. Billy was four years older than he which meant he was young enough to "inherit" those clothes his cousin no longer wanted. For all of the children, the clothes of others were not only new to them, but seemed new to their friends in school. Only Volkmar had a problem because of his size. Emilie had to patch his pants when they wore out on the seat, or on his knees. But other than "these hard times" the family stayed together. Friederich paid his yearly interest on the mortgage. Emilie kept silent about what she might have seen or known concerning Friederich's sexual proclivities. The conspiracy of silence continued between the two of them. Not only did Emilie feel safer by not revealing what she had learned about her husband. But she remained in denial that he could have done such things to his relatives. Their bifurcated life style continued as if nothing untoward ever happened. She continued to find solace in her children, her garden, her piano playing and church attendance. Friederich continued to work on the farm until called to employment as a tool maker on the eve of World War II. He used what opportunities he could to "visit" his daughter in the darkness of the night. He thought no one could hear him, or would know what he was doing to her. And she never told anyone until years later.